Watch out for these
NEW & UPCOMING RELEASES FROM
GL WILLIAMS

AVAILABLE NOW

SYMPÁTHEÍA
(Book One of the Lady Justice Saga)

SARALAND

AVAILABLE SOON

STARFALL
(Book Two of the Lady Justice Saga)

MARIPOSA

FORGET ME NOT

Follow, Like and Share on Instagram, Facebook, Tumblr, Pinterest, Snapchat and Twitter @realglwilliams

Visit me at **www.realglwilliams.com**
for exclusive content, author branded apparel and up-dates. Don't forget to join the G Squad for members only perks, like author giveaways, prizes and swag.

CADEJANT
PRESENTS

A NOVEL BY

GL WILLIAMS

Saraland

Saraland

Saraland is a work of fiction. Names, characters, places and incidents either are the products of the author's imagination or are used fictitiously. Any resemblance to actual persons, living or dead, or to events, or places, or locales is entirely coincidental.
Copyright © 2019 by GL Williams
Cover photograph courtesy of Lorri Lang Photography, featuring cover model Sarah Buer
Cover Art and Design by GL Williams
© GL Williams. Book design and layout by GL Williams, adapted for paperback. ® All rights reserved.
Reproducing, scanning or distributing any part of this work in any form without written permission of the author is a violation of copyright law.
Printed in the United States of America.
Published by CADEJANT Media & Entertainment

www.realglwilliams.com

Paperback ISBN 978-0-578-51513-7

First Edition: December 2019

Chic-Lit Fiction | Beauty-Fiction | New York-Fiction | Romance | Careers | Social Media | Socialite | Adult-Fiction | Young Adult-Fiction | Southern Gal-Fiction | Comedy | Drama | Fashion-Fiction | Small Town-Fiction | Teenage Fiction | High School Fiction | Rural-Fiction

COPYRIGHTED MATERIAL

*"If you want something said, ask a man; if you
want something done, ask a woman."*

MARGARET THATCHER

one

SATURDAYS ARE FOR SUCKERS ♡

I'm not a morning person. Sure, I get up early every day, bolting out of the comfort of my bed to spend the next few hours getting ready for the madness of the grind. But I don't relish it. At all. Especially on Mondays 'cause weekends are way too short. Most definitely on Saturdays, because, well, working on any day following one of my Friday nights is a hard lesson about the dangers of hangovers and poor choices.

Thankfully, today I didn't wake up dry heaving into a ceramic dookie bowl with a pounding headache like I had just spent the beginning of the weekend in a mosh pit. I woke up with regret. Regret that I went to bed with my makeup on, especially since I could feel my mascara caked into my eyelids, scorching my retinas, turning my crusty eye boogers black.

Reluctantly, I opened my eyes and with a squint I tilted my head enough to look for the familiar bright light of my cellphone screen sitting on the nightstand, buzzing and screeching with that ridiculous ring tone I picked out just to make sure I got up.

That isn't what woke me up, though. It was the obnoxious alarm clock going off like a madwoman beside it. Probably as bad as a gazillion New York alley cats, with their razor claws screeching against a high school chalkboard.

Maybe not that bad, but regardless, I am most likely the last person on the planet with a digital alarm clock.

It was only ten years ago that I stepped into my freshman dorm room for the first time during move-in weekend. I'd start classes with my side of the room decked out with absolutely nothing but that old Radio Shack relic.

Unlike most of everyone else arriving at NYU to take up residence with all of their accessories, comforters and fluffy pillows from IKEA and *Tarjay*, I moved in with my guitar and the same massive, overstuffed gym bag I brought with me to New York. I had the same clothes in it that I had worn through the last two years of high school.

Most were gifted to me from Auntie Beanie, who was by far the most fashionable person in my family. By fashionable, I mean that she bought all of her clothes from outlet malls and high end department stores. Everything she passed down to me was brand named, including the brown leather cowboy boots she gave me that last Christmas before I left. Like most of the things she gifted, she had only worn them once, so they looked brand new.

She'd taken another trip to Texas and bought those in the shopping Mecca that was San Marcos, along with some cute sun dresses, jeans, skirts, hats and other shoes, and practically hosted a private fashion show when she picked me up and took me over to her hotel room for the few days she was there. We wore the same sizes, so everything she brought fit me perfectly.

She never stayed at our house when she visited. There was always this tension between Auntie Beanie and my momma, and I never knew the story behind it.

Armed with my debit card loaded with the financial aid refund of leftover scholarship money, and the extra cash from Auntie Beanie, I took the bus crossing the Holland tunnel to Jersey to satisfy my overwhelming shopping urge at a real mall. I needed a decent sheet set and a comforter, and I had to replace some of the clothes Auntie Beanie gave me that could no longer tame my country derrière.

I took the PATH train from 9th Street Station through the tunnel to Newport Station and made the short walk to Newport Centre. It was less than three dollars for the trip, which was way cheaper than a taxi. One way, it took less than half an hour.

After hitting Forever 21 and Hollister, I stopped at Claire's for some shiny stuff before finding the comforter and sheets on a clearance shelf at Sears. That uneventful trip took the whole day, but not because I was a certified shopaholic in need of therapy. Although I loved the mall, I was reluctant to go back through the tunnel.

I wasn't sitting on the train for long, but it seemed like entire decades had passed and I was freaking out. Admittedly, I'm not a fan of tubes that go underwater for people to travel through. I saw *Daylight*, that Sylvester Stallone movie from the '90s. The fear is real and totally ridiculous, but it made me super anxious whenever I went with my family or friends through the I-10 and Bankhead tunnels back in Mobile.

The train tunnels were different. They were claustrophobic, ominous and dark, which is why I never crossed the Hudson ever again after that. For about a year or so, anyway.

Some friends of mine had invited me to this lavish party over in Guttenberg or Edgewater somewhere- I'm not exactly sure which, but all I know is that I was like, *no. Never again*. Besides, it wasn't long before I discovered that there were endless shopping options in New York, from the shops, malls and boutiques up and down SoHo, Midtown and Madison Avenue to Brooklyn and the Village.

I often browsed Canal Street's fare, haggling with the street vendors over a two for twenty deal on sunshades, way below clearance on defective Coach or Prada bags and perfume dupe fragranced oils. I grew up being accustomed to having hardly anything, but once I had that first fix, I could easily drop like half a grand in one hour.

Poor choices. New York, and watching too much Sex and the City, can make you into a monster.

I regretted accepting those generous *Platinum This* and *Cashback Rewards That* offers in the mail. Swiping all that plastic was a huge mistake, and I knew I would have to find a job that would let me work doubles on the weekend to pay those credit card statements with the grown woman-sized APRs. And finals would be here before I knew it.

With a slap, I hit the button on top of the alarm clock, and it went crashing to the floor. Aggravated, I reached for the cellphone to slide the bar up to silence it and knocked it off of the nightstand too. With a groan, I laid back until my head hit the pillow, flailing my arms in total misery, and felt the tips of my fingers touch rough grossness. I kept feeling around with the back of my hand and found a face. My eyes closed tightly as I let out a breath, pursing my lips.

I slowly turned my head to the right to find my thumb and pointer finger grasping a pointy honker attached to a bronzed face with dark hair framing the temples. I had blackout curtains on my window so I could sleep better and for privacy from pervs, but the sunlight peeked around the edges just enough for me to see the grizzly mesh splattered all over a chiseled Superman jaw.

I pinched the nose hard.

He woke up, his eyes shot open, and he looked at me in confusion for a moment, before he settled back down and made himself comfortable. Then, he smiled at me.

I didn't smile back.

"Dude, you gotta go," I said, shoving him in his shoulder.

"What?" he muttered, confused.

"You gotta go, *man.* Come on, get up!" I growled, pushing at him again. Reluctantly, he rose, rubbing his eyes.

"I've gotta get ready for a meeting," I said.

"On a Saturday? Can't you cancel and chill with me? I can make us some pancakes."

I frowned at him with narrowed eyes. *Are you for real? Pancakes?*

"Dude, no. I don't even know you," I said. I crossed my arms and waited as he bent down over the edge of the bed to search for his socks, pants, undies, shirt, and whatever else.

Then, he stood up, and I was gifted with an unflattering view of the cheesy, pale imprint of his bikini briefs from his waistline down to his thighs. It was hideous. When my eyes traveled farther down, they discovered a farmer's tan. He looked like a little lea-guer wearing crew socks up to his kneecaps. Wow. Just wow. Where did this guy come from? The freakin' Midwest?

He turned around and sent me a look like he was sexy or some-thing. He wasn't. I mean, he was okay, but not great. That scratchy beard thingie made him come off like a bad impersonation of Adam Levine, and the ridiculous butt chin hovering over his knobby neck did him absolutely no favors.

I could think of six people. *Six.* Travolta, Demi Lovato, Blake Lively, Vanessa Hudgens, John Stamos and Taylor Swift. They're probably the only people who can rock that and look sexy getting away with it. But, most definitely not this guy.

His chin looked like it could easily consume a whole person.

"Dude, can you just *hurry up*?" I barked, exasperated. I pulled the covers more tightly around my body, covering everything up to my collarbones.

He smirked, shaking his head. When he had slid into his undies, pants, socks, shoes and shirt, he headed toward the door.

"You got my number?" he asked, holding on to the door frame to turn around and watch me for a moment.

I glared at him, on purpose, to make him as uncomfortable as possible.

"Yeah, I got it. You put it in my phone last night," I lied.

He smiled, then disappeared. I listened to his footsteps on the wood floors as they faded through the living room, then for the sound of the locks on the front door to unlatch, unbolt, unlock, and for the door to open and close before I tossed the comforter and sheets off of me to bolt out of my bed.

I reached down and grabbed my cellphone from where it had fallen under the nightstand, tapped the screen to silence the alarm, and then again to FaceTime Angie.

Angie laughs at me when I use voice assistant, telling me Siri and everybody else in New York can hear me 'cause I yell at the phone like an idiot. It's a habit, and I know I do it.

Occasionally, Siri can't understand my accent, which comes out now and then when I'm pissed or excited about something. Words tumble out and I start ramblin' as my momma called it. Then I would have to repeat myself, slowly, and Siri sometimes still doesn't get it right.

Sashaying through the living room with my bare feet slapping against the floor, I listened to the phone ring as I walked over to check the locks on the front door. The knob didn't budge, so I twisted the top latch, sliding the bolt into place.

After three rings, Angie answered.

"What up, *gurrrrl!*" she purred, breathing heavily into the phone. Her face was a shadow against a bright background.

"What are you doing? Working out? You're supposed to be on your way here," I said, heading back to my bedroom.

"I *am* on the way there. I'm actually heading up now. Got stuff for tonight with me." She raised the phone up, changing the angle so I could see her without the glare. Her long braids sat twisted into a bun at the top of her head, and something she was holding in her arms was making loud crinkling noises. Sweat dotted her forehead.

I passed the kitchen and smiled. Charlemagne was busy going to town in his bowl, pushing it up against the cabinet. He turned to look at me, licked his chops, and went back to crunching his breakfast. I checked his water bowl quickly and reached down to scratch his head.

"So, tell me why you let me go home with some *rando* dude last night?"

Angie laughed into the phone with a slight snort.

"He's not a random. He was the bouncer. That's Thirst Trap

Frankie.”

I stood back up to continue to the bedroom, putting the phone on speaker.

“The bouncer? I can understand *maybe* the bartender. A strong maybe. But the bouncer? What kind of bestie are you?” I yanked my bedsheets and comforter off of the bed. I'd have to wash them or burn them. I hadn't decided yet on which.

“I'm sorry, but you're the one so insistent on fornicating with guys you don't know. I was going to minge block you, but you looked like you were having a good time. Blame it on the Tanqueray, not me.”

“I don't drink Tanqueray,” I said with a sniff.

“You did last night. Slamming down Cranberry Pineapple Gin and Juice like it was Kool-Aid.” I could hear Angie's little snicker. *Punk. Not funny.* I frowned.

“Never let me drink that stuff again. *Capisce*?” I narrowed my eyes at her image on the phone with a menacing glare.

“Like I can stop you,” she said, laughing.

“I thought we were in SoHo all night?” I asked, rubbing my head as I stepped into the bathroom. I was getting a headache, but it wasn't from a hangover. It was from disgust. With myself. *Frankie?* For real?

“For a while. Then we hit up the Pegu and had a few drinks, caught an Uber to East Village and ended up at the Rumpus Room. You said you wanted to go dancing, so we did, and it was total hilarity. When you get drunk, your country always comes out. You were all like, *Hey ya'll!* Hugging everybody like a stoned bridesmaid. I'm legit surprised you aren't over there hugging the toilet,” Angie said. “Hey, buzz me in. I'm outside with my arms full.”

"How far did you *walk*, fruit cake?"

"Far enough. Nutcase dropped me off like six parsecs away. I kept telling him to stop," Angie said. "Almost ended up trapped in the sequel."

"Stop catching cabs, man. They don't understand English," I said with a laugh.

"Oh, they understand perfectly fine. He just wanted an extra couple of ticks on his little meter."

"I don't know why you don't just take an Uber. Or Lyft. Your pick," I mumbled.

"You hear about all those crazy drivers? All those assaults? Catching one with a group like last night is one thing. But alone? Nope. I'm good. Better luck with the cabbies. They're too scared to try anything stupid," Angie said.

"Scared of *what?*" I asked.

"Scared of *me*," Angie chuckled.

"You make like, no sense," I said with a laugh. "Are you saying they're scared of you because all the cab drivers are immigrants?"

"At least I support them," Angie replied. "Restaurants. Little corner stores. Even the dry cleaners. I mean, we're all freaking immigrants, to be low key honest. Unless you're Native American, not one person walking the soil of this country can say they or their ancestors didn't arrive here from somewhere else."

"Well, Mexicans," I said.

I found the shirt and jeans from last night laying next to the closet door, so I put them on and grabbed my keys to head out barefoot and meet Angie at the entrance to the building.

"I think they count as Native," Angie said. "Europeans came

here to get a trade route to Asia through the Pacific and did horrible things to Native Americans and Mexicans to do it."

"Weren't they escaping persecution? In the sixteen hundreds, Protestant Christians wanted to break away from the Roman Catholic Church's oppression. The Puritans opposed the rituals and liturgy and believed in the supremacy of GOD. During the rule of King Charles I, Puritans with moola fled executions in England for America," I said.

"Looks like you know your white people history," Angie teased.

"I mean, Oliver Cromwell, Roger Williams. The Mayflower. Anne Hutchinson, John Cotton. The Puritans persecuting the Quakers, like Ann Austin and Mary Fisher. The early Salem church and the Salem Witch Trials," I chuckled. "That stuff was drilled in our heads in high school."

"That's unnerving that you know and remember all of that," Angie snickered. "I could tell you all about Frederick Douglass and Nat Turner though. Should I be regretting that I know you?"

"You are so basic sometimes. I swear. People should learn the *whole* history of this country in school."

"I was talking about the ones who came to America long before the people you're talking about. How'd they get here?" Angie asked.

"I don't know. That land bridge thingie. Captain James Cook. Learned about all that in high school."

"I think that's just a theory," Angie said, the amusement clear in her voice. "That's a long walk to South America. Anyway, how long are you gonna make me stand out here discussing the New World? Been out here for the last thirty minutes."

My apartment was on the ground floor, right next to the front entryway of an upscale art deco brick building on King Street. There were only a few feet from my door to where I could see Angie through the glass, standing outside on the concrete steps holding two grocery bags, with her cellphone on speaker tucked between her shoulder and neck.

I could've peeked out of my bedroom window at the right angle and saw whoever was walking up, but once they were in the entryway, they were beyond my early warning system. The buzzer box was the last line of defense.

I opened the door and grabbed a bag.

"You feel better now? It hasn't been *that* long. You're such a whiner," I teased.

"You had me standing there so long, my toe nails grew out through the front of my sneakers. You owe me a mani, so thanks for that," Angie muttered under her breath, hanging up and tucking her cellphone into her back pocket. I smirked, propping the door open for her with my foot as she slid by me.

"I had to put some clothes on. You don't want me to come out here naked, do you?"

"I'm sure it wouldn't be the first time," she said as I moved to get ahead of her to open my door and let her into my apartment.

She shuffled past me and headed to the kitchen as I kicked today's copy of the New York Times sitting on my welcome mat into the doorway. Charlemagne plodded through the living room to meet her as I closed the door behind me and locked it.

"Oh, you won't budge for me, but you'll come out and give her a warm welcome," I said, cutting my eyes at him, reaching down to pick up the newspaper. He ignored me, following Angie into the kitchen. After she set the bag onto the counter, she shoved her hand in and pulled out a bag of doggie treats.

"That's 'cause he's spoiled rotten. Ain't that right, Charlemagne, AKA Charles the Great, AKA King of the Franks?" She ripped open the bag, took out a little meat morsel, and squatted down to let him take the treat from her palm.

"Well, I gotta get a shower so I can get to this meeting," I said, setting the newspaper and the other bag next to the one on the counter. "You're not cooking tonight, are you? I thought we were getting take out."

"I found this neat recipe on Pinterest that I wanna try," she said, pulling out her phone to silence a notification. She stood up.

"Um, no. You're not touching that stove. We can get an Uber Eats driver to drop something off," I said, turning to head toward the bathroom. "Chinese. Or we can take a walk and grab some slices at Joe's."

"First of all, I'm not down with the Sweet and Sewer Chicken. That new place we ordered from put pickles in the sweet and sour sauce. Who does that? Besides, even when I bring things over, you hardly ever eat it. God forbid I mess up your shiny little stove."

I stopped and turned around, looked at her, then laughed. I couldn't help it. The look on her face was classic. She was totally wounded. Poor thing.

"I just don't like the smell of cooked food in my kitchen. I don't want to get my stove dirty, and I hate when that black, crusty crud gets caked on it. It's super disgusting. My momma always had that black gook all around the burners, and it would never come off completely, no matter how hard you scrubbed at it. Plus, I hate that *smell* that just *lingers*." I wrinkled my nose. "It's gross. Like a fart that won't go away and follows you into the elevator."

"We get Thai food, and that funky grifter foot smell stays in your place for days. What's the difference?"

"It doesn't mess up my stove," I said with a smile.

"Still smells like sweaty butt and nacho toes," Angie said.

"Gross. Thanks for that mental image," I said, rolling my eyes.

I tossed my hair over my shoulders and spun around to prance to the bathroom.

I could hear Angie talking to Charlemagne, asking him how he puts up with me, and I couldn't hold back the giggle. I absolutely relished getting under her skin 'cause she let me.

As I climbed out of my dirty club clothes and plopped them into a haphazard pile on the bathroom rug, I rechecked my phone, then tossed it on the counter next to my toothbrush before stepping into the shower.

My first few weeks in this place had me scalding myself almost every night. The water came out boiling, so I had to be careful with the positioning of the knobs. Afterward, I'd be sitting there fuming in bed looking like a straight up pissed off lobster, running aloe gel all over my arms, shoulders, and legs. So, I started taking arctic grade showers to prevent myself from looking like a total beet. At least until I got the hang of getting the knobs just right. Then it felt good to let the water run all over me.

Reaching for the shampoo, I let the spray soak my head. I could feel the tickle and itch as it plastered my long blonde mane to my back. I leaned my head back and pushed my hair away from my face, then lathered it up, twisting to pull it all around so I could reach the lower lengths.

I frowned as golden strands collected around the drain. I was long overdue for a stylist visit. My ends needed trimming. Bad. And it wouldn't be long before I'd have to color my roots again to hide my natural reddish brown-blonde hair color.

It could be from all the stress. A case of the bubble guts had me debating whether or not I should skip my usual morning five-minute walk up 6th Ave and Bedford for macchiato and breakfast of either coffee cake or cardamon pistachio bread at Prodigy on Carmine.

Although I sometimes work on Saturdays, never ever do I take a meeting on the weekend. Everybody knows that Work Saturdays are for suckers. This Work Saturday meeting was important, though.

Providence, a beauty and cosmetics brand in Charlotte, North Carolina, had been following my Instagram posts and my YouTube and Facebook Live video blogs. They contacted me a few weeks ago about possibly collaborating on a new product line. Meeting with them would most definitely be worth sacrificing a Saturday for.

After I rinsed the shampoo out, I grabbed the color protecting conditioner, ran it through my hair, soaped up my body to wash that dude off of me and rinsed off, quickly getting out of the shower to get my now crazy looking hair tamed. It took magic to knock out all the ridiculous frizz and curls.

Jackie and her cousins worked Puerto Rican voodoo on me. They used products in their salon meant for ethnic hair, but they did incredible things never done before to my mane. I could finally let my hair grow out well past my shoulders, feather it, and wear it in sexy styles I wouldn't dare try when I was in hell hot Alabama.

I slapped on leave in conditioner, ran it through with my fingers and massaged it into my scalp, feeling the tea tree oil tingling my follicles as I breathed in the soft smell of coconut.

While my hair was still wet, I slapped on cocoa and shea butter lotion from head to toe as I sat on the edge of the toilet seat. I could feel the razor wire coming back on my shins, so I knew I couldn't get away with not shaving my legs past today.

Next, I grabbed the ceramic blow dryer with the styling combs and dried my hair, then spent what felt like an eternity running sections of it through the straightening iron. When my looks were on point, I headed back into the bedroom.

My walk-in closet was a catastrophe. There was zero organization going on in there. I had my shoes still in their boxes stuffed on shelves and on the floor wherever they would fit, with totes stacked up to one side and my dresses and skirts hanging in no particular order from the racks.

I grabbed the pair of black slacks hanging on one of the lovely wooden hangers that I had swiped from a hotel room in the Village when a few friends and I pulled an all-nighter. I had already ironed them. Kind of. I let the dryer do all the work.

Moving on to my dresser, I yanked out a frilly cami top made of a light material with a wide neck. It was cream with blue floral print splattered all over it. Hopefully, the heat outside wouldn't make me sweat my boobs off. That would be *horrific*, more like an extinction level event.

No one enjoys chafing, those unsightly red pimples in the creases between your titties and your chest, and the itchy scratchies at the place where under-wire slices into flesh. Most of my bras were the wireless type, but that was a useless feature on a hot day. And judging by this past week so far, today would be flaming.

Central Park broke a seventeen-year record last May around this time with ninety-degree temps. Following record snowfalls, freak winter storms and blizzards, this year should prove to be no different. With it being so much hotter than last spring, everything growing leaves and blooming flowers will arrive unfashionably late.

Once I had slipped on my cami, I changed my mind about the black slacks. After working my bootie into slim, coordinating chinos, I styled my long hair into a cute up do with a messy twist at the back of my neck to prepare for the scorching, clammy heat. I hit it with holding spray to make it stay long enough to get this meeting over with, and then I put on my business face with subdued eyeliner, natural tones, and nudes for a fresh look.

I grabbed a pair of nude strap sandal heels strewn near my closet door and slid them onto my big feet. Checking the mirror to make sure I was the total package, I spun around to see Angie standing there looking at me with Charlemagne in her arms. He watched me with his ears perked up and his tongue hanging out.

"What?" I said, looking down at my outfit. "It doesn't look right?"

"You realize you have like a zillion followers now on Instagram? That's insane," Angie said, scratching Charlemagne's head.

"Stop exaggerating. I barely have a quarter large. But it *is* hella crazy, although I have to figure out new content. I feel like I'm at a total standstill. Everyone's posting these exotic trips and vineyard lunches with mimosas and kale salads. I've gone nowhere outside of New York in forever, so I can't compete with that," I said, reaching for my lint roller. I swiped it down my right leg to catch some renegade golden hair strands.

"You haven't gone outside of New York, *ever*. Just saying," Angie said.

"You know what I mean," I said, cutting my eyes at her with a scowl.

"Just keep being yourself. You don't need all that extra *BS*. You're building this incredible following without it, just by show-ing people how to make things work for them. They like you for you. So will these people. This meeting you're about to go to could be that *thing* for you. You're about to launch your own *brand*. It's your dream, right? That's a total game changer. You're gonna need me to dog and house sit a lot more."

"Angie, I appreciate you doing that for me, but you're my best friend. I don't need you to babysit my dog and watch my place. I can hire someone to do it," I said, slapping the lint brush back onto the dresser.

"But I want to. I like helping you out. Plus, frankly, do you re-ally want someone you don't know up in your house handling Charles The Great and your stuff? Oh, wait. You already let people you don't know handle your stuff, so I can't really say that can I?" She giggled. I wanted to cut her.

"Oh, it's on when I get back," I said. "Get the strap."

"Okay, Fifty," Angie smirked as she followed me to the door. "I'll get your sheets washed too, so you don't have to smell ball-sack and Axe body spray when you go to sleep tonight. Or at least have it fresh for the next one."

"Look, hooker. You don't have to do that, I can wash my own sheets," I said. "You're always doing too much. What? Are you in love with me?"

"I'm in love with Charles," Angie said, squinting her eyes at me.

I opened the door, turned around, cut my eyes at her again, and shook my right knuckle sandwich in her direction with my lips pursed.

"Do that at the meeting," Angie said, smiling. "I double dog dare you."

"Bye, Angie," I said, closing the door behind me.

two

I LOVE NEW YORK ♡

I decided to skip Prodigy. That was probably a mistake. I don't do very well without my morning macchiato fix, but thanks to waking up late because of last night's indiscretions, I was pushing it close this morning. I should have been out the door as Angie was walking in.

Luckily, I didn't have far to go. The Spring Street subway station was only a few blocks down 6th. I walked to the corner of 6th and King and made a right. Three minutes later I was in the elevator holding my breath against the sharp, pungent odor of piss for the quick ride into the slightly cooler, stale, dank disgustingness of the underground MTA station, with its signature mosaic tile artwork decorating the walls. The art was gorgeous. The funk was just trifling.

Maybe an Uber would have been better. Brisk feeling, cold AC from my doorstep to my destination would have been a superb option over braving the scorch of the concrete, steel, and asphalt that was the spine and frame of New York. I didn't want to arrive to this meeting with my updo all jacked up, stray escaping strands plastered to the nape of my neck, and wet patches spreading from my armpits to my hips.

Too late now.

The schedule placed the train at 42nd around 11:18, so I knew to be waiting on the Spring Street southbound platform at 11 on the dot to stand for twenty minutes, give or take 'cause, with New York subways, you don't take chances. Even though waiting could have me pulling my switchblade on super gross creepers and what-nots from the Upside Down.

Not that long ago, there was an incident on a subway in the Bronx where a 24-year-old woman fell asleep on the way home at around two in the morning and woke up to some nasty butt-licker with his hands in her undies. She screamed and he ghosted at the next station.

And it's not just the Bronx. There's all those super gross, serial subway pervs prowling New York trains at all hours seeking to horrify women with their masturbating prowess.

I preferred sidestepping Godzilla-sized rats on the sidewalks of the city to constantly having to keep a mindful eye on everyone and everything around you, with your butt pressed into a corner and your switchblade held out in front of you to cut anything that dare comes near.

Since graduating NYU, I try to avoid the subway trains as much as possible, especially the Lexington Avenue Line, the F train, and the R. These routes were the most perv-infested out of all of them by far.

Riding any of the subways made me want to scrub every last inch of my body with Clorox wipes. The stations themselves were probably hoarding mutated versions of tuberculosis and gonorrhea, and it was a miracle that New York didn't look like Raccoon City.

Unfortunately, getting to the Bronx to hang out with Jackie on weekends required me to take the 6. Unsuccessful at finding a safe place to sit, I would stand with other women in a protective cluster to avoid being groped or grinded on, or find a spot out of arm's reach of nearby sleazeballs, clutching my knife at my side.

I absolutely *never* step foot in Grand Central or Union Square. Those two stations are quite possibly the pervert capitals of the world, where there have been the most arrests for sex offenses.

After sliding my MetroCard through the reader slot and awkwardly slipping through the turnstile, I stood at the platform and waited, vigilantly watching every nook and corner with my ears on high alert.

This station was notorious for not being as worn, filthy, and skanky as others, which is why I gave it a chance. It was much cleaner and more pleasant, somewhat maintained, and usually staffed. It was a gamble though, sometimes having limited weekend service or no service at all 'cause of maintenance or construction.

Although it had an open underpass, I wasn't foolish enough to get caught in the easy trap, leaving me running for my life to escape some super crazy loonie trying to steal my iPhone or worse, stick a grimy finger down my hipsters. Or, even worse, kill me after doing God knows what to my unconscious body. Thus the switchblade, ever ready. Just in case.

But I love New York.

The train was on time and packed. I stepped in and literally, mere seconds after grabbing the bar, I was moving with a group to fight the mass of on boarders to exit out onto the platform at Canal Street station.

I tried not to touch any surface whatsoever as I made my way through the crowded station, with its foul combination funk of dirty laundry, moldy undead zombies, Chernobyl and musty cigarette ash to get to the light of day above.

Once back on 6th, I reached into my clutch and took out a tiny bottle of Limoncello hand sanitizer Angie got for me from Bath and Body Works, slathered it all over my hands and lower arms, then dabbed just a smidge under my nose to clear my palette.

It would be another four minutes before I was standing in front of the Roxy in Tribeca. That was my first time ever riding the subway to Canal. It would also be my last time riding the subway to Canal, or maybe anywhere, for that matter. There was another twenty or so left on my MetroCard. I was almost ready to just give it away. I was definitely getting an Uber back home.

When I first arrived in New York the summer before my first semester at NYU, the subway was the way to get around. There was also the bus, cabs and walking. Most people on campus, and in New York in general, rode bikes. But then I would be on the bus, watching how close cabs and buses got to bike riders, watching bikers smash into parked cars or get sideswiped despite the bike lanes. I saw way too many bikers sprawled out on the road looking like someone just sucker punched them and stole their lunch money after some idiot cut them off and sent them wobbling to the pavement. That was enough argument for me to pass on that option.

Time has gone by in a flash. It felt like it was just yesterday when I was living on campus in the dorms, going to parties, clubs, getting to work, and spending the weekends and summers with Jackie and her family in the Bronx.

Who am I kidding? I *still* live in an apartment that feels like a dorm, go to parties, clubs, go to work, and spend some weekends at Jackie's in the Bronx.

I met Angie during my freshman year at NYU, and we hit it off right away. She lived on my floor in Weinstein East, directly across from the elevators in 834. She was probably seven rooms down from me but on the other side.

I was always hanging with her and her roommate, Tynique, because my roommate, Trish, was super quiet and totally anti-social. A perfect specimen of an extreme introvert. I don't even know where she was from. Probably Upstate New York. Like Syracuse. Or maybe she was from Idaho. I don't know. She had a thing for barbecue corn chips, pickles, and Slim Jims. It made the room feel stifling and smell like nacho taco Nikes.

Whenever I came into the room, I would find her huddled up on her bed facing the window with her iPod, her laptop, and a textbook. She never said hi, and never looked up, no matter how much I tried to get her to interact. So I gave up.

Angie and Ty called themselves the 834 Clique. Whenever I'd stop over, they'd cup both their hands around their mouths and be like, *"What's going on in the 816?"*

I'd always respond with *"Not a thang!"* There was never anything going on in 816 but straight up silence, broken only by the crunching of feet smelling Fritos.

Sophomore year, I hit pay dirt when I was assigned to Palladium Hall with Angie, but we didn't get the roommate request we submitted. We ended up separated by six floors, so we agreed to get an apartment together ASAP. It took us both forever to save up first month's and lasts month's rent plus security deposit totaling the cost of a used Hyundai, but we managed to pull it off during our senior year. We found an apartment right near campus in the Village. Uber launched during our junior year, so by the time we were seniors, we were catching Ubers, busing it, and walking more than riding underground.

Not long afterward, Angie and her boyfriend, Stu, started talking babies and family, and eventually Stu moved in. So I moved out to SoHo. By then, my internship with Frost, courtesy of the hook-up from the Wasserman Center in Palladium Hall, had become a paid job.

Frost was a fashion upstart on West 40th across from Bryant Park. I assisted the marketing staff with the catalogs, emails, and shoots during the day dressed in heels, and then hobbled over to The Grill at Bryant Park with throbbing feet for waitressing duties to make that SoHo rent.

Taking the job at Frost was the dream I didn't know I had. I gained a plethora of skills working with lighting and product that helped me set up my online content later.

I finished up at NYU with a music degree in business but ended up working somewhere totally left field. New York was getting more expensive by the second. I didn't have time to wait.

Along with several other music publishing jobs that popped up, I applied for a job opening with Flavor Unit in New Jersey to get in the door as a receptionist, hoping to connect with the Queen herself. I got called for an interview with Flavor but cowered out at the last minute. Then, the opportunity with Frost came.

Although Frost paid less, between that and the restaurant, I was pulling in just over a grand a week with tips included. Somewhere else, I probably would have lived like a boss with that kind of cheddar coming in. This was New York. Three weeks of pay went to rent. After utilities, the rest was just enough to eat like I was on SNAP.

But then Jackie and I came up with an idea that changed things. She had been fooling around with her family's recipes, making essential oils and lotions. I was hanging out at her place in the Boogie Down, her family's nickname for the Bronx, on Sundays after she got out of church to catch up.

Seeing what she was doing, I started trying my hand at different things and ended up with creams, lotions, and lip balms that smelled like southern comforts, desserts, and drinks from growing up in southern Alabama.

Two years after I graduated from NYU, Jackie and I were selling on Etsy and eBay. Not long after that, we launched our Instagram blog and YouTube channel doing tutorials on how to use beauty and cosmetic products, in particular for people with sensitive skin like mine and for women who had dry skin and darker skin tones like Jackie's.

People wanted our moisturizing creams and lip balms. It wasn't long before we needed extra help and I stopped working for Frost.

Then last year, after I started my mini-boutique renting space in the corner of a salon selling our beauty products and doing make-up like a mini-Sephora, Stu and Angie were no more. Stu was most definitely not someone who fit the description of being baby daddy material, so I was super-psyched that he didn't knock Angie up.

She caught him Snapchatting and sending eggplant emoji's to a high school senior.

Sneaky Snapchat. Genius way of cheating, as long as whoever you are cheating on isn't looking over your shoulder at your Snaps.

Angie's from Queens. You can't hide anything from her; she can smell a lie a borough away.

I was never into Snapchat. I thought it was for kids, mostly as a way for them to get away with hiding who they were talking to and what they were posting from their parents, especially since opened Snaps vanished by the next day. And Stu was very much a kid, spending most of his time at her place invisibly tethered to his Playstation Pro. I don't even really know if he actually had a *job*. He got money from somewhere.

Angie used to have all kinds of gigs going on, but now she worked for an IT company from home. She worked from my place when she was dog sitting Charlemagne, using my wifi. I noticed her laptop stuffed in one of the grocery bags, so like me, she would be doing work stuff on a Saturday.

Neither one of us was doing what we went to NYU to get a degree to do.

Angie graduated with an art degree, but she was a total computer geek, which worked out great for me. She helped me build my website.

My music degree remained a relic, and I stuffed the custom-made guitar I came to New York with into my closet, right behind all those boxes of shoes. It was the last gift I ever got from my daddy, just before he left when I was twelve and leaking marinara into my gym shorts for the first time. I haven't touched it in about five years.

three
A GIRL CAN DREAM ♡

I wiped sweat from my brow as I stood in front of the Roxy Hotel, perched on the converging point where 6th Avenue intersected White Street, right near the point where 6th branched off from Church at Franklin Street.

The retro-looking lettering on the front above the doors made me feel like I had walked into a bygone era. The red brick looked new.

They completed the renovations three years ago, but it was incredible how timeless it looked, even with the updates.

A uniquely vintage looking brass luggage cart sat parked near the doors next to the marquee.

I made my way through the wood-framed glass front doors and immediately started drooling as the fragrance of coffee coming from Jack's hit my nose, making me regret not getting up earlier to grab my favorite at Prodigy. I made a mental note to stop by Jack's for a latte on the way out, after the meeting.

I reluctantly shuffled past, letting the refreshing air inside the building dry the sweat from my face.

Stepping out into the lobby past a pool table on the right perched near quaint crescent-shaped, luscious looking booths, I noticed that the air suddenly grew cooler. I admired all the exposed brick that ran down the right wall to the Roxy stage where musical instruments sat, arranged as if waiting for the next performance.

It felt like a vintage movie theater, but with beautiful stone and wood floors. The lounge area was cavernous and moody, with gorgeous decor. Looking up, floor after floor rimmed by railings rose into the atrium. The Oyster Bar sat in an area that appeared to me to be an overturned grand piano, open and airy with windows framing all sides.

Tables and booths were everywhere. I squinted as I scanned the Roxy Lounge to look for the group from Providence.

A tall, red-haired, slender girl with freckles walked up to me and smiled. I have no idea where she came from. It was almost as if she came from beneath the floor.

"How are you today? Welcome to the Roxy. Can I get you anything?"

I then realized this lounge also served as a restaurant, thus the tables, chairs, and booths everywhere.

I smiled.

"Um, no, I'm just meeting with some people," I said.

"Oh, what group are you with? Maybe I can help you find them," she said, clasping her hands together in front of her just above her belt.

"Providence," I said, as her eyebrows raised.

It was then that I saw a long arm with bracelets jingling at the wrist, waving at me from a table sitting beneath a large mirror toward the back of the lounge.

She followed my gaze.

"Ah, it looks like you found them," she said. "Can I help you with anything else? Would you like a tea or a coffee?"

"Nope, I'm good, thanks. I appreciate it," I said. The girl smiled, nodded, and sailed off. I headed toward the waving arm and jingling bracelets. Turning around for a moment in the direction I had come, I discovered that the red-headed girl had vanished as if she disappeared into the floor. It was either highly bizarre or amazingly efficient.

When I reached the table, a tall, bronzed, blonde-haired man, with muscle trying to burst through his button-up Oxford and chinos, stood up. He extended his hand as the woman next to him stood up. She was also tall and blonde but timelessly gorgeous in a Michelle Pfeiffer kind of way. They both towered over me like a two Eternals from the MCU.

I held out my hand to accept his and shook it.

"You must be Amanda," he said with a distinctive southern accent.

Yummy. *Mr. Grey will see you now.*

"Yes, it's good to meet you, finally," I said, almost curtseying like an idiot before I caught myself. He was making me sweat all over again. Suddenly I felt hot, like everywhere.

"I'm Richard," he said, smiling. "And this is Alexa, our COO. She's also in charge of branding," he said, extending a hand toward her.

Alexa nodded with a broad smile as I took her hand.

"It's my pleasure," she said, also with a deep southern accent. "So, I see you've developed a following on social media," she said, sitting down.

I pulled out a chair and sat as Richard smoothly sank back down and adjusted himself in his seat. I cleared my throat.

"Not quite. I wish," I said, sheepishly.

"Well. What you've done, it's commendable. Positioning your-self as a kind of go-to guru for both women of color and women with fair skin tones is amazing. I love the broad crossover appeal of your reach," Alexa said.

I wondered if anyone teased her about her name, saying *'Hey, Alexa'* before proceeding to order flannel socks.

"Thank you so much for that," I said.

"Would you like anything before we get started? We were about to order lunch," Richard said. "Dinner was great last night, so I'm sure lunch will be just as incredible."

I smiled.

"No, thank you. I've had a late breakfast," I lied.

"Well, we can wait until after our meeting to order, if that's al-right with you," Alexa said, looking at Richard. He nodded.

"Perfectly fine with me," he said, pushing his menu further to the right. "Well, we can get right to it, then."

Alexa clasped her hands in front of her on the table. Her blue eyes fell on me.

"Well, Amanda, as we discussed in our last phone call, we have been working to position Providence to reach a broader audience. Mainly, the fast growing number of young adults and teens with disposable income and an aesthetic for the less is more, minimalist philosophy. They have an attraction to mid-market brands with a social conscience and clean insta-fabulous packaging. Recent re-search details the influence of this VSCO girl trend. Are you famil-iar with the term?"

I rose my eyebrows at Alexa in confusion.

"VSCO? I've heard of it, but not familiar with it," I said.

"It's a term from an app called Visual Supply Company. It describes the girl that wants fewer products cluttering up her vanity. She wants transparent ingredients, clearly understood on simple labeling. She likes socially conscience brands that aren't well known. She's all over social media, with very little make-up, comfortable clothes, an allowance to burn, and she's totally disrupting the cosmetics industry," Alexa said.

I nodded.

"Basically, she's all the girls that are liking your posts and buying your products," Alexa added. "She's the girl that likes relatively unknown brands like yours, and people like you."

"Ah, I see," I replied.

"That research I was talking about? It shows a 21% decrease in spending on cosmetics among female youth year over year. Large cosmetic retailers are seeing their stock plunge across the board. The biggest one is looking at a stock drop approaching 30% by the end of this summer. So, we can admit that makeup right now at least, is dying.

"This year, Providence saw a plunge of 12% profit over last year and we're looking to lose a lot more. That doesn't sound like a lot when compared to the much larger brands, but our sustainably sourced cosmetics are completely vegan. So that says a lot."

Richard took a quick sip from the glass of water that sat in front of him, watching Alexa speak as he nodded in agreement.

"This VSCO girl trend reminds me of the current trends in home design and decorating. Magnolia. Marie Kondo. Less is more. She's moving away from bold cosmetics in favor of honeysuckle lip balms, rosewater spritzes and products she can use for multiple purposes. Takes up way less space on her uncluttered and organized shelf," Alexa said. Following Richard's cue, she took a sip from the glass in front of her.

"Are you sure you don't want anything to drink? A glass of water or a tea?" she asked.

I shook my head.

"No, really, I'm fine," I said, although my mouth felt like it was stuffed with cotton and mulch.

"To address the trends, we've developed a new brand that we believe will benefit the demographic we are trying to reach," Richard said.

I nodded again.

"It's a critical time. We've recently partnered with larger big-box retailers to gain additional footholds in the market, but as a somewhat newer brand compared to other more seasoned beauty labels, we want to do more on a personal level, and really connect with our audience and client base," Richard added.

"I'm sorry," Alexa said, cutting in. I looked at her as she rested her hand on my arm. "I have to ask, what is that you're wearing? The fragrance? It reminds me of something my husband bought me for our anniversary."

"Oh, um, it's a lemon fragranced perfume. Not sure which. I think it's Italian," I lied again.

She nodded.

"Have you tried Amber Aoud Absolue Precieux? It's from Roja Parfums. My absolute favorite," Alexa said. She held a wrist out for me to smell.

I bent and sniffed. It smelled lovely. And ridiculously expensive.

"No, I haven't tried it. I'll have to look it up," I said.

"When my husband bought it for me, I fell in love with it," she mused as she crossed her legs. "So, when you were doing some of your reviews in the past, have you worked with fragrances?"

I smiled.

"In a way. I've worked with mostly essential oils. I try to create real scenarios when I review different products by testing them on myself for others who have sensitive skin types like mine. It's more authentic," I said.

"And for women of color, you have your associate. What's her name?" Richard asked.

"Jacqueline. She's Puerto Rican and where her family is from, it's very tropical. My followers who have darker skin always say how dry their skin is regardless of the climate where they live. Jackie is good with putting together moisturizing oils and botanicals to help calm skin and treat the dryness," I said.

"She tests them on herself and her family. They have a very long history in creating amazing creams and oils back in Puerto Rico. It's part of their heritage. Her family came to New York when she was small and brought their traditions with them." I smiled as I cleared my throat. I felt parched.

Alexa nodded with interest, smiled and continued.

"With our product, we have a R&D team that conducts trials, never on animals of course, and we source our products from sustainable resources to nurture the environment. For instance, we create our cleansers with all natural oils that are broken down easily and absorbed."

Richard held a finger up and cut in.

"We also manufacture locally in the Charlotte area, to lower cost of development. We recently purchased hundreds of acres of rural farmland just outside the city for our new state-of-the art facility. We'll be launching our new line of beauty and skin products in stand-alone boutiques within flourishing mixed-use developments and town centers across the country," Richard said. "Like farm to table, only with skincare."

They were speaking my language, and that was exactly what I wanted to do. Set up AJ Rush boutiques within town centers. A girl can dream.

"That's great to hear because the products that Jackie and I have developed are perfect for what you are trying to achieve. Transparent, sustainably sourced from all natural, organic, vegan ingredients and oils. And, they're produced locally, right in the Bronx. We even use herbs we get from local urban farms right here in the city. The amazing thing is we work hard to create something that everyone can use, especially people who are socially conscience," I said.

I reached into my portfolio and pulled out a folder. Alexa looked at it and I noticed a hint of a frown on her face. I slid it over to her.

"What am I looking at?" she asked as she flipped it open.

"It's my product outlook, map, and five-year plan. We have a growing product portfolio, and it's worth checking out. Great investment potential with the reach we are achieving with our social media platforms."

She flipped through a few pages, and looked over at Richard. He smiled at me.

"We love what you're doing. We think it's great. And you being so influential this early on is astounding, especially building something so amazing in such a short time.

"We're launching a new line for our prestige boutiques to promote a new line of fully organic, sustainably sourced vegan products. We have new insta-worthy packaging that is fully recyclable. The packaging itself is clean and sustainable. We feel that you understand our culture and we believe you can help us re-position our brand." Richard smiled, taking the portfolio from Alexa, and pushing it back toward me.

I stared at him for a moment.

"I'm sorry, so this wasn't a meeting about collaborating with me on my existing product line?" I asked.

"Amanda, your product is amazing, but we already have a wonderful product. We would like to bring you out to Charlotte to tour our Uptown headquarters, our labs and our facilities, and see what you think. With your unique perspective, we think you would be a great fit as our brand ambassador. We want you to use your social media savvy as an influencer to assist us in extending our reach to new potential clients we haven't reached before as we seek to position ourselves on a growing playing field," Richard said.

My eyes went from Richard to Alexa, and I watched as she crossed her legs and adjusted herself in the chair. Her bracelets clinked and clanged against each other with every movement, and her perfume wafted in the air with every motion.

"We are totally re-envisioning Providence. You have new upcoming brands like Millie Bobbie Brown's Florence by Mills. Cruelty-free, clean, totally vegan, and super affordable. She offers natural looking make-up because right now, it's all about natural beauty. She's launching sometime this summer and will probably sell out for quite some time. The anticipation is high.

"You also have Kathleen Fuentes. The YouTube and Instagram influencer known as KathleenLights with over a million followers. She's launching her Lights Lacquer brand of cruelty free, vegan nail polish later this year. Again, crazy buzz. Brand awareness is more important than price to Gen Z," Richard continued, before clearing his throat.

My eyes shot back to Alexa, as she cocked her head to the side, and she returned my gaze for a moment, almost expectantly. When I didn't respond, she chimed in.

"It's a three-prong approach. You would head up the social media aspect as an influencer, reaching people on a personal and street level. We will brand this prestige line and position it as a destination experience in trendy neighborhoods, and the last thing is growing that experience aspect of it," Alexa said, then took a moment to exhale slowly, almost as if emphasizing her point. Or to calm her own inner turmoil, since delivering this spiel to me seemed to be next level frustrating for her.

That was probably because my eyes were boring a tunnel through her exasperated forehead. She annoyed me, in every sort of way. I wanted to rip the bangles off of her wrists and play ring toss on the church steeple that passed for her nose.

Namaste to you, too, lady.

"People connect with celebrity endorsements, but the biggest influencers are those who connect with their public, like you, and others like you. You can help us grow that, too, by finding others like yourself and coaching them in our business model," Alexa said. "People like your colleague, Jacqueline."

I nodded, trying my hardest to check my facial expressions.

"It sounds like an amazing opportunity," I said.

"When you come to Charlotte, you'll also meet some of our staff and the new out of the box thinkers we've brought on board. There, you'll get a feel for our culture and identity. We can show you our flagship boutique, give you a taste of what Charlotte has to offer, and go from there," Richard said.

"That sounds really nice, thank you," I said, smiling. Actually, I was massively disappointed. I thought this would be my big break. Seriously. I thought I was about to get out of the corner of the salon and into Neiman Marcus. Nope. Not today.

Richard and Alexa stood.

"Well, we'll be in touch soon with the details. After our lunch, we're off to look at a few possible locations for a new boutique. Are you sure you don't want anything? We'd love for you to have lunch with us," Alexa said as I stood up to shake her hand again.

"No, I'm still processing breakfast. But thank you. I look forward to talking to you both soon," I said, reaching to shake Richard's hand.

"It was a pleasure to meet you, Amanda," Richard said.

"You as well," I said.

"We know you're not from New York, with that accent that keeps peeking out on your Instagram stories. I heard it a bit while we were talking. Whereabouts in the south are you from?" Alexa asked.

I grinned.

"Alabama," I said.

Richard raised his eyebrows.

"I would have never guessed. What part? Birmingham?" Richard asked.

"Um, no. Saraland. Right outside Mobile. Just north of Chickasaw and Prichard," I said.

"Wow. Alabama. Are you a Crimson fan?" Richard asked.

I shook my head.

"Nooo," I said.

Richard chuckled.

"I'm actually a Duke fan. I used to dream of playing basketball for the Blue Devils. I played in high school, but, well. NYU," I said grinning.

"So, you played for NYU?" Alexa asked.

"No, I didn't. Music scholarship."

"Wow, go figure," Richard said.

"I was a Lady Gamecock," Alexa said. "But that was almost thirty years ago. Power Forward. Back when we were dominating championships in the Metro Tournament. "

"Wow. That's amazing. I was a Power Forward, too," I said, smiling.

"I can tell. You have the legs and arms for it," Alexa said, smiling.

"So, the Lady Gamecocks. That's South Carolina, right?" I asked.

"USC. University of South Carolina. Yes," Alexa said, as Richard signaled for the waitress. The red-head from earlier was back. Probably from under the floor somewhere. I don't know where she came from, but she was fast.

"That's really incredible," I said. "Well, again, it was nice to meet you both, and I look forward to seeing you in Charlotte," I said.

"Talk soon," Alexa said as Richard began placing his lunch order.

I stuffed my portfolio back into my bag and spun around to head back toward the entrance.

Wondering if they were watching me leave, whispering possibly horrible things under their breath, I turned back to see them busily ordering their lunch. I was now an afterthought.

It was piteous that I would even be so paranoid in the first place. The pair from Providence seemed to like me, although the meeting was maddening.

I get it, kind of. They were busy people. Probably on a tight schedule. Meeting with me was like killing two birds with one stone.

I was unable to resist the smell of fresh brew no longer. Stepping over to the counter of Jack's, which was hailed as New York's first 100% organic coffee shop and vegan bakery, I pulled up the Uber app on my phone and hailed a driver. While I waited for them to arrive, I perused the offerings through the glass.

Organic and vegan frittatas, toasted almond peach scones, and strawberry crumble muffins sat on the bottom row below mixed berry torts, oatmeal cream pie cookies, and apple turnovers. Every last thing on either shelf made me drool incessantly.

I ordered a cold brew iced coffee to cool me off and calm my nerves and a scone to nibble on. Then, I stepped out into the entryway and waited just inside the door for the driver to pull up to the curb, because the heat outside was blasphemous.

four

ALL ABOUT PERCEPTION ♡

My Uber driver, Shelly, looked like a muppet. Her facial expressions in the rearview mirror were incredibly animated in the one-way conversation that she obviously didn't realize she was having with herself. My mind and focus were elsewhere.

She continued to jabber on about whatever, through the crawling traffic on 6th, and while we sat in the total ridiculousness that was the Canal and Laight Street intersection.

At said intersection, I thought of stepping out of the Black Ice fragranced Honda Accord, leaping across the sidewalk, barreling through the throng of pedestrians, and diving headfirst into a Double Bacon Black with a side of fries and a banana shake. It was a perfect combination for nursing wounds.

Just on the other side of the wedge-shaped building perched off to my right beyond a line of trees, Black Burger sat next to the Fresh Food Deli and Grocery, on grid locked Canal Street near the corner of West Broadway.

It was open until 2am from Thursday to Saturday, and recently, after a night of early weekend bar crawling, Angie and I found ourselves at B Flat for drink specials. An hour later, I needed some meat, and Black Burger was only about a block away. It hooked me with the first bite.

Shelly pulled up in front of my place on King a while later, after sitting for decades at each light. I tipped her with cash and left her a four-star rating because I was an insanely nice person, and within moments, I was inside my apartment, where I heard Angie and Jackie laughing like drunk hyenas.

As usual, Charlemagne didn't even greet me at the door. The little gremlin perched on Angie's lap as she leaned her head back, laughing. I'd give that dog away if he weren't so stinking cute.

Jackie smiled at me.

"What's up, homie," she said. "How was the meeting? We gonna be rich?" Jackie shifted over on the sectional and tapped for me to sit down next to her.

I tossed my portfolio down on the coffee table and kicked off my heels, curling my legs under me as I crashed down between her and Angie. Charlemagne leaped up from Angie's thighs and bounded over to me, plopping down in my lap after licking my face.

"Now you wanna come over here and act like you know me," I said. "Just for that, I'm dropping you off in the alley behind the Chinese buffet. Their daily specials are suspiciously inexpensive. I have my thoughts about that."

Charlemagne looked up at me with wide eyes, then laid his head down. The heat from his belly blasted my thighs. He was such a cuddle monster. Occasionally.

Jackie was looking at me, expectantly. So was Angie.

"Okay, so the meeting went well," I said.

"Well, that's good, right? We're gonna be rich?" Jackie reached over and scratched Charlemagne's head.

"Not exactly. I don't know. I mean, it wasn't what I thought it would be. It wasn't about our product line, what we've done. It wasn't about collaborating on a new line with them, either. It was actually about *their* product line." I frowned.

"So they led you on?" Angie asked.

"No, not like that. I think I misunderstood them, maybe? I don't know. Providence basically wants me to be a brand ambassador or influencer on social media to promote their stuff. They want a group of ethnic people with varying skin tones and me."

"Like a model?" Angie asked.

"No. Kind of. I don't know. Yes, I guess, in a way, but it sounds more like maybe doing what I'm doing now. Just with this new beauty prestige line, or whatever, they developed for basically every skin type out there. It's supposed to be all natural, vegan and cruelty free," I said.

"That's weird that they want you to do this with a group of ethnic people. It's almost like they are implying that you're ethnic," Angie said. "Or more than likely, they want to get at least one white person in the mix for racial inclusion."

"How much money are they talking?" Jackie interrupted, smiling.

"You *would* ask that," I smirked. "Honestly, I have no idea. We never got around to talking about that. They were getting ready to have lunch."

"They didn't invite you to lunch? I thought it was a lunch thing?" Angie asked.

"They did. I was just too nervous to eat. My gut's been in an uproar honestly since I got up this morning. I felt like my face was on fire."

"That's that guilty shame, right there, that you're feeling," Angie said with a chuckle.

I almost flicked a middle finger at her, but stopped myself. And I wasn't going to tell Jackie about my Friday Night Fling. I wouldn't hear the end of it.

"That's a natural reaction. It's okay," Jackie said, shaking her head at Angie. "So, what are you going to do?"

"I don't know. I mean, they want me to come down to Charlotte to their headquarters and all that to visit. But that kind of cuts you out, Jackie. We did all this together."

"No, *chica*, you did all that yourself. You had the ideas. You did all the online stuff. I just helped you put it together. It was all you. You deserve to shine," Jackie said.

"That's not fair. You did a lot. Angie did a lot. I definitely don't think I feel comfortable doing all this and leaving you guys behind."

"You have to move to Charlotte?" Angie asked.

"I don't know. Maybe? I don't think so. It's all social media, so I don't think I have to be there to do what they're asking me to do," I said.

"Only way to find out is to go down there and see," Jackie said.

"How are you okay with this?" I asked.

Jackie looked at me, raising her eyebrows.

"AJ, look. Like you said, we helped you. That's it. You're our friend, and we care about you. We want to see you succeed. It's not about us, and it never was about us. You do what you have to do to make it in this world, and we got your back, just like that. You don't have to worry about anything else. Just do what your heart tells you to do," Jackie said.

I loved her thick Puerto Rican accent. It made everything she said sound magnificently meaningful and deliberate.

I scratched behind Charlemagne's ears for a moment.

"What about you guys?" I asked.

"What about us? I got my salon. Angie's got her techie hacking nerdy stuff. We're good. We just wanna make sure you're good," Jackie said. She shrugged. "I mean it would suck if you moved away and all, but we can visit you, and you can visit us. It's no big deal. Angie's able to take her work with her. I've got my family to help with the salon. No problem."

Jackie paused for a moment, her eyes focused on me intently. When I didn't respond, she inhaled slowly.

"Besides," she added, "all that flying back and forth to Puerto Rico racked up my rewards, so I can be down there to see you pretty often."

"I don't really want to move away," I said.

"That's your decision, *mija*. Your choice. Whatever you decide, I told you. We got you," Jackie said. "Oh, and you got some mail that came. I brought it for you. It's on the counter in the kitchen."

"Mail?" I handed Charlemagne to Jackie. He turned and bounced over to Angie. Then he jumped to the floor, yawning.

"Well, forget you, then," Jackie said, waving her hand to dismiss him. He ignored her.

On the counter were two envelopes addressed to me at Jackie's house. One was junk mail. I opened it to find that it was a loan offer from some Native American tribe in North Dakota with an eye-watering interest rate. In large, bold type at the top of the notice, was a declaration to borrow up to fifteen hundred.

Deceptive fine print hidden in the bottom few lines required that borrowers pay them back over eight grand over 36 months. Nope. Nobody's credit was bad enough to justify jumping off a cliff like that. I set it aside to slip it into the shredder.

The next envelope was from Saraland, written in handwriting. The address was familiar. It was the house I grew up in.

I tore open the envelope to find a very short and blunt, cryptic, handwritten letter from my momma.

She told me I needed to come home, and for me to call her so she can send me money by Western Union to get there.

I thought the only people who used Western Union were migrant workers on work visas and immigrants sending money back home to their families. I sent money to Angie with Apple Pay from my iPhone to cover stuff she would get that I ran out of, like dog food or toilet paper.

Plus, I had my own money. I didn't need my mother spending her cash assistance and disability check to get me down there. And, really, who the hell writes letters? It's quicker and easier to send a text or a Snap, or a message on Facebook or Instagram, or even call with FaceTime. There's email. Twitter. I even get super pervy messages on YouTube. Nobody writes letters anymore. Especially by hand. That's so nineties.

My momma can easily Google me. I've got all those IG followers, many of whom write stupendously creepy, inappropriate smut on my comment feeds. I block and delete regularly.

"You okay, AJ? You seem a little bothered over there," Angie said from the sofa. "I can see steam coming from the kitchen."

I shook my head.

"I'm okay. I just got a letter from my momma," I said, walking back into the living room to sit between Jackie and Angie again.

"From your mom? What's it say?" Jackie asked.

"She just says she couldn't call me 'cause she doesn't have my number, and that I need to come home, and to call her so she can send me money Western Union to get there on a bus," I said.

"A bus? It's better to fly or drive. Buses take forever, and they reek of diesel, sex offenders, and pee-pee. I wonder what's so important. Did someone pass away?" Jackie asked with a frown.

I shrugged. Charlemagne was at his water bowl, making slapping noises as he drank thirstily. Then I heard him shuffling around in his food bowl, pushing it up against the floorboards like he usually did to really get in there.

"I don't know," I said, finally.

"You gonna call her?" Angie asked.

"I don't know," I said again. "She didn't even write the phone number down. Guess she thought I'd remember it."

"You haven't talked to her in like what? A few years, right?" Angie turned away to watch Charlemagne for a few seconds before covering her mouth, giggling like a toddler.

"Try ten," Jackie said.

"Ten years? What the hell, AJ. That's crazy," Angie said, returning her gaze to me.

"I never told you everything about my momma, have I? Or my family? There's a reason I don't talk to them," I said.

"You don't have to get into that," Jackie said, waving her hand.

"No, maybe Angie needs to know so she can understand," I said.

"It's never good to pick at a scab," Jackie warned.

I ignored her.

"So, as you know already, I grew up in this little bitty town. Saraland. It's just outside of Mobile, actually. I went to school in the sticks. There were a few Hispanic, Asian and black kids, but in the area where I lived, all you saw really were rednecks and coal rolling lifted diesel pickups with large confederate flags flapping in the wind.

"Anyway, to sum it up, my family sucks. The cops are racist. Me and everybody I knew think they did something horrible to a guy I was talking to for no reason at all other than because he was black. They arrested him and suddenly he just disappeared. I absolutely hate it there. As soon as I had my high school diploma in my hand, I was like *deuces*," I said, holding up two fingers in a peace sign.

"Dang, AJ. That sucks," Angie said. "I mean, you told me a little bit, like you grew up with nothing, about your grandpa when he passed away, and how you had to wear hand-me-downs that your aunt wore in the seventies and eighties, but I had no idea they were like Nazis."

"Worse than Nazis," I said.

"No one is worse than Nazis, and I don't think they're that bad. It's all about perception," Jackie said.

"Yeah, and I grew up with them, and I perceive that they are all bigots. I'm good. That settles it. I'm not going back," I said.

"What if your grandpa left you like some huge inheritance you didn't know about?" Angie winked.

"No one there has a pot to piss in. Plus, I'm the youngest. If my granddaddy left anything for anyone, it would go to my daddy or my momma if it didn't go to my Nana Jane. *Maybe* my oldest brother. And he's the worst," I said.

"Man, you really got it in for them, huh?" Angie said.

"My best friend drove me here the day I graduated. We were on the road all night and got to New York at 10:30 the next morning. No one went looking for me. No one filed a missing person's report. Nothing. They didn't even care that I was gone," I said.

"It's probably 'cause your BFF told them where you were and that you were safe," Angie said.

"Nope, she wouldn't have done that."

"I'm sure it isn't what you think," Jackie said. "Family is always family."

"It's different for you, Jackie," I said.

"How is that?" She looked at me with her eyebrows raised.

"Well, for one thing, you all get together, all the time. You spend time with one another, you guys never fight, and no one is selfish. You all think about one another, and put everyone else before yourselves. You do holidays, dinners, cookouts and it's wonderful. I love spending time with you and your family. I love the celebrations, the quinceañeras. You have *traditions*. I love all of that. My family? They're horrible," I said, frowning.

"First of all, my family is far from perfect. We've got our issues, just like the rest. But people change. And you don't know how anyone else feels. Your family probably misses you. It's been a long time," Jackie said.

"I doubt it," I said.

"Only one way to find out for sure," Jackie said.

"You're always saying that," I said, sniffing. I was fighting back tears of anger. Fear. I don't know. Probably both.

"It's 'cause it's true. Look, you don't have to go down by yourself. We can go with you," Jackie said.

"I can't go. Unless you're taking Charles the Great with you, I have to stay here and dog sit and watch the crib, plus someone needs to run the boutique," Angie said.

"I don't plan on being gone for more than like two days if I *did* go. In and out, covert style black ops mission. But I'm not going," I said as I tossed my hair over my shoulder for emphasis. "And you don't need to run the boutique. It can be closed for a couple of days. Or I can phone a friend."

"Then I'll go with you. We can fly down tonight or tomorrow, rent a car when we get there. Whatever you want. I can look at flights real quick online, and we can book out of JFK," Jackie said.

"I'm not going, so it's okay, Jackie," I said.

"AJ, what if your mother is dying or sick, and she's not saying it to you? You need to go." Jackie frowned. She pointed her finger at me as if to drive the point home and watched me for what seemed like an eternity.

"You don't want the regret of knowing you could have been there one last time to see her and didn't do it. If it's the worse case scenario, and I really pray that it isn't. But, when people we love are gone, they're gone. There's no getting them back. And there's no goodbye. It's too late," Jackie said, shrugging. "And that's your *mother*. Nothing she ever does will change that. It's a fact of life."

"Wow. Why so *morbid*, Jackie? Nobody's dying," I said, rolling my eyes. Jackie straight up ignored me.

"Trust me. I know. I was angry with my brother for joining that gang. He did things he shouldn't have done. My parents taught him better than that, but he chose his life. And I didn't talk to him anymore after he got sent to Rikers. I never visited him in that place, and you know what? He died while waiting for his court date," Jackie said, her eyes beginning to gloss over. I felt a sudden pain in my gut, and I was ashamed that I never knew that detail of her life.

"What happened to your brother? How did he die?" I asked, unsure if she would even want to answer me. I wouldn't blame her if she didn't.

"Someone took a toothbrush, sharpened it, and stabbed him, over and over again. Now he's gone, over contraband pages ripped out of a porno mag. I can't get him back, and I can't say I'm sorry to him. All I can hope and pray is that GOD tells him for me," Jackie said with a sadness I had never heard from her before. She was always so positive. Seeing her like this, I was mortified.

"I'm so sorry. I didn't know. You never talked about him," I said.

"It was hard to bring up. But, anyway. You don't want the regret, AJ. You never get over something like that," she said, almost as a whisper.

We fell silent, listening to the click of Charlemagne's feet on the wood floor in the hallway.

"Well, after all that, some libations are required," I said.

"Oh, okay. If you're drinking, I'm leaving," Jackie stood up.

"Jackie, no, don't go," I said. "Just 'cause you're a church girl, that doesn't mean you can't still hang out with us while we drink. I've got Sunkist for you in the fridge. It's your favorite. Come on, seriously. Don't go," I said.

"For someone who used to *be* a church girl, you know I don't love being around that stuff," Jackie said. "But you two have fun. I will see you later. Plus, I want to get a head start on the traffic back to the Boogie Down. I always get stuck on the FDR."

"It's the weekend," I said.

"This is New York. You know that never matters. I'm not taking any chances," she said, reaching into her purse for her keys.

"What I'm saying is, you seriously paid like forty bucks to park for a few hours. Might as well stay the whole day."

"It was more like thirty-three, but it's still way cheaper than catching an Uber, Lyft or Juno over here. And I hate the train and buses. Too many Stranger Dangers."

"When I come out to see you on the weekends, the subway takes about the same time it takes you to drive. And I carry Suzanne." It was my nickname for my switchblade.

"You should just move out of SoHo. You can have a house with a garage out my way for what you pay here if you don't mind the barbeques, block parties and chilling with all the *boriqua*."

"Then, I would have to drive an hour to the shop and pay forty bucks a day to park."

"Move the shop. Simple. You need your own space, anyway. Instead of camping out in the corner of a salon. She's practically charging you booth rent."

Exasperated, I blew out a long breath and shook my head.

"Well, I love you. Thank you for the talk, and the mail," I said.

"You're welcome," Jackie said. "And I love you too. You should go and see your family. Call me if you change your mind, and I'll go with you."

"Okay. Drive safe," I said, standing up to follow her to the door. I walked with her outside to watch from the stoop as she walked back down King toward the valet parking garage three blocks down near the corner of Greenwich.

As she reached the end of the block, I stepped back inside and found Angie on the floor, on her hands and knees, looking under the sectional.

five

"You lose your crack stash, Angie?" I asked jokingly.

"Funny. No, I can't find my phone."

"You want me to call it?" I asked, reaching in my pocket for my cellphone.

"My ringer's off and I think the battery's dead," Angie said. "But you can try."

I flicked up the white bar on the screen of my iPhone with my thumb and stared at it to unlock it, then called Angie's cell. A distant, intermittent buzzing came from the kitchen.

Her cell was on the counter, so I retrieved it and brought it to where she sat on the sofa. It had ten percent battery left, with 48 missed call notifications that were all from Stu.

When I handed her the phone, I looked at Angie with a knowing look on my face.

She saw my glare, and her eyes grew wide.

"What did I do?"

"What's up with Stu?" I asked.

She looked at her phone.

"Seriously?" Angie rolled her eyes, using Face ID to unlock her phone.

"You two getting back together?"

"Hell, no. I can't believe you even asked me that. He's probably gonna ask me something stupid about Fortnite. He's been stalking me when I play online. Go get the liquor," she said.

"Um. Block him," I said with a smile as I headed into the kitchen to pull out a bottle of Robert Mondavi Napa Valley Cabernet Sauvignon. I bought two of them to celebrate after Providence called to schedule the meeting. Now I wasn't sure there was anything to celebrate.

I reached into the cabinet above the sink and produced two wine glasses, then dug in the drawer where I keep all of my silverware for the corkscrew.

"So what are you gonna do?" Angie said as I walked back into the living room.

"About what?" I asked, setting the glasses down. Angie reached for the corkscrew and wine bottle, ripped off the foil wrapper, stuck the corkscrew into the cork and began twisting.

"About your mom. Are you gonna go home?" She popped the cork out with a yank, and poured wine into the glasses, filling them both halfway.

"I really don't want to go back. Seriously. I left the boonies for a reason," I said.

"But Jackie makes a valid point," Angie said. "Actually, she made several valid points. Okay, all of her points were valid. You get what I mean."

"I get it," I said, reaching for the wine glass closest to me.

"Do you hate your mom?" Angie asked.

I frowned at her.

"No, I don't *hate* her," I said as my voice cracked. The glass clicked against my teeth sharply as I sipped some wine down to wet my throat.

"But you hate your family," Angie said over the rim of her glass. She sipped it like she was sipping coffee, cupping the bowl of her goblet in both palms the same way she drank the last bit of milk in her cereal. Adorable.

"No, I don't hate my family," I said. "I hate how they act. And I can't stand my grandmother. She needs to just die already. If she isn't already dead. She's like the Crypt Keeper so highly unlikely."

"Wow. That's pretty harsh. So you hate your grandmother," Angie sniffed.

"Maybe," I said.

"What exactly happened to you there?" Angie asked.

I laughed.

"What didn't happen?" I snorted.

"Really? That bad?"

"You have no idea."

I took a sip and set the glass down.

"So tell me," Angie said.

She tucked her legs beneath her and shifted her body to face me, laying her arm along the back of the sectional.

I groaned, totally reluctant to get into this with her right now. All I wanted to do was to run to the bathroom. This whole thing twisted my guts into knots, and I was behind a few episodes of Fear of the Walking Dead on the AMC app.

Angie sat there looking at me expectantly like she was waiting for me to reveal the sex of a baby. I matched her stare for a moment before I finally caved.

"So, you know I told you about how my family's poor? All that, right?" I said.

"Yeah," Angie said.

"And they're practically racists?"

"Kind of, but not really," she said with a smirk. Angie's sarcasm was next level, to say the least.

"Okay, so I was in high school. Junior year. And there was this boy. Wait. Let me back up."

I breathed out, slowly, and started over.

"So my best friend I had back in Saraland. Her name's Rebecca, but everybody called her Becka for short."

"Had?" Angie interrupted.

"Yeah, we haven't talked in a long time. I don't know. Anyway, I nicknamed her Becka Snacks 'cause she stayed snacking on munchies. I called her Snacks for short. You wanted something, she usually had it in her locker or backpack. She was like a walking vending machine."

Angie snorted.

"Why didn't you keep up with her? You two have a falling out?" Angie asked.

"I got busy with school. And she went away to UA Birmingham for pre-med, I think. After that, we lost touch. I don't even think she's talked to Jackie in a while, either," I said.

"What's up with you Alabama people not talking to your fam?" Angie shook her head.

"I don't know. We used to be really close," I said.

"You think it has something to do with how close you got to Jackie since you've been here?"

"I don't know. That sounds ridiculous."

"But possible."

I frowned, downing the rest of the wine in the glass. Angie poured more in both goblets.

"I mean, you guys grew up together. You were like sisters, right? Then you move over a thousand miles away for college. You probably didn't talk to her as much due to your classes, and then you were with Jackie every summer and on weekends when you weren't hanging out with me."

"I don't know, Ang," I said, sipping. My stomach was starting to growl. I was about to get into Charlemagne's bowl. It would probably be better than whatever Angie brought over in those mysterious grocery bags.

"I didn't even really know much about her until now, and you never once went back home. I mean, she might've felt abandoned or something. Like, you kind of left her behind and moved on with your life. I'd probably feel that way if it were me," Angie said.

"That doesn't sound like Becka. I mean, she didn't visit me up here either."

"My mom used to always tell me that with friendships and family, everything's a two-way street. You can't always expect everyone else to make the first move. Like in the situation with your mom. Speaking of which, so about that."

"Yeah, right. So, my momma. Well, growing up wasn't exactly easy with her. I mean it was different when my daddy was around, but even then, she worked a lot. So after he left, my Nana was always over our house with Granddaddy, and she'd always be watching everything I was doing, making racist comments about me watching Fresh Prince all the time.

"She wouldn't let me watch any of the black shows or movies on TV. She completely freaked out about Jungle Fever and Save The Last Dance when they came out. Save The Last Dance was like my favorite movie. I bought the DVD later with birthday money from Auntie Beanie and kept it at Becka's. I watched all the shows and movies I wasn't allowed to watch at home, at her house."

"Sounds like your grandma had something against black people," Angie shook her head. "Maybe something happened to her that traumatized her. Made her form some sort of bias. I mean she's old enough to remember segregation, right? My mom was born the year it officially ended."

"No. She was just outright racist, period."

"But your mom wasn't like that."

"She never said anything. I mean, I think she was."

"Did she ever, like, make comments like your grandma did?"

"Not really. I hung out with friends that weren't white from the schools in the area, and she knew about them. They can't control who you're around when you're away from home, no matter what my Nana said.

"But when my daddy left, my momma- she just changed. She lost jobs left and right. She was always loopy from meds and sleeping. Always tired. She got on disability and I, to this day, have no idea what she was disabled with. I'd get home from school and she was in the living room laid out on that nasty smelling sofa. I think she pissed herself a lot. My older brothers and sister just went out doing whatever. My sister got knocked up and eventually moved out. My brothers were never home. So I got the brunt of my Nana's evil."

"So this boy you liked? What happened with that?" Angie asked.

"That's where things hit the fan. Becka's boyfriend, Wayne, he was a black kid that stayed over in Prichard, not far from where we stayed. He played football for Vigor High, and we met him freshman year, after one of the games. It was like a month after Katrina hit.

"Anyway, his brother, Terrell, had his license. He drove this really nice car, so he started bringing Wayne up to see Becka. After a while we all started hanging together- my crew and his crew. Terrell had this girl he was with. I started basketball my sophomore year, and then I found out he and his girl broke up, so Becka planned this sweet sixteen party and set it up so that me and Terrell kissed."

Angie laughed.

"She set you guys up? Talk about a wingman," she said.

"I think that whole party was a way to get us together. She knew I liked him. It worked, though. But we had to sneak around."

I finished the wine and set the glass on the table, flicking loose strands of hair from where it tickled my earlobe.

"You had to sneak 'cause of your grandmother?" Angie asked.

"Because of everybody," I said with a sniff. "Plus Terrell was older than me. In college."

"Did your grandfather know about it?"

"Nope. No one did, at first. Just my friends."

She shook her head.

"Did you guys do it? 'Cause that's statutory rape."

"Not in Alabama. Plus, my daddy was in college when he and my momma got together. She had her first kid when she was 16," I said. "It was legal."

"History repeats itself," Angie said.

"No, it didn't. I never got knocked up," I said.

"I was talking about your sis," Angie smiled.

"Oh, yeah, right. Well, anyway. Then, Momma had four more to that same guy," I quipped, debating whether or not I should grab the other bottle of wine from the cabinet. Or just make the switch to vodka.

"Your dad. So, why'd he leave?"

"No idea."

"He just up and left?"

"Yep. Didn't even take his crap with him. Left all his clothes, everything."

"That's weird. You sure he's not dead somewhere in the Alabama swamps?"

"Positive."

"How do you know?"

"He ain't that lucky," I said.

"Your country's coming out. You getting mad, there, AJ?"

"Just a little."

"We can change the subject."

"Let's do that," I said.

"So, how about those Steelers?"

I looked at Angie with a smirk, and snort-laughed.

"*What?* You're so random," I shook my head, wiping at my nose. I was sure that a whole stream of snot had flown out. Thankfully, it hadn't.

"It's a good question. Pittsburgh sucks this year," she said.

"You don't even watch football," I said, shaking my head again.

"Stu got me into it. He's a Giants fan. Diehard. Constantly trying to figure out if he was Blood or Crip," she said.

It took me a while to figure out what she meant.

"Oh, yeah, the colors," I said, frowning.

"*Duh.*"

"You think you're so funny. But you're not," I said as I stood up to head to the kitchen to find some liquor in the cabinet. The wine had me buzzing, but now I needed something to kick my butt into 'don't think about stuff' mode.

"You know, I read an article that says the Steelers might come back and get ten wins by the end of the season," I said.

"Fake news. Still not getting to the playoffs," Angie said.

"Probably not," I agreed.

"So, are you going back home?"

She knew how to snap me back to reality just when I was trying desperately to legitimately escape it.

I turned around and sneered at her.

"No, they can all die for all I care," I said.

"Wow. So hateful," she smirked. "I know Jackie offered to take you. But I'll drive you down next weekend, so that I can protect you from the confederates. We can take Charlemagne, I can take off work for a few days and rent a car. Get a hotel that allows pets. Stay a couple of days. Unless you feel like flying. Then you're on your own. I was in fifth grade for 9-11, but I still remember it like it was yesterday. All the smoke, the ash, the chaos, and the *sound*. I thought it was the end of the world. Horrible. I'm not flying *nowhere*." Angie visibly shook as if a bitter, cold wind had caught her off guard.

"I mean, I know you lived here, but you never talked about that before. I'm so sorry you went through that," I said.

"No worries," she said. "I don't like to think about it."

I nodded that I understood.

"You don't have to worry. I'm not going," I sniffed. I reached into the cabinet to find an empty bottle of vodka. The second bottle of Robert Mondavi sat perched next to it.

"Sure you are," Angie said, standing up.

"Nope," I said, grabbing the wine bottle before slamming the cabinet shut. Charlemagne barked in protest from his crouch at my feet, as he tipped over his empty food bowl. Such a diva.

six

DON'T GET SYPHILIS ♡

"My butt hurts so bad, and I seriously have to pee. This drive is ridiculous," Angie said, squirming in the driver's seat.

"I tried to tell you it was an 18-hour drive. You're the one who was bent on driving straight through. Oh, it's no *problem*, we'll just do it *overnight*," I said, mocking her and shaking my head as I rubbed the little stretch of skin under Charlemagne's chin.

"Yeah, well, I thought I could do it. Your friend back in Alabama did it. And I did it. We're almost there. But, for real, this seat isn't doing my butt any favors." Angie grimaced.

"There's a McDonald's at the next exit. We can stop for a while, and I can drive."

"With what license?" Angie's eyebrows rose. "I'm not dying in the car with you. No way."

"I know how to drive, Ang," I said, adjusting myself in the seat.

"Well, luckily, GPS says we only have like an hour left to go. So that's good."

The sign for Exit 57, Alabama 21 to Atmore and Uriah, came up quickly. Angie took the off ramp and made a left at the intersection to cross beneath the underpass. On the other side, a Holiday

Inn Express sat to the left, and McDonald's was on the right, just past the Waffle House. All you smelled was grilled food, even with the windows up.

Angie pulled into the parking lot of McDonald's and got out, stretching. I rolled down the window two inches or so just before she turned the car off so that Charlemagne wouldn't suffocate, and as soon as I stepped out of the car, I realized I was pathetically overdressed.

I needed to be wearing a swimsuit, or just my underwear. It was fierce as fire down here, and it was so hot that I actually saw the heat waves bouncing off my skin. There was no way my foundation was going to make it in this broiler oven. It was as if I had slathered cookie dough on my face before leaving New York.

Angie locked the car, armed the alarm and bolted for the door without me. I followed her inside and found her in the bathroom with her leggings bunched up around her ankles, squatting over a toilet with a wad of tissue in her hand. She was trying not to touch anything.

"You know, more than likely there was a bathroom at that hotel we passed. It probably would have been a whole lot cleaner."

"Yeah, I didn't think about that until it was too late."

"Don't get syphilis," I said, reaching for the sink to wash my hands. I wasn't going to risk squatting the way she was. My luck, I'd pee all down my legs in these jeans. I needed to get a pair of shorts on, fast. My legs were smoking, and the only way these jeans were coming off at this point was with a pair of scissors.

"I thought you had to pee, too," Angie said. She wiped, pulled her leggings up, and the toilet automatically flushed when she moved away.

"Nope, I'm holding it," I said, as she reached into the sink to wash her hands.

"You can hold it that long?"

"Watch me," I replied.

She shook her head.

"You better not pee in that seat and try to blame it on Charles the Great, 'cause I'll know when I see the crotch spot."

I laughed loudly.

"Sadly, the seat's already soaked. I'm like totally sweating through everything. I forgot how hell hot it was down here," I said with a snort.

"Yeah, so much for warning me. The black is melting off my skin and my braids are coming loose. I'm about to cut the legs of these leggings. By the time we get to your mom's house, I'll look like a bottle of milk with an afro," Angie said with a chuckle.

The line inside was ridiculous, so we walked out of the restaurant, deciding not to order anything to eat there. Outside, the drive-thru was packed. We slid between two waiting cars to get to the parked rental.

After taking Charlemagne for a quick little stroll to pee, feeding him and giving him water, we plopped down in the hot cloth seats. Angie snapped the AC dials to the max, and suddenly I was glad we didn't get the Maxima with the black leather, even though the seats were cooled.

We stopped by Sonic across the street from McDonald's for double cheeseburgers, tots, and Route 44 slushes, and then we were back on Interstate 65 heading west without any fanfare, eating to a soundtrack. Angie had plugged in her iPhone for Apple

CarPlay and we listened to her usual playlist that included Cardi B, Halsey, Bey, Jay, Fat Joe and Camila Cabello.

I never listened to any of that back at my place, when I was alone. I played the greats. Dizzie. Coltrane. Duke. Miles. Monk. Herbie. Louis. Billie. And when I wasn't engulfed in jazz music, it was old school Whitney. Nineties R&B. I wasn't a fan of what the radio was currently playing. None of it sounded like real music to me. It was more like noise.

My band teacher in high school, Ms. Whittle, was the one who got me into jazz and classical. Playing it in jazz band and symphony orchestra embedded it into my soul. I also played that style in church on my acoustic guitar, when I was on the worship team. I loved taking the old school church hymns and putting a soulful, jazzy twist on them, singing in my three octave mezzo soprano range.

People said I sounded like a white Erykah Badu. I was totally okay with that comparison. She was a queen, and one of my favorite artists.

My Nana despised my music taste and collection, but I couldn't care less. She always told me to turn it down, and I would just turn it up more to spite her.

I finished eating and gathered up the wrappers, napkins, and trash to put it all back in the paper bag the food came in. After tossing the bag onto the floor behind Angie's seat, I watched her as she grasped the steering wheel in both hands, bouncing her shoulders as she danced in the chair.

Smiling at her, I reached for my slush. I sipped, got instant brain freeze, clutched my forehead until the pain was gone, then set the slush back down in the cupholder.

I looked back to see Charlemagne sniffing at the bag on the floor. I should have known not to toss it back there.

"You know what?" Angie asked.

"What?" I asked.

"Maybe you'll get to see your dad again while you're here."

"Highly unlikely," I muttered.

"You never know," Angie said.

"I love your optimism. But realistically, probably not gonna happen," I replied. "Nobody knows where he is."

"Someone knows. Child support," Angie said as she adjusted herself in the driver's seat.

"Maybe," I replied softly.

Charlemagne found his way to my lap and decided the view out of the window was better as he slapped his paws on the glass, standing on his hind legs with his tail wagging. His head went from side to side as the trees whisked by in a blur.

A sign perched on the side of the road for Exit 31, Alabama Route 225 to Stockton and Spanish Fort made my stomach do somersaults. We were getting close.

Suddenly I felt the urge to tell Angie to turn around and head back to New York, and the next few miles happened quickly, like the last bit of bathwater draining out of a bathtub.

Within what seemed like seconds, we passed over the Tensaw and Middle rivers. The car's tires click-clacked over the girder joints as we crossed the long, low bridge into Mobile County, as both the northbound and southbound sides straddled over a wide, sparkling canal.

A short while later, the bridge rose steeply and soared high over the Mobile River. As we passed under the arches at the highest crest of the deck, I craned my neck to peer over the concrete divider at the winding brownish water as a barge slowly crept toward the supporting piers below. Blazing sunshine seemed to vanish, and suddenly the sky grew overcast and cloudy ahead of us, despite the brightness.

Angie was excited. Her dancing got more intense, while the Sonic double cheeseburgers and tots set my stomach in turmoil.

When I saw the sign for Exit 22 to Creola, I began to feel dizzy. It was like I was overcome with some unseen, heavy weight that seemed to get heavier as the miles continued.

The next junction, Exit 19 for US 43 to Satsuma and Creola, would take us straight to my old high school. The signs were now familiar, as roads I had taken before with friends either hid beyond the trees to either side or crisscrossed the freeway over the next few minutes of driving.

Memories, smells, tastes all came flooding back, and my hands began to sweat and shake nervously when we exited at the next interchange for Saraland and Citronelle, at Exit 15. It was Celeste Road.

Me and my squad used to hang out at the Dairy Queen on the weekends and after school. It was to the left at the light, just past the freeway. To the right was the Shell station where Terrell and I had gotten pulled over that last night I saw him.

Following the directions from the GPS, Angie made a right at the light onto Celeste and then made another right onto Forest Avenue. We followed that into my old neighborhood, where I had ridden my old ten-speed up and down the roads with my older sister and friends in the neighborhood.

Everything was still as it was, with the woods to the left as we passed the Wyatts' house. I stayed the night there for sleepovers with Madison and Allie, girls I grew up hanging with in their backyard because they were one of the few homes in the neighborhood that had a pool. Their set up was probably the nicest, and the pool house was an added bonus. It was a popular make-out spot.

"This is my old neighborhood," I said.

Angie nodded.

"I figured," she replied.

I pointed back toward the Wyatt's with my thumb.

"That house we passed with all the nice cars out front. I used to hang out there a lot with my friends that lived there."

"Oh, yeah? You still talk to them?"

"Not since I left," I said.

"You wanna go back and see if they're around and say hi?"

"Nah," I said.

"Okay."

She hit the turn signal and made a right onto Martha Alleyn Drive. Most of it hadn't changed, except for a brand new modern brick rancher that must have been built recently, sitting awkwardly as a brazen anomaly among older homes on the right.

The partially wooded lane continued on as we passed Harriet Street, and Angie pulled into the driveway of what should have been the house I grew up in. The address was the same, but the house wasn't.

What had been a sandy, patchy yard was now a large, lushly landscaped greenway. Flowers blossomed from well-manicured bushes and shrubs arranged as if planned along the now paved driveway and walkway. Spreads of dark mulch gathered around the base of the foliage.

The house I remembered was an old single-story brick rancher with ugly wooden slats and a pale brown roof in desperate need of replacing. It had a front porch with an old rocking chair, a ridiculous looking old sofa, a card table and checkered garage doors that looked like something out of Alice in Wonderland.

This house was different. It was modern, like something out of a Magnolia magazine. The old oak towering in the front yard was the same tree, but there was a new two-car garage with gorgeous doors and a second story above it.

The roof looked new, the brick was now white with dark wood featured in a lovely wraparound porch, and the front of the house was different, clean and modern, extending out further toward the street.

I reached for my purse and pulled out the letter from my momma to double check the return address. This was the correct street address. But it was the wrong house.

Angie looked at me, confused.

"This house. It's not right. It's different," I said.

"What do you mean? It's freakin' nice, girl," Angie said, turning the car off. "I thought you said your family was poor."

I looked at her with confusion on my face, then I jumped at the sharp sound of tapping on the window.

seven

WILDFIRE IN A DRY BUSH ♡

I turned to see my momma standing there, bent over with her finger pointing downward. I followed her gaze and unlocked the door. She opened it and I was dumbstruck.

The last time I saw her, she was wearing her crusty pajamas to my high school graduation, and her hair looked like she had spent her whole life soaking wet, plugged into a socket.

She stood there in gorgeous strapped sandals, trendy jeans and a really fly top with a dainty emerald necklace hanging from her neck. She looked like she used a professional MUA, there were thick, blonde highlights in her sandy hair, and it was on point, styled and pulled into an updo like she had been to Serge Normant up in Chelsea.

"You just gonna sit in there, looking at me wide-eyed like an owl in an oak tree, or are you gonna get out of the car?" Momma said, smiling.

It was then that I realized I was holding my breath.

Angie clutched Charlemagne as I practically spilled out of the car and collapsed into my momma's embrace. She held me tightly, and I breathed in the expensive perfume on her skin. The smell of fruit and summer filled my nostrils, and I hid my smile in the wing of her shoulder.

After a bit, she held me at arm's length, inspecting me with her eyes wide, just the way she used to.

"Other than that long hair, you haven't changed a bit," she said. Her eyes watered up with actual tears. My eyes stung, and my heart pounded in my chest. It was hard to breathe. Even though I told Angie I didn't, I missed my momma despite the fact that I hated her so bad. I wanted to shake the urge to hold on to her longer. It made my stomach feel like it was being torqued from the inside out.

She wiped my eyes with her hands. They were softer than I remembered. She hadn't aged a day. Actually, she looked much younger than she did when I left.

"Momma, you look so beautiful," I said after a while. "Who are you, and what did you do with my *mother*?"

"Aw, thank you, sweetheart. Come on, let's get you inside. It's hot as a devil's nightmare out here. We can get all your bags later," she said.

She nodded as she turned her attention to Angie, who had just shuffled around from the driver's side, balancing Charlemagne in one arm with a wide grin on her face.

"Who's your friend?" Momma asked.

"Hi, I'm Angela," Angie said, reaching out her hand.

"We hug around here," Momma said, reaching to embrace Angie. "And the little one, here?"

"That's Charlemagne. Charles for short," Angie said. She nodded toward me. "Her dog."

Momma looked at me and smiled.

"Ah, I see. Well, do you have a crate for your little guy?"

"I didn't bring one," I said. "I don't have him in a crate at home. He does fine without one."

"Well, I'm sure we can pull something together for him," Momma said, reaching out to scratch Charlemagne's head. "By the way, I'm Bethany Jane. But you can call me Beth," she said to Angie.

"Everyone calls her Angie," I blurted.

"Well, it's a pleasure to meet you, Angie," Momma said with a little nod, leading us to the front door.

"What happened to the house?" I asked.

She held the door for us to go inside.

"I remodeled," she said as I stepped into the foyer, followed by Angie and Charlemagne. I looked around in disbelief, my mouth hanging open in shock.

The house was cool and airy and looked nothing like it used to.

"How, Momma? You win the lottery?"

She closed the door behind her as she stepped inside.

"A lot has happened in the past ten years. We have some catching up to do," she said.

I looked around again.

"Yeah, I guess we do," I agreed, still awestruck.

The old, ugly, smelly, stained tan carpeting was gone. The entire house now had dark wood flooring. The lovely, chalky white walls were smooth to the touch, and the wood paneling was gone. The front living room wall had been removed, and the kitchen was now the central focus of the newly open space.

Beautiful modern furniture sat in the living area, and there was now a large bar with bar stools perched along the side of it, separating the kitchen from the front living space. In the center of the bar was a sink with satin silver fixtures and an ornate chandelier with elegant, fragile looking balls of light above it. Beyond that, white cabinets lined the back wall where the stainless steel fridge and wall mounted double oven stood. There was another sink and a matching stainless dishwasher.

The cabinets were embellished with nickel hardware, and another oven and microwave were tucked into the cabinetry next to the pantry. To the right, the hallway leading to the bedrooms was still there.

There were new, updated, much larger windows. The once horrifying sparkly popcorn ceilings were redone and a dark wooden beam crossed where the wall separating the kitchen and dining room from the living room once was.

I walked over to the left side of the house where the stuffy old garage had been, with its strong gasoline odor that seemed to come from the floor and walls. It was converted into a formal dining room that opened up to a decorated stone patio.

From where I stood, wood-framed outdoor furniture with dark red pillows and flower accents easily visible and the yard was totally green. Lush landscaping surrounded a stone and tile outdoor living space. Chairs, an umbrella, and a dining table sat perched near the edge of a sparkling pool.

I beamed as my momma stood next to me. She placed a hand on my shoulder as I looked over at what was now a staircase leading up to a second floor above the new two-car garage that had been added on.

"Your room is up there. In the FROG," Momma said.

"What's a *frog*?" I asked frowning.

"It's a finished room over the garage."

"You moved my room? All my stuff?" I asked.

"Well, some of your things are still there. Go have a look," she said, turning toward the kitchen area.

Angie followed me as I plodded up the staircase.

At the top of the stairs, chilly air greeted me as I stepped out onto a dark wood finished floor matching the staircase and the rest of the house. There was an Oriental rug in the center of the room. My old bed was gone. A queen-sized bed sat perched against the wall opposite a floor to ceiling wall of glass at the back of the house overlooking the large backyard and pool. On either side of the bed were two additional windows with views of the front yard.

I headed over to the large window to take a peek outside, shaking my head in disbelief. Trees had been planted against the rear property line, and a new looking large shed sat near the edge of the yard.

Angie squeezed in next to me to look out, and I felt her breath bouncing off of the glass back into my face. I stepped away and looked back toward the windows facing the front yard.

My old dresser, with its busted drawers, pencil carvings, and missing knobs, was gone. A matching dark espresso colored chest, armoire, vanity, and desk all sat neatly arranged along the wall to my right, and a door to a full bathroom sat next to what looked like a walk in closet to the left.

"Wow, AJ. This room is pretty nice. I think you need to take back all you said about your family," Angie said. "Unless we just stepped into some sort of alternate reality, your mom is amazing."

I didn't know what to say.

Nothing was as it was before. And that made me have a thought that might make a ton of sense.

"I wonder where my Nana is," I said.

"Your grandmother?" Angie asked.

"Yeah. Like, is she dead?"

"I don't know. Maybe you should ask your mom and see."

"My Nana being dead would explain the Love It or List It home makeover. Insurance money."

"I don't know, AJ. I think she would have told you. All you can do is ask."

I frowned at Angie, then tapped my finger against my chin, crossing my arms in speculation.

"I'm seriously afraid to ask her that right now. She's like a whole different person. Not trying to light a wildfire in dry bush, know what I mean?"

I caught myself, hearing the words as they were dribbling out of my mouth. I sounded just like my momma. Gross.

Angie exhaled.

"I think you can ask her, and she'll tell you. Are all those your trophies?"

I followed her gaze. My momma had set up all of my basketball trophies neatly on stands on top of the desk, and my plaques hung up on the wall above them.

"Yeah. MVPs mostly. All-Star," I said.

"Dude, I've known you for ten years and had no idea you played ball. Why didn't you play for NYU? You would have killed it," Angie said, smiling.

"I didn't get in on a basketball scholarship," I replied.

"I know that, but you didn't have to get a scholarship to play for the team. They let you try out as a walk-on. You'd be playing in the WNBA by now," she said.

"Easier said than done," I replied.

"You were *that* good, you definitely would have made the team."

"Good enough for Satsuma doesn't mean good enough for NYU. You see where we are? Very few humans out here at the edge of the galaxy. It's mostly droids and the occasional Wookie."

"Okay, Last Jedi," Angie smirked.

I grinned, spun around on my heels, and bounded back down the stairs. Angie followed me, and when I stepped back into the formal dining area, my momma was nowhere to be found.

I turned to Angie.

"Can you wait here with Charles the Great? I'm gonna check the other side of the house."

"Yeah, that's cool," she said. I nodded and headed through the archway down the hall to where my old room was.

The first door on the left was the room that once belonged to my older brothers. I peeked inside. It used to be a tiny room with a bunk bed and a twin crammed in, basically blocking the closet. It was dangerous to dare step inside, with G. I. Joes, Star Wars figurines, X-Men, Power Rangers, Beyblades, Pokémon, Legos, and Transformers all over the floor.

When they got older, it was a HAZMAT catastrophe of dirty clothes, stinky sneakers, textbooks, earphones, CDs, Slim Jim wrappers, X-Box and Nintendo games and God knows what else hiding under all of that.

Who could forget the smell of sweaty socks and ball sacks hanging in the air of the hallway outside their room like the stench from the petroleum refineries lining the bay. My brothers seriously *stank* that bad, and Allen was always torturing the other two about how disgusting they were.

Now, their bedroom had been updated like the rest of the house, with new windows, new closet doors, a new ceiling fan, fresh paint, and new wood flooring.

A single full-size bed replaced their rickety bunkbeds, with a nightstand next to it and a matching dresser on the opposite wall, where a flat screen TV was mounted above it.

It looked like and smelled like no one had slept in that room in a long time. Momma must have made it into a guest room.

I continued walking down the hall to the next room on the right. It used to be my older sister's room. It was remodeled too.

There were paintings on the wall that looked like they were from Europe. The bed itself was a queen with plush pillows and a Neo-patterned comforter. An Oriental rug lay on the floor, and espresso furniture similar to the furniture in my new room sat perched against the wall. A Sony Bravia flat-screen television hung mounted to the wall with an Xbox One X and Sony stereo system wired up to it, tucked neatly behind glass doors of an entertainment stand. A basket of clothes sat on the floor near the closet door.

A distinct, feminine fragrance lingered in the air. It was either hair spray or body spray, but it smelled like Jolly Ranchers.

The room felt lived in, and I wondered if my sister had come back home. I turned and headed to the next room, which would have been my old room. When I stepped inside, I stopped and caught my breath.

Momma had just dropped a stack of towels into a linen basket next to the elevated bed by the window.

Nana Jane lay in the bed dressed in a nightgown, silently staring up at the ceiling with the sheets pulled up and gathered around her waist. Next to the bed sat an ash-colored nightstand that matched the dresser against the wall near where I stood. A bowl of what looked like half-eaten apple sauce sat next to a glass of something sparkling.

There was a machine with an air tank next to the bed, and a clear tube ran up from it to Nana Jane's nostrils.

My momma straightened the sheets around Nana Jane and looked up. She smiled when she saw me.

"What do you think of your new room?"

"It's nice, Momma. I like it. What's wrong with Nana Jane?"

She exhaled.

"Your grandmother got sick not that long ago. She started forgetting things. Kept having these anxiety attacks and shaking real bad, and then she got pneumonia, and after that, she's been like this, on oxygen to help her breathe, not really doing much or saying anything," she said.

"She still sick?"

"Not like she was, but she can't get pneumonia again. It could kill her."

I sniffed.

"Can she talk?" I asked.

"She hasn't said anything in a while. She's just there, but not there, you know what I mean?"

I didn't.

"Why don't you put her in the hospital or nursing home?"

"Because it doesn't work like that. Besides, she's better off here with me, where I know I can keep watch over her," Momma said.

"Well, that's what they have nurses for," I replied. I stepped in a little closer to the bed, and Momma straightened herself.

"She's here, and that's all there is to it."

I nodded, watching Nana Jane's chest rise and fall.

"Does she know I'm here?" I asked.

"I don't see why not. She can hear you."

I stepped closer. I watched Nana Jane's eyes as she continued to stare up at the ceiling. Then her gaze went to my momma. I moved closer. It was then that I noticed that she wouldn't look in my direction.

Wow.

"Nana?"

She blinked.

"Nana Jane, I'm back."

She blinked again, keeping her eyes focused on my momma.

I shook my head. She knew she was wrong. She remembered what she did, which is why she couldn't bear the sight of me. I wanted to snatch that oxygen mask off of her and let her fight for air. And choke.

I felt my face getting hot, so I backed away to head out of the room.

"Give her time, she'll warm up. She hasn't seen you in so long."

"Hasn't been long enough," I muttered under my breath, stepping into the dark of the hall.

I walked back into the living area, where Angie sat on the chaise lounge with Charlemagne in her arms.

She looked up at me, smiling. Her smile faded when she saw my face.

"What happened?" she asked.

"What didn't happen? My Nana is alive and well, kickin' it in my old room, living life as a cauliflower."

"Aw. I'm sorry," Angie said.

"Don't be. This was a bad idea. A really bad idea. We should just go," I said.

"AJ, I don't think that's a good idea, I mean, your mom is clearly happy you're here. Look at all she did for you with your room and all that, not even knowing if you were really gonna come down or not. It would be totally rude to leave. Not when you still don't know exactly why she wanted you to come back here so bad."

"Dude. My bedroom's a nursing home, and that other room, FROG, or whatever, is really a low key guest room. Seriously, I'm about to scream. I can't be here. We gotta go," I said.

"I don't think you should leave either," Momma said from behind me, causing me to jump again. I didn't even know she was there. She was still a stalker.

I turned around to look at her, embarrassed and unsure of how much she actually heard.

"I know it's been a long time. Too long. A lot has changed. And there are things I think it's time you knew about." My momma was wringing her hands.

I frowned.

"You mean about the letter?" I asked.

"We can talk about it later. Not right now. We gotta go pick up your niece. She's over there hanging out at that pizza place over on Celeste with her friends, over by the library. I told her as long as her grades were good, she can hang out there right after school, and then do her homework when she got home."

"My niece?"

"Yes. Your sister's daughter. Ivy. Did you forget you had a niece?"

"Wow," I said. I hadn't even thought about her. "She was so little when I left."

"Yes, she was."

"Where's Taylor? At work?" I asked.

"No. She's in jail."

"What? In *jail*? What the hell did she do?" I crossed my arms.

"She's in there for shoplifting and drugs. Had some prescription pills on her," Momma said.

"*Your* pills?" I asked, then quickly flinched as Momma cut her eyes at me. She looked like she was about to slap my face.

"No," she said.

I glanced over at Angie and met her look of discomfort just as she raised her eyebrows at me. I shook my head in disbelief.

"How long's she been locked up?" I asked, turning back to Momma.

"Just a few weeks. They might let Taylor go at the hearing. She's taking these classes now, so that should make her odds a little better."

"You didn't bail her out?"

"No. She needs to be right where she is."

"Why would you say that? Why would you leave her in there? That's insane," I said, my face getting hot again as a massive headache started coming on. My freakin' *mother*.

"Actually, she asked me not to post her bail. The public defender said that if she sits, she's more likely to get off on probation, especially if she completes those classes."

"A public defender? You know they work for the system, right? And a real lawyer would've gotten her out. And off." I shook my head, exhaling sharply.

"You say all that without really knowing the full story and how she got arrested in the first place," Momma said. I looked at Angie again, who looked apologetic.

"Still. She needs a real lawyer," I said.

"Maybe. But what good would that do her in the long run? This way, she gets the help she needs."

"There are drug rehabs for that," I said, clearing my throat. It felt like my mouth was full of sand.

"That's true. But a nice, cushiony rehab won't put the fear of GOD in you. Sitting in a concrete box with no daylight, phone or freedom is a whole different story. She's not gonna want to go back after that."

I frowned.

"Your perspective makes absolutely no sense whatsoever," I said.

"I think it does," she snapped back. "Your sister is no criminal. That boyfriend of hers, well, he's double trouble in a dump truck. Being away from him will get that influence off of her. Being in that cell will isolate her enough so she can think about what kind of life she really wants. So she can be a better mom for Ivy."

I exhaled slowly. Nana Jane's sick. Taylor's in jail. What's next?

"What about my brothers? Allen? Wyatt? Tanner?"

My Momma's face changed, and she smiled.

"They're all fine. All have jobs, all working. All living on their own. Allen is down in Mobile. He works for the Port Authority. Wyatt is the manager at the Verizon store over by the police station, and Tanner drives truck over the road."

"So how did Taylor end up in jail exactly? She steal something from Walmart with someone's codeine prescription in her pocket?" I asked, after a short pause.

"Well, like I said, Ivy's daddy was a big influence on that."

"Figures. Where's he?"

"He's in jail, too. For a much longer time."

"Geez. What did *he* do?"

Momma scrunched her face up in thought.

"You know, I'm not really sure. I know he had a lot of warrants and violated his probation. He's been in and out of jail since you did that little vanishing act of yours."

"So, how did he get my sister locked up?"

"Taylor told me he slipped a lighter into her pocket before they left the store. The sheriffs were right next door having lunch, so that was convenient. As far as the meds go, he had a plastic bag of fentanyl on him, some marijuana and some other pills that somehow ended up in her jacket. None of the pills were in a prescription bottle, and he didn't have a script for them."

"So, he basically set her up to cover his own anus," I said sharply.

"As I said, he's a heaping mess of trouble."

"If he had all these warrants, why would he go somewhere with the police right next door?"

"I never said he was the sharpest tool in the shed," Momma said with a chuckle.

I paused for a little bit, watching Angie stroke Charlemagne's chin.

"I'd like to see Taylor," I said.

"Well, she's at Mobile County Metro. They only do video visits. We usually schedule it on the app, and then you just plug in on your scheduled time. It's like Skype or FaceTime."

"They don't let you see her in person?"

"No. Not unless you're a preacher or a lawyer. I can set it up for Saturday, and we can do a video call on my phone."

I nodded, then sat down, letting my head sink into my palms. Momma nodded toward Angie.

"You know, you can set him down. It's perfectly okay to let him wander around and stretch his legs," Momma said.

Angie laughed, releasing her grip on Charlemagne, and he quickly leaped down onto the wood floor. He looked up at me, then plodded over to my momma's feet, sniffing at her sandals.

"You have feeders for him?"

"Yeah, we have a bowl for his water, and one for his food."

"Well, you can put them over there in the kitchen, so he can get to it when he wants," Momma said.

Angie stood up and headed out the front door to the Nissan to get Charlemagne's bowls and his food from the floor behind the front seats.

Momma sniffed and looked down at me as I sat on the sofa with my head in my hands. I felt her eyes on me, so I looked up.

"You okay there, Sugarbear?"

I hadn't heard Momma call me that in a very long time. Surprisingly, it made me smile.

"Yeah, I'm okay. Everything's just overwhelming."

She sat down next to me, placing an arm over my shoulder and squeezing me to her breasts. She smelled so freaking good.

"I'm glad you came. You should have come home a long time ago," she said.

I didn't respond. Just breathed her in.

"You hungry? After we get Ivy, I was gonna stop by the store for a few things for dinner. I can grab you something quick to hold you over while we're out."

"We had Sonic just before we got here," I said. "I won't be hungry for a while."

"Well, I'll make dinner early, so that way, when you do get hungry, it'll be ready. How do you feel about having pasta?"

"Sure. Sounds good. You putting sugar in it?"

Momma looked at me like I had lost my mind.

"Why? You don't like my spaghetti?"

"I've gotten used to New York and real Italian food. No sugar please," I said. "With the sauce on top, not mixed in. And the noodles al dente."

Momma shook her head and laughed.

"As you wish. Garlic bread, then?"

"Well, of course," I said with a smile. "But I don't really feel like going with you to get Ivy. You mind if we just hang here?"

"Okay, then. Be back in a bit. Can you check on your Nana every once in a while? Make sure she's drinking fluids?"

I exhaled again.

"Sure," I said.

Momma stood up, walked over to the pantry door, opened it, and grabbed a key fob and keys hanging from a key hook. She walked over to a door near the staircase to the upstairs room.

"I'm gonna grab Angie an air mattress while I'm out," she said.

"Momma, that's not even necessary. We have a hotel reservation."

"That's a waste of money. You've got a bedroom. You're not staying in a hotel."

How's she gonna tell me where I'm staying? I'm a grown woman. I can stay wherever I feel like it.

She looked at me, expecting a response.

I rolled my eyes.

"That bed is big enough for the both of us. It's like, ridiculously humongous. Don't need an air mattress. *That's* a waste of money," I said.

Momma smiled at me, and I got the sense that I may have been testing her nerves. Good. She spent most of my childhood existence constantly testing mine.

"Well, I'll grab one just in case."

She opened the door beside the stairs leading to the upper level and stepped out into the garage, then softly closed the door behind her. I listened for a short while, until I heard the clanging of the garage door as it opened and the sound of an engine as it roared to life.

nine

MAYBE SHE'S A METH DEALER ♡

I quickly climbed onto the sofa to peer out the window through the drapes to watch Momma as she pulled out of the garage.

A black Mercedes SUV slowly backed down the driveway, maneuvering around the Nissan Altima rental, and out onto the street. Momma was wearing stunner shades, casually looking both ways before she slipped off in the direction Angie and I had come.

A freaking Benz. It looked brand spanking new.

How the hell did my momma afford something like that? With Nana still alive and well, there were only a few options left that I could think of. Either she got some huge payout from my granddaddy's insurance when he passed, she found herself a sugar daddy or she got lucky at a slot machine.

Spinning around to sit straight, I tucked my legs underneath me, slid out my iPhone and held it up to my face to unlock it. Then, I opened Safari and pulled up the Mercedes site to look through the SUVs to try to find the one my momma was driving. When I found one that looked like it, I scoped the listings on the website for the Mercedes dealership in Mobile.

After sorting by model and thumbing down for what seemed like entire centuries, I found one that looked just like hers, but silver. It was an AMG GLE 63, with an atmospheric price, at well over a hundred grand for the sloped roof SUV.

I tucked my iPhone back into my pocket just as Angie was stepping back inside, shaking my head in disbelief. She had the dog food in one arm and the bowls balanced in the opposite hand as she shuffled over to the kitchen.

"Your mom's car is really nice," she said.

"Yeah, I know. I wonder how Momma got it. It's like a six-figure truck," I said, getting up to join her in the kitchen.

"Wow. Your mom is a *baller*," she said as she squatted down to push Charlemagne's bowls further apart. "What did you do? A little detective work?"

She poured dog food into Charlemagne's bowl. He came from wherever he was down the hall to the kitchen as soon as he heard the sound of chunks hitting stainless steel.

"Yeah. I looked it up online. Thing's expensive," I replied.

"I don't know. I mean she probably got it from working. Maybe it's a lease," Angie said. She turned on the tap and filled the other bowl with fresh water and set it down for Charlemagne.

"She was on disability for whatever reason when I left." I watched Angie as she stood back up.

I seriously struggled to wrap my head around it. Going from a doped up drool queen to bling in Momma's situation just made little sense to me.

"Maybe she went back to work and got a high-paying job. People do that, you know. I wouldn't keep reading into it. It's probably

not what you think, so there's really no need for you to be so paranoid," Angie said, reassuringly. It wasn't enough.

"*Or* — maybe she's a meth dealer," I said. It would make
sense. This area was full of meth labs back then. There was probably one on every corner now, like McDonald's on the East Coast.

"That would make this entire house smell funky as hell. Totally
doubt that," Angie said with a disgusted look on her face.

"Since when do you know what a meth lab smells like?"

Angie ignored me and smoothly changed the subject.

"I guess I need to cancel the hotel room since obviously we're
staying here." She located the pantry and placed the bag of Blue
Buffalo dog food inside the door, closing it softly.

I nodded as I watched her tread back over to the living room
area.

"Yep, looks that way. But I want to leave after I see my sister
on Saturday.""Okay. Whatever you want to do, AJ," Angie said.

I leaned onto the kitchen island with my elbows, clasping my
hands in front of me while I listened to the slapping noise of
Charlemagne drinking from his bowl. Shortly afterward, the sound
of stainless steel being pushed against the wall accompanied loud
crunching and sniffing as he ate.

Angie stood in the living room area facing me and thrust her
hands into her back pockets like a schoolgirl.

"So, do I get to meet your grandmother, or what?"

I grimaced.

"Sure," I said. "Why not?"

I reluctantly straightened up, adjusted my shirt and led her
down the hallway toward my old room.

Once we were inside, Nana Jane focused her eyes on the window.

I watched her for a while. Angie posted up next to me so close that I heard her breathing.

"So, this is my Nana," I said with a sniff.

"What's wrong with her?"

"She got pneumonia, started getting scatter-brained or whatever and then ended up like this. That's all I know. She has some sort of breathing machine, or whatever that is, sitting on the floor."

"Oh, man. That sucks. Can she speak?"

"Don't know. Try it. Maybe she'll talk to you. She likes black people," I joked.

Angie shook her head, laughing.

"Everybody likes black people. Don't you watch Netflix?" She walked over to the bedside and reached for Nana Jane's hand. Nana let her take it.

"Hi, I'm Angela. Amanda's friend. Everybody calls me Angie," she said, holding Nana Jane's hand.

Nana moved her hand away.

Angela turned toward me.

"Told you," I said.

She wrinkled her nose and moved to stand next to me again.

"She won't even *look* at me," I said.

"I'm sure she can hear you," Angie replied.

"Good," I said, turning to walk out of the room.

Across the hallway from my old room, my momma's room sat with the door closed. Being nosy, I turned the doorknob and pushed the door open to peer inside.

The room Nana and Granddaddy usually crashed in when Momma was laid out drooling in a stupor on the sofa had once been a cluttered mess. It was the purgatory for all the baskets of laundry as they eventually found their way there to be folded.

An old turntable used to sit on top of the antique looking dresser in front of a large mirror with a crystal lamp perched near the end of the dresser. Speakers sat on the floor on either side and a framed portrait of a blue-eyed Jesus with Fabio hair hung near the closet.

Now, a nicely appointed queen sized bed sat against one wall flanked by ash wood nightstands on either side. The bed had a simple white comforter and light gray pillows stacked against a headboard that didn't look out of place in a W hotel.

Dark hardwood floors matching the hallway replaced the old brown carpeting, and the walls were painted an off white. A large gray ottoman with a cream colored faux fur throw folded over the cushions was at the foot of the bed. A Peleton stood in the corner facing the large window with an HDTV suspended above it angled toward the bed.

"Where'd your mom go, by the way?" Angie asked, peering over my shoulder to look into the room. "Wow. This is nice. Must be your mom's room."

"To get stuff for dinner, pick up my sister's daughter. Probably a crate for Charlemagne that I'm not gonna use and an air mattress for you. That way we can't do anything suspicious in the bed," I replied.

I closed the door quietly and turned to head back down the hallway.

"Gross. I'm not spooning with you ever again. You slobber so bad. And you fart in your sleep. I have never in my life met someone so gassy. Nope. I'll take the air mattress for four hundred dollars please," Angie said.

"I do *not* fart when I sleep," I retorted as we reached the living room.

"Oh, yes. You do," Angie chuckled.

"You're such a liar," I replied, sinking back down onto the sofa. Angie reclaimed the chaise. Charlemagne was eagerly waiting for us, and when I tapped my thigh, he jumped onto my lap and licked my cheek. Such a snuggle bug.

"Plus, none of the guys I messed with said anything," I added.

"That's cause you got that *good good*. And you're model hot, not one of them THOT's. No dude's gonna turn down the goodies just 'cause you let out a couple of seat heaters. Besides. Usually when I smash someone, they pass the hell out right afterwards. I put that *thang* on 'em, so a guy wouldn't hear me fart, anyway."

"Yo, have you been low key sleeping with other dudes since Stu? I thought you turned celibate?" I said, breaking out into a loud laugh.

"I'm not a nun, AJ. I got needs, girl. I mean, I don't bang the whole bar like you do, but I get it in when I need it. I got a regular booty call," she said.

"Um. I don't bang the whole bar. So fight me. Keep talking out the side of your mouth and you're gonna get it. I know where my granddaddy kept his rifles. So, who's this booty call of yours? Someone I know?" I asked, being nosy.

"A lady never tells," Angie responded with a chuckle. "So what are we gonna do until your mom comes back? Go play with your grandpa's gun collection in the backyard? Hunt some squirrels?" Angie asked.

"Dude. The pool. We can go out on the patio and chill."

"Probably should put Charles on a leash."

"Oh no. We're in Alabama. I'm not letting him out there with all those chiggers, ticks and fleas. Or worse, the vultures will snatch him right out of the yard. He's staying inside."

"Well, dang, if it's *that* bad, why are we going out there?" Angie laughed, standing up. "I don't want anything chewing on my legs, thighs and sides. Got any bug spray?"

We headed out through the patio doors and stepped out onto the tile. The sun's heat pricked through my skin, and it was agonizingly humid. I knew it wouldn't be long before my hair was all jacked, looking like an old wet mop. It had gotten a lot hotter than it was this morning when we stopped at Sonic. Like crazy hot. And it was only the last half of May.

Wearing sunscreen was an exercise in patience on the Gulf Coast, often requiring frequent reapplication. All the sweating compromised any real benefit. Alabama and New York summers were two different nightmares. Alabama had that hot, stifling, can't breathe kind of heat and humidity that seemed to bear down heavily on your shoulders, whereas New York summers were oppressive and hit you from above and from the sides, like slow roasting in a concrete and steel oven.

Summers for the past ten years have been sweltering in New York, but it was nothing like this. The sun bites viciously down here in the farthest reaches of the South, where winter is not really winter at all, and summer sticks around, lingering like a kiss on a porch swing.

People down here in Mobile used to always say that winter was more like a distant relative. Momma once told me about a blizzard that hit when I was a toddler. It happened in the spring before I turned three years old, dusting us with around two inches of snow. That would get laughed at in New York, where a blizzard meant total white out conditions, snowdrifts, and snow piled up by the foot.

I had gotten used to knowing what winter truly felt like while living in the city of insomniacs. I never owned an actual winter coat until I moved to New York and experienced real, lingering snowfall for the first time. Since then, the biggest winter storm I'd experienced was three years ago in January. It dumped almost three feet of snow in Central Park on top of what was already there.

That year, after forceful prodding, I finally went out with Angie and Jackie to ice skate at Wollman Rink on the East Side near the Central Park Zoo. I was afraid to skate on the ice, although I had roller bladed often when I was younger.

Ice skating became my new winter addiction.

But, even now, between New York and Alabama there were obvious stark differences in the effect the sun had on my body. In New York, I had to hit the tanning bed to get a nice bronze. Growing up in Alabama I spent most of the year looking like I had rolled around all day in a bowl of nutmeg.

Angie stooped down at the edge of the pool and looked at me with a blank expression as she dipped the tip of her finger in the water. The sweat rolled down her temples from her braids.

"It's hot out here, girl. Like this is for real. The pool water feels like you can boil eggs."

I grinned.

"It's too hot even for me. I feel like all the fluid in my body is evaporating through my pores," I said.

"Why you ain't tell me it gets this hot down here? Got me wearing leggings when I should be wearing nothing at all. And you got on jeans, so I know you're 'bout to spontaneously combust," she said.

"In my defense, it's always been hot down here, but I forgot it was this bad this early. It's not summer for a few more weeks. The forecast said it would be 86 today. It feels *way* hotter than that."

We went back into the house to escape the solar oppression.

"I don't know how I stayed outside like that all day during the summers. Eating watermelon with salt," I mumbled, desperately trying to fan myself with my hand. Sweat dripped from my brow and matted my hair to my temples.

"New York has made you soft, girl," Angie said. "We should get swimsuits and use the pool if your mom doesn't mind. After we find like fifty bags of ice to dump in there."

"When she gets back, and it cools off a little toward the evening. That's probably the best time to do it," I said. "Maybe we can get in after we eat," I added. I walked over to the fridge to take a peek inside, looking for something to drink. Sweet tea and milk. I grabbed the sweet tea pitcher and set it on the counter.

"You're not supposed to swim after you eat," Angie said, looking through the cabinets for glasses. She placed them on the counter next to the pitcher as I poured us some tea and took a sip. I hadn't had sweet tea in years. It was so smooth. New York didn't know what real sweet tea was.

"Who told you that? I swam with Madison and Allie in their pool after eating ribs and pulled pork. No problem," I said. "Their dad was always cooking something in the smoker."

"Pulled pork? Sounds gross. And you didn't have any problems 'cause you're country as hell."

"Don't knock it till you try it," I said. "You've never had barbecue?"

"Of course," Angie said. "My dad grills all the time during the summer. Ribs and chicken."

"You never had pulled pork?"

"No, and I never ate chitlins either. My mom eats it like it's the best thing since Wonder bread, making noises like she's having multiple orgasms. She in there cookin' that, got the whole house smellin' like trunks of dunks. I'm talking FEMA level. Never will I ever put that doo-doo smelling slop in my mouth. Soon as she came home with them buckets with the red lids, I was like, *peace*!" Angie said, throwing up deuces.

"Oh, you're eating pulled pork. I'm taking you to this spot we used to go to. If it's still there," I said.

Angie's face turned up into a disgusted frown, and she fake gagged.

"I'm not eating anything you have to pull off of something."

"You are seriously too much," I said, feeling the cold air conditioning making my soaked back feel like I was wearing an ice jacket. "I'm going to have to change into another top."

"It'll dry eventually," Angie said, rolling her eyes. She sat down on the edge of the chaise. Her back was just as soaked as mine was and sitting against anything would just make it feel that much colder. I shivered as Charlemagne leaped into her lap.

I sat on the floor at Angie's feet and curled my legs under me, laying my head against Angie's knees as I reached up and stroked Charlemagne's fur.

After we had dried off a bit, Angie curled her legs up and laid down on the chaise and I moved to lay beside her on the attached sofa, with Charlemagne posted up behind Angie's thighs.

The long drive had taken its toll on both of us. Angie was the first to fall, and I listened to her gentle breathing coming from her parted lips as her head began to grow heavy against mine, her braids pressing against the crown of my head.

We both smelled like the sweaty outdoors, but within minutes, I was lulled by the quiet of the house and memories of riding my ten speed up and down Martha Alleyn in the summers. I always wore my favorite denim shorts, Auntie Beanie's hand-me-down cut-offs from when she was my age, with my frizzed out hair up in a messy ponytail, balancing my gallon jug of partially frozen sweet tea as it dangled off the bike's handle.

It wasn't long before I was completely passed out, and the memories began to fade into a dreamless sleep.

ten

The smell of marinara, basil, and sautéed garlic filled my nostrils, and I sat up, rubbing my eyes. Momma was in the kitchen with a towel draped over her shoulder, her right arm swishing something around in a large skillet as it banged against the burners.

Angie was standing next to a blonde-haired, short girl with freckles, giggling together as they chopped at whatever on the countertop.

I sat up, looking around for Charlemagne. Then I heard him, lapping away at the water in his bowl out of sight beyond the kitchen island and bar.

My stomach growled impatiently, and I stood up to head over to the kitchen and be nosy.

Momma looked up and smiled when I slapped my hands on the kitchen bar and island.

"You get enough beauty sleep?" she asked.

"Haha, hilarious," I said yawning. "How long was I out?"

"Couple of decades. Whoopi Goldberg's the president now. You missed the election. It was insane," Angie said, shaking her head.

"You've got jokes," I said, standing up. My head was throbbing and I felt dizzy.

Momma cleared her throat.

"Ivy, aren't you going to say hello to your auntie? You were very small last time you saw her," Momma said, holding her hand out as if to present me to the court. Sauce dripped on the countertop from the spoon she was using to stir. It coordinated with the rest of the silicone tipped utensils, with their solid wood handles and the matching cookware. I knew that Chrissy Teigen Cravings set anywhere. I had bought it for myself and never used the utensils because of my OCD attitude toward my kitchen. It set me back like nearly three hundred bucks, but it was pretty.

"Hey. What's up?" Ivy said with a little wave and a smile, as Momma quickly wiped up the droplets of sauce with a cleansing towelette.

"What's up?" I replied with a nod in her direction. She didn't look like I remembered her, at all. She was a little chubby thing that I probably only saw maybe a few times since my sister was never around. Ivy was a little hottie now. I just hoped she didn't inherit her mom's penchant for bad choices. Or mine, for that matter. Beauty always comes with a price.

"What are you cooking? It smells good," I said, peering into the large skillet. Scallops, calamari, shrimp and clams all rolled around in a buttery sizzle as they browned, and Momma set the spatula down and turned the burners to the lowest setting. Red sauce bubbled in a pot on the next burner.

The gas burner grates were clean. I watched with my eyebrows raised as she took a small cloth and wiped around them. Then, I turned my head toward the wall-mounted oven as the mouth-watering smell of garlic bread hit my nostrils.

"It's Pescatore, just without the mussels," Momma said, dumping the red sauce that had been simmering in the pot into the skillet with the seafood, and she quickly stirred. "If you'll reach over there and grab that oven mitt and take the garlic bread out for me, that would be phenomenal."

It was comical that my mother had just said *Pescatore* like she was from Italy or something. There was no getting over it. I was literally dead at that point.

I slid my hand into the oven mitt on the counter and glanced at Angie and Ivy as I squeezed by Momma to get to the oven. I turned it off and reached in to take out the garlic bread.

Momma set a large serving dish down on the counter in front of me with a maple cutting board and bread knife next to it. Taking the cue, I set the bread on the board and sliced, looking over again at Ivy and Angie huddled together like they were best friends.

I cleared my throat.

"So, how are you liking high school?" I asked.

Ivy looked up at me and snorted.

"Like, it's okay, I guess," she said. Her braces glinted in the kitchen lighting as she spoke. "My last day is Thursday, and it's only a half day. Can't wait, to be honest."

She and Angie had just finished chopping up and assembling a salad in a bowl. Ivy took the bowl over to the dining room table and set it down in the center, inserting a pair of tongs into the greens.

"So, just three and a half days left of class. That must be agonizing. You playing sports next year, right?" I said.

"Yeah. I mean, we got workouts starting in August for volleyball, then I got fast pitch again next year in the spring."

"Nice," I said. "When do you go back?"

"The seventh of August, which sucks. But, this year will be cool 'cause we're starting blocks, so we get out earlier. Like before 2:30," Ivy said as she adjusted the salad bowl to center it on the table.

"Wow. That's early," I said. "So, what are your plans for the summer?"

Ivy looked confused.

"Like, I don't know. I guess hang out," she said as she glided around the kitchen island to the counter, reaching into a drawer to select silverware.

"Ivy, tell her about this past season," Momma said, licking a finger as she tossed a towel over her shoulder and began serving plates.

"I played with a twisted ankle, and didn't tell anyone," she said. "And we took home the championship trophy for the Invitational tournament. I had like four home runs."

I looked at her in shock.

"So, this year, you're a sophomore?" I asked.

"Yeah. Tenth grade," she said, setting the silverware and napkins as Momma placed the plates on the table.

"That's awesome," I said. "You gonna play in college? At an *Ivy League* school?"

"I don't know. Maybe," she replied, oblivious to my sneaky tease.

Angie apparently didn't get it either. She took the sliced garlic bread from me and set it up in a basket lined with cloth to place in the center of the dining area table.

Momma got the joke. She smiled and chuckled softly as she placed a pitcher of lemonade and a pitcher of sweet tea on the table, then headed back into the kitchen to come back with glasses. She set these on the table next to the pitchers.

"You didn't make any *drank*, Momma?" I asked.

She looked at me with her eyebrows raised.

"What are you talking about? I just put two pitchers on the table. If you're looking for soda, I don't have any. I can get some from the store later. You just have to tell me what kind you want. You girls go ahead and sit down and eat. I'm gonna check on Nana Jane right quick," Momma said, slapping the towel that was lying on her shoulder down onto the edge of the kitchen sink before heading toward the hallway.

Angie sat next to Ivy. I sat down across from both of them. Momma's steps were heavy as she plodded down the hallway, her heels smashing into the wooden floors with every step.

Charlemagne had perched himself on the chaise lounge. He watched me with his tongue hanging out, before yawning and returning his gaze to the table.

When Momma returned, she sat silently at the head of the table, shuffling her chair on the wood floor as she reached for a linen cloth to lie across her lap.

"Can Nana Jane feed herself?" I asked.

"Your grandmother? Sure, she can eat on her own. She doesn't eat much, and she's finicky, but she'll eat when she's hungry." Momma pointed toward the garlic bread.

I grabbed the basket and held it out to her, and she took a few slices and set them on the edge of her plate.

"And she can't walk," I said.

"Not well. Your Nana's had a few knee surgeries. Hip replacement. She's got a walker, but she doesn't get around much like she used to," she said. "You wanna say Grace?"

I looked at her like she'd lost her mind.

"Um. No, I'm good. You can say it," I said.

"I got it," Ivy interrupted. "Dear Heavenly Father, thank you for this food that we're about to receive and the blessings throughout the day. God is great, and God is good, and we thank You for this food. By His Grace we all are fed. Give us LORD our daily bread. Amen."

Angie and Momma both responded with an 'Amen' while I watched Ivy for a little longer. Although she looked like she'd easily pass as her twin, she was nothing like Taylor. Or her felonious daddy. At all.

That was a very good thing.

"Nicely done, Ivy. Well said. Thank you," Momma replied.

Ivy smiled, placed the linen napkin over her lap, and reached for the garlic bread.

I picked up the fork laying next to the plate on the linen napkin, twirled linguine pasta onto the prongs, dipped it into some of the extra sauce and put it to my mouth. Momma's Pescatore was so flavorful. The fresh basil and garlic exploded onto my tastebuds, and the seafood wasn't the typical flash frozen, chewy textured monstrosity that I avoided.

The shrimp, calamari, clams, and scallops tasted fresh. I tasted just a hint of the wine she cooked with as well.

This was a far cry from the store brand chalky tasting boxed macaroni and cheese and cut up ninety-nine cent hot dogs she used to make us all the time when my daddy was still around. That and the *not real* bad imitation of Kool-aid that left permanent red mustaches on helpless innocent children.

We never exactly knew what it was, so we just called it *drank.* I'd watch as Momma poured half a pound of sugar into a gallon pitcher of water, then rip open and pour that tart whitish powder into the mixture. It would turn red the minute it hit the liquid, and she'd stir it with a wooden spoon, permanently stained from mixing up *drank.*

After playing outside, if Nana Jane's sweet sun tea was all gone or brewing on the front porch, we could always count on Momma to provide the alternative.

"Momma, can we have some *drank*?" we'd ask. She would hop over to the old brown fridge that looked like it belonged in the fifties and pull out that plastic pitcher with the yellow spout and pour *drank* into the glasses Nana Jane got from McDonald's. They matched the old scratched up, faded plastic plates in the cabinet illustrated with creepy throwback McDonald's characters.

When I checked the cabinets earlier, the only plates and glasses I found were from Pottery Barn and Crate and Barrel. Looks like Momma messed around and found kitchen and culinary religion.

"Wow, Ms. Rush, this is so good," Angie said.

"Beth is just fine," she said. "I'm not *that* old. Yet."

"Where'd you get this recipe?" I asked.

"I have a lot of recipes I've picked up over the years. A magician never reveals her secrets," Momma teased, scrunching her nose up at me.

"She gets them from watching those cooking shows on Hulu," Ivy said.

"Snitches get stitches," Momma curled her lips up at Ivy, who just smiled, stuffing her mouth with a slice of garlic bread.

"Why not open a restaurant?" I blurted with my mouth full. "It tastes fantastic."

"Who's got time for *that*?" Momma said with a laugh.

"Gramma Beth, after we do mom's visit tomorrow, can we go to the mall? I need a new pair of flats and work shoes."

"Work shoes? You have a job?" I blurted out.

"Yeah, at Publix," she said. "I don't work again until Monday night."

"What's that, and what do you do there?" I asked.

"It's a grocery store that just opened up here a few months ago. Off of 158 by the freeway. Really nice place. They've got good sushi and hot food. It's where I usually shop. Before they even opened, Ivy applied and got hired on the spot. It's about the only place you can work being fifteen that doesn't involve cows, chickens or picking stuff from trees. And she hates babysitting."

"Oh, okay," I nodded.

"We'll see about the mall. Might be better to go after church on Sunday when we have less going on."

"We always go out to eat after church, though," Ivy said. "And malls close early on Sunday."

"The Shoppes at Bel Air are open until 5:30. We can eat somewhere near the mall after we get your shoes," Momma said.

"I'd rather go on Saturday," Ivy said with her mouth full. "That way I have more time to look."

"Ivy. We're not going on an all day shopping excursion if all you need is a pair of work shoes. So, we'll see," Momma said.

I reached for a glass and poured myself some tea. In New York, you can never find real sweet tea, and most people I know who drink tea drink it unsweetened. Or with milk in it. To me, that's just despicably nasty. Might as well just suck on the tea bags. Or sprinkle tea on Frosted Flakes.

Momma's sweet tea was pure diabetes. It was super sugary and stupidly addictive. I drank two glasses down before pouring a third glass, as my Momma watched me in amusement. I was caramelizing into candy by the second.

"If you're *that* thirsty, drink water," she said.

"I haven't had tea like this in a long time," I replied between sips.

"Shouldn't stay gone so long," Momma sniffed.

"So, Momma, what do you do for a living?" I changed the subject.

"Real estate," she said.

"Really? As in selling houses?"

"Exactly."

"Since when do you sell houses?"

"Since I got my real estate broker's license."

I sipped down more tea, feeling myself getting full, fast. I still had linguine on my plate.

"When did you get your license?" I asked.

"A few years after you left home, not long after your grandfather passed away."

"Did Granddaddy leave you a lot of money?" I asked.

"You're getting carried away, now," Momma warned.

"I'm just asking a question, Momma. I mean, the house is like a whole different house, you're driving a brand new Benz. I'm just catching up, that's all."

Angie kept her head down, eating in silence. Ivy watched the both of us in amusement, visibly eager to see where this ended up.

"Your grandfather got his pension when he retired. He'd been saving up money for a long time. The house needed a lot of work, so he started working on it with your brothers shortly after you left home. I think that's how he coped with you leaving like that.

"When he passed away, his pension and his social security went to your Nana Jane. His death benefit and life insurance policy were enough to cover his funeral expenses and finish the renovations he was doing on the house.

"I went through therapy, and when I got better, I used some of the money to take real estate classes and get my licensing. I sold some homes, invested more money in this house, set up Ivy's college fund, started my own realty company and treated myself to my Mercedes this past Christmas. I deserved it after all the hard work I put in."

She watched me as I sat there staring at her in silence.

"Satisfied?"

I cleared my throat.

"I was just asking, Momma," I whispered.

"Well, now that we have *that* out of the way, I have something for you."

She excused herself from the table and walked back down the hallway. Not long after that, she returned, sliding keys and an envelope across the table toward me.

"That's your key to the house. The other key, is the key to your grandfather's Camaro, sitting in the garage. He wanted you to have it. I've kept it maintained and did some work on it that it needed. It runs fine, looks good as new. In that envelope is the title, registration and insurance to the car and your part of the deed to the house. When I pass away, you'll get my portion and be the majority owner. I expect you to keep it up and make sure to take care of it. It's to stay in the family."

Suddenly everything started making sense. The letter. Everything.

"Momma. When you pass away? Why are you giving me all this now, is there something you're not telling me? Are you sick?"

"Girl, hush the nonsense. I'm giving you all this now so you'll have it since you're so adamant on leaving out of here like a second term president."

"I said I would stay and leave Sunday," I said. "I don't see what the problem is."

Momma stood back up with her finished plate and took it over to the kitchen sink to wash it. I listened to the water running in silence and glanced at Angie, who watched me with a pained look on her face. Ivy was scraping the last bit of linguine from her plate with a slice of garlic bread. She stuffed it in her mouth and downed the last of her lemonade before joining Momma at the sink.

Momma took her plate from her, and Ivy headed toward her room, pulling her phone out of her pocket.

"Maybe I should leave Sunday, and you stay for maybe a week or two and catch up with your mom," Angie said in hushed tones. "I mean, I can take care of everything there, and take Charles back with me. And me and Jackie can deal with the boutique while you're away."

"I don't want to stay here past Sunday," I said firmly.

"I get that, AJ, but I mean, it seems like your mom needs it. You need it. You guys clearly have stuff to work out. You should stay."

I stared at Angie as if she had stolen my lunch money.

"I'm just saying," she said with a shrug, getting up to take her plate and glass to the kitchen.

I sat there fuming as Angie and my momma cleaned up, put food away in storage containers and into the fridge, cleaned the table, and removed my now empty plate.

When everything was done, Momma headed back down the hallway.

Angie curled up with Charlemagne on the chaise lounge.

I stared at the Camaro keys.

Angie smiled.

"Yo, how you gonna have a Camaro with no license?"

"I guess I'll have to get one."

"Where you gonna park it? Parking's a nightmare in SoHo. And it's expensive. You're gonna have to move to the BX, Queens or Shaolin. Unless you wanna grow hair on your legs commuting from Strong Island or become a Nutmegger and move to the Cut. Or you can pay them tolls and cross that bridge to Dirty Jerz."

"Queens, Staten, and the Bronx are too far for work. And there's no way I'm living in Jersey. It's bad enough we have to go back through there to get back to New York. You can forget the Cut, and I'm definitely not doing Long Island."

"You shop in Jerz and party over there all the time."

"Not really. And, that's not living there," I said with a laugh.

"Well, you're gonna have to figure something out. Anywhere you go it's gonna be expensive to park that car unless you leave the City or come across the bridge. Are we gonna check out your muscle car, or what?"

"I guess," I said, pushing myself up out of the dining room chair. I grabbed the keys and stuffed the envelope in my back pocket and followed Angie through the garage door.

She clicked on the light.

Momma's AMG GLE 63 sat perched next to a ceramic white, 1970 Camaro SS. Granddaddy used to have this car under a tarp in the garage, with that old, crusty Chrysler Town and Country van parked out in the driveway. It used to be a dull white, with two thick, fading blue racing stripes running up the hood. My brothers all thought he would give this car to them. They always made bets on who would get to drive it first, but no one ever did.

Here it was, completely restored, looking showroom new and tarp-less.

"You gonna let me drive it?" Angie said.

"So you can put it into a concrete barrier? Nah," I said with a laugh. "That thing is a beast. It's like 450 horsepower at the wheels. And I know Granddaddy put more into it. I'm scared to drive it myself," I said.

"So what? You just gonna leave it here to rot in the garage?"

"Um, no." I took out my iPhone and started taking pictures of the car from every angle that came to mind. "I'll get my license and drive it."

"So when are you gonna get it? Tomorrow? Are you even ready to take the test?"

"I've *been* ready to take the test," I said. "Just never took it 'cause who really needs a car in New York," I said.

"Well, a quarter of New Yorkers drive themselves to work," Angie said, checking to see if the doors were unlocked. They were.

"Your family's house has a garage, and they've got like three cars parked out front," I laughed. "You're like the Queen of Queens. I should just keep the car at your parent's house."

"I wouldn't even trust a valet to park that Camaro safely. And it's probably a rare classic, so you might find it jacked up on blocks with nothing left but the carpet mats if you park it on my parent's street."

"I'll put it in storage, I guess, and just drive it once in a while. I don't know," I said.

"That's no way for a Camaro to live," Angie said, sliding into the passenger seat. "This thing is nice. These seats are like Land O' Lakes."

"Or Country Crock," I said as I slid around to the driver's side and plopped down into the seat, sinking into the buttery custom leather. The carpet was even thick and lush. The leather on the dashboard was fragrant, and the steering wheel was velvety in my hands. A pair of lamb's wool women's driving gloves sat on the middle console next to the automatic shifter embroidered with the SS logo. The gloves were my momma's size.

"Maybe I'll get Momma to drive us to the mall in this," I said.

"I don't think anyone but a midget can fit back there in the back seat," Angie said.

"For the love of muscle, we'll make it work," I said, opening the door to get out. Angie reluctantly followed me, and I locked the garage door behind her.

"You gonna stay past Sunday?"

I looked at Angie and shook my head, following her up the stairs to the room above the garage.

eleven

ADULT LEVEL OF COMPREHENSION ♡

I awoke to find Angie snuggled up next to me, and Charlemagne posted up at the foot of the bed. The television was still on, and the FOX10 News was doing a Saturday morning newscast. It was something about a new Mobile River Bridge because of several accidents on I-65.

Last night, before passing out in the enormous bed, we stripped out of our sweaty clothes, took showers and changed. I had fallen asleep in my cut-off shorts, tee shirt and socks. Angie was laying underneath the covers in her panties and tee shirt.

Her socks were in the middle of the room on the floor. Her sneakers sat next to my sandals next to the dresser. Our dirty clothes sat in a heap near the bathroom door.

Angie's head rested on her arm, and she was drooling down the side of her face.

When I stretched, Charlemagne perked up, his mouth opened, and he began to whimper. I knew what that meant.

I crawled over Angie, who just moaned and resettled into her spooning position, grabbed a poop baggie from my purse and led the way as Charlemagne plodded down the stairs.

Momma was rustling around making noise in the back room with Nana Jane. I scanned where Charlemagne's bowls were and saw his leash sitting on the counter near the bag of Blue Buffalo dog food.

I grabbed his leash, clipped it to his collar, and followed him out the front door, just as Ivy shuffled into the kitchen, her hair disheveled and all over the place. She looked like a madwoman.

Seeing the look on my face, she frowned.

"Don't judge me," she murmured, yanking the refrigerator door open. "They called me into work on my day off."

"What time did you go to bed last night?" I asked.

"I don't know," Ivy replied, slapping a quart of orange juice on the counter before rifling through the cabinets for a glass. "I was catching up on Empire and Star. I missed a whole lot from softball. Don't hold the door open. You're letting in flies. Grandma Beth will blow a kidney. For real."

I smiled. That's something I would say. I shook my head and closed the door behind me.

It was blazing hot already outside. Global warming is real. Charlemagne tugged at the leash, leading me to the left down Martha Alleyn toward where there were more elegant, newer brick homes, with their vaulted ceilings, perfectly symmetrical sidewalks and concrete driveways. They sat tucked among the tall trees and pines, just before the street curved to the south toward Robert Williams Drive and all the older ranchers.

Sauntering over to a utility pole just inside of our property line, Charlemagne lifted a leg to soak the dark wood, all the while looking at me with an amused expression, curling his lips up into what appeared to be a naughty smile.

I rolled my eyes at him as he let out the last few sprinkles, then let him lead me as he went about looking for a place to let his poops loose.

About twenty feet down the road, in the wooded area adjacent to the house, he found a spot at the edge of the ditch and squatted, his little hind quarters quivering with effort as he dropped a few turds in the grass.

When he finished, he trotted off toward the asphalt, and I stooped down to retrieve his turds with the poop baggie, and tagged along as he trotted down the street a little more before I tugged the leash for him to head back the other way.

Back inside the house, I dropped the poop baggie into the trash after tying it closed. In New York, I always found a public trash can to do that. But these were quality baggies, so I knew they wouldn't smell up Momma's house.

I took the leash off and let Charlemagne roam, and immediately he went to his water and food bowls.

Momma came into the kitchen, fully dressed and made up with her hair done.

"Hey, Sugarbear, I have to take Ivy to work. I'll make breakfast when I get back unless you don't feel like waiting. There's cereal, oatmeal, and grits in the cabinet. Milk in the fridge. Bread for toast in the bread box. If you would rather cook, eggs and bacon are in the fridge. I've got an errand to run after I drop Ivy, so it may be an hour or so."

"Okay, Momma," I said.

"Check on your Nana for me, please. Oh, and I registered us for a video call with Taylor at 3:30."

"Cool," I said.

Momma disappeared through the door to the garage. Shortly after, I heard the Benz bark loudly as it started up, and the garage door hummed as it raised.

Ivy came from her room and headed toward the door.

"Have a good day at work, Ivy," I said.

"Yeah, right," she replied, adjusting her ponytail and running a lint brush down her pants before grabbing her purse from the stand near the door.

"See ya," she said, and then she was gone.

I went to the window to peek through the blinds as the Benz slowly backed down the driveway and headed toward Janey Lane.

Angie shuffled down the stairs from the second level room in her socks, and plopped down on the chaise lounge, rubbing her eyes.

"Your mom is so *loud*," she complained.

"Yeah, her voice carries. How'd you sleep? You got a little drool right there," I said, pointing at the sliver of white crust running from the corner of Angie's mouth to her chin.

"Fight me," she said.

"You want breakfast now, or you want to wait for Chef Beth to cook it when she gets back?"

"Where'd she go, anyway?"

"To take Ivy to work. She got called in. And Momma had an errand to run. Probably a bootie call at one of her properties."

"You watch way too much Netflix," Angie said. "I can wait for your mom to eat."

"What, you don't trust my cooking?" I said with a frown.

Angie looked at me with her eyebrows raised.

"You don't cook."

"I *do* cook. Just not at my place."

"Heating up a frozen dinner in a microwave means you don't cook, fool," she said.

"I cook sometimes for the dudes I date," I said.

"No, you don't. Liar," she said. "I wouldn't call your little game of Tinder roulette dating. You just smash."

"Wow. *Judgy much?*" I replied. She stuck her tongue out at me.

I smirked at her, before twisting back around in the chair and holding my hands out for Charlemagne, who bounded into my lap like a cat from the floor.

"We should sneak the Camaro out and take it up and down the street while your mom's gone. Wake up the neighborhood," Angie said. "Do a couple of donuts."

"You and that Camaro," I replied with a sigh.

"Life is short," she said.

"So is your adult level of comprehension," I remarked. Angie punched me in my shoulder. I slapped her back in the tricep.

"Ow, *butt licker*," she whined.

"That's what you get."

"I'm gonna tell your mother you assaulted me," she said, scooting away from me. "Freak."

"Such a crybaby."

"So what's on the agenda today, besides talking to your sister?"

I shrugged.

"I don't know. Ivy's working now, so maybe just chill here, I guess."

"You should show me around your hometown," she said. "It doesn't look that big. We can drive around."

"There really isn't that much to see," I said. "This place is the worst. And everything floats down here. Kids disappear. We're safer inside."

"It's not *that* bad. Definitely quiet," Angie replied.

"Yeah, that's what will drive you insane," I said with a light chuckle. "Make any noises and they will hear you. And find you. And *eat* you."

"You're already insane."

"Fine, we can go out and see stuff. Probably take less than five minutes. Go get ready and brush your freakin' gophers, girl. Your breath smells like Similac and Tic Tacs," I said. "But first, I gotta tell you something, and I'm afraid to talk to Jackie about it."

Angie frowned.

"Uh oh. You fell in love with Thirst Trap Frankie and now you wanna get married and move down to FiDi with the rest of the millennials."

"Um. Can you not ever mention Frankie ever again? Actually, I wanted to talk about Cola. Jackie's cousin, Collette."

"What about her," Angie asked.

"We were low-key working on a clothing line called Rush & Cola," she said.

"So that's *extremely* random. Why would she be mad about that? She knows about it," Angie said.

"Yeah, but she doesn't know that me and Cola started making calls and got in touch with this beauty company in Texas. Right after that meeting with Providence. They have labs and facilities in Austin to make lip balms, beauty creams and lotions, essential oils, serums, scrubs. Even hair care. They work with brands to create custom products and they handle design and packaging," I said.

"Wow. That sounds like a nice hook up. But I'm sure it costs a fortune up front to get started, right?"

"Well, I don't know. There's an application to fill out and about an eight to twelve month turnaround to get a custom product ready to sell from scratch. Or you can use their own formulas and bases to do private label and start a beauty line the fast way."

Angie nodded and rubbed her chin as if she were a scientist speculating the solution of an equation.

"So by private label, you mean slapping your own label and packaging on their already made product and selling it as your own?" she asked.

"Exactly," I replied.

"And they can custom manufacture your formula," she added.

"Yes."

"You know the big beauty brands do this all the time with manufacturers in Asia, right?"

"Of course," I replied.

"It's probably way cheaper to go through a manufacturer on Alibaba. Like all those Amazon sellers."

"With some of those companies, there's no guarantee of where the ingredients they use really come from," I said. "And Jackie would have a conniption. She probably wants to keep making this stuff by hand, but I want to go large scale with it, especially after that conversation with Providence. I've been thinking about it more."

"She's gonna tell you what I'm about to tell you. Start small, use what you have, do what you know and work your way up from there. Wise advice, paraphrasing from the words of Russell Simmons."

"He also said sell what you love to other people. Give people what you wish you could buy but isn't available. For me, since store stuff doesn't cut it, that means the right products for my dry and sensitive skin and for my crazy hair, but responsibly manufactured. Sustainably sourced. Vegan, organic. Clean. Jackie has something incredible with everything she makes with none of the extra garbage you find in stuff sitting on shelves. Selling it on Etsy and out of a salon in SoHo isn't getting it major distribution. I thought Providence would be the key to that," I said.

"You know you could still do that Providence thing and learn the industry for a few years, stack your cheddar first. Being an ambassador or influencer for a large beauty brand like that will get you *props.* Just think of all those industry contacts you'll meet who can back your brand," Angie said. She sounded more excited than I did.

"Maybe," I replied. I let my eyes wander around the room as if that would somehow change the subject.

"And you didn't tell Jackie all this why?" Angie asked. "I mean, she said she had your back and that she was doing all this stuff for you to help you get up."

"Really, I didn't start seriously thinking about it until on the way here. I don't want to attempt taking this mainstream and not bring her along. I mean, you, that's easy. I know you'll ride with me. But she's got so many ties in the Bronx and it means letting those ties go to take things to the next level. Family is important to her. I don't have those tethers holding me down," I said.

Angie's eyebrows raised.

"You think having family is a setback that holds you down?"

"Well, yeah. My family didn't do anything to help me get where I am today," I replied. "They were toxic, and I left. I know if I had stayed, I definitely wouldn't have gone far in life. Probably be serving ice cream part time for minimum wage."

"Your aunt. She helped you get where you are and she's family. Did you forget about her? Your best friends growing up? And Jackie's peeps *became* your family. *I'm* your family. We got family we're born with, and family we pick up along the way. Either way, it's still family."

Angie punched me in the shoulder again. I raised my hand to get her back, but she bolted off of the chaise lounge and stomped up the stairs back to the room above the garage.

A few seconds later, she was back downstairs and out the front door, getting the rest of our luggage out of the trunk of the Nissan. We were lazy last night, only grabbing something to change into after our showers, and leaving the luggage in the trunk. I followed her outside to help, grabbing the forgotten Sonic bag from the back seat that now had the car smelling like funk and mustard.

I helped her drag the luggage upstairs, and we got ready.

We both got dressed in clothes light enough to keep us cool in the Alabama heat. Angie pulled her braided hair up into a tight bun at the crown of her head and I wrapped mine up in a messy bun at the nape of my neck. I put on a little mascara, lip balm and eyeliner, leaving the foundation off so I didn't walk around with cheesecake stuck to my face. After Angie put on eyeliner and lip balm, we were ready to go. Then, I heard the garage door opening. Momma was back.

She wasn't alone.

twelve

YOU AIN'T THAT BROKE ♡

I tromped downstairs to find Momma standing in the living room next to Becka. My breath caught in my throat.

Becka looked at me and smiled. She looked the same as she did when I left Alabama, as if not one day had passed since Graduation.

"What's up, *Manda Pants?*" she giggled, holding her arms out wide. I ran into them and grabbed her, embracing her tightly. She smelled like the outdoors and burning wood.

"Where have you *been*?" I asked, holding her at arm's length to look at her. Her jet black hair was long now, her skin was olive from the sun, and she looked like a Jenner.

"Whatchoo mean? I've been where I've always been," she said.

"You know what I mean," I said.

Momma headed into the kitchen and washed her hands before pulling pans out of the bottom cabinets and setting them on the stovetop, just as Angie came downstairs to see what all the fuss was about.

"Well, you know, I finished up at UA Birmingham. Then I started working across the bridge at Infirmary Eastern Shore. They built a new medical center here in Saraland just over a year ago, and they just started building a 24-hour emergency department. When it's completed around Christmas this year, I'll be transferring there," she said.

I hugged her again in total disbelief.

"Where's little Tyree? He's ten now, right?" I asked.

"Yep. He's with his cousins. They had themselves a little sleepover last night. I'll pick him up after dinner tomorrow since he's staying the weekend."

She pulled out her cellphone and scrolled to show me a few pictures of him.

"Dude, he's so big. He's gonna be tall. Like his daddy and uncle."

"Yep."

"How'd you know I was here?" I asked.

"Yo' Momma put you on blast on Facebook," she said. "Posted a picture of you laid out on the sofa like you drunk or something. She even used a hashtag. *#sheback*."

"Oh my god. She's so crazy. So, how's Wayne doing?" I asked.

She laughed.

"That's been over for a long time. He lives in Phoenix now. Plays for the Arizona Cardinals."

"The NFL?" I asked, my eyebrows raising.

"Yep," she said.

"That child support must be ridiculous," I said with a knowing smile.

Becka smiled back. That explained the Jenner swag she had going on.

"We do okay," she said.

"What happened between you two?"

"Them fast *thots* at UA got a hold of him," she said.

I frowned.

"I really thought you two were meant to be," I sighed.

"Yeah, you and me both," Becka said, looking at Angie.

"Oh, so this is Angie. We met in Weinstein Hall at NYU during my freshman year. We've been together ever since."

"*Together*, together?" Becka asked with raised eyebrows as she hugged Angie.

"No, not like that. She's my second bestie," I said, laughing.

"Oh, okay. Thought you were rolling on the other side for a minute there. You better be specific girl, being all Insta-famous now," Becka said.

"It's nice to finally meet you," Angie smiled. "I've heard a lot about you."

"Yeah, probably all bad stuff, right?" Becka laughed.

"So you driving a Benz like my momma?" I teased.

"Noooo," Becka said. "I'm a simple girl. I don't need all that. I got a Jeep."

"A Jeep's still nice," I said. "You buy a house?"

"I'm actually buying one from your mom. She's showing me a few properties on Monday."

I looked over at Momma, who glanced up at us and smiled.

"Ah, I see you, over there getting it," I said. She ignored me.

"So, where are you looking?" I asked.

"Close by. There's actually a house on Spartanburg Drive that I have my eyes on. It's like five years old, brick, on a half acre. Four beds, three baths. It's like around 280 grand. Almost three thousand square feet. It's gorgeous. You should go with us to see it," Becka said.

"On Monday?" I asked.

"Yep," she said.

"I won't be here. Heading back to New York on Sunday." She frowned.

"You suck," she said. "Well, before you leave, you have to come through and see Tyree."

"I will," I said.

Momma cleared her throat.

"I hate to interrupt your reunion, but I'm fixing grits, eggs, and bacon. How do you want your eggs, ladies?" Momma plopped open a two dozen carton, set them on the kitchen island and produced a spatula and whisk from the drawer.

"I'd like my liquid chicken scrambled," I said.

"Same," Angie replied.

"I'm good, I already ate," Becka said. "And actually, I have to head out in a bit. I can't stay long."

"Okay, then," Momma said. She got busy cracking eggs into a bowl while Becka, Angie and I sat at the table.

"So are you working later?" I asked as my eyes went to Becka's wrist. Her Apple Watch was going crazy with notifications. She checked it and smiled.

"Actually, it's a funny story. Pauline's having a little get together at her family's house in Bayside. I'm heading down there when I leave here. They just fixed it up from all that hurricane damage."

"Yeah, I heard about that in the news. Harvey was terrible," I said.

"Yeah, there were more than that. Gordon was just in September. It's been chaotic lately," Becka said.

"Yeah, I see. Man, I haven't seen Pauline in so long. I thought she was moving to California," I said.

"Who's Pauline?" Angie asked.

"OMG. For real, the three of us were inseparable throughout junior high and high school. She moved here in what? The middle of fifth grade? Her family's freakin' rich. They're like from Lebanon or the middle east or somewhere. They're big developers. Most of the reason Saraland started blowing up so fast right after we graduated high school. Remember Prom, Manda?" Becka rolled her head back in laughter and produced a snort.

Angie smiled in amusement at our reminiscing.

"Yeah. We all went to JC Penney to get dresses, and she shows up to Prom in a two thousand dollar prom dress from some French designer. Lanvin. It was nuts. There's no telling what she did with the one she bought from JC Penney to make us feel better," I said. I shook my head.

"Yo, she probably took it back," Becka laughed. "With her boujee self."

"Probably," I said. 'Or sold it on ebay."

"Girl, Leenie don't even use eBay. She all about poppin' tags. So, since you deserted everybody and didn't bother callin' nobody, I can bet you ain't got her number," Becka said, pulling out her phone.

"I don't have anyone's number on this phone," I said.

"What the hell is *wrong* with you? We was your best friends, yo. You know, you only live once. Time is short. Shouldn't do that.

Don't do it again," Becka said, swiping up on her screen. "Digits, please?"

I rattled them off after a few seconds of thinking. I almost forgot my own number.

"Ain't that exactly what Jackie and I were telling you?" Angie said with her hands cupped over her mouth as if she were sharing a secret.

"I get it," I said. My phone vibrated with the text Becka sent me. I saved her and Pauline as new contacts.

"You know," Momma said, chiming in as she spooned eggs onto two plates. "Pauline's family is how I got into real estate. They have quite a few connections here."

"Really?" I said. "So that means, you, Pauline and Becka are all swimming in money. I'm barely paying my bills."

"You ain't *that* broke, girl. I've seen your Instagram stories," Becka said with a loud cackle.

"You chose to live in the most expensive city in the country. What did you expect? You're just throwing away money when it costs next to nothing to stay where you grew up," Momma said.

"It's kind of starting to get more expensive here, though," Becka said. "I noticed home prices going up super fast."

"My rent is $2700 a month for a one-bedroom apartment, and that's 'cause they cut me a deal," I said.

"You know what I can find you here for that? You'd be in a house so big that you would need a shuttle to get from one end to the other. I'm exaggerating a little but you get my drift," Momma said as she set a plate of bacon and eggs with buttered toast on the dining room table.

"There's no life here," I said, turning to head toward the dining area. "It sucks."

"Girl, now I know you're trippin.' We were always doing something together," Becka said. She turned to Angie. "Don't let this chick fool ya, we chilled at the beach on weekends, Pauline's beach crib, the Floribama Shore, Pensacola, went to the malls, the parks, the bay, the bayou, Dauphin Island. Gulf Shores. Crabbing. Oysters, fishing, swimming. Don't even let me get started on Cry Baby Bridge and the Neversink Pit. Cathedral Caverns? There's so much to do here. It's impossible to be bored. Manda had tons of friends, she was the basketball star, played them strings in band, sang and played guitar in church, *and* she was super popular."

I pulled a chair out and sat down with Angie and Becka at the dining room table, scooting up to the second plate Momma placed in front of us.

"First of all, you're naming like *all* of Alabama and part of Florida. I'm talking about stuff to do right around here. In Saraland. There's nothing. And, I was *never* popular," I corrected her. "She's exaggerating," I said, as Momma sat bowls of grits down on the table, along with a crystal dish of butter.

Angie stared at the bowl.

"What's this?" She wrinkled her nose as she bent over to sniff it.

"It's grits," I said.

"Like Cream of Wheat?" she asked.

"Not even close. Those are made of the obvious. They make grits from corn," I said.

"Gross," she said. "No offense to the cook."

Momma laughed, putting the pans in the sink to wash them.

"Seriously, try it," I said. "It's good."

I looked down at my plate, shocked that Momma didn't over-cook the eggs to the point of being brown and crispy like she used to. I had to slather mine with ketchup and cut them up with a butter knife to force myself to eat them. On cue, Momma set a bottle of Heinz next to my plate.

Angie shook her head at me.

"You're really not going to put that on there are you?" she grimaced. "It was bad enough watching you dump ketchup on a perfectly good steak. Who does that? What's wrong with you? You need a psych eval. Stat."

I took a bite of the fluffy eggs. They were perfect, no ketchup necessary, and I didn't even need to salt them. Alternate realities are real.

"Doesn't need it," I said with a smile, stuffing another forkful in my mouth.

"What time are you planning on leaving tomorrow?" Becka asked.

Charlemagne appeared from wherever he was hiding and sniffed at Becka's shoes. She reached down to pet him.

"I'm not sure. That's Charlemagne AKA Charles the Great AKA King of the Franks by the way," I said as I bit into a slab of thick applewood smoked bacon.

"That's a *really* long name," Becka said.

"He has a really long personality," I replied.

"You thought you were on to something, huh? With that little play on words," Becka said with a loud cackle.

"I know, right? She swears she's a comedian," Angie added.

"All of you suck, so whatever," I said as I added a glob of butter to my grits. I stirred it while Angie watched me with a disgusted look on her face.

"That's a truck load of butter. What are you trying to do? Lube up your esophagus?"

"Shush," I said, putting a spoonful in my mouth. It was so creamy and smooth.

I remember Momma making grits back in the day. They stuck to the spoon in the worst way and were usually thick and coarse like beach sand. I always added water and milk before tossing them into the microwave to resurrect the dead.

Worse, my sister put a mountain of sugar on hers, which was a cardinal sin in its own right. That's not including the cheese. I'm surprised she didn't live life in a perpetual state of constipation.

"Hey, you know what? Why don't you leave Monday and come with me to Pauline's? It's gonna be sweet. We can hit up the Grand Mariner tonight for dinner." Becka clapped her hands together with the prospect of me sticking around.

"What's the Grand Mariner?" Angie asked.

"It's this place off Dog River by the bay, down past South Marina. They've got this nice little restaurant, that's what she's talking about. It's a great seafood place. Their fried fish, oysters and shrimp are so good. We usually sit on the outdoor deck so we can watch the boaters. Also, their burgers are *the* bomb," I said as I slathered strawberry preserves onto my buttered toast.

I folded the toast in half like a taco and dipped it in my grits. Angie grimaced again, shaking her head before slowly putting a forkful of eggs in her mouth.

"You are *way* more country than I thought you were," she said.

"Aww, don't let the Alabama scare you," Momma said with a laugh. She had finished cleaning up and was pouring herself a cup of coffee. I didn't even realize she had made any.

"You mind if I have a cup?" I asked over my shoulder.

"Not at all," she said, reaching in the cabinet for a ceramic mug. "Cream, sugar? I have Butter Pecan flavor."

"That's fine," I said. It ain't Starbucks or Prodigy on Carmine, but it will do in a pinch. I was trying to fight the thoughts that began surging in my head. They were vivid memories of Terrell. He liked the burgers at the Grand Mariner.

The first time we ever went to that restaurant was the weekend he met up with us at the vacation home Pauline's family owned on the bay. His burger was so juicy and thick that it fell apart. We watched him eat it with a knife and fork like he was fancy, and I teased him the rest of the night.

After we ate, we all headed over to Hollinger's Island park nearby to enjoy the peace, collect seashells and sea glass, and snuggle on the sand while watching the waves under the starry night.

It was a romantic evening, one I would never forget, and my heart began to burn again with the hurt from his loss. It had been so long, but now these feelings were flooding back as if no time had passed at all. And I didn't like it.

"You alright?" Angie asked. "All that cholesterol starting to get to you?"

I smiled, realizing my eyes were watering up with tears.

"I'm okay. Just a memory," I said.

Momma was watching me with growing concern on her face, and Becka reached for my hand, knowingly.

"Memory of what?" Angie asked.

"It's nothing. I'll tell you later," I said. Then to Becka, I smiled.

"I'll stay until Monday if that's okay with Angie," I said.

Angie smiled.

"I'm good with that. I just have to call Enterprise and extend the rental, that's all. No biggie. And we should probably call Jackie, so she has a heads up with the shop and all," she said, scraping the last bit of egg from her plate.

"I texted Jackie last night before I went to sleep. Everything's good over there," I said. "She's going by to get the mail out of the box and check the apartment later today."

"Well, like I said before, I can always head back, and you stay here another week or two, and I'll just come back and get you. I have plenty of vacation days," Angie said.

"Monday's fine," I said, feeling Momma's eyes on me.

Becka batted her eyes at Momma, clasping her hands beneath her chin.

"Can I steal them today and bring them back tomorrow night? *Purty* please?"

Momma shook her head.

"What about your call later with your sister?" Momma said, focusing her eyes on me.

"I mean, why not do a call with her Monday before I leave, if you scheduled it? And if you show me how to do it, I can talk to her when I get back home," I said.

"You haven't talked to your sister in ten years," Momma replied with a frown.

"I hardly saw her before I left. Seriously, I doubt she'll have much to say to me now," I said sharply.

"People change, Amanda," she said. "Your sister would be thrilled to hear from you."

"Doubtful," I said as I finished up the last bit of grits and stood up. I grabbed Angie's plate and bowl, stacked it on top of mine, and used my fingers to pluck up both of our glasses with my waitress skills from The Grill at Bryant Park.

Momma stood up to take the dishes from me.

"You go ahead with your friends. You have a key to get back in," Momma said. "I'm gonna go back there and check on your Nana. Probably time for her meds. And congratulations on your shop. What is it?"

I smiled.

"It's a beauty pop up shop boutique in SoHo near where I live. It's in part of an upscale salon and spa. I sell vegan, cruelty-free, all natural and sustainably sourced skin creams, oils, cleansers and moisturizers that I make with Jackie, Becka's cousin," I replied, proudly. My face was beaming.

"Impressive," Momma said with a nod.

"So Becks, about that Instagram stories thing. You've been on IG all this time all up on my feed and never reached out to me?" I said, shifting my attention to Becka.

She sniffed.

"So Manda, *about* those Instagram stories. You've been on IG all this time all up on your feed, seeing my follow, my likes and comments, and never reached out to me?" she said, folding her arms across her chest.

"*Touché,*" I replied with my voice low and my eyes to the floor.

She was right. We all set up Facebook accounts during the end of our Sophomore year of high school in the computer lab. Becka and Pauline sent me a friend request right then and there, and we began to connect with just about everyone we knew.

Terrell had a private Facebook account, but he rarely used it.

Instagram became a thing not long after I moved to New York. Although my Facebook account was still active, I barely used it, and rarely signed in. I began using Instagram more often. Becka and Pauline eventually abandoned Facebook completely. They followed me on Instagram, liking and commenting on my IG posts.

At first, I liked and commented back. But after awhile, I got busier, and it faded.

Being here with them now was surreal. I felt a hint of remorse for not keeping up with my friends over the years. It was surprising that they didn't hate me for it.

Or maybe they were planning to get payback by drugging me up and leaving me abandoned and tied up somewhere in a marsh where the gators would find me.

With a sigh, I led Angie and Becka up the stairs to my room to get ready and pack a bag for the night.

thirteen

BALLER WAGON ♡

I pulled my hair up in a messy bun to handle the stifling heat after spending what seemed like an eternity to get the frizzies out, and Angie rocked her signature braided bun.

She moved the Nissan over so that Momma was able to get in and out of the garage without driving into the grass, parking behind where the Camaro hid beyond the garage doors.

Momma insisted that I leave Charlemagne with her. He didn't complain, posted up in his adopted spot on the chaise lounge, the perfect perch to see everything happening from a dog's eye view.

Parked along the street, partially in the grass, was a black Range Rover with LED lighting in front and enormous black rims on all-terrain tires. The windows were tinted so deeply that it was difficult to see inside.

I slapped Becka on the shoulder.

"You are such a *liar*," I said. "That's not a Jeep. A Jeep is like a Wrangler or a Cherokee. That's a baller wagon."

Becka snickered.

"You say tomato, I say tomah-to. Potato, potah-to," she said, clicking her key fob to open the rear hatch.

"Whatever," I said, moving around to the rear hatch to toss my overnight roller bag in the cargo area, next to a backpack that was already there. Angie set her beach bag next to mine, stuffed with everything she thought she'd need.

We climbed inside and sank into the soft leather, and I was met with the richly feminine fragrance of body splash and lotion from transporting a female wherever she felt like going. There was an undertone of school backpack and sports equipment, and it was all tainted with the smell of burning wood from Becka's clothes and skin.

"Hey, why do you smell like smoke?" I asked, finally.

"My dad's been out smoking meat since early this morning. I was out there helping him. My parents are having a cookout tonight, and I was supposed to be there, but I ain't going, and they don't know it yet, but they're about to find out," Becka said with a giggle.

"Girl, you're crazy," I said.

"I don't wanna be around all them *primos locos*. Those kids are freakin' *bad*. No home training. Last time, there was poo all over the bathroom floor from one of those *pequeñas mocosas* taking their pull up off, and my parents tried to make *me* clean it up. Nope. I'm not the one," Becka said.

She started the Range Rover, and it barked to life, the supercharged V8 rumbling, sending pops and crackles out through the exhaust.

I glanced over at Becka in the driver's seat, who was adjusting the air conditioning, bopping her head to music that wasn't playing yet. Behind me, Angie was texting on her phone, smacking her gum.

"Hey, Ange, can I get a piece?" I asked her.

Without looking up, she reached for her purse, rummaged around in it for the package of chewing gum and handed it to me. I took a stick out, unwrapped it and popped it in my mouth, then offered some to Becka, who shook her head and showed me the gum she was already chewing through her teeth.

I passed the gum back to Angie, and she tossed it back into her purse, and resumed texting something lengthy to *whoever.*

I was trying to investigate, but she held her screen at an angle that kept me from viewing it. I decided to let her know I was being nosy by flat out asking.

"Dang, girl! You writing a synopsis?"

"Naw, I'm just responding to this idiot," she replied.

"What idiot?" I asked. "You aren't texting Stu, are you? 'Cause I will straight up beat you down in this truck."

Becka snorted as she pulled away and headed toward the west end of the street where it met Forest Avenue. The stop sign had the words 'Dirty South' spray painted on the back side of it in a faded white. Whoever did it misjudged the amount of space and had to add the 'th' smooshed into the upper corner of the octagon above the letter u.

"It's not Stu," Angie said. "Haven't talked to Stu in a while."

"Define a while," I said, scrunching my face into a stern look. She shook her head.

"I don't know. A while," she said. I pointed at my eyes with two fingers and then at her with the same two fingers.

"I don't like that answer," I said, turning around to face forward. Becka pulled out her Samsung Galaxy and plugged it into the USB charger. Her phone paired with the Range Rover's bluetooth on the large infotainment screen in front of us, the music began to play, and she pulled up the navigation to check traffic.

Then, she clicked on a playlist.

Bass pounded from all sides as she cranked a Camila Cabello song up, and I leaned back in the seat, soaking it all in.

Much of Forest Avenue, with its cracked asphalt, looked the same as it always has. It was a wooded neighborhood with older ranch homes, some brick and others covered in siding, nestled beneath the thick oaks and pines that spread out over the rooftops and landscape.

The old narrow bridge over the muddy creek was still flanked on either side by rusty steel railings. Before long we reached the Circle K on the right, where they served "down home chicken," just before the intersection with Celeste Road.

Making a left on Celeste, Becka danced in her seat as she rode the rear bumper of a slow driving Corolla in front of us for a short few seconds before we reached the Dollar General, the Shell station and the freeway. When she made a right on to the ramp, the Corolla continued forward toward the heart of Saraland.

Construction barrels, with their orange and white stripes, lined both sides of the on ramp and the north and southbound sides of I-65. Becka accelerated uncomfortably close to the barrels as we joined the dense traffic.

"You sure you know how to drive this thing?" Angie asked with a laugh.

Becka ignored her, passing a slower moving semi-truck in the right lane as we approached the exit for Alabama 158 and 213 for Citronelle and Saraland, with pines towering over both sides of the freeway.

Becka used to take that exit in her old Camry when she would drive me out to the University of Mobile to meet up with Terrell after his classes. Chickasabogue Park was also off of that exit where I spent hours with my granddaddy, daddy, and older brothers while they fished. I was much smaller back then, dressed in those frilly little flower dresses Momma always bought for me, long before I was old enough to wear Auntie Beanie's hand-me-downs or shopping spree gifts.

That was back when fireflies glittered in the fields as the sun set beyond the horizon. It was like stars at your feet. I can't recall the last time I saw a firefly or a lightning bug. I wondered where they all went.

Maybe it was global warming and climate change.

When we reached the overpass, Becka pointed off to the right, where the new Infirmary Health building stood beside the freeway, visible through spaces in between the pines.

"That's where they're putting up the new ER, where I'll be working," Becka shouted over the music. "So, I won't be far away at all."

"That's awesome," I said. "Everything is so different, now."

"Yeah, that's true. So much has changed since you left, but so much has stayed the same, too," she said. She turned the music down. "Have you seen the new high school where Ivy's going?"

"Not yet," I said, as I glanced at the new Hampton Inn and Suites off the exit where there were several recently built hotels and restaurants, along with a megachurch.

"Saraland's got its own high school now. Satsuma has this sweet new stadium. New buildings. Citronelle is all new. All the schools here split off from Mobile County Public Schools right after we tossed our grad caps, so everything changed fast after that."

"That's insane," I replied.

"Yep. There's so much new stuff going on in this area, and they're building more," Becka said.

"It's like I move to New York, and come back here to visit and discover the Multiverse," I said.

"I know right? Pauline's family is still bringing in more investors. They're even putting up a huge stadium and sports complex, partnering with all these secret people nobody knows. It's so big, it's gonna take up space in both Saraland and Prichard of all places."

I nodded in silence as I tried to see more on the opposite side of the freeway as we crossed the overpass.

"Be careful if you ever drive through here. There have been so many accidents on this bridge," Becka said. "Mainly tractor trailers."

"Why?" I asked.

"There was this newsfeed article where a truck driver said the bridge is too narrow. He's right. It is. They're supposed to be fixing it, finally, but I ain't sure when they'll get around to it. I hope it's soon with the area blowing up like it is. Traffic is gonna be like Montgomery."

I nodded again, trying to figure out if the massive building past the overpass was a church or not.

"It's the perfect time for you to come back. They've got a six hundred million dollar Airbus plant in Mobile now, and they're getting ready to build a new Mobile River Bridge and Byway. Supposed to be a two billion dollar project. Not to mention everything that's been going on in Downtown Mobile. A lot has happened in the past ten years, and I can't wait to show you around," Becka said.

The freeway opened up to three lanes, a concrete divider began between the northbound and southbound lanes, and traffic eased a bit.

My heart began to pound a little as I looked up to see the sign for the I-165 exit to Prichard and Downtown Mobile.

Terrell and I had passed that exit so many times. I would often ask him about where he lived, what his house was like, what the rest of his family was like, but he never had much to say about them. He never talked about his momma or his daddy.

It was almost as if he was ashamed of them, or maybe scared of what I would think of them.

He and Wayne, along with everyone else from Vigor High, called where they lived the Trap. He refused to take me through his neighborhood, or anywhere else in Prichard, saying it was too dangerous and that I, or anyone else white, would be shot if anyone saw me there, especially with him.

He told me that even the police didn't dare go through the Trap for fear of being shot at.

I had always wanted to see what his neighborhood looked like, what his room looked like, and what the inside of his house looked like. I wanted to meet his momma and his family. He said that wasn't in the cards.

Whenever we went anywhere together, it was far away from Prichard or Saraland. Wayne and Becka didn't have any problems being together. Becka's family was Puerto Rican. She easily rocked an afro or braids, and most everybody in her family was just as dark as he was.

I understood why Terrell kept me away from his world, even though it pissed me off. Saraland and Prichard were very different from each other, despite how close they were. It made me hate Alabama even more.

Becka turned the music back up. Camila Cabello faded into Cardi B, and we continued down I-65 as the city of Mobile stretched out all around us.

I closed my eyes and let my mind drift. Memories of Terrell and high school started flooding back faster. Things I had forgotten and pushed into the corners of my mind were now vividly fresh as if they had happened yesterday.

The I-10 split to Florida and Mississippi came up quickly. The drive from my momma's in Saraland to Pauline's place in Bayside was only about thirty minutes, but I'd forgotten how little time it took to get anywhere. It seemed like time went much slower back then, and it was a deep contrast to the decades of life you forfeit sitting in New York traffic.

After joining West I-10's four lanes toward Pascagoula, we were exiting on Alabama 193 to Dauphin Island and Tillmans Corner.

My excitement grew, but a sudden sadness overcame it. This would be my first time going to Pauline's after what happened to Terrell. I hadn't been able to bring myself to come back this way, knowing that everything would remind me of him.

Becka must have sensed my mood change. She turned the music down and stopped dancing and bouncing in her seat.

I looked over at her, and she smiled and patted my left hand, squeezed it, then returned her grasp on the steering wheel as she settled in her seat.

We arrived at Pauline's house on Bay Road. Becka slowly turned onto the white gravel drive and continued up to the brick house on the bay, with tall pines towering over the coastal cottage style home on all sides.

A nightmarish, dark gray Shelby GT 350 sat parked in the shadows of the open garage to the right. I know that car anywhere because I've wanted one since I saw one sitting on the curb in front of the Westfield World Trade Center Mall.

I scoped it out when it first opened, taking an Uber to spend a Saturday shopping when the weather was cloudy and depressing. I quickly found out how pricey the mall was and walked out with a few things from Sephora and Bare Candle and a pack of cozy chenille socks from UGG Australia.

The menacing car lurking in the shadows could only belong to one person. She'd always driven a modded out Stang since the day she got her driver's license. Pauline.

fourteen

MAYBE IT'S A PELICAN ♡

The house was just as it always was, except for the new landscaping and young trees growing close to it.

Becka rounded the circular drive and parked on the shaded concrete pad in front of the garage. We climbed out, grabbed our luggage out of the back of the SUV and headed toward the front door with our overnight bags. Angie looked around with a smile.

"This house is *dope*," she said as she deeply breathed in the bay air. I knew the smell changed further up closer to the industrial areas, where the putrid stench of petroleum refineries made you want to hurl.

I shifted my bag in my hands while Becka rang the doorbell. After a short wait, a tall, deeply tanned brunette with wide eyes and thick lips answered the door. Her eyes grew even wider when she saw me. She pushed past Becka and nearly collapsed onto me, wrapping her arms around me and squeezing. She's been working out. A lot. I couldn't breathe.

"Oh my god! Where the hell have you been? You never called, never texted, no Snapchat, no nothing," she said with her distinct middle eastern accent.

"Hey, girl," I said, breathing in the soft citrus smell of her hair and skin. She held onto me for a few more moments, before pulling away to give me a visual inspection.

"New York, huh? Why so *far*?"

"I didn't have enough money to get to Paris," I said.

"Personally, I thought you hated us. The way you left like that. When Becka texted me and told me you were coming, I totally freaked," Pauline said, pushing a few loose strands of hair from my temple.

"Okay, ya'll over here actin' brand new, so can we go inside now, 'cause it's hot as fire," Becka said in her fake whiny voice.

"Yeah, yeah, go ahead. My bad," Pauline said as she stepped aside and held the door open. Becka and Angie shuffled past Pauline, followed by me.

Inside the house, it smelled like fresh paint and new house. The floors were refinished, replaced with a lighter walnut. The cream walls were now a light gray, and the windows facing out toward the back deck were new.

Pauline closed the door behind us and glided toward the back windows.

"It's all been renovated. That hurricane tore everything up here," she said. "My parents gave the house to me, but I'm going to sell it when it's all done. They're still working on things."

"Why sell it? It's so nice," Angie said.

"We have a house on Dauphin Island, and we're selling that too. It's been horrible here lately with all the storms. There was Hurricane Nate, then Gordon was just like six months ago," Pauline let out a long sigh.

"Made a mess of everything. Look, I'll show you," she said, opening one of the two doors out to the rear deck.

We set our bags down on the living room floor and followed her outside.

She showed us that there was a new screen wrapping around the porch, and there were new ceiling fans installed, but all of the repairs were obvious. Most of the open deck was new boards that were a stark contrast from the older wood. The patio tiles and pillars looked new, and the pier and covered boat dock, where they had added a porch swing, were both new. The repainted trimming and replaced siding were all a brighter white than the surrounding fixtures.

Pauline's parents had also reinforced the bulkhead.

"My dad's breaking ground in Tampa on the waterfront along the canal for a high rise development. He's involved in a massive downtown revitalization project, so we'll be moving that way sometime soon. Not sure when, exactly," Pauline said.

"So, you're moving? That sucks," Becka said. "First Manda, now you. Leaving me here to rot."

"Florida sounds nice," Angie said.

I nodded in agreement.

"It *is* nice," I said with a knowing smile. Angie saw my expression, and her eyebrows rose.

"You both should come down when we get set up. It'll be nice to have you around," Pauline said with a smile, leading the way back into the house. "I was gonna get the grill set up later if you want to throw on some steaks."

"Or, we could just go back to our spot. The Grand Mariner," Becka said.

"They're open. It's the time of year when they get crazy busy," Pauline said, hunching her shoulders. "I don't know. It's up to you guys. But I've got steaks," she added.

"Since when do you *grill,* Leenie?" I couldn't help but crack up. Just imagining Pauline standing in a pillar of smoke flipping meat while trying to keep her acrylic tips from catching fire was too much.

"I learned from my dad," Pauline said. "He's a beast with the spatula."

"Well, that settles that," Becka mused, as Pauline slid the patio door open. Becka stepped back inside. "I hope you have citronella cause these mosquitos are fierce out here. I think I just got bit up all over my legs."

"I've got bug spray in the kitchen under the sink. I keep getting chewed on in the morning on the way to work. It's like they hang out and wait for you," Pauline said. "They're supposed to be spraying."

"Well, tell them to get on the ball, sister," Becka said as Pauline stepped inside. I hesitated, then hung back, turning toward the pier. Angie watched me as I began to walk out toward the dock before sliding the glass door closed.

Angie followed me down the long pier in silence to the covered boat dock. When we reached the dock, Angie sat on the wooden swing while I stood at the dock's edge, looking out over Mobile Bay, breathing in the sea's briny fragrance.

The last time I had stood in this spot, I had his arms wrapped around me. It had been so long and it was hard to remember his scent, but I knew the last gift I ever gave him was a bottle of his favorite cologne, Versace Metal Jeans.

I once looked for a bottle of it in New York, but I found out they discontinued it. I found the little bottle of the lady's version on Amazon for a just over forty bucks, but it wouldn't be the same.

I would give anything to see him again. Being here brought it all back like a flood, and it seemed like every second, I relived some long ago memory from the past.

Angie watched me quietly. I felt her gaze on me, and I knew she was concerned. She was a good friend and knew when to give me my space, but she protectively stayed close by me in case I needed her.

It used to annoy me. I always thought she was hovering and crowding me before Jackie reminded me that Angie was an only child, and didn't have many close friends because of where she grew up, and I was like the sister she never had and always wanted. I had never seen it in that perspective before, and it made sense.

It still bothered me a little, but I'd grown used to it.

Like an unspoken language, I turned and gave Angie a quick smile, taking a step to the side. On cue, she jumped off of the swing and stood next to me, putting an arm around my shoulders. I was hit with the floral and fruity scent of the Caribbean from her braids. It was calming.

"You okay?" she asked.

"Yeah, I'm good."

"You sure?"

"Copacetic," I said.

She released me, letting her arms fall to her sides.

"Okay," she said. "It's relaxing out here. I could just fall asleep on that swing."

"It's nice at night. Snuggling under a blanket, watching the stars. Or the pelicans in the evening."

I turned to head back. She followed.

"I don't think I've ever seen a pelican. Except at maybe the zoo," she said.

"You'll definitely see them here," I said with a laugh. "There's a lot of them."

When we got back inside the house, Pauline and Becka were in the kitchen, laughing hysterically.

"Yo, you gotta see this meme! Check it out," Becka said as she leaned in, holding her cellphone horizontally. Angie and I shuffled around the counter to see what all the fuss was about.

On her phone screen was a cereal bar floating in a bowl of milk. Someone had texted someone else asking if they ever used a cereal bar, and how it worked.

I snorted as Pauline burst into laughter again.

Angie let out a giggle while shaking her head.

"I can't even with that," she said.

We grabbed our overnight bags, and Pauline led us upstairs to the renovated bedrooms. Immediately at the top, on the left side of the upstairs loft was the door to the master bedroom facing the front of the house, with its lavish custom bath. The guest bedrooms were on either side of the loft, each with a private bathroom and balcony.

Angie and I claimed Pauline's old bedroom. It was to the right of the loft, above the downstairs bedroom on the lower level. The covered balcony sheltered the outdoor patio beneath it. The other bedroom where Becka slung her bag onto the bed, was above the dining area. The terrace of that room extended over the screened in patio on the lower level.

We followed Pauline back downstairs, and she headed out onto the back deck to get the gas grill started. Becka disappeared for a while, probably to the bathroom. Angie stretched out on the sofa in the living room in front of the entertainment center and started texting. I texted Jackie to check in with her, then opened Instagram to see if there were any updates.

I hadn't posted anything since last weekend.

Planning a post would be simple. All I'd have to do was just head out to the end of the pier and post a few updates there when the sun was going down, use my favorite Mayfair or Amaro filter for dramatic effect, and then use IG Layout to make it all fit together nicely.

In my first post outside of New York, I wanted it to look good.

The shadows stretched out as the sun quickly slid toward the horizon. Pauline finished grilling a few New York strips, and we sat down at the dining room table to finish them off, with a Greek salad and grilled tomatoes and asparagus.

Pauline seriously threw down in the kitchen and on the grill. Last time I saw her, during our senior year, the most she cooked was a box of Mac and cheese or a package of ramen. Her dad did all the outdoor grilling, while her mom and older sisters slaved in the kitchen.

She was the youngest like me. The only difference was, she was born with a silver spoon in her hand. Her grandparents on her daddy's side were wealthy immigrants.

After dinner, Pauline and Becka cleaned up while Angie and I got mimosas ready. We moved to the patio to relax and watch the boats and the evening sink into the night.

We talked about high school memories, filling in details that Angie never heard from me. She laughed as Pauline and Becka shared stories of our teenage shenanigans, like the day we had a tornado drill towards the end of sixth grade.

We had known Pauline about a year by then and quickly discovered she liked trouble.

She swiped the substitute teacher's keys to the classroom and hid them in the trash can on the way out to the hallway. When the tornado drill was over, we were all locked out of the room. It took like an hour for the maintenance dude to come and unlock the door.

"Hey, Pauline, what's up with Cali? I thought you were moving there." I said, after taking a long sip of mimosa. I stretched out my legs on the folding chaise lounge chair and adjusted myself.

"I *went* to Cali," she said.

"Why did you come back?" I asked.

"Cause people over there are so plastic," she said.

"I figured you'd fit right in," I snickered.

"You want to get thrown off the edge of that dock? Keep playing," Pauline said, sloshing her mimosa around before putting to her lips. She sipped, smacked her thick lips, then let out a long, exaggerated sigh.

"Where'd you end up going? USC?" I asked.

"No, I went to UCI."

When she saw the confused look on my face, she clarified.

"University of California Irvine," she said. "Same place…"

Becka nudged Pauline sharply in the arm with her elbow. I frowned at them, wondering what that was about.

"Same place that has all those important *alumni*," Pauline said, finishing the sentence.

"Oooo, *fancy*," I said. "Whatever happened to USC?"

"I didn't get in," she said with a shrug.

"You had the grades, though."

"They've got like a seventeen percent acceptance rate. Top tier celebrities get in, no problem. I didn't even stand a chance," Pauline said.

"Well, you look like a Jenner. Should've sent in headshots with your application. You would've practically slid right through the doors," I said.

"Did you even apply?" Becka asked as she scrolled up on her phone screen, the light illuminating her face in an eerie glow.

"No," Pauline said.

"So why would you say you didn't get in, when you never applied in the first place?" I asked.

"I just know. It wasn't worth the embarrassment," Pauline said.

I shook my head.

"A little of that Lebanese charm would have gotten you in," I joked.

Pauline held out her hand.

"Wait. What? Did you say I was *Lebanese*?" She closed her eyes, cocked her head back and laughed loudly, shaking her head. "You are too much," she added with a snort.

"What? Isn't your family from the middle east?" I looked around at everybody, confused.

"Uh. *Yeah*," she said as she began to cough from laughing so hard. "Oh, man, that was funny."

"I don't get it. From where then?" I frowned.

She took a sip of mimosa and sighed before answering.

"You've known me for how long? And you don't remember what I am? Wow. Anyway, here's your refresher. Take notes. My family is Persian. My parents are from Iran. They moved to California in the '80s, before I was born, during the Iranian Revolution. We're Iranian Jews. I'm from Beverly Hills. That's where I was born and where we lived until we sold our house there and moved to Mobile. My family still owns a lot of investment property in LA. That's why I went to college in Cali. That's where I'm from, and it's home to me. Eventually, I'll go back for good. Just not yet," Pauline said.

"What about your accent?" I said.

"My *Cali* accent? You're a freaking goofball," she said, adjusting herself in the chair.

"What about all that talk about people in Cali being plastic?"

Pauline finished the last few drops of mimosa before setting the flute down carefully on the patio tiles.

"Manda. I was kidding. I mean, yeah, people are plastic there, but not everybody. I definitely like it better there than here. After I help my parents in Florida, I'm moving back to L.A. to do my own thing while my parents stay in Tampa. You should come with me when I go. You'd like it out there. It's better than New York. I can promise you that," Pauline said with a smile as she climbed out of the lounge chair to stretch.

"Are there Cali rats? 'Cause New York rats are the worse. They pop up from behind fire hydrants and scare people. A few of them deliver for Postmates. Anyway, totally sadistic. The nice ones will stop a cab for you. The bad ones will jack your purse and steal your Airpods. You don't know *who* to trust," I said.

"First of all, there's probably no such thing as a *nice* rat—" Pauline began.

"Lab rats," Becka interrupted.

Pauline shot a finger up toward the sky. As always, her gel tips were on *point*.

"Umm. Firstly, *no*. Disgusting. And secondly, there are no rats in Cali. It's too freaking hot," Pauline said.

"I don't know about Cali. First off, earthquakes. Then every time you fart, there's another wildfire popping off," I said.

"Live where it's wet," Pauline replied.

"It never rains in southern California, and umm, sea level rise. Then there's the inevitability of the coast breaking off and floating toward North Korea," I added.

"What lame newsfeed did you get that from?" Pauline re-marked, laughing with a snort.

"It'll probably just fall off into the ocean, but that's another discussion. You better not leave me in New York by myself," Ang-ie said with a croak. She had been silent so long that when she fi-nally spoke, her voice sounded harsh.

"Awww, Angie. Don't get all choked up. No one said I was leaving you," I said, pinching her arm.

"Girl, do that again and I'll pull your hair straight out your scalp," she said with a hiss. "All you'll have left is them jacked up edges."

I chuckled as I adjusted the reclining angle of my chair. The sky was getting darker. I watched two pelicans gliding southward, just above the surface of the bay. I tapped Angie's shoulder and pointed. She followed the direction of my finger and craned her neck as she squinted her eyes.

"Don't you see them?" I asked.

"See what?"

"Herons. Right there near the pier," I said. Then something caught my eye at the end of the pier, where the swing hung from the covered boat dock. I thought I had seen something earlier, thinking it might have been a heron or a well-fed seagull resting. But now, whatever it was, had shifted, and it looked like it was something much larger than a bird.

I stood up and moved toward the edge of the patio.

"Do you see that?" I said as I squinted, trying to see better in the waning light. I pointed toward the end of the pier.

"See what?" Pauline asked, her hand poised on the patio door handle to go back inside and refill her glass.

"There. I swear someone's over there chilling on the boat dock."

"I don't see anyone. Maybe it's a pelican," Becka said, sitting up in her reclining chair.

"Dude. That's not a bird." I stood up, setting my glass of mimosa down on the patio tiles. Angie stood up with me.

"I think there might be someone down there. I don't know. I can't really tell," she said, craning her neck to see what I was seeing.

"You're bugging out, girl, and that's only one drink. It's not even *that* alcoholic. You rollin' and not telling anybody? Where the bomb kush at?" Becka chuckled as she leaned back, curling her legs beneath her.

"Look, *bruh-tina,* I'm not tripping. Someone's over there," I said. I cupped my hands around my mouth. "Hey!" I yelled toward the shadow.

I saw movement again.

I leaped toward the pier, pulling my phone out to turn on the flashlight, illuminating the wooden planks as I stomped toward the boat dock.

"Hey, *stalker*! I've already called the cops!" I yelled again, quickly closing in on the shadow.

The shadow suddenly grew larger and taller, a looming silhouette against the deepening purple of the sky over the bay.

When I reached the boat dock and held the phone to light up the trespasser, I stopped short. My heart immediately pounded in my chest, and I felt myself start to shake uncontrollably.

With my throat suddenly parched, my voice was nowhere to be found.

Beginning to water, my eyes burned savagely, blurring my vision.

The gravelly, deep voice that came next confirmed the impossible.

"You haven't changed at all," he said, gripping a bouquet. "It took you long enough to walk down here."

I trembled at every word.

Every thing I tried to forget for what now seemed like ages came rushing back like a flood, and in an instant, I was back at the beginning of my freshman year of high school, 14 years ago.

Freshman Year

fifteen

SEPTEMBER TO REMEMBER ♡

Vigor V Satsuma, September 2005

I was super psyched. It was the first home game of the season, and Momma actually let me go. I don't know what got into her, but I was convinced that she was gonna say no.

I mean, she was laid out on the sofa watching Judge Judy. I wasn't sure if she was actually really watching the show or not. When I squatted down near her head, drool drizzled lazily from the corner of her mouth, elastically base jumping toward the floor.

She was seriously out of it. But when she mumbled the word yes, and asked me not to come home later than eleven with slurred words that made even more saliva run down her chin, I honestly didn't even care. She smelled funny again, which meant she desperately needed a shower. Matted to her head, her hair looked greasy.

I stood up and headed to my room to call Becka and tell her it was on and popping, and then I got ready, throwing on jeans and an oversized hoodie. I dabbed on a smidgeon of eye shadow around my eyes, eye liner and some lip gloss I stole from Taylor and Ivy's room since she was never home and usually always with her shady boyfriend, then I grabbed my New Balance sneaks.

Out of the two pairs of shoes I owned, they were my favorite pair, honestly because Auntie Beanie bought them for me. The other pair of shoes I had, I refused to wear except to run around outside. They were plain flats from Walmart.

I slid on my kicks and nearly flung myself out the front door to wait for Becka's mom.

While I waited outside, Tanner pulled up to the house in Momma's six-year-old Buick Century, parking it in front of the garage next to Granddaddy's old Chrysler minivan.

Nana Jane had a 'For Sale' sign on it, but it seemed like no one wanted it. Granddaddy replaced the transmission, water pump, thermostat, heater core and God knows what else. Nana and Granddaddy bought a brand new Chrysler 300C to replace it.

They thought by selling it themselves, they'd get more than the dealership offered them for it.

Good luck with that.

When Tanner got out of the Buick, he nodded at me and smirked.

"Why you outside?" he asked me.

I looked at him and rolled my eyes.

"Why are you *nosy*?" I asked, annoyed.

"It's my job to be nosy." He pulled a pack of cigarettes from his jacket pocket, slid out a stick and lit it up, dragging on it deeply with two fingers like he was smoking a spliff. He was oblivious to how much of a total butt hole he looked.

"Are you even *inhaling*, stupid?" I asked him, kicking at a rock embedded in the soil surrounded by a clump of clover as I leaned against the porch support column.

I refused to sit on that ratty old red sofa on the porch. The boys and Granddaddy sat on it to chill out and sip on glasses of *drink*, but I wouldn't go anywhere near it. Might be snakes or raccoons hiding in it. Or worse. I wasn't taking any chances of anything crawling up into my cooter and hosting a fundraiser.

"You want one?" He stepped forward to hold out the pack.

"Dude. No. Momma's gonna rip drag strips out of your butt flesh when she sees you out here smoking. Nana's halfway freakin' blind, so she'll just accuse *me* of doing it. And Granddaddy's never here, but if he was, he'd probably ask you for a short."

"One. I'm grown. Two. She's high as a jet on them pills, so I know for a fact she ain't never getting off that couch. At least for the rest of the night. Which is why I'm inviting a friend over. You better not say anything, or I'll beat you with a switch." Tanner bent over, snorted, and spit out a loogie.

I frowned at him in disgust.

"Threats, threats," I said, sliding down the column to sit in the grass. Suddenly, I giggled.

"Yo. Why are you wearing a jacket? You look super suspicious. It's like 80 degrees out. And what are you gonna do when Nana Jane and Granddaddy come over later? You know they always stop by at night to check on Momma to make sure she's still alive," I said with a wide smile.

"They're not coming into my room, so what I got to worry about?"

"Okay, Tiger," I said as Becka's momma pulled up into the grass in her Subaru Outback. I stood up as Tanner tossed his cigarette butt into the yard.

"Sure, go ahead. Start a brush fire and burn the house down. Fool," I muttered.

"Seriously, where you going?" he asked.

"Oh my god, dude. To the *game*," I yelled, exasperated.

"Calm down, Charlie Brown. You got your cell on you?"

"Yep," I said, blowing out a breath. He annoyed the hell out of me.

"In case of emergency?"

"Dude, I don't need another daddy. I've been doing just fine without one."

"Just looking out for you," Tanner said.

"Look out for yourself, with your hoochie hooker tonight," I said as I stepped through the grass toward the Subaru.

Becka rolled down her window.

"Sup, Manda Pants!" she hollered loudly through the half-open window. It wasn't even necessary to be that boisterous.

"What's up, Snacks," I said, as I climbed into the back seat behind her. Becka's momma smiled at me through the rearview mirror.

"How are you, Amanda?" She pulled away from the grass and used the driveway to make a U-turn.

"I'm good, Mrs. Canales," I said. "How 'bout you?"

"Can't complain. You excited about the game?"

"Heck, yeah!"

"Becka said something about you guys getting pizza after," Mrs. Canales said.

"Pizza sounds good, Mrs. Canales," I said with a smile.

"Okay," she replied, then reached down to turn up the Latin music.

Becka danced in her seat with her arms up, snapping her fingers, her large hoop earrings making clanging noises as she moved her head to the music. I watched her in amusement, before looking out the window.

The short drive out of my neighborhood and down Celeste took us over Interstate 65 without incident and onto Saraland Boulevard.

A few minutes later, we were heading down the drive where the buses dropped off students at Satsuma High. The little main building was to the right. The football field was straight ahead.

Mrs. Canales pulled up at the field next to the tennis courts, telling Becka to call her when the game was over, and that she'd pick us up and take us to Benzi's for pizza after the game. Becka and I climbed out and headed straight for the bleachers.

Under the bright lights, the worn grass was a dusty yellow, and the field's patches of dirt and faded white markings were a stark reminder of how country this area was.

Satsuma High had a student population that was ten percent black, and about four percent other, with less than seven hundred students total crowding the small main building during class. Seemingly, every dark-skinned male student I had ever seen walking the halls was out there on the football field wearing crimson on white.

The stands on the opposite side of the field, where the visiting team, the Vigor High School Wolves, the Vigor High spirit squad, cheerleaders, marching band, and everyone that appeared to be from Vigor High, were a stark visual contrast to the side of the field Satsuma High occupied.

I wondered what would happen if we went to sit with the Vigor High group.

The bleachers on either side were a sad sight. There weren't that many spectators, and it seemed like miles separated pockets of a handful of people scattered on the old metal seating.

Below at the scrimmage line, the marching band played a slow melody that made the snooze fest even worse. I looked at Becka, my excitement for the first football game I had ever attended starting to wane quickly.

Breaking the monotony, I heard our names being called from above us in the middle rows of the bleachers. Sitting in a group was Pauline.

"Hello, hussies! Up here!" She stood up and frantically waved her arms as if she were hard to spot. Becka and I laughed as we stomped over the lower bleachers to reach Pauline.

"Took you long enough to get here, geez," she said with a giggle.

"You're the only person who would be here before anyone else, nerd," Becka said as she settled in next to Pauline, leaving space for me to sit between the two of them. "We're going to Benzi's after for pizza. You coming?"

Pauline smirked.

"I don't know. Maybe. It's tough being spotted around town with you clowns. Too much trouble for a girl like me. You're ruining my future *and* my reputation," she said.

"You get your own self into trouble. You don't need us to co-sign," I said. Pauline snort laughed as I turned to Becka.

"Where the snacks at, *Snacks*?"

"At the concession stand, Manda," Becka said, reaching into her pocket for a stick of gum.

"You guys want anything? I think I might get a hot dog or pretzel or something," I said.

"Where do you think we are? That concession stand down there has been closed for a hot minute," Pauline said.

"Closed? Since when?" I asked.

"Um, since freaking *Katrina,*" Pauline said. "Like, it just happened. Where the hell you been, Manda? Exploring the rings of Saturn?"

"How would a hurricane make them close the concession stand? All the way up here."

"I don't know, but it's closed," Pauline said. "I mean, there was a whole lot of damage up here, too. People losing roofs and trees falling on their trailer park shoe boxes. Little squirrels getting blown away into oblivion."

I was quiet for a while. I'd never been more scared in my life, than when Katrina hit. When it was all over, there were tree limbs on our street and the power was out for days. That was about it for my neighborhood.

"I'm sure someone is gonna be selling something from somewhere down there. Wait till a little later, and I'll walk down with you and see," Becka said. "Meanwhile, want some?" She held the gum out for me to take a stick. That would just make me hungrier.

"No, I'm good," I said, leaning back as the announcer spoke through the loudspeaker.

Soon, the home team spilled out onto the field. The dude posted up in the box announced the players and their numbers as they left the bench. Shortly afterward, the visiting team was on the field.

Becka reached up and started slapping my shoulder like she had lost her mind. Hard.

"Dude, what?" I rubbed my shoulders and contemplating slapping her back.

"Look at that right there. You see him?"

"See who?" I followed her nod toward the field.

"Him," she said, pointing. "Standing next to 32. The other team."

"Who? 43?" I asked, focusing my eyes on a skinny dark-skinned dude with thick braids flowing down his back from where they sprouted out of his helmet.

"Yeah. Ain't he sexy, for real?" Becka started fanning herself with her hand.

"How can you see him with his helmet on?" I asked. Pauline snickered.

"I wasn't looking at his helmet. Them legs and thighs. That's where my eyes went first, then I caught a glimpse of that baby back booty. Then I seen them guns that boy is packin' and just about lost it," Becka said.

"Don't you go to church like three days a week?" Pauline tossed her hair back and smirked.

"I'm a sinner saved by grace," Becka said.

I shook my head.

"You might need to get you like, *way* more grace," Pauline said.

I finally decided to hit her back. I smacked her shoulder so hard it sounded like a baseball being cracked by a bat and it hurt my fingertips, nearly making her tumble down the bleachers.

"What the *hell,* Manda? Freaking Hulk. You need to lay off the red meat," Becka frowned, rubbing her arm.

"That's what you get, *sucka,*" I giggled. "Oh, and that dude who's butt you're so obsessed with probably has a lazy eye and a serious hair follicle infection. You won't be able to tell who or what he's looking at."

"I'll tell him you said that," a deep, gravelly voice said from above and behind us.

I twisted around with Becka and Pauline to find a tall, chocolate skinned Omar Epps looking dude with a chin strap beard sitting next to what looked like Gabrielle Union. Surrounding them was a group similarly dressed, as if they were going to some ritzy jazz spot in New Orleans.

"You better not say anything," Becka said.

"But you like him, right? You wanna get them digits?" he asked.

"Yep, she clearly does," Pauline said.

"Well, I can make that happen," he said confidently. The girl next to him pinched his arm.

"Little boy. Do you always insert yourself into grown folks' conversations?" I asked him. He looked at me and cut a broad smile that suddenly made me feel like I was choking.

"Nah. We just like trolling the other team from their side of the stands," he said.

I cleared my throat, suddenly parched and desperately thirsty.

"Well, you should go back to your side of the field and sit with the posers. That way you can comfort one another in solace after the Gators eat you alive," I said. Then I realized how ridiculously corny I just sounded. What the hell was wrong with me?

Becka slid me a sideways glance.

"Umm hmmm," she mumbled under her breath.

"What?" I asked, my eyebrows raised defensively.

"I see you, *playa,*" she said, pointing two of her fingers at her eyes, then at mine.

"Whatever," I said.

"You want the hookup, I'll take you down after we win to introduce you to him," the boy said.

"You're crazy," Becka said.

"Alright, then. You change your mind, let Big Tee know," he said. The girl next to him pinched him again.

"Okay, *Big Tee,*" she said. Then, she waved her hand at us. "Please ignore my boyfriend. He's the epitome of graciously stupid. Hi, I'm Lexi," she said.

"Hey," I said.

"Nice to meet you, Lexi. That's Pauline on the end. This is Amanda, and I'm Becka," Becka said as she pointed to each of us.

"Nice to meet you too. This is Terrell," she said, pointing to him. He waved casually.

"Sup," he said. I nodded. He smiled at me again, and my skin began to get hot.

"You guys are juniors?"

"Freshmen," I said.

"Oh, wow. You look older," she said. "I thought you guys were parents." I hoped she was joking, cause if she wasn't, it was a long way down those bleachers. Head first.

"Are *you* seniors?" Pauline asked.

"Sophomores. At U of M," Lexi said.

I frowned.

"What ya'll doin' all the way up here?" I asked.

"That's my little brother, Wayne, down there playing. Number 43. I come to most of his games," Terrell said.

"Oh," I nodded.

I twisted back around and faced forward as I watched Satsuma make another touchdown. They were leading 14 to 7.

After a while, Becka nudged me.

"Snacks?"

I looked at her with raised eyebrows.

"Do. You. Want. Anything?" she asked, mimicking sign language as if I didn't hear a word she said.

I ignored her and turned toward Pauline with my hand outstretched. She reached into her pocket and pulled out a wrinkled ten-dollar bill and handed it to me.

"Whatever drink you find that's not diet. Doesn't matter. And whatever you want," Pauline said.

I took her ten and stuffed it into my pocket.

The bleachers were making my butt sore, so I eagerly stood up and followed Becka down the stands. The concession building was closed, but there were tables set up along the track surrounding the football field. Students sat behind the folding tables selling slices of cake on small styrofoam plates wrapped in cellophane, bags of chips, popcorn, sodas, and candy bars.

I bought a Three Musketeers and two cans of Coke with money I had in my other pocket, while Becka grabbed a bag of Doritos, a Sprite, and a bag of caramel popcorn. On the way back, we stopped at the edge of the field near where the cheerleaders were getting ready to start another set.

Becka craned her neck to pick Wayne out of the mass of players on the field as we headed back up to our spot on the bleachers. After plopping back down on the hard metal, I handed Pauline her Coke and her ten-dollar bill.

"Why didn't you use the ten?" Pauline asked, refusing to take the money.

"What I wanted cost twenty," I lied.

"You're ridiculous. Keep it," she said, snapping open her Coke and taking a long drag. I stood there holding the money for her to take like an idiot. When she ignored me, I sighed and stuffed it into my pocket, deciding to slip it into her purse later when she wasn't watching.

"Dang, you couldn't get us nothing? I mean, that's just shameful and impolite," Terrell said from above us. I twisted in my seat again to face him.

"You didn't ask," I sneered.

"You didn't give me a chance to ask, girl," he said. "I would've paid."

"Well, you can pay for our pizza after the game, since you're losing. How about that, Mister," Becka said, peeling open her bag of Doritos. The smell of cheese and corn chips wafted into the air.

"Pizza sounds good to me. Where we going?"

"Benzi's," Becka answered, stuffing a few chips in her mouth.

"Where dat at?" he asked.

"It's not far. Couple of lights down, I guess," she replied with her mouth full.

"Oh, so it's local?"

"Yep."

"Okay, then. My treat," he said.

Lexi laughed.

"You got money?"

"*What*, girl? I'm ballin' for real," he said. "And you know this."

I twisted to face forward and watch the game, not even trying to hide the smile on my face.

Satsuma got another touchdown, gained a conversion and held their lead. Vigor was playing well, but their defense began to struggle after a flag from the referees threw off their momentum.

Becka, thirsty as ever, kept nudging my arm every time Wayne was in view,

The game progressed as we snacked, with people all around us screaming and the marching band playing signature upbeat football anthems. The cheerleaders kicked, jumped, flipped, screeched, and hollered, suddenly invigorated.

The stands vibrated as proud daddys, and over-enthusiastic mothers pounded their feet into the metal so hard, it shook my SI joints out of place.

Satsuma High was on fire, and the Gators ended the game with a final score of 24, just three more points than Vigor.

We stood in the stands for a while watching people exit the bleachers and crowd around the field to socialize. Terrell finally stood up and stepped down toward us with Lexi holding his hand.

"So, we gettin' this pizza or what? I'm meeting my brother at the buses. You got a ride, or you want to ride with us? We can squeeze into my hooptie," Terrell said.

"Um, I gotta jet, sorry," Pauline said. "I gotta get up early to-morrow. We're still trying to deal with the damage from the hurri-cane. So much to clean up. The beach house is a disaster." She pulled out her flip phone and called her mother, stepping off to the side.

"Can you even get through there? Isn't Dauphin Island still closed off? I thought the roads were completely washed out under all that sand. I saw on TV that a bunch of houses basically got ripped right off the island, and I heard that the Causeway and the Bayway were closed, and everything down there at Dog River Ma-rina and Harbor Landing was torn to pieces," I said, picturing the horrifying images on the news about the widespread damage from Katrina.

"Our beach house is still standing. Barely. There was a ton of water damage. The windows are all gone, and everything inside is ruined. But my dad says someone else's whole roof is smashed up against the house. He's been down there a few times to fend off the looters. It's really bad. But he wouldn't let any of us go with him. He said it was too dangerous. That ticked my mom off, royally. We were going to go down with the truck and try to get something accomplished," Pauline said.

"That sucks," I replied, shaking my head.

"Probably gonna end up selling it. I feel horrible for the people who own the houses next door to ours. My dad said that on one side, all they had left was the front steps and a few pilings. The entire house was gone. On the other side, you couldn't even tell there was ever a house there," she added after a short silence.

I watched her as she seemed to space out. It was hard for me to even begin to fathom what she was going through.

When Katrina hit, my brothers hunkered down wherever they were, Taylor and Ivy stayed home with me and Momma, and Nana Jane and Granddaddy paced the house praying under their breath.

Momma slept through the whole event. I've never heard anyone cry as much as Ivy did, and Taylor was freaking out, which terrified me even more.

The howling wind, the endless rain, the pounding against the windows and things flying through the air were all compounded by the threat of tornadoes everywhere and not knowing when one would touch down and rip your house apart.

They had opened emergency shelters in Saraland at the elementary school.

After the storm, we went through a few weeks of total madness with Momma bugging out like a psycho. I ended up spending most of the time at Becka's while we waited for the utility company to restore the power.

Katrina hit just a month ago, but the terror was still fresh. I still shivered from the experience of thinking you were safe with a Category 1 storm approaching, weakened from its slog across southern Florida that Thursday, and then suddenly seeing your grandparents at your house, praying like you wouldn't live through the weekend.

Newspaper articles would show that people were still chilling and relaxing on Dauphin Island and Gulf Shores beaches on Friday and Saturday under deceitfully sunny skies. Unbeknownst to them, Sunday would reveal the true, inevitable, terrifying nightmare of extraordinary proportions that was bearing down on Alabama's coast.

That Sunday morning, forecasters warned of storm surges of up to ten feet on Dauphin Island. Weather specialists said that the storm would be a wrecking ball as much as 200 miles inland.

That following Monday, New Orleans was nearly obliterated. Within an hour away from my house, entire communities in Mississippi were scraped right off the coast. Dauphin Island looked like it had been raked through like dead leaves in the autumn.

There were rumors that Biloxi and Gulfport had been completely washed out into the Gulf of Mexico, never to be seen again, like a modern Atlantis.

Downtown Mobile was completely flooded, and dumpsters sailed the streets like barges in the canal. For New Orleans, though, the nightmare was only just beginning.

Racked by a sudden chill, I shivered as I turned to Becka.

"Oh, don't even look at me like that, you know I'm down. Question is, what's your mom gonna say?"

I hesitated before answering her. I was trying to shake the memory of Katrina.

"I gotta call her."

"So, get to it," Becka said.

I pulled out my Blackberry and called the house phone because my mother never answered her cellphone.

There was no answer. It went to voicemail, so I left a message telling her I would be at Benzi's for pizza and home afterward.

"So, where do we go?" Terrell asked.

"How'd you get here?" Becka asked.

"The freeway," he said.

"Well, that's vague," I said.

"Only way to get here. Unless you take the long way." Terrell rubbed his chin strap beard.

"You probably took the Saraland and Citronelle exit, right?" Becka asked.

"Yeah," Terrell replied.

"Okay, so then you go back the way you came, except, when you make that right, don't take Celeste going back toward the freeway. You want the other street right next to it, on the other side of the gas station. That's Route 213. Sheldon Beach Road. You'll know you're going the right way. You'll see a Rite Aid on the left in a shopping plaza. Anyway, keep going. You'll pass a Church's Chicken, a car wash and then you'll come to these plazas on both sides. There's a street there. Ennis, on the left. Make that left and turn into that plaza right there on the right with the brown roof.

Benzi's is on the right side of the building. If you see the big red brick church with the white steeples you went too far," Becka said.

"Look at you, Dora. I'm the map, I'm the map, I'm the *map*," I sang.

"You suck. Call me Dora again and you die. Anyway, I'm getting my license soon. Might as well be ready. Plus, I've been secretly driving my cousin's car without my mom knowing," Becka said.

"You better not get pulled over, Becka. Cops around here don't play around," I said.

"I got a permit. Duh," Becka said. "Mom only wants me to drive with her, but I'm like, *syke*."

"You're crazy. Having a permit means you have to have someone twenty one or older in the car with you," I said.

"Yeah. My cousin," Becka said.

I had no idea which cousin she was talking about, because all of her cousins that I knew weren't even old enough to drive.

"Okay, let's go. I'm starving," I said.

"After all that garbage you just ate? Where you puttin' all that?" Terrell snickered.

"I can eat, dude," I said. "You just don't know."

"Hey, come on, that's my mom," Becka said, pointing in the direction of the parking lot where her mother pulled up.

"Alright. Well, we'll see ya'll at Benzi's," I said as I hugged Pauline. She was still on the phone arguing with her momma.

"Everything okay? You need a ride?" I asked.

"She's coming. She's just being a punk about it," Pauline said. "My brother was supposed to pick me up, and he's out with his whoever doing whatever."

"Sounds like my family sitch," I said. "That's why we all need cars."

"For real," Pauline said. "I'm about to break down and get one."

"You got your permit yet?" I asked.

"I will soon. See ya girl," she said as she hugged Becka and turned toward the parking lot to wait for her mother.

"We can wait with you, if you want," I said.

"Nah, she's almost here. Not necessary. Go have fun. See ya in church," Pauline said as she walked away waving her arm.

I followed Becka to her mom's car and climbed in back.

"Pizza, right?" her mom asked.

"Yep," Becka replied, snapping her seatbelt into place. "We're about to get pepperoni wasted."

"How was the game?"

I looked up to see that Mrs. Canales was talking to me through the rearview mirror.

"It was good. We won. By three points," I replied.

"Huh. Not bad," she said, then turned up the Latin music.

We made the trip back down Saraland Boulevard into Saraland and to Industrial Parkway listening to a mix of Shakira, Daddy Yankee, Wisin Y Yandel, Calle 13 and Frankie J, before pulling into the parking lot in front of Benzi's. It took that long because Becka's mom drove like a snail in a golf cart.

As expected, it was busy. The parking lot was full.

Terrell and Lexi were standing outside with Wayne, who had changed out of his uniform and was wearing a Nike shirt and shorts. Terrell was standing, posted up against a big, shiny, black Mercedes, with his arms around Lexi.

Becka and I climbed out of the car and walked up to them.

Terrell watched me with an unsettling gaze, and I looked away.

"Yo, this is Dwayne Wayne," Terrell said, patting his brother on the shoulder. Wayne shook his head.

"Yo, chill wit dat," he said, chewing on a straw. He was holding a nearly empty paper cup, shaking the remaining ice. Wayne stepped forward and reached his hand out to shake Becka's.

"Hey. I'm Becka," she said.

"You guys are so corny," I said, stepping past them to head toward the door. They followed me inside where it was total chaos.

People were waiting for pick up orders, all the tables were taken, and there was one booth empty that still had napkins, cups, and a pizza pan sitting on top of the table.

We grabbed it before anyone else did.

"So, whatchoo guys getting?" Wayne said, twirling the straw around between his teeth.

"I like cheese," Becka said. "Amanda's a meat eater. So, I guess we can get whatever."

"She's a vegan, so she'll have the salad," Terrell said, flicking his thumb at Lexi. She smacked him in the arm.

"Shut up! I am *not* a vegan. I eat meat on my pizza, too. You're the worst," she said.

I looked at her and immediately thought of Hilary from Fresh Prince.

"So, where'd you two meet?" I asked.

Terrell grinned.

"There was this party off campus. I was there. Lexi was there. Everyone was high. She wasn't. I was. So she took advantage of my highness and got me to give her a lap dance," Terrell said.

Lexi, on cue, and predictably, smacked him in the shoulder again. I was sure it was probably black and purple by now.

"We *did* meet at a party. It was on campus, so no one was high. That I know of. And he can't dance to save his life," Lexi said. "At all. Which is shameful for a brotha, if you ask me."

"I can dance. Want me to show you right now?" Terrell began to slide out of the booth.

"No!" Lexi grabbed him by his shirt and held it tightly, then grabbed it with both hands as he tried to out-muscle her.

Holy cow. She was strong.

"You're not embarrassing me," she said.

It was too late. People were watching us as Terrell acted like a total goof. But he still made my skin hot.

"You're gonna get us kicked out of here," I said.

"Their loss," he replied.

"I don't know you people. On that note, I'm gonna order," I said, standing up to head to the counter.

I ordered a large cheese and a large pepperoni with large drinks.

I felt someone behind me and spun around to find Terrell standing a little too close for comfort. His cologne smelled super expensive.

"Yo, I told you I got you," he said, pulling out a credit card. He handed it to the cashier, who gave me five large cups. I passed three of them to Terrell. He took the cups, retrieved his card and receipt, and headed over to the soda fountain, laughing.

I don't know what he found funny, but it was unsettling.

I poured Cokes for Becka and I and returned to the booth, sliding in next to her, across from Terrell and Lexi. Wayne was watching Becka cooly, with a new straw to chew on.

Wayne was giving off his relaxed vibe as Becka tried to make conversation. I watched them as they fired off three to five-word sentences at each other, with Wayne periodically responding with "That's dope, that's dope."

I thought about the first person I crushed on. Disney David. He was this cute boy in my neighborhood that once looked like he belonged in an after school series. He now tragically suffers from insufferable amounts of acne on his face to the point that they caused hideous pits and craters. High school was unkind to him.

David used to hang out with Becka and me when we spent the summers chilling in Maddie and Allie's pool. His family was seriously into racing, and they'd be out working in the garage on their go-carts and stock cars, sending the thundering noise of a revving V8 engine and exhaust pipes throughout the neighborhood at all hours of the day.

My sister was into those races growing up, often tagging along with the boys. She would come home after late nights out at the track, covered in sweat and smelling like dirt and gasoline.

Disney Channel David was replaced by Will Smith, LL Cool J, Taye Diggs, and Sean Patrick Thomas by the time I was eleven.

The pizzas came, and for the rest of the evening, I sank into the background and watched as Terrell made jokes, Lexi slapped him in the shoulder for every little thing he said out of character, and Wayne and Becka did whatever it was they thought they were doing.

seventeen

Signing up for varsity basketball tryouts was a huge mistake.
Coach Freddie had it in for me the minute I stepped up to the table in the hallway for sign-ups. She stood next to Kayli Jordan, the captain of the team who sat in a scratched up blue plastic chair. In front of her were forms for parent permission, immunizations, and physicals.

Kayli looked at me and smiled as I reached for the clipboard and the pen dangling from the string attached to it.

"You're a sophomore, right?" she asked.

"I'll be a sophomore in the fall," I said.

"Weren't you in my chem class?" Kayli watched me as I scribbled my name on the next available line of the sign-up sheet.

"Yep," I said.

"You're taking junior classes?" She popped her gum.

"Just that one," I said.

"Wow. How'd you pull that off, being a freshman?"

I looked at her as I slid the clipboard toward her.

"They advanced me. I'm ahead in science."

"Oh. That's cool. You must be super smart." She looked at the clipboard, then handed me one of each of the three forms.

Coach Freddie was watching me. I looked at her as she smiled.

"Tryouts are this Wednesday and Thursday. Three to five," she said, without blinking.

I nodded, avoiding her glare.

"You sure you can commit if you make the team? You're the symphony and jazz band's only string instrument. You might not be able to do both," Coach Freddie sniffed.

"I think I can manage," I said.

"Playing basketball ain't nothing like flicking your fingers across that oversized fiddle," Coach Freddie said, her face expressionless as her eyes went to the students filing by in the hallways.

"It's not a fiddle. It's a cello," I said. "And a double bass."

Coach looked at me and humphed, before returning her gaze to the herd of underclassmen shuffling to beat the next bell.

After I chose jazz band as my elective at the start of the school year, on the first day of class Ms. Whittle pulled out the best of only two violins sitting in the band closet collecting dust. She offered it to me, and I quickly declined. Initially, I didn't feel like dealing with shouldering a midget guitar while dragging an oversized chopstick with horsehair running down the side of it across its strings.

I told Ms. Whittle that I played guitar in church, and she calmly sniffed and said, "This isn't church, my dear. This is the Orchestra."

She assigned me to the cello and double bass, made arrangements to get them from somewhere seemingly off world, and reached into the bottom drawer of her desk. Ms. Whittle pulled out a Ray Brown vinyl album, handed it to me and told me, "This will give you a head start. He's all you need to know. That's your new religion, right there."

On the cover of the record was a charming, handsome cocoa brown man in a gray suit, smiling with one arm wrapped around a smaller, sand-colored cello and the other around a deep, dark bass.

Later that night, after stealing my momma's turntable buried deep in her closet, I played the 1960's record while sipping *drank* from a small glass, pretending like I was drinking a goblet of wine.

Listening to Ray Brown and Ella Fitzgerald forever changed my perspective on music and greatly influenced the way I performed in church. I had always been drawn to R&B, jazz, and soul. Now, they were in my bones.

"Wednesday and Thursday. Don't forget," Kayli said, interrupting my nostalgia. "We need another point guard."

I smiled at her as I stepped away to brush past a group of students clustered near the table. They were looking at another sheet taped to Coach Freddie's classroom door with a list of names. It was the sign-up sheet for next season's varsity teams Spirit volunteers.

I took the next few steps and entered the stuffy algebra classroom. Summer wasn't officially here yet, but it was already scorching outside, turning some of the school's classrooms into saunas.

Becka was sitting in her usual chair by the window. I slid into the desk next to hers.

"Yo, homie, what's up?" She smacked her gum and smiled, watching me get organized. I sat my algebra book on top of the desk, opened it to the chapter that we were on, and flipped to the next empty page in my notebook.

"Not much. What's up with you?" I asked, clicking my thumb to expose a small length of the lead in my mechanical pencil.

"I wanted to see if you wanted to head out to my house after class. My mom's making mofongo, and dad's grilling carnitas," Becka said.

"That would be awesome, but I think my sister's bringing Ivy to the house. I haven't seen my little niece since she turned two. Now she's about to be three." I blew out a breath, watching the substitute teacher scribble the even-numbered math problems out of the textbook onto the dry erase board. I assumed that the odd-numbered problems would be for homework, considering what our Math teacher, Mr. Foose, would do. Regardless, it was like four pages of math. I wasn't thrilled, to say the least.

"Man, where does your sister go for months at a time?"

"Years, you mean? No idea." I said. "When she's gone, my momma acts like an even worse psycho hypocrite than she already is."

"What do you mean?" Becka dug into her backpack and produced a tootsie roll, handing it to me. While she rummaged around for another one, I unwrapped mine and popped it into my mouth.

"I thought she was going out to interviews for jobs. Last week, she comes home all shady, disappears into her room for hours, then comes out when my Nana Jane and Granddaddy stop by, and she's all trashed. They, of course, take care of her. My granddaddy gets the grill going and barbecues some pork chops, and then Nana Jane is laying it on me like it's my fault Momma left out to do whatever she was doing." I snapped the lead off my pencil after realizing I was scribbling at the top of the page in my textbook. I quickly erased the mark and clicked more lead out, placing the mechanical pencil onto the desk.

"I don't get why your mom doesn't just go get help. I mean, I know it's only been like three years since your dad left. But still. You gotta move on, you know?" Becka chewed daintily as she flicked her tootsie roll wrapper onto the floor.

"It's easier said than done. I'm not even over my daddy leaving," I said as the substitute teacher cleared her throat.

She began calling on people to come up and answer the problems she had written on the dry erase board while showing their work.

I slumped down in the chair, hoping she wouldn't point in my direction.

Algebra seemed to drag on for decades before the dismissal bell finally went off. After class, I followed Becka to her locker, then out through the front entrance toward where her bus would be.

Before she climbed up the steps into the bus, she turned to me and picked a speck of lint from my white button up uniform shirt.

"If you change your mind, call me. My mom said she'd come to get you as long as she's not tied to the kitchen," she said.

With a nod, I watched her disappear past the bus driver, and then I headed toward the parking area to look for my sister in whatever she was driving now.

Taylor was waiting for me, parked near the buses. She was behind the wheel of a black Pontiac Sunfire that had a Road Runner steering wheel cover, matching floor mats, and Ivy crammed into a car seat in the back. She was facing forward, holding something that melted all over her hand. When Ivy saw me, she reached out with both arms and eagerly fluttered her fingers in her standard toddler greeting.

Taylor's hair was a greasy mess. She was wearing a wife beater, and new tattoos graced her right forearm. They were swollen red and glistening with petroleum jelly. Her lip was pierced.

The hint of weed reached my nostrils and in disgust, I wrinkled my nose at the odor that to me always smelled like a skunk and sweaty armpits.

I climbed into the passenger side and clutched my backpack to my chest as Taylor pulled away from the curb and cut a U-turn in the middle of the roadway, heading back out toward Saraland Boulevard.

"How long you need me to watch her for? I've got a ton of math homework, and a paper to write for Spanish," I said.

"I have to work extra hours tonight, and my babysitter bailed on me last minute," she said, as she aggressively cut someone in a Suburban off to change lanes. They blasted their horn at her in protest. She shot her middle finger up at the rearview mirror and smacked her gum.

"So does that mean real late?" I asked.

"I dunno, Manda. Maybe," she said. "Mom can't watch her. She's toasted."

"Looks like you're a little toasted yourself," I replied.

"Not hammered like she is," Taylor said.

"Did it hurt?" I asked, changing the subject. I knew Taylor was high. She was driving like she didn't know which lane to be in, while smelling like the Amazon. I began to doubt she was even going to work, and if she actually had a job.

"Did *what* hurt?" she sniffed, annoyed.

"The tat."

She glanced at her arm, then ran her fingers through her grungy hair.

"Nope."

"What is it?" I asked.

"It's Ivy, with her face surrounded by poison ivy and flowers. And her birth date," she said, holding out her arm to show me.

I frowned. That looked nothing like Ivy.

"You might want to get your money back," I said.

"Why? It looks tight," she said.

"Okay." I disagreed. "Does Ivy have clothes to change into? She needs a bath."

"She was playing outside earlier, and I gave her a popsicle, so she's sticky. Got clothes in her diaper bag."

Ivy was turning three, and Taylor still used a diaper bag. I shook my head. She must've been wearing custom made Huggies or something, because there's no way they made diapers to fit her tush.

"Is she still drinking from a bottle?" I asked.

"I've been working with her to get her off of it," Taylor said.

"She's way too old for that. That's going to ruin her teeth," I snapped.

Taylor looked at me and laughed.

"You're something else," she said, her eyes returning to the road.

"So that means she's probably still in diapers, too?"

"She's got pull-ups. She knows to take them off and go potty," Taylor said. "Some girls aren't ready to be potty trained until they're four. Every kid is different."

I didn't believe that.

"She should've been out of diapers a year ago, and off the bottle long before that."

"Who died and made you a child specialist?" she snapped.

"Why haven't you been by in like, a year?" I asked, ignoring her.

She ran her fingers through her hair again, glanced out the window, and balled her left hand into a fist and covered her mouth, coughing harshly.

When her coughing fit was over, she cleared her throat.

"I've *been* stopping by. You're always at school," Taylor said.

"Momma says she hasn't seen you."

"She probably hasn't seen much more than the back of her eyelids lately."

"You're one to talk," I said.

Taylor cut her eyes at me sharply.

"Don't get at me, Manda. I do the best I can," she said.

"You can do better," I said under my breath.

"Yeah, cause you're Miss Perfect, right? You don't know anything. And you're not a mother. You don't know what it's like."

"I know a lot," I said.

She frowned and grew silent.

The brakes screeched as she pulled onto the dirt and gravel driveway. She slapped the gear shifter into park, snatched the keys out of the ignition, slid out of the seat and reached beneath it to grab the handle to yank the seat forward.

With a few motions, she had Ivy unsnapped from her seatbelt and free of her booster seat.

Ivy climbed out and onto the grass. Her face and hands were covered in what I hoped was chocolate and not poop.

Taylor slammed the diaper bag into my arms and marched up to the front door.

I grabbed Ivy's less grimy hand and led her behind Taylor into the house. Momma was passed out on the sofa snoring loudly with drool caked around her mouth and her hair sprawled out all over the sofa armrest. On the old floor television, Judge Milian was yelling at a trio of women who appeared to be related, standing at the podium, fighting over an heirloom antique china set on The People's Court.

Nana Jane and Granddaddy weren't here yet. I knew they'd probably be at the house just before five.

Other than the television being on, the house was silent.

I heard the door slam behind me.

Taylor was gone without saying another word. I exhaled slowly, leaning my head back with my hands cupping the back of my head to close my eyes for a few minutes, almost as if to reset myself.

It was just Ivy and me, and my half-dead momma.

"Ivy, you wanna take a bath?"

She nodded.

After tossing Ivy's diaper bag onto the stained coffee table in front of where Momma snored, I dug inside of it carefully to find a mismatched outfit that smelled like it was clean.

Shaking my head, I pulled out all the clothes inside of the bag, dumped them into the washing machine in the laundry room, and poured in a cup of vinegar with the detergent. I turned the washing machine on, and then led Ivy to the main bathroom to start her bathwater.

The Johnson & Johnson's baby shampoo that Nana Jane had brought over to the house months ago sat on top of the shower rack all this time, unused. After pouring some into the water to make bubbles, I stripped Ivy down to find grass and dirt in her pull-up.

I carefully lowered her down into the bath water after testing the temperature with my finger. She began playing with the bubbles while I tossed her pull-up in the trash and added her chocolate soiled clothes to what was already in the washer.

Returning to the bathroom, I slid down onto the floor to watch Ivy play with the suds for a while before I began washing her hair. Small rocks and dirt hid in her hair along her scalp, so I used my fingertips to scrub her head gently to get everything out.

I soaped her up and washed her with a small terry cloth, then rinsed her off, took her out, patted her skin dry, slipped her into a pull-up and wrapped her in a fresh bath towel to hang out with me in my room while waiting for her clothes to finish.

I gave her a coloring book and crayons, and while she scribbled, I got to work on my Spanish paper.

A little while later, my flip phone vibrated. I pulled out my red Motorola RAZR and answered.

"Yo, whatchoo doin'?" Becka asked. She sounded like she was out of breath.

"Nothing. Just finished giving Ivy a bath not that long ago, and now I'm working on my Spanish paper while Ivy colors," I said.

"Cool. Can you come outside in twenty minutes?"

"Why? What's up?"

"My mom's bringing over some mofongo, carnitas, and rice for you and Ivy. There's more than enough. You want some butter rolls with it?"

"You didn't have to do that," I said.

"You know my mom. She's gonna make sure you eat. She'll be there in a little bit, so watch out for her," Becka said. "I've gotta get back to ping pong. I'm kicking my uncle's *culo.*"

"Okay, you do that," I laughed, hanging up.

"Hey, Ivy. We're about to eat good tonight," I said. "Do you like meat and rice?"

She nodded.

"Yesss, I likes meet an whysss," she said softly in toddler lingo. She smiled at me, made a cute little humming noise, then went back to drawing red squiggly lines all over Snoopy.

Sophomore Year

eighteen
FRIDAY NIGHT LIGHTS ♡
Vigor V. Citronelle, September 2006

"Yo, are you ready?" Becka stood at the door, her hands on her hip, being all dramatic.

"We're not going to be late. I don't know what you're bugging about. The game doesn't start for another hour."

"Yeah, but I'm trying to get there early, know what I'm saying?" Becka clicked her teeth, and I looked at her knowingly.

"Dang, girl. Why you so _thirsty_?"

"Wayne's meeting us there early so we can chill for a few minutes before the game."

"I thought he rode the bus with the rest of the team? How's he getting there?"

"He's got a ride," Becka said. I knew that look on her face. She had something up her sleeve.

"Who's the ride, _Becka_?" I asked.

"Come on, girl, let's go," she said, reaching out to pull on my arm.

"Dude, I don't have my shoes on, I need my cellphone, and I gotta get a different shirt. This one's not working for me today," I said, prying her claws away from my wrists.

"So, hurry up. You need my help?"

"No, I got it. Geez," I said, as Becka followed me into the house. I closed the door behind her, and she stopped short, staring at my momma.

She was sitting up, her eyes looking beyond the television and into inter-dimensional space. Family Feud was on, but I turned the volume down. Drool hung from her chin and drizzled onto her v-neck sweater.

She had to be hot in that, but not even a drop of sweat glistened on her brow. I left her like she was, without wiping the stream of saliva from her face.

"Is she okay?" Becka asked.

"Yeah, she's fine. She'll be like that for a while, then she'll get up, probably get a Coke from the fridge. She might snack on something, then she'll pass out on the sofa as usual. That's her new normal," I said.

"That doesn't look anything *near* normal," Becka replied.

"It really isn't," I said, heading toward my room at the back of the house, across the hallway from my momma's room. She never slept in there, so Nana Jane and Granddaddy used her bed whenever they stayed over.

"How's Ivy doing?" She asked while I looked under the bed for my Steve Madden black flats. They were my new favorites, along with the black and burgundy Jordans Auntie Beanie gave me to match my uniform for basketball. She brought over a bag of brand name clothes and shoes for me last weekend when she visited from Florida. The days of hand-me-downs were officially *sayonara*.

"She's good. Haven't really seen her much since those couple of times I babysat," I said. I found the flats and sat on my bed to slip them on. They were comfortable.

"That's crazy," Becka said. "I hope your sis gets it together."

"Yeah, me too," I replied, standing to follow her out to the Subaru.

Her momma was talking on her cellphone as Becka slid into the front seat next to her. I got in behind Becka and closed the door.

Mrs. Canales nodded and hung up.

"You guys have plans after the game?" she asked.

"Don't know yet," Becka said.

Mrs. Canales backed out of the driveway and onto the street.

"Well, since it's Friday, we can all head down to the shore early tomorrow morning. I just got off the phone with some family friends. They're leaving for the weekend and wanted to know if I would house sit. They said it was okay for all of you to come along," Mrs. Canales said.

"Pensacola?" Becka asked with excitement.

"A little farther. Destin," she said. "Somewhere new. We've never been there before."

Becka twisted in her seat to look at me, her eyes sparkling with excitement.

"You wanna go?"

I smiled.

"I don't know. I mean, you know my situation," I said.

"Yeah, so that means you can go," she said with a smirk.

"I still have to ask," I replied.

"For what? It ain't like she hears you when you do," Becka said.

"Rebecca Denise, watch what you say to people," her momma snapped.

"I'm sorry, but it's true. Her mom's basically a cauliflower," she said.

Mrs. Canales pulled over and put on the hazard lights.

Then, she turned to glare at Becka, who seemed to shrink into the seat cushions.

"You never know what someone is going through. You're on the outside looking in. You don't talk about anyone like that, ever again. Do you understand me, *mija*?"

Becka nodded.

"*Say it*," Mrs. Canales said, with a sting.

"I'm sorry, Mama. I understand," she mumbled. Becka twisted around and looked at me as if she were in pain.

"I'm sorry about what I said about your mom. I didn't mean it," she said.

"It's okay," I replied. I reached out to touch her shoulder. She faced forward, and Mrs. Canales turned off the hazard lights and pulled away from the side of the road.

The rest of the drive north up US 45 through Mauvilla, Chunchula, and Gulfcrest was done in silence. Nearly forty minutes after leaving my driveway, we pulled up to Citronelle High, with its almost one-hundred-year-old brick buildings still standing.

"See you after the game, Mrs. Canales," I said as I slid out and onto the sidewalk. I followed Becka through the grass and around the buildings to the football field.

"So about this weekend," I began. "I think I have basketball practice too."

"It won't hurt to miss one practice, Manda," Becka said.

I stopped walking. Becka turned around and a look of concern dawned on her face.

"What's wrong?" she asked.

"You know, I still can't believe I made the team. I traveled on like every lay up during tryouts. I couldn't dribble to save my life, and I messed up my thumb trying to catch a pass."

Becka stepped toward me.

"Give yourself more credit. Coach saw something in you. Kayli wanted you on the team real bad, for a reason. You'll be fine, I promise," she said.

"You know what the worst part is? My momma doesn't even know I'm playing. I brought my uniforms and practice suits home and she was spaced out as usual. My Auntie Beanie bought me a pair of Jordans to match my uniform. I have no idea where she got them from. You'd swear they were custom made," I said. My eyes began to sting, and I quickly brushed away at the corners with my fingertips, fighting to get control of myself.

Becka saw me shaking and reached out to squeeze me tightly. I held her for a split second, before pulling away.

"My Auntie Beanie flew up from Florida to make sure I got my physical done, paid my athletic fees and signed all of the forms for me to play," I continued with a sniff.

"She even bought me a couple pairs of shoes for practice and my game shoes. New sports bras and undies, my warm up suits. It ain't like my own momma was gonna do it. No way I could've asked my Nana. Granddaddy's not really coming around anymore."

I shook my head as Becka nodded, a soft look on her face.

"I'm about to have my first two games and then a freaking three game tournament before Thanksgiving, and I'm pretty sure no one from my family will even be there."

"I'll be there," Becka said. "Leenie will be there. We're your family, too. And all your crazy soon-to-be raging fans will be there."

"Coach says I have chicken legs. She laughed at me, saying that I look like a hen trying to get to a high branch when I made lay ups at practice last weekend. She said they were more like *give ups*. I can't deal," I said.

"Coach Freddie can be the worst. She's a freaking drill sergeant. Everyone on the volleyball team says she's really mean. And they've been killing it. I can only imagine how she is to you guys.

"The varsity girl's basketball team is the embarrassment of the athletic department. You notice there are never any pictures of the team in the school newspaper? They're like the ugly stepchild. So, I'm sure it's not directed at you. Maybe she's just frustrated." Becka wiped at my cheek with her hand.

"No, it's me. At practice, she's like, 'I can't for the life of me figure out how your ugly shots are getting in the hole. Throwing all those rocks up there is working for you, but it's not pretty. At all. You need finesse. There's a beauty to it.' How do you say something like that to someone and expect them to even *want* to get better?" I sniffed, after imitating Coach's strong, redneck country accent.

"That just means she believes in you and sees potential. I think you're taking it all wrong. Coach Freddie is a total butch, but I know you're gonna slay it this year. Just watch," Becka said. "Kayli tells everyone you never miss a shot. Which is freakishly impossible. So, that's saying something."

Standing near the entrance to the field, Wayne and Terrell talked quietly near a group of people walking toward the bleachers.

When Wayne saw us, he chuckled.

"What took you so long?" he asked as Becka flung herself into his arms.

"My mom drives really slow," she said.

I felt Terrell watching me as I moved over to lean against the fence, putting Becka and Wayne between the two of us. He leaned forward to look at me directly. I wrapped my arms around my chest.

"Yo, what's up?" he asked, casually.

I looked at him, shaking my head as I raised an eyebrow at him.

"What's up with you?" I replied. He sniffed loudly, then grinned.

"You smell good. I can smell whatever you're wearing all the way over here," he said loudly.

"Oh, yeah? Huh. Soap will do that, I guess," I said. He laughed in response.

"So, why you all the way over there?" Terrell asked.

"Where's your girl, Luxury Toyota?" I fired back.

"Lexi? We broke up," he said, kicking his right leg out to pound the ground with his heel. I watched him as he fidgeted, then looked away, shaking my head in disbelief.

"For what? You cheat on her?" I asked.

"Nah. We're just going two different places," he said.

I nodded, watching more people arrive in lifted diesel trucks with their aftermarket HID's and floodlights spraying the gates with piercing brightness. I turned my head away and twisted around to face the field, waiting for the irritating flares in my field of vision to go away.

Wayne gave Becka a kiss and headed off toward the locker rooms to get ready, and I followed Terrell and Becka toward the bleachers.

We sat on the visiting team's side near the top of the stands. The Vigor High marching band was settling into the middle rows, adjusting straps and instruments as their spirit squad huddled up in the rows below them, laughing and talking.

I watched as the Vigor High cheerleaders ambled out on to the edge of the field to practice routines before the game.

On the other side of the field, the bleacher rows began filling up as Citronelle High students, friends, families, teachers and the community began arriving.

The Citronelle marching band was on the field with the cheer-leaders, the ribbon throwers and flag team. The spirit squad was setting a few boxes down in between the rows, and someone pulled out and unfolded a t-shirt from inside one of them.

This game felt more exciting than the Satsuma home games Becka and I attended this year. Last Friday, we lost to Daphne by 33 points, and at the first game of the season, we lost to Baker by 7. In two weeks was the next home game.

My first basketball game wasn't until the second week of November, so I was trying to use football games as a way to escape the house when I wasn't at basketball or band practice.

I smelled her expensive perfume before she was even halfway up the bleachers to where we were sitting.

Pauline plodded up the metal past Becka and me, plopping down to sandwich me between the two of them as usual. She laid her head on my shoulder. I felt it bobbing up and down as she chewed her gum loudly, the aroma of spearmint wafting up with every flex of her jaw.

Becka snorted.

"You two should get a room," she said.

"I agree," Terrell said from behind me.

"Both of you can kiss my caboose," Pauline said, raising her head to smack her gum with an obnoxious crack. "You two get a room. How 'bout that?"

Becka laughed, knowingly.

"I'm not the right candidate for the job on that one," she said.

"I hear ya, girlie. So where the snacks at?" Pauline sat her purse down between her legs and sniffed. "Whatcha got in that bag of yours?"

"Yo, you just got here. What do you do, skip dinner?" Becka asked. "Them kale salads ain't enough to satisfy?"

"You got some tamales in there? Some taquitos? Doritos? Ranch dip? Hook a girl up," Pauline held her hand out in front of me, and I leaned back to give her room to beg.

Becka cut her eyes and unzipped her backpack, holding it open in front of me for Pauline to peer inside.

Pauline looked, rummaged around, then frowned.

"You got nothing. What's up with that, *Snacks*?"

"We're getting concessions, girl," Becka said.

"Well, you suck," Pauline said with a smack.

Terrell laughed, shaking his head in amusement.

"Mind your business," Pauline said, pointing her finger at him. He held his hands up in surrender as I smiled, standing up to head down the bleachers toward the concession stand. I heard they had funnel cakes, and I wanted one. Pauline grabbed my arm and handed me a twenty-dollar bill.

I tried to hand it back but she smacked my hand away.

"You know what I like. Hook me up, and get whatever you want. You know how we do. I got you," she said.

I nodded and turned to take a step, when Terrell stopped me.

He handed me a twenty-dollar bill.

"Hook me up too. Surprise me," he said.

I raised my eyebrows at him as he held the bill out, waiting for me to take it.

"Do I look like a waitress?" I snapped. "You've got legs, dude."

"Oh, I see how it is," he said, standing up with a wide grin on his face. He followed Becka and me down to the concession stand.

Becka bought a Coke and a bag of popcorn, Terrell bought a few slices of pizza and a Mountain Dew, and I grabbed two bags of Doritos, a Coke and a Sprite, a Snickers, a funnel cake, and two hot dogs, gripping it all to my chest as I balanced to get back to where Pauline was waiting.

When we returned, Pauline reached to take a few things from me so I didn't drop them. Once I was settled down, she handed me my funnel cake just as the announcer started talking. I offered some to her, and she snapped off a chunk from the edge, sticking her gum to the rim of her soda can.

When Becka saw Wayne on the field, she lost her mind and started screaming hysterically.

"Dang, wish someone would cheer for me like that when I make an entrance," Terrell said from behind her as she stomped on the bleachers, making my butt hurt.

She sat back down. I looked at her with a smirk.

"You get that all out of your system?" I asked, smartly.

She smirked back and popped a few kernels into her mouth, crunching loudly on purpose.

Terrell leaned forward.

"Ya'll ignoring me?" he asked.

"Yes," I said.

"Why you doing me like that?"

"Cause you're annoying," I said, simply. "You need to get Lexi over here so she can calm you back down to your regular self. You're being weird."

"*I'm* being weird?"

"Yep."

He sniffed, then laughed.

"No, I think it's the opposite. *You're* being weird," he said.

"You're both being weird, so shut up and watch the game. My boyfriend's about to score a touchdown," Becka said, snapping open her soda.

Pauline leaned into me and I felt her lips brush my ear.

"So, I see chickie-chick isn't here. What's up with that?" she whispered.

I turned to tilt my head toward her, and she pressed her ear up against my face. I giggled, then put my lips to her ear.

"He said they broke up," I whispered.

She nodded, then pressed her lips against my ear.

"Soooo, you gonna ask him out or naw?"

I moved my head away from hers and looked at her with a horrified expression on my face.

"What? No," I said sharply, but loud enough for Becka to look at us with her eyebrows raised.

"Ya'll over there sharing secrets," Becka muttered, smacking me in the temple with a kernel of popcorn. "Do tell."

"Pauline thinks she's a Def Jam Queen of Comedy," I said.

With a giggle, Pauline nudged me in the arm.

"Don't act like I ain't hit a home run with that," she said. "I know you."

"Apparently not that well," I snorted.

"I can just feel the vibes," Pauline replied, before sipping her Coke. Then, for no reason, she punched me in the shoulder.

"Okay, Lexi," I said.

Terrell caught on to that, and leaned his head back and laughed.

"Oh, man, you're cracking on my ex, now, huh?" he said.

"I don't know what you're talking about," I said with a snicker as Wayne crossed a line of defenders and stormed up the edge of the end zone to score a touchdown for Vigor. The visiting side of the field went wild, standing, screaming and yelling as the bleachers quaked beneath me, making my butt hole ache.

Terrell stood and whistled sharply, piercing the air above my head. I finished the last bit of my funnel cake before setting the plate down. Pauline gestured toward it with her hand, and I gave it to her. She took it, balled it up with her wrappers, and handed me my hot dog and the bag of Doritos.

As I ate, I was suddenly aware of Terrell's cologne. It was different from what he usually wore. This time, it reminded me of the ocean.

I closed my eyes as it reminded me of the family trips to meet up with Auntie Beanie at the resort in Clearwater. We packed into the minivan with coolers, beach toys and luggage, some of which went into the ridiculous wedge-shaped contraption on the roof.

The boys where obnoxious the whole way there, crammed into the three seat bench in back, and I had to sit on Taylor's lap between Nana Jane and Momma. Daddy drove with Granddaddy riding shotgun.

I instantly became hooked on Florida's gulf coast beaches, with bright blue water clear as glass and powder white sand as soft as flour. It was like a Caribbean post card.

I was nine years old back when we made our first trip to Clearwater. It was the summer after my third grade year, back when Momma had me in those flower dresses all the time, with the white sandals that had the daisies on the front straps.

Nana Jane had that big family photo album we looked at every year during Thanksgiving, when I was reminded how curly and blonde my hair was back then. The sun bleached it nearly white during the summers when I was small, and I tanned so much darker than everyone else that I looked like I was a foreign exchange student with albino hair they were hosting from some third world country.

Over the years my hair darkened, and once I was in New York, I spent ridiculous amounts of money getting color, blonde highlights and blow outs after discovering the expensive salons of the Dominicans. Eventually, Jackie and her cousins found out about my hair struggles and rescued me from financial ruin.

I turned to find Terrell's eyes on me. He unsettled me in the worst way.

Quickly returning my gaze to the field, I wondered what it would be like to feel his arms around me. I didn't trust him. Everything about him unraveled me and annoyed me and I hated that I was so aware of him.

A long while later, the game ended with Vigor winning by twenty. Wayne snagged three of those touchdowns. We celebrated after the game, with Mrs. Canales dropping Becka and me off at Benzi's to meet up with Pauline, Wayne and Terrell. It was hard to focus on food and eating with all the thoughts running through my head, and with all my attention devoted to avoiding Terrell's gazes.

I didn't want to like him.

But Pauline was right, as always. And I wanted to kick her for it.

nineteen

SWEET SIXTEEN ♡

November 2006

"Why you running up and down the court like that, girl? Like a bow-legged gazelle in a baby walker," Coach Freddie blasted her whistle and the screech immediately got under my skin.

She irritated the hell out of me. All I wanted to do was walk right up to her with this basketball, give her a swift uppercut to the chin and then dribble the ball on her face while she lay sprawled out on the wood floor.

I was sweating my mascara off. Darkness and stars pressed in at the edge of my field of vision, as if I was about to pass out. Just the act of breathing in and out proved to be an arduous affair.

"And pull your shorts up! It's like you're wearing an apron. You 'bout to bake a cake, Duncan Hines?" Coach screeched at me again as I flung myself past her. I was in the middle of doing suicides after missing too many passes.

As I approached her again, she jabbed an arm out to stop me in mid-stride. She almost clothes-lined me, and I almost reached up to choke her neck.

"What's your *deal,* Rush?" she asked.

I looked at her oddly and hunched over to grasp my knees, desperately trying to keep myself from coughing. Sweat burned my eyes, my chest was heaving, and the blood pulsed in the vein straddling my temple.

"What do you mean?" I asked hoarsely.

"I mean, why you afraid to catch a pass? You scared the balls gonna take your face off?" she asked with a grunt.

"No, ma'am," I said, attempting to straighten myself back up and face her directly, eye to eye.

"You could've fooled me. A pretty girl like you? You look crazy running up and down that court like that. You've got raw talent. You just need some spit shine. I'll have you right by the end of the season, I promise you that," Coach said, slapping me on the back. "We're gonna do something new."

She turned and blew her whistle, then yelled for Kayli.

"Hey, Jordan!" Coach screeched.

Kayli stopped shooting at the free-throw line and jogged over to where we were standing mid court.

"Yes, Coach?" Kayli replied

"Alright, look. Miss Jordan's gonna to be your partner for this. Here's what you're gonna do," Coach said, signaling for a ball.

Keisha, a point guard, passed one to her. Coach Freddie nudged me to the line at the half court center circle. She directed Kayli to the opposite side, then showed us the passing and sidestepping maneuver she wanted us to do.

When I tried it, I nearly tripped over my own shoes.

"There's hope for you yet, kid. Keep at it," she said, tapping her clipboard to her legs.

She blew the whistle and signaled the other girls to gather around her at the top of the key, while Kayli and I passed the ball and sidestepped along the half court line repeatedly from one side to the other.

Kayli smiled at me.

"Check you out! You go Rush!" she said, loudly.

"What?" I asked.

"You're catching the ball," she said.

"That's 'cause we're close to each other. It's a whole different scenario when you're farther away," I said.

Kayli took a step backward and passed.

I caught it.

She took another step backward.

I passed. She caught it, then took two more steps backward and passed.

I caught it.

"You were saying?" she snickered.

"Still too close," I replied, passing the basketball back to her.

She stepped back three steps, took a step forward and hurled the ball toward me with far more force from her chest. I ducked away to avoid the ball.

"That's the problem," she said. "You've got trust issues. Trust your teammates. Nobody's trying to hurt you, Manda."

"Do you have to pass so *hard?* Trying to take my head off?" I asked, hopping over to retrieve the ball.

"The farther away you are, the more force the ball needs in a pass, especially if you're trying to keep the other team from stealing," she said. I stepped to the line and sent the ball back to her.

She held the basketball over her head and passed it, and I reached up to catch it. It went straight to my hands. My palms stung as I sent it back to her the same way.

She nodded.

"See, you're getting it," Kayli said with a smile. "Stop being such a girly girl and muscle that thing, lady."

Then, she stepped further away toward the opposite key, raised the ball with one hand, and held it over her head.

"Don't be afraid," she said. "I'm gonna send you a rocket, but I know you got this. Are you ready?"

I spread my legs and lowered my body, holding my hands out in front of me.

"No, you want to be flexible and loose. Not all rigid," Kayli said with a chuckle. "And you don't have to stand like that. This ain't football," she said. "It can come at you like this at any moment, in the clutch, so you gotta to be ready."

I relaxed and straightened up a little as Kayli raised the ball.

Kayli flexed and fired her arm with velocity, sending the basketball tearing through the air. I leaped with my toes a little, reached up and caught it with both hands.

"See? Not so bad, right?" she laughed.

Suddenly, there was loud applause, and I turned around to see Coach Freddie and the rest of the team clapping and whistling.

"Keep at it, Rush. We could use another strong Power Forward. I'm throwing you to the wolves tonight, when we play Leflore. Get your head in the game," Coach said.

She turned to address the others.

"Alright ladies. That's it for practice. Get ready for tonight. See you on the bus. Be on time."

Kayli flung the ball into the bin at the side of the court and I followed her to the locker room and the showers.

Just before stepping inside, I was hit with the sharp pungent combination of chlorine, musk, mildew and sweat. I hated the school's showers, but I didn't want to walk out of the gymnasium smelling like Funyuns and Fritos.

When I reached my locker, I pulled out my gym bag. I stripped out of my sports bra, warm up tee, socks, sneakers and shorts, stepped into my shower sandals and quickly scrubbed down, washed my sweaty hair, conditioned, and rinsed off.

After I toweled myself dry and slapped on some Bath and Body Works Sensual Amber body cream, I slipped into a fresh pair of clean cotton panties and a bralette.

Standing barefoot in my undies, I pulled my cellphone from my gym bag and called Taylor's phone. She didn't answer. I called the house number, then my momma's cell. Nothing.

I wasn't dialing Nana Jane, and it was too early to call Granddaddy. I tried Becka's cell. She answered after the first ring.

"You need a ride?" she breathed into the phone.

"Yeah," I said. "What are you doing? You're all out of breath."

"I was chasing my cousins. We were playing manhunt in the back, but we were waiting for you to call. I'll get mom and we'll be there in a sec," she said.

"Okay," I replied, hanging up.

Kayli walked by, drying her sandy hair with a towel, with the smell of roses and candy following close behind her.

"You got a ride, Rush?" she asked.

"Yeah, someone's coming to get me," I said.

"Okay. Well, see you tonight," Kayli smiled as she grabbed her duffel bag. She flung her towel over her shoulder. "Oh, and happy birthday."

I looked up at her.

"How did you know it was my birthday?"

"For real? Come on, Manda. I've known you like, forever."

I laughed.

"You mean since my freshman year?"

"Girl, no. You might not remember me, but I knew you from elementary school and Adams Middle. We weren't in the same classes or obviously, the same grade, but I always saw you in the hallways," Kayli said. "And you were in the Christmas program like *every year.* You always sang those two songs. 'Let it Snow' and 'Winter Wonderland.' Everybody in Saraland knows who you are."

I never knew,

"Wow. Well, you're the only person who noticed my birthday," I said.

Kayli smiled.

"I'm sure I'm not the only one," she said as she shuffled out of the locker room in her burgundy colored flip flops.

I finished tying my shoes, grabbed my backpack and towel, and headed out to the front entrance to wait for Becka and her momma to arrive.

I didn't have to wait long. They pulled up in the Subaru and I slid into the backseat behind Becka.

"So, after the game, you're coming to my house," Becka said.

"Why?" I asked, as if I didn't know what was up.

"It's a surprise," Becka squealed with delight. I shook my head, trying not to laugh.

"Your surprises are never surprises because you warn me that they're surprises, so I'm never ever surprised," I said.

Mrs. Canales giggled, covering her mouth with her hand.

Becka twisted around in the front seat to glare at me.

"You know what? I do something nice for you and you're just so ungrateful. If I don't tell you I have something planned, you'll find some ridiculous way of being busy." Becka stuck her tongue out at me and spun around in the seat to face forward.

"That's not true, I don't make myself busy. You see how my life is set up," I said.

"Yeah, you've got basketball, jazz band and symphony orchestra. There's playing the guitar and singing in church. And you babysit Ivy," she said.

"You think I'm busy now, wait till I get a job," I said with an evil cackle.

"How are you gonna have time for a job, Manda Pants? Oh. I'm getting my license next week."

"What? Dude, that's awesome. You getting a car too?"

"She's lucky she's getting her license," Mrs. Canales said.

Becka frowned at her, then reached down to turn up the Marc Anthony playing on the stereo. I sat back in the seat and grinned.

After a satisfying dinner and a few minutes chilling with Becka and her family, I was back in the gymnasium for the game against LeFlore at 6:00 pm.

Keeping her promise, and confirming how crazy insane she was, Coach Freddie took me off the bench for the first time this season and threw me into the game after the second quarter.

My time on the court was fast-paced, but otherwise uneventful. Keisha, apparently not in her right mind, kept passing the ball to me. I somehow made six shots inside the key, but lost the ball more than a few times.

On one occasion, I missed a pass, and the ball bounced off of my shins, ricocheting across the line toward the bleachers. Keisha trotted over and patted me on the back, saying "It's okay, great job," while one of LeFlore's guards laughed at me on her way to retrieve the ball and take possession.

Kayli nailed a few layups, nine rebounds, and six assists while Keisha had a few shots outside the post and we still lost by twenty-two points.

I didn't even break a sweat. The defeat was that easy and that swift.

After the game, Becka and her momma met me at the entrance near the locker rooms and I headed out toward the parking lot sulking behind them. I had showered and changed out of my uniform and into a pair of cut-off jeans, an Aeropostale tee shirt, and flip-flops. I walked clutching my gym bag by the handles, letting the shoulder strap skid along the floor.

A little while later, we pulled up to her house, where Pauline's blue Mustang GT sat parked along the curb. Another car, a low slung, silver Infiniti G35 with custom rims, sat behind it.

"Who's that?" I asked, nodding toward the Infiniti.

Becka snorted.

"Kayli just got her license too," she said.

"That's her car?" My lower jaw dang near struck the curb in shock as I stepped out of the Subaru, quickly walking over to ogle the sport sedan.

"Yeah, she just got it," Becka said. "You know how she and her brother race at the drag strip where your sister goes, right?"

"I didn't know that," I said. "I thought her brother was a pro for NASCAR or something. I've seen their semi-truck around at the fair a few times."

"Well, no. He drag races, but they also compete in car shows together across the country. You should see all their trophies."

I shook my head. Kayli was a winner, that's for sure. Lady Gators Team Captain, star Power Forward, Fast and Furious Drag Racing and Car Show Queen.

Becka and her mom opened the front door as I stood waiting. We stepped inside to the spicy aroma of charcoal-grilled meat, garlic, cumin, lime, cilantro, and Sazón.

Becka's dad stood in the kitchen with her uncle and brothers, tearing into cielito lindo and chips. I saw their delicious homemade guava dip sitting on the coffee table in front of Kayli, so I dropped my gym bag on the floor, grabbed a club cracker from the plate and dug in.

"That game gave you an appetite I see. Good. There's plenty, so eat up, chica," Mrs. Canales said with a giggle. "If you want hamburgers or hot dogs, they're coming off the grill next in just a few minutes."

"Thank you, Mrs. Canales. You didn't have to do all this," I said as she walked over to me, reached her arm around my shoulders and gave me a squeeze.

"You are family. Family takes care of one another."

"No one from my actual family is here, though," I said.

Mrs. Canales smiled at me, her eyebrows arching with softness.

"Amanda, not everyone understands what the concept of family truly is. But that's not your fault. And it doesn't mean they don't love you. People are complicated. Right?"

"Yeah. I guess," I said, with a sigh. My thirteenth birthday was the worst. It was the year before we got hit by Hurricane Ivan, and the first year that I didn't get a party or a cake. By then, Momma was sinking hard and fast and Taylor was deep into her pregnancy with Ivy. My dad had been gone since Christmas Eve the year before, and life for me was spiraling into formulaic misery.

"Crazy game, huh?" Kayli said, interrupting my thoughts. I gladly welcomed the distraction and nodded as I sat down next to her, reaching for another cracker.

"You did good, though. Like, you never miss a shot, girl. You were on fire," Kayli said, reaching her cracker into the guava dip to scoop out a chunk. She put it to her mouth and took a deliberate bite, wiping at the corner of her lips with her finger.

"Keisha was on beast mode, too. Shame we lost though. Their defense is insane," I said with my mouth full.

"Yeah, but we'll beat 'em next time. Once we get you comfortable with the ball and movement, Coach is gonna start you on plays. By the time I graduate, you should be ready to take my spot. Next Team Captain."

"Nice," I replied, as Becka flicked my ear.

"Girl, I will straight up choke you," I barked as she laughed and plopped down next to me on the sofa. I flicked her ear in retaliation.

"Shouldn't Keisha be Team Captain after you? She's really good," I said.

"She graduates with me next year. So that leaves you," Kayli smiled, munching on a cracker.

"Wait. So you're graduating next year, but you were in my Chemistry class last year," I said.

"Right," Kayli replied. "I was in Honors Chem. Couldn't deal, so they put me in regular Junior Chem. You're not the only smart girl at Satsuma."

"Ah, okay," I snickered. "Well, I'm not in Honors classes, or AP classes, so, I can't compete in your league."

"Give yourself credit, Manda. You're way smarter than you think you are. You've got a lot going on. But if you didn't have all that, you'd probably be in Honors and AP classes all day," Kayli said.

"How do you know so much about me?" I asked.

"Your girl Becka is a major snitch. Can't keep nothing to herself," Kayli teased. "She's been telling *all* your secrets."

I turned to Becka.

"Yo, you should see that freaking ginormous cake my mom made for you. Like I don't even get cake that big. What the hell, Manda? You think you're special or something," she said, reaching for the guava dip.

"Whatever, Becka," I said. "You're lucky I don't connect your butt hole to your eyebrows with a bobby pin and dental floss."

"See! I swear, you are so *abusive*," Becka said. "Where do you come up with this stuff?"

"When's the last time you saw Wayne," I asked, redirecting the convo.

"Funny you should ask. He's on the way here, right now."

"Your mom is letting him come over?"

"She's *been* letting him come over. As long as she's here or my dad's here, they're cool with it. Just can't go in my room with the door closed. They're paranoid that we're gonna make some Lil' Waynes."

"First of all, *gross*. Second of all. How's he getting here?" I asked.

"You'd like to know that wouldn't you? One of his friends is dropping him off," Becka said, licking her fingers.

"Oh," I said. I was hoping that his brother would have been the one to bring him up, so I could at least catch a glimpse. Shameful as it was, I hated that I wanted to see him. More so than that, I hated that I was actually upset that I wouldn't.

I reached over to tap Kayli's bare shoulder. Her blush colored spaghetti strapped cami, with its plunging bust, showed off her bronzed boobs. It was worse the way she was sitting. I envied her. Mine were nowhere near that luscious.

"So, is that your Infiniti parked out front?" I asked.

Kayli smiled.

"Yeah. Just traded in my hooptie for it."

"What hooptie?" Kayli wasn't the kind of girl you'd catch driving anything beat up.

"That Ford Taurus. The white dinosaur," she said with a giggle.

"What Taurus? Last car I remember seeing you in all the time was that Nissan coupe."

Kayli nodded and cleared her throat.

"Oh, yeah. That was my brother's. We took that to the track all the time. The Taurus was mine, but I hated driving it. So my brother let me drive his car sometimes. He felt sorry for me," Kayli said. "But we just put in coil overs, spark plugs, Motordyne ART pipes and exhaust. It's *loud*. Taking it to the track next Sunday. After-wards we're going to Cry Baby Bridge. You should come. It'll be fun."

"Um, I'll pass on Cry Baby Bridge. I'm not going ghost bust-ing with *nobody*. I saw the Blair Witch Project," I said with a chuckle.

"As far as the track is concerned, maybe, if I can get out of go-ing to church. I'm supposed to be leading worship service again because its youth Sunday or whatever," I said. "Pastor Corbin lets the youth run service once a month and has the youth pastor deliv-er the sermon."

"You still go to the Village Church, right?" Kayli asked, reach-ing for a napkin to wipe her fingers.

I nodded. The church was a small building near the fire station, right off of Saraland Boulevard. It didn't look like much from the outside, but on the inside, it was usually packed wall to wall with people in attendance. I saw a lot of familiar faces from school sit-ting in the pews with their siblings and parents.

"We were going to change churches. My mom was talking about going to the Village. We haven't been to church since my parents divorced. My dad is on the board at the old church, and it was hard for my mom to see him, so we just stopped going," Kayli said, balling the napkin up and rolling it in between her fingers.

"I'm sorry, Kayli. I didn't even know. You'd like the Village. And you, your mom and your brother can get involved. There's always something going on," I said.

"We'll have to check it out. But seriously, next Sunday. I'll pick you up at six," she said.

"Sounds like a plan," I replied as Becka checked her cell. She looked at me and grinned, then quickly got up and bounded for the front door.

She yanked it open, and Wayne stood on her porch with his arm extended, his hand in a fist, preparing to knock. He smiled at her and reached his arms around her to hug her. Then he brushed past her and nodded at me.

"Happy Birthday," he said.

I smiled back.

"Thanks," I gushed as he handed me a small bag with tissue sticking out of the top. "Aww. You didn't have to get me anything."

"Wasn't sure what you liked. Becka had to hook me up with the inside scoop," Wayne said, plopping down into the loveseat near the window, spreading his arms out across the top of the cushions.

I reached into the bag and pulled out a package. It was a Ralph Lauren Polo pajama set. I smiled. It looked super comfortable, and expensive. The only people to ever buy brand name clothes for me was Auntie Beanie and Pauline. Becka and her family always gave me jewelry, candy, snacks and food on special occasions and holidays. That was nothing to complain about. I loved to eat and wear bling.

"Thank you Wayne. You didn't have to spend crazy money," I said.

"Oh, I didn't. Got it from Burlington, on clearance," he said. "I ain't got it like that. I'm broke, for real."

Becka laughed.

"He's far from broke. He just got a job working at some packaging place off Airport," she said.

"Aw, man, congratulations! I want a job," I said. "Momma won't let me get one. I'm gonna find a way, though."

"Well, anyway, we all sitting in here chilling. Somebody's outside waiting on you," Wayne said, grinning at me.

"Who?"

"Go find out," he said, pointing his thumb to the door.

I shook my head at him and stood up.

Kayli and Becka stood up as well, and shuffled over to the window just as Pauline walked out from the back of the house.

"Sorry, I didn't even know you were here, yet. I was back there playing Barbie house with the little people," Pauline said, quickly moving toward me with her arms spread out. She hugged me tightly and kissed my cheek. "Happy Birthday. I gotta get your present out of my car."

"Pauline, you didn't have to get me anything," I said.

"Girl, shut up and go outside," she replied, shoving me toward the door.

I grabbed the doorknob and stepped out into the pleasant night air. It was still rather mild, with a slight chill in the air. Heading toward mid-November, the temperatures during the day hovered in the low seventies, and at night slipped into the forties. It was probably in the high sixties as I closed the door behind me.

The older, black Mercedes S Class sat perched along the curb. Terrell stood leaning against the passenger side, cooly clutching a large gift bag in his hand.

"Why you got me standing out here all night, about to freeze to death," he said with a snicker.

"It's not even cold outside. Stop whining like a baby," I said.

"Just for that, I'm taking all this back. I kept the receipt," he said.

I stepped toward him, aware that Becka and Kayli watched us through the window. Pauline slipped past us to trot over to her car.

"You're not funny," I said. "You didn't have to get me anything."

"It's your sweet sixteen. That's a big deal," Terrell said, just as two vehicles pulled up and parked behind his Benz.

The girls from the basketball team piled out of the first, a red Ford Expedition and the second, a beige Chevy Suburban, followed by a few students I was cool with from my classes.

Another car pulled up behind them. It was the twins and their brother from my neighborhood, being dropped off by their daddy.

Keisha led the basketball team toward me. One by one they hugged me and walked inside.

I couldn't believe all these people showed up for my birthday. It was going to be a packed house.

Keisha stood looking at me and Terrell, before chuckling.

"Ya'll two should get a room," she said as she skipped off toward the porch.

I shook my head as the twins, Madison and Allie, walked up to hug me. Then, their brother, Alex gave me a pound with his right fist and threw up a peace sign in silence to Terrell as he followed his sisters inside.

Terrell chuckled.

"Well, here. I can't stay. But I wanted to give you this before I left. I'll be back later to pick up my little bro," he said.

"Why can't you stay?" I asked.

"Got something I gotta take care of real quick," Terrell said, handing me the heavy gift bag.

"What the hell is in here? A Tonka truck?" I asked.

He smiled, leaned forward, and kissed me on the corner of my mouth, sending flames of fire up and down my neck and spine. I almost dropped the bag from the shock. And from my legs going numb.

"See you later," he said, stepping back and smoothly walking to the driver's side of the Benz, before disappearing inside.

I stood there in silence, my eyes wide and my skin burning hot as he watched me with that sly grin on his face, the car's chimes going off as he started it up. It roared to life, and he slipped off quietly down the street, leaving me to stare at the space on the pavement where the water from the Benz's AC unit sat in a puddle.

I took a peak inside of the bag just as Pauline walked up to stand next to me, clutching an oversized gift bag.

"What did you get?" she asked.

I held the bag open for her to peer inside.

There was a large, wooden jewelry box, a bottle of Yves Saint Laurent Elle Summer, a bundle of roses, and a box of Godiva chocolates.

"Dang, girl! Your boy got some class," Pauline said, slapping me in the shoulder. "Better hold on to that. My boyfriends always turn out to be total butt lickers."

She handed me her gift bag.

I looked inside, pushed away the tissue paper, and pulled out a Coach Khaki and Mahogany Park Signature Hobo shoulder bag with matching heels and a bottle of Chanel Beige.

"I can't top your gifts from the Prichard Taye Diggs, but I hope you like them. You can wear those on your next date with boom-shak-a-laka. I saw them when I went to New York before school started and thought of you."

I smiled, and reached my arms around Pauline, squeezing her tightly. This was the best birthday ever.

"Thank you, Leenie," I breathed, unsuccessfully fighting back tears.

I heard the door to the house open behind me.

Becka put an arm over my shoulder. She guided me back toward the front door, followed by Pauline, just as Auntie Beanie pulled up behind the SUV's and honked her horn. When I thought my birthday couldn't get any better, she arrived as the icing on the cake.

I turned and watched as she got out of the Pontiac G6 she was driving, grabbed bags from the backseat of the car and walked up to where I was standing.

Pauline and Becka smiled at her, and she gave them a little wave.

"Hi, girls," she said, her voice quiet and cracking. She stood there clutching the bags before Pauline and Becka grabbed them from her and headed back inside the house.

"You were amazing out there, on that court," she said. "I'm so proud of you."

"You were there? At my game?" I said as she reached her arms around me and hugged me. We were exactly the same height, and she had beach blonde hair styled in layers. Her tanned skin was bronzed and shiny from the Florida sun and moisturizers. She smelled like coconuts and chocolate.

"Of course. I wouldn't miss it for the world," she said with a smile. "I called Coach Freddie and found out she was putting you on the floor, so with it being your sixteenth birthday, this was extra special. I recorded the whole thing with my camcorder. I'm surprised you didn't see me there. I was right behind the bench."

"I can't believe you're here," I said.

"Why wouldn't I be?"

"Well, I know you're busy," I replied.

"I'm never too busy for you," she said, wiping away tears at the corner of her eyes. "You're growing up so fast. I try not to think about the fact that you'll be graduating in another two years."

"Yeah. It's crazy right?"

"You know where you want to go to college, yet? Any ideas?"

She grabbed my arm, looping hers through mine and we stepped onto Becka's front porch.

"Not yet. I have a few in mind. Far from here," I said.

"I totally understand that," she replied. "Do you plan on getting a basketball scholarship? Or academic?"

"I don't know. Haven't talked to any recruiters yet, and I'm taking the ACT and SAT my junior year. Already took the PSAT last month, and I scored pretty high. A little over 1200," I said as I opened the door to let Auntie Beanie step inside ahead of me.

"That's incredible, Manda. I mean, wow. You know the top scores on that are like, what? 1400? You were only a few points off of a National Merit Scholarship. You should take it again your junior year. You'll score higher and get that award," she said as she stepped inside.

Boisterous laughter and loud jíbara music playing from the stereo greeted us.

Becka and her momma were dancing in the middle of the living room with Kayli and four of the girls on the basketball team. Everyone was huddled in the kitchen, living room, dining room and den of the crowded house. Becka's little cousins were running around chasing each other with toys in their hands, screaming and cackling like little gremlins on Christmas Eve.

"It's a madhouse here," Auntie Beanie said with a giggle.

"Yeah," I agreed.

"I booked my hotel room through the entire weekend. I'll be heading back to Clearwater on Monday. If you don't have any plans this weekend, when you get out of school tomorrow, why don't you come back with me and we can hang out those three days. I'll drop you off at school on my way back to Florida Monday morning after we have breakfast."

"I'd love that. But there are a few issues with that whole plan," I said.

"What's that?" Auntie Beanie asked.

"The Thanksgiving Tournament starts Saturday. I have a game Saturday night, Monday night and Tuesday night. And Kayli and her brother are racing this weekend and invited me. It's on Sunday."

Auntie Beanie smiled.

"That sounds like fun," she said. "I'm in. I'll take you to all the games for your Tournament and watch you play, and I'd love to go with you to Kayli's race. All I have to do is extend my hotel room until Wednesday morning. No biggie. Now, wait till you see what I brought you."

twenty

CREAMED LIKE CHEESE ♡
Lady Gators V. The Wolfpack, January 2007

"Calm down, ladies!" Coach Freddie yelled as we piled into the bus.

Kayli plopped down next to the window and slapped the space next to her when she saw me. I squeezed in next to her, slinging my gym bag into the seat in front of us, next to her burgundy duffel.

"You ready for the big show? This is our first time playing Vigor in a few years, and I heard those girls are no joke," Kayli said.

"It's weird, going to Prichard. I heard it's dangerous over there," I replied.

"Who told you that?" Kayli asked. "That's a bunch of bull. I mean, everywhere has its neighborhoods, but me and my mom go to Prichard all the time to eat at this place called Annie's. It's soul food and it's delicious. My mom grew up in Prichard."

The signature snorting sound came from the brakes, and the bus lurched forward, slowly making its way out of the Satsuma High parking lot.

"That guy I'm talking to? He's from Prichard. He swears its super dangerous, like I can never go there, ever," I said.

"That depends on where in Prichard you go. There are a few sketchy spots, but I mean, we've got a few of them up here, too," Kayli replied, gripping the seat backs in front of us.

I sniffed.

"I mean, they can't be as bad as the spots in Prichard," I said.

"Manda, you can go to Prichard. Just don't go places you absolutely know you shouldn't go. I mean, we go Downtown, up Wilson and Turner and never have a problem. You'll be okay. If you want, you can come with me and my mom next time we go to Annie's or Cozy Brown's to eat. I'm sure she won't mind," Kayli said. "Your boyfriend needs to take a chill pill. Unless he has something to hide, there is no reason you can't go to Prichard. That's just dumb."

I nodded and settled back down into my seat.

Saraland Boulevard was void of any real traffic for the most part, until the bus reached the area near Norton Creek and Industrial Parkway. Beyond that, it seemed like the closer we got to Chickasaw, truck and commercial traffic became heavier.

As we traveled along US 43 South across the Smallwood, Sr. Memorial Bridge over Chickasaw Creek, I leaned my head back and peered out the window as Kayli busily texted someone on her phone.

I noticed the bus driver slowing to a crawl through Chickasaw, an area notorious for police patrolling. All my brothers got speeding tickets coming through Chickasaw on Route 43 driving Momma's Buick when we were younger, and Daddy was pulled over once with a warning while we were heading back from Christmas shopping right after the Halloween before he left.

Since then, my brothers and my sister didn't drive through Chickasaw unless they had no choice.

It wasn't long before we were passing through the heart of Chickasaw and veered right on to Craft Highway. An abandoned shopping center sat on the left, before we passed through an un-countable number of semi truck trailers sitting lined up in rows along either side of the street, backed up to the docks of steel buildings.

Monotonously depressing, the rest of the journey into Prichard was full of commercial and industrial sites, tractor trailers, vast stretches of dirt plots for lease or sale, abandoned buildings and warehouses, and apocalyptic scenery. I spent most of the time yawning every few seconds. Kayli watched me with an amused smile.

"Pretty boring, huh?" she said.

"Oh my god, yes. I can't believe the bus driver went this way. Nobody goes this way," I replied.

"It's a straight shot to Vigor down US 43," Kayli said. "We're almost there."

I looked out the window again as the Prichard water tower came into view as Craft Highway became Wilson Avenue.

There were more enormous, empty lots for sale or abandoned on both sides of the street, and the area seemed desolate and empty.

"My mom said there used to be tons of houses through here," Kayli said. "She told me they moved out of Prichard when she was a kid during the seventies. Around the time she was born, white people began moving out of the area as black people from the less nice areas of Prichard began moving in.

"Some laws were passed that allowed them to move into areas that they used to be restricted from living in. Before my mom and her parents moved, Prichard was mostly white. Soon after they left, Prichard was mostly empty, and mostly black, and anyone white that remained in the area put their kids in private schools to keep them from being mixed in with the black kids."

"That's messed up," I said, frowning so hard it made my temples twitch.

"Well, there's more. Right when my mom's family moved, Prichard elected its first black mayor. That really got people twisted up. But I guess around the time that you and I both started kindergarten and first grade, they finished building Interstate 165, and it helped redevelop the eastern side of Prichard. You know, where all the nice shopping and hotels are.

"But around 20 years ago, downtown Prichard was mostly empty. A couple factories closed, and many people lost jobs. The city declared bankruptcy. They demolished housing projects for the poor. A lot of other things happened that mom told me about, like something about Prichard not paying people's pensions. Anyway, that's why you see all this poverty."

"You know a lot about Prichard," I said.

"I saw you looking around at everything all sad, and like I said, my mom grew up here. So I thought I'd tell you why it looks like this."

She leaned in close to me.

"Honestly, I think your boyfriend, or whatever, tells you that you can't come to Prichard because he probably doesn't want you to see where he lives. He's probably embarrassed, and feels bad about how his neighborhood looks," Kayli said, quietly.

"Most of Prichard is blighted, but it's not the fault of the people who live here. From everything my mom has told me, it's the county, the government and the minds of hateful people who let Prichard fall to the wayside. I mean, I just watched a news reporter talking about how Prichard doesn't even have proper trash services, so garbage just gets thrown wherever," Kayli said, settling back into her seat.

"I didn't know any of that," I said as we entered the gate surrounding Vigor High School. The neighborhood around the school looked similar to the area around Satsuma High. My nerves calmed down following Kayli's reassurance, but seeing the neighborhood and how nice the school looked from the outside helped to settle me further.

Within a short few minutes, we were inside the gymnasium which to my pleasant surprise smelled like coconut.

The bleachers were filling up on both sides as people piled in to watch the game.

We performed warm-ups on the court while Coach Freddie gave us some last minute stats, advice and plays, and she chose the starters.

The twelve of us headed over to the visitors locker room to climb out of our warm-up suits. I noticed a small spot on my burgundy Lady Gators jersey and quickly wiped at the smudge, discovering it to be lint.

Back on the court, Kayli and Keisha gathered around the center court line, along with Joy Post, Heather Roye and Brittni Landon, the other three starters.

Keisha stood opposite Vigor's point guard, number 18, who was a teenie little hottie with flawless cocoa skin and calves the size of cantaloupes. The whistle blew and Keisha smacked at the ball.

The taller Vigor Wolves guard got the best of her and sent the ball flying toward a waiting teammate who caught it, quickly spun around, and dribbled uncontested toward a first layup.

It was a sour start to what would be a challenging game.

I watched as we took possession of the ball. Coach was firing off suggestions from the line as Keisha passed the basketball in to Joy, who dribbled it down from the opposite basket toward center court.

Vigor's other guard, number 33, with her hair tucked into a plastic headband, approached Joy to defend against her from the top of the key.

Vigor's center quickly moved toward the free-throw line as Joy fired off a pass to send the ball to Brittni, who was down at the left side of the lane.

Before Vigor's forward could stop her, she sent a high arcing shot and landed a three pointer.

I jumped off the bench, whooping and howling loudly. Coach Freddie sent me a sharp look, and I sat back down with a smile, clapping.

I flashed a thumbs up sign as Brittni and Joy passed me on their way to defend.

The first quarter ended a short while later with Vigor leading with eight to three.

The game picked up in pace at that point.

While watching Joy get stopped at center court by Vigor's forward, who had suddenly been injected with a dose of major aggression, I noticed three familiar faces grinning at me from across the court in the opposite bleachers, four rows up.

Becka sat next to Wayne, who sat next to Terrell. They waved when they discovered I had found them.

I waved back, smiling.

Wayne put up a peace sign and nodded with his signature cool head bob and I shook my head at him, returning my gaze to the court.

That quickly, I missed a foul that sent Vigor to the free-throw line. Their forward made both shots.

Coach Freddie made a substitution and swapped Joy and Heather for Amy Ciccone and Consuela Ruiz.

Consuela took Heather's place as center, and Amy took point at the top of the key, opposite Keisha. Brittni continued on as forward across the key from Kayli.

The referee called foul on the play when one of Vigor's forwards checked Amy with a painfully loud arm slap as she attempted to steal the ball outside of the paint, and Amy sauntered over to the free throw line, rubbing her arm.

Vigor's coach replaced the offending forward, and Amy sunk both shots at the free throw line.

Not long after Vigor's guards crossed the center line, Amy intercepted a pass and bolted to the opposite goal, taking possession. The Wolves quickly scrambled, sprinting to catch up to her in the paint as she tossed up a layup that bounced off the backboard.

Brittni was suddenly there to assist. She rebounded and missed, and Keisha retrieved the ball before Vigor's forward could grasp it.

Keisha twisted, fighting away a defensive swipe from Vigor's power forward, and managed a jump shot that got nipped by Vigor's center. Somehow, it still bounced roughly off the rim, barely slipping through the hoop to raise us by two points.

It wasn't long before we were at halftime, with Vigor leading twenty to thirteen.

Coach Freddie approached me.

"You ready to play, Rush?" she asked.

"Yeah," I replied.

"You sure? These Vigor girls are no joke. We're getting creamed like cheese. I'm gonna send you in for Brittni. She's doing a great job, but I think you could use some time on the court," Coach Freddie said.

I nodded, and she turned and approached the table.

I was sent in to relieve Brittni, Amy was replaced by Renee Peters at the top of the key, and Carla Thompson took Keisha's place as the other point guard.

Kayli remained on the other side of the key from me as we posted up on either side of the basket.

We were now twenty-seven to forty, with Vigor leading, and we had possession.

Carla and Renee trotted down and crossed center court and immediately met defense from Vigor's two guards. I could tell that they were going man to man, and we adjusted our play accordingly when Carla called it out.

I was embroiled in a battle of clothes line with Vigor's power forward defending against me as her long arms pressed into my larynx. She was taller and more muscular.

Her skin smelled lovely, though. I breathed in cocoa butter and perfume whenever she moved, and her nicely braided hair blocked my vision as I tried to get around her to be available for a pass.

In a quick move, I spun around her back and found myself inside the key with my hands out.

Carla was quick.

Her pass came at me with such force that the ball slapped against my palms. I caught it and without thinking, twisted and leaped into the air, curving my elbow and flicking my wrist in a hook shot that sent the ball arcing high over my head.

Vigor's power forward was too late to react.

The ball made a *thwick* sound at it touched nothing but net.

As I landed on the balls of my feet, a roar thundered from the bleachers on both sides.

Kayli slapped my arm.

"Okay, *Magic Johnson*! I see you," she said with a giggle, as she trotted off to the opposite court to defend. I quickly followed her as thunderous pounding continued from the bleachers.

The ladies of the Vigor Wolves didn't like the crowd's reaction to my shot, and made sure I knew it when they arrived offensively to embarrass us in the key with solid passes, and a beautiful, unopposed jump shot right in front of Consuela's face.

Coach Freddie pulled Consuela out and sent in Lourdes Mendoza, who usually played forward but was tall enough to be in the middle of the key.

Not long after that, Consuela had a foul called on her when she stopped one of Vigor's forwards from going to the hoop.

They got a quick boost in score when she made one of the free-throw shots, sending the other bouncing off of the rim and into our possession.

During the last quarter, Kayli switched positions to point guard, Sara Arkland was sent in to replace Carla up top, Brittni returned across the key from me, and Heather returned in the center of the key.

With Vigor's super aggressive center in place, Heather couldn't get a clean shot to the basket, so Kayli, Brittni and I made a few more to finish out the game at thirty-nine to fifty-two, with the Wolves maintaining their thirteen point lead during most of the game.

We lined up to cross the court and high five the Vigor Wolves, our burgundy uniforms contrasting their clean white jerseys with green trim as we headed toward the visitor's locker room.

After climbing back into our warm-up suits, we headed to the Satsuma activity bus with our gym bags and duffels.

Wayne, Terrell, and Becka were waiting to greet me outside the hallway entrance.

"Yo, that was a tight game," Wayne said, reaching his fist up to give me a pound.

"Thanks," I said, quietly. "Even though we *lost.*"

"Those shots, though. Girl, you're off the chain. Everything you put up was all swishes," Becka said with a huge grin on her face. She reached her arms around me and hugged me. "I'm so proud of you. You're gonna be in the WNBA."

"I don't know about all that," I replied, my eyes going to Terrell, who stepped closer.

"It's good to see you. You were amazing out there on the court," he said.

"I'm surprised to see you here," I said.

"Why wouldn't I be? I'll be at your next one too. It's a home game, right? Against Vigor?" Terrell said.

"Yeah. In like three weeks. Look! I'm in your hood, and I haven't been shot. See? I can visit you here," I said.

He shook his head.

"*This* is a nice neighborhood. *Mine* ain't so nice," he said.

"Naw, girl. We in the trap, you *feel* me?" Wayne said, reaching up to grip Terrell's hand in one of those black people hand shakes I always saw Becka doing with her cousins.

"No doubt," Terrell replied, licking his lips and returning his gaze to me. "I'm sorry, babe. I mean, I'd love it if you could come through. But it's not safe for you."

"Mmm hmmm," I responded, with one eyebrow raised.

Kayli brushed past me and rubbed my arm in a gesture that I knew to mean, *let's go*.

"Well on that note, see ya when I see ya," I said, reaching my arm around Becka and squeezing her quickly before slipping away toward the bus.

"Oh, it's like that?" Terrell asked, sounding slightly wounded.

I chuckled.

"Yep," I replied, before stepping onto the bus behind Kayli.

Junior Year

"Let Garrett take you."

I cut my eyes at Pauline.

"Seriously? I watched him eat his boogers in Bio Lab. Plus, he's a Smurf," I smirked, watching Becka's face curl up in disgust as she bent over and stuck her finger in her mouth, gagging.

Just the thought of his funky fingers made me want to puke all over the dress.

"I like, can't with you right now. Now I have Smurf Garrett stuck in my head. Thanks for that," Pauline said, flipping open a shoe box to pull out a pair of strappy, shimmery I. Miller Ricole Buckle open toe heel pumps. She eyed them for a moment before slinging them back into the cardboard container.

"So, I guess that's a no on Picky Smurf?" Becka teased, taking the shoe box from Pauline. They wore the same size, so Becka took them out and quickly tried them on. She twirled around like a ballet dancer, lifting her leg to look at the shoes from every angle. They had already selected their dresses and were patiently waiting on me to figure out my life.

"Well, it's going to be weird, all of us going together in the limo, and you going without a date," Pauline said, watching me totally eyeball Becka's feet as she pranced in the pumps. "I think those shoes come in a light pink color, too. So you can wear them with that super hot dress you have on. You know you want it. You've been walking around with it on for like an hour."

"Dude, it has not been an hour. And I'm wearing my lucky Jordans. I've got big feet. And yeah, I like it," I said, tucking at the strap over my shoulder to adjust it. It was a sexy, satin sleeveless City Triangle party dress. The blush color and trimming made it a stunner. The front cut showed off my muscular lower thighs, knees and sun-kissed legs, sure to piss my momma off.

The part that really stole the show was the inner lining in the back, with gorgeous floral print that I couldn't stop looking at. It peeked out from behind my legs as it flowed down to my ankles like a train.

"So then, that's the one," Becka said. "Let's check out and get out."

I quickly tugged the dress off in the fitting room, changed back into my shorts and tee, and bought it at the register with Auntie Beanie's JC Penney card, smiling at the discount.

On the way out of the entrance by the kids clothes section, I stopped short.

Terrell stood there, cooly posted up on the curb against his black Benz, clutching a bouquet of lilies, sweat running down his forehead into his squinted eyes.

The word Prom was scrawled next to a question mark on the passenger side of the car in washable white marker.

Becka grabbed Pauline's arm, pulling her toward her parked Camry.

"Laters," Becka said, with a mischievous cackle.

I watched her walk away as Terrell stepped toward me. He already knew my answer. My trembling gave it away.

I smiled as he cocked his head, with that cool smirk of his, the corner of the right side of his mouth turned up. When he talked, his marvelously white teeth peeked through on just that side. His swagger was fierce, and he knew it.

My cheeks felt like they would melt away into the February air.

"Are you seriously pulling a promposal right now?" I asked with a grin.

"You like my style, huh? Not too flashy, but with just a touch of baller swag," he said with a chuckle. I shook my head.

"You are hardly balling. And anyway, why're you sweating? It's only 67 degrees," I said, grimacing at his shiny forehead.

"Cause I've been running around all day in your mind," he replied, wiping at the sweat with the sleeve of his shirt.

"You're such a dork. I swear you can't be any cornier," I laughed. He was wearing a red paisley print long sleeved button-up shirt with a sleeveless tan v-neck sweater over it. I bought it for him when he turned 22 last November. He loved his v-necks.

"You're probably hot in all those layers. Maybe you should take off that sweater," I said, reaching out to pull at the bottom seam.

"Yeah, you just want to get me out of my clothes," he replied with a chuckle.

I sucked in my teeth sharply.

"Whatever," I said, rolling my eyes.

He smiled with that crooked smile I had grown to adore, but he still annoyed the hell out of me. I resisted the urge to wipe his face with his own sweater by sadistically pulling it up over his head.

"So, I heard you're going to prom without a date," he said, chuckling.

I shook my head at him and rolled my eyes again, hiding the dress bag behind my back for no real reason at all.

"Well, I wasn't. 'Cause you can't go with me. You're too old. Age limit is under 21 for someone from another school, *grandpa*. Plus, there's this paper you have to sign showing you're still in high school, and you haven't been in high school for *a while*, so yeah," I said, letting out a loud sigh.

"Sounds like a lot of bureaucracy."

"Did you just learn that big word today? I'm impressed, smarty pants," I replied, adjusting my grip on the bag in my hand.

"You're awfully snarky today. Should I text Becka to come back and get you?"

"You know. My homies suggested that I take a booger eater to Prom. Maybe I'm better off just going with him instead of you," I said with a giggle.

"Hey, I get it. I understand completely. Who am I to stand between a girl and her salt intake? Just take a pack of M&M's for balance."

"You're such a clown. Hope that marker washes off," I said. "I know how you like to keep your ride clean."

"Yeah, it comes off. It's one of those washable ones for glass. Got it at Michael's. Why you changin' the subject?" He held out his hand, thrusting the flowers toward me.

I took them in my free hand and held them to my nose, deeply breathing in the lovely, soft fragrance. He watched me with an amused look on his face, his eyebrows raised in expectation.

"I didn't change the subject. I just didn't give you a direct answer," I said, wrinkling my nose at him.

"Ah, is *that* what you call it?"

"Yep," I said. "And you're really sweaty. You seriously need a shower."

"It's freakin' hot, girl," he said.

"It's really not. Seriously. Take that sweater off. I'm getting heatstroke just from looking at you," I replied.

"You're getting heatstroke 'cause I'm so *fly,* girl," he said as he backed up a few steps and opened the passenger car door of the big Benz for me. I shook my head at him and hesitated.

"You're so stupid. I've gotta get back home. My Auntie Beanie is up visiting from Florida, and I've still got her credit card. Won't be long before she sends the Army National Guard after me." I bit my bottom lip as he reached up with his left hand to rub the back of his neck.

"You're killing me," he said.

"I'm sorry. It is what it is," I replied as he looked away.

"Alright. Well, I can drop you off at Becka's since I can't go anywhere near your neighborhood," he said smartly.

"Well, you won't let me anywhere near *your* neighborhood, either," I retorted.

He exhaled slowly, looking down toward the pavement.

"You know why. I told you. It's too dangerous. I can't take you through there. You'll get shot at. Nobody white every comes through the trap. Neither do the cops," he replied.

"That's hard to believe. Nobody from Prichard acts like that at the football games. Or at the two basketball games I've had playing at Vigor. I've been to Prichard more than a few times now, with Kayli and her mom, to eat."

"That's a whole different scene. The people I'm talking about, you won't find them in the hallways of Vigor. You'll find them on the corner, on the streets. If something happened to you, I couldn't live with myself," he said.

He was sincere. His voice had lost its usual deep bass and had taken on a pitch that made my eyes tear up. Someone, or something, bad had happened to him there. Maybe one day he would find the courage to tell me about it. For now, I decided that I wouldn't push.

I finally nodded, stepped forward to slide into the leather seat, set my bag and purse on the floor between my feet, and snapped the seat belt into place. He closed the passenger side door softly, got in on the driver's side, and adjusted the climate control.

"So, since I can't go *inside* with you to prom, I got a plan," he said, his voice still soft.

"Oh yeah? And what's your plan?" I asked, sniffing the lilies again.

"I'll meet you at Becka's, drop you and your squad off at Prom. You'll chill with your peeps, then about midway through, you'll come back outside where I'll be waiting. Save the last dance for me. I have somewhere special to take you."

I looked at him with renewed interest and curiosity, smiling at the shout out to my favorite movie of all time. I felt my heart pounding in my chest like a jackhammer.

"You're so corny," I said. "But I like your plan. Are we all going, or just you and me? You know Becka's going with your little brother. Pauline's taking Allie. Kayli is going solo with me. Can all five of them fit back there in the back seat?"

"She's a big car. We'll make it work. Pack it like a church van," he said. "You hungry?"

I smiled.

"Not really."

There was no way I could eat with my stomach doing gymnastics. I hated that he did that to me. I didn't like not being able to control my body's reactions around him.

"Well, you wanna chill with me for a just few minutes? I promise I'll drop you back at Becka's after."

"Yeah, I'll chill with you. Where do you want to go?" I asked.

"I dunno. Maybe just ride since you're not hungry. Or we can go to that park you like so I can spend a little more time with you. I haven't seen you that much really except for my birthday, Christmas, New Year's and that last game against Citronelle. Oh, and Valentine's Day. I didn't see you at all last summer 'cause I was in Cali."

I nodded. He was right. That's probably six times since the end of last school year. But it was hard to see him when he worked after classes, and we couldn't be seen together anywhere near where I lived since we became a thing, or whatever this was. I was even paranoid to have him drop me off at Becka's since it was so close to my house.

I resorted to reclining the seat down all the way so no one would see me and I had him drop me off near the corner of Tavares and Spanish Trace to walk around the short curve to Becka's from there.

Terrell swore it wasn't necessary to do all of that, but I wasn't taking any chances. My momma might be splattered across the sofa, spaced on prescription meds, but my nosy Nana got around just fine. So did my brothers, and there's no telling what they'd do if they found me with Terrell.

"Well, I mean, I've had basketball games and practice all winter. You could've come to my games," I said.

"Couldn't. I had my internship. Plus, I had to catch up on core electives to graduate on time, and then there's my job," Terrell said with a sniff.

"We've been busy," I mused as I glanced out of the passenger side window. He reached for my left hand and clasped it in his.

"I know. But I want to see you as much as I can," he said with his voice low enough to vibrate my skin.

"We'll see each other. It's just been hard, but basketball season is over now. So it's all on you."

He sunk back into the seat cushion and let out a deep breath.

"But I still have to work," he said, after a short silence.

I found his eyes and held his gaze as he caressed my fingers.

"We'll figure it out," I said, finally. I released his hold on my hands to adjust my bag so that my dress wouldn't get jacked up. "With what you're wearing, it's too hot for the park. You're dressed like there's frost on the ground. We can just chill somewhere near here."

"Where do you want to ride to?"

"I really don't care," I said.

Terrell nodded, reached for my left hand again to hold it as he always did, and settled back into the driver's seat. Steering with his left hand, he maneuvered the big Benz away from the curb and around the Bel Air Mall complex toward Airport Blvd.

I watched as the silver bracelet I bought for him for Christmas last year from Piercing Pagoda slid up and down his wrist with every movement.

The holidays had been a total calamity. Auntie Beanie had come up from Florida, Nana and Grandpa were visiting, and all three of my brothers were there. Taylor and Ivy showed up just in time to witness Momma go at it dramatically with Auntie Beanie over something, leaving Auntie Beanie to hand me an envelope as she hurried outside in tears to her Buick LaCrosse perched on the curb.

Inside the envelope I found a couple hundred dollars in a handwritten Christmas card.

I ran outside after her, but she was already in her car, spinning the front tires in the gravel along the curb as she peeled off with the engine roaring in protest. I watched her disappear as she turned left onto Harriet to head out of the neighborhood.

I decided not to spend the money she gave me. I held on to it, pulling up the corner of the carpet near the closet in my bedroom to tuck the money beneath the cheap Berber. I had a feeling one day I would need it.

As Terrell coaxed the '97 S 500 onto Airport road, I focused on the feel of his large, warm hand grasping mine. The veins seemed to pulse with his heartbeat. I let my eyes travel up his arm to his neck and his ear, then over to his eye and nose, then his lips.

He kept the car at an easy pace as we headed toward the airport, smoothly gliding past all the shopping centers, hotels and restaurants along Airport Blvd. Beyond the Pinebrook Shopping Center, everything faded seamlessly into wooded residential developments that sprawled out on either side.

I watched as a mix of shopping plazas, hotels, restaurants, developments, and neighborhoods whisked by until Terrell turned onto Terminal Drive to enter the airport. He took the loop around to exit back out from the other side, and we headed back in the direction we came.

I closed my eyes, and my thoughts went to Prom as I wondered what Terrell had planned for that night. While I was lost in my thoughts, the big Benz covered the length of Airport Blvd back toward the freeway, and then drifted along on Interstate 65 heading north to Becka's house on Spanish Trace.

He felt my eyes on him and he looked over at me and smiled. I smiled back and sunk down further in the seat, feeling a sense of euphoria wash over me.

twenty two

DON'T GET PREGNANT ♡

Auntie Beanie flew in from Clearwater early in the morning. She called to wake me up and surprise me, and to make sure I was ready when she arrived. I quickly took a shower, washed and conditioned my hair, put it up in a wild looking pony tail, threw on a pair of khaki shorts and a t-shirt, and grabbed my flip-flops.

Momma wasn't on the couch when I trampled down the hallway into the living room. I turned around and went back to check her bedroom. She wasn't there, either.

Taylor had been home for a while now with little Ivy, but she wasn't in her room, either, and none of my brothers were home.

I stepped out into the kitchen and peered out of the little window into the backyard.

Momma sat in her robe on the concrete patio floor with her hair a tangled mess and her frail looking shoulders hunched over as she stared out at the woods behind the shed. Something resembling a cigarette dangled from the pointer and middle fingers of her right hand.

I checked the door next to the kitchen to make sure she wasn't locked out, and then I headed out the front door to wait for Auntie Beanie on the porch, leaning against one of the columns.

She pulled onto the gravel a while later in a Chrysler 300 rental, and after picking me up, followed by Becka, Pauline and Kayli, she took us to Nouveau on Dauphin for a full day of massages, facials, manis and pedis, followed by shampoos, hairstyling and makeup. Afterwards, Auntie Beanie drove us out to Wintzell's Oyster House for lunch.

Terrell had originally planned to pick us up at Becka's as promised, but Auntie Beanie had other plans. A black Cadillac Escalade limousine sat perched outside of Becka's house when we got back to change into our prom dresses.

Auntie Beanie nearly begged me not to wear my lucky Jordans when she saw me in the City Triangle party dress. Pauline presented me with a box containing a pair of blush colored I. Miller Ricole open toe cone heel pumps identical to the ones Becka was wearing from JC Penney, but sized to fit my big feet.

I sat on the sofa in the living room, reluctantly strapped into the pumps and when I stood up, I found myself four inches taller. Auntie Beanie took my Jordans and moved them away from my field of vision, probably hoping that I wouldn't grab them on the way out the door. I thought about it, but the look on her face when I stood in the pumps was priceless.

Maddie and Allie arrived in their color matching gowns just as we stepped back outside. They climbed out of the back of their parents' Silverado and lifted their gowns up to dance over to the limo. Lucas, Allie's last minute date, got dropped off a few minutes later.

We had decided earlier that Pauline, Kayli and Maddie would be my plus three's tonight. I gave them osiria rose corsages that matched mine as they giggled in excitement.

With everyone present, Auntie Beanie took pictures of us in our dresses in Becka's backyard with her Canon 40D, then a few more with us in front of the limo.

When Terrell arrived, the disappointment was clear on his face, but he was a trooper, reminding me to look for his text on my cellphone later. I felt horrible. In the flurry of excitement, I had neglected to let him know that plans had changed.

Auntie Beanie, as perceptive as ever, signaled for Terrell to join us in front of the limo. I slipped the matching boutonniere I had hidden away in my purse on to the lapel of his white tux jacket, and after a few group shots, she took pictures of him with just me.

I heard him chuckle in his throat as I shivered against him from nervousness and anticipation, feeling the solidity and strength of his body and becoming intoxicated with the musk of his cologne.

After she finished taking pictures, she and Terrell watched as the rest of us piled into the limo. I gave them a final wave, and the driver closed the door behind me.

Inside the Cadillac, a long, plush leather bench ran from the front to the back on one side beneath the windows. A bar stocked with water bottles and soda ran along the length of the opposite side. I sank into the perforated, pillowy cushions between Pauline and Becka, with no way to pull my dress over my legs to keep out the cold air in the cabin. The front cutaway that exposed my legs had one drawback. As I watched goosebumps spread across my thighs, I wished for a blanket.

At least the pumps were hella comfortable.

Above our heads, recessed rose colored lighting in the ceilings surrounded a long mirror. They pulsed with the beat of a T-Pain song as it played over the speakers.

The intimate space within the limo erupted into laughter, conversation and giggles as we made the trip down Interstate 65 to Interstate 165, continuing until it became Water Street coming into Downtown Mobile.

With the city's skyline rising just a few blocks away, we veered to the right onto Congress Street and made an immediate left onto Royal. Palmettos lined the street on both sides, and buildings towered over us as we continued through Downtown.

After a while, on the left, we passed the valet parking area for the Riverview Plaza Office Building, with its dazzling jade-hued portico, and rising high next to it, the Renaissance Riverview Plaza Hotel. Just beyond that, the limo made a wide left turn at the light onto Government Street, then another left back onto South Water Street.

The driver stopped at the front of the Mobile Convention Center before the pedestrian bridge to the Renaissance, near the steps leading up from South Plaza.

He walked around to open the door, offered his hand to help us climb out, then reminded us that he would be close to this same spot waiting for us when the night was over.

I thanked him, and as we walked toward the South Plaza, I stopped and gazed up at the Renaissance Riverview Plaza Hotel, with its newly completed spire reaching into the sky. Not far beyond it, a few blocks down Water Street, the RSA Battle House Tower, with its coordinating spire, stood gracefully over the city.

Despite the excitement, Prom proved to be a political affair. Stacy Freeman, Senior class president, stood on the tiered steps to the second level in her long trained, silver gown littered with rhinestones, with a neck plunge so deep that ski resorts should've been put on notice. She passed out ballot forms to all the Satsuma juniors and seniors walking up the steps to elect the Prom Court.

I reached up and accepted a ballot as I whisked past her, followed by Kayli, Pauline, Maddie, Allie, Lucas, then Becka and Wayne.

As we worked our way up the stairs to the outdoor terrace, everyone we walked by kept staring at my dress and hair, even though Pauline was the one wearing a two thousand dollar gown and heels with red bottoms.

Once inside, we filled out and dropped our ballots into the box, exchanged our tickets for purple rubber wrist bracelets and walked through the concourse lobby area that spanned over the train tracks running beneath it. We avoided the rest of the student council members aggressively handing out more Prom Court ballot forms, shuffled past one of several super silly photo booth set ups, and headed down the hallway to enter the Grand Ballroom.

An usher checked our bracelets as soon as we stepped past the double doors. Immediately, I was greeted with a cool waft of air as it fluttered against my temples, immersing me in various fragrances of perfume, cologne, foundation, concealer, hairspray, body spritz, conditioner and lotion.

The middle of the dance floor was a cluster of seniors, juniors, their dates, and parent-teacher chaperones.

Rihanna's "Umbrella" pounded from the speakers and shook the floor as lights blazed and shimmered across the ballroom, and hazy smoke drifted in the air.

A DJ stood behind a laptop and turntables, holding large headphones to one ear while bobbing and bouncing, perched on top of a small platform.

"Yo, it's crazy, right?" Becka said.

"No doubt," Wayne replied as she grabbed his hand and led him past me toward the thickest part of the crowd.

Maddie stepped beside me and looped her left arm through my right arm. Kayli did the same on my left side, and Pauline laid her palms on both of my shoulders and nudged me forward. I could smell the Dolce and Gabbana perfume on her shoulders and neck as she shuffled her feet, bopping to the rhythm.

"Do we have to dance like, right now? We literally *just* got here," I complained with a pout.

"Yes, ma'am! Time to show off those sexy legs and those ridiculously cute heels you're wearing. Like this is a Honey sequel," Pauline replied.

I let out an exasperated sigh as she shoved me toward where Becka and Wayne were already twerking to a T.I. song. By the time we reached them, a cluster of jerking, writhing and twisting Prom pounders surrounded them and Justin Timberlake was bringing SexyBack.

I lifted my arms and danced in what became a private circle, with Pauline, Maddie, Kayli and I facing each other. Becka and Wayne joined in with Allie and Lucas, and the rest of the Prom crowd made room as we danced, gyrated and bounced under the flashing lights.

It wasn't long before my throat was dry from all the screaming we were doing at each other to be heard over the music. I turned to look around to find where the refreshments were being served.

Pauline figured out what I was looking for and tapped me on my shoulder. She leaned in to yell close to my ear, gripping my elbow.

"I'll go with you. Tables in the back," she said, leading me away from our circle twerk.

Pauline noticed me walking funny.

"You okay, there, Manda Pants?" she asked, a frown furrowing her brow.

"I'm good. Think I twisted something. Not used to these shoes," I said.

"Ah," Pauline blew out a breath and snapped her fingers. "I wanted it to be a surprise, but I should've given them to you earlier so you could've broken them in."

"That's a thing?" I looked at her with a disbelieving grin on my face.

"Yep. It's real. I kid you not. You're supposed to break in your heels before you wear them. I always walk around the house in mine for a few days before I wear them out," Pauline quipped as we reached the long table with the refreshments.

I stared at the large bowl of red liquid perched near the end of the table. Cups sat stacked up next to it along with another large bowl of ice and a pair of tongs. Arranged near the punch were dishes with cut meats and cheeses, cheese rolled up in prosciutto, celery, broccoli and carrot sticks, crackers, and a chocolate fondue fountain.

Another ballot box stood near the table to the left.

"You think someone spiked the punch?" I asked as I grinned at Pauline. She let out a little giggle.

"If not, I'm about to," she said, tapping her thigh.

"You got a flask hidden in your panty hose, Pauline?" I smirked.

"I'll never tell," she said, reaching for the ladle and a cup to pour herself some punch. Seemingly out of nowhere, a freckled kid in a frilly tux shirt and blue bowtie stood up and snatched the ladle up before she could grab it, and retrieved a cup, pouring punch into it. He gingerly handed it to her with a smile.

She looked at him oddly.

"What are you? Harry Potter? Where the hell did you come from?"

He cocked his head to the side and guffawed, and we took a step back in case his head exploded from laughing so hard.

"Yo, chill, mama. I was just organizing the extra cups under the table. I ain't no wizard," he said.

"I don't know. You've got smoke still kind of floating in the surrounding air. If you're not Harry Potter, you're definitely Gandalf. Stop scaring people, man," Pauline said as he poured another cup of punch and handed it to me.

"Just for that, you're cut off," he said.

"Yeah, we'll see," Pauline snapped back as she turned around to drag me back toward the others.

"I wonder what else he was doing under there," I teased.

"Don't think I even want to know," Pauline replied, sipping punch.

"Anyway, why are you pestering the freshmen?"

"He started it. Jumping from under tables in the dark."

I shook my head as we reached the group.

Wayne looked at me and clicked his teeth.

"For real? You ain't bring me none?"

I glared at him, then took a deliberately slow sip of punch.

"Oh, it's like that? I see you," Wayne said, spinning around to put his back to me. "I'm telling. Next time you wanna see my bruh, you're catchin' a cab."

"Good luck with that," I smirked.

"Did you see Matt from first block? He almost fell into the speakers," Kayli snorted.

I glanced over in the direction she was nodding. I didn't see him.

"What the freak was he doing?" I asked.

"I don't know. That's Matt for you. I swear he has no sense of balance. Remember the hallway? When he dropped that science project all over the floor and it looked like a Xenomorph jizzed all over the place for a week before they replaced the tiles?" Kayli giggled.

"It's too early for that," I said with a laugh.

"He's always high, anyway. Won't be long before he does something else super stupidious," Lucas said.

I looked at him with my eyebrows raised.

"Whoa. Since when do you speak? I didn't even know you could talk," I said.

Lucas laughed.

"No, you haven't been around him long enough. He talks way too much," Allie said.

"Why you clownin' on your date like that, yo?" Wayne said, spinning back around to dip his hips in some crazy dance move. I shook my head at him. It was hard to imagine how he and Terrell could be from the same parents. They were nothing alike.

"I can clown on him whenever I want," Allie said, wrapping her arms around Lucas. "You don't mind, do you, Lukie-Wookie?"

"Yo. Did you seriously just call him a Wookie? He's not even hairy. At all. Ain't even a mustache growing in. Not one hint of puberty," Wayne teased.

Lucas didn't like that. He twisted away from Allie and walked off toward the refreshment table.

"*For real*, Wayne? Say you're sorry," Becka said.

"Yo, I'm just messin' with him," Wayne said. "Can't take a joke?"

"He's real sensitive. People mess with him in gym class. That's why I offered to go to prom with him. I felt bad," Allie said.

"A charity case? I thought you actually liked him," Maddie frowned. "You told me you liked him."

"I *do* like him, a little. I mean, he's nice. I watched him ask this girl out, and she laughed at him and told him he should finish fourth grade first. In front of a whole group of people in the hall-way. That was brutal," Allie said.

"That makes you any better?" Maddie snapped. "I mean, you could hurt his feelings. Mess around and scar him for life."

"Mess around and be the next mass shooter," Wayne said under his breath.

Becka cut him a sharp glare and he looked down at his shoes as if something there was suddenly worth investigating.

"I thought I was doing something nice," Allie replied. "I don't see what the problem is."

I interrupted before the block got too hot.

"Hey, ya'll. Let's just calm down. Really. We're here to have fun, not cut at each other's throats over whatever. Wayne, be nice. Say you're sorry. Allie, be nice. Say *you're* sorry," I said.

"Say I'm sorry for *what*? I didn't do anything," Allie sniffed.

I turned around to see if I could spot Lucas in the direction he went. When I didn't see him, I headed over to the refreshment table. Pauline and Maddie followed me.

We found Lucas standing at the table, sipping a cup of punch in one hand, holding a chunk of cheese in the other.

He looked at us and let out a slow breath.

"Hey, Lucas," I said in a singsong voice. He ignored me. I moved around to stand in his line of vision until he recognized my existence.

"I don't know why you're bothering. She didn't even stand up for me," he said.

"Allie asked *you* to the prom, right? And now you're here. It's beautiful. *A Night To Remember*, right? Come on, we're here to have a good time. Not stand here guarding the snacks," Maddie said.

"What's up with that dude Becka's with? He doesn't even know me," Lucas said.

"Wayne's a dork. Ignore him. He's a total goofball. Doesn't mean anything by it. He likes to joke around," I said.

"Well, it wasn't funny. At all," Lucas replied.

"I know, and he's sorry. Come on, for real," Maddie said, grabbing Lucas' arm.

He resisted, then reluctantly let Maddie lead him with us back to where Wayne was gyrating his hips to Becka's sloppy salsa dance. The DJ began mixing Young Jeezy into a Ciara song. Kayli was dancing, looking at Wayne like he was crazy, and Allie watched Lucas as he avoided her eyes.

She stepped toward him and put a hand on his arm.

He caved and started moving his hips off tempo. Allie grabbed his hand and guided him to the beat of the song as she danced.

I smiled at them, then settled into a little groove of my own while raising my hands in the air after I downed the rest of the punch.

With everyone getting along now, all I could do was count the minutes until my cellphone buzzed with the text I was waiting for.

It wasn't long before they announced that the last of the ballots had to be turned in for counting to elect prom court. It was then that my cellphone vibrated. I took it out from where it was tucked into my bra and read the text from Terrell, fired off a reply, then smiled as Pauline and Becka gave me knowing grins.

"Have fun! Don't get pregnant," Pauline said with a smirk as she wrapped her arms around me and squeezed me tight. "I'm so happy for you, girl."

When she let go, Becka hugged me, followed by Maddie, Kayli and Allie. They headed toward the outdoor terrace flanking the ballroom overlooking the bay, and I waltzed over to the concourse lobby area to meet Terrell outside in the South Plaza.

When I got to the doors leading outside, security stopped me.

The two butt holes in uniform firmly directed me back toward the grand ballroom like a wayward toddler.

twenty three
SPRING BREAKERS ♡
April 2008

I don't know why I even bothered. Laid out as usual on the sofa, drool drizzled toward the floor as Momma's head hung off the edge of the cushions. There were several prescription bottles strewn all over the coffee table, along with a can of soda and a plate with dried up cheese spread on it. Balled up tissue paper was scattered on the floor. I wasn't cleaning it up. I'd had enough of picking up after my momma.

She missed prom. She missed all of my basketball games. She missed everything. And Nana Jane acted like it was my fault, somehow.

"Momma," I shook her shoulders again to wake her up.

"Just go," Taylor said, standing next to me biting into a piece of toast with a grossed out expression on her face. "She won't even remember you asking, anyway."

"Yeah, but then I won't hear the end of it from Nana Jane," I said.

"Nana ain't your momma," Taylor replied.

"She tries to act like it. If she had her way, I wouldn't do any-thing at all," I said, shaking again.

Momma sniffed and sucked drool back into her mouth, then whimpered something under her breath.

"Momma, wake up," I said. "I wanna go away for Spring Break."

"It's last minute, anyway. Go pack a bag. I'll deal with Momma," Taylor said.

"Dude. You won't even be here. Soon as I'm out the door, you'll disappear like usual, and then when I get back, Nana Jane will try to pop me with a switch. Make me wanna fight somebody," I said, frowning at Taylor.

"I'm not going anywhere. Ain't got nobody to watch Ivy," she said.

"You'll just take her with you," I replied. I knew her more than she knew herself.

"I'm telling you, Manda. I got it. Just go," she said, shoving me in the arm.

"Yo, watch your hands," I snapped.

"Or you'll do *what*?" Taylor popped the rest of the toast into her mouth, bent over and thumped Momma in the forehead. I sucked in a breath in shock.

"*What*?" Momma muttered, disorientated as she started pushing up on her elbow attempting to sit up.

"Hey. Amanda's going away for Spring Break to Florida with Auntie Beanie. She's trying to say 'bye' before she leaves," Taylor said, loudly.

"You're goin' with your Auntie? That's real nice," Momma slurred, licking her lips, trying to focus on Taylor, who I began to believe she thought was me. "Ya'll be careful now… on them roads."

"Okay, Momma. We will," I said, looking at Taylor strangely as she flicked her hands in my direction, shooing me away.

I turned on my heels, realizing I had grown accustomed to the musty smell of Momma's hair, and the tart smell of the dried up saliva on the sofa cushions. She probably hadn't showered or taken a bath in a few days. It was getting harder for Nana Jane to drag her up off of her perch. Grandpa stopped coming around. It was too difficult for him, emotionally. Taylor wouldn't touch her even if she fell on the floor.

I was too angry with her to do anything but let her sit in it. I was done feeling sorry for her. She did it to herself.

Back in my room, I grabbed my gym bag from the chair in the corner and slung it onto my bed. I pulled out my basketball uniforms, my warm-up pants, sports bras, deodorant, and everything else in the bag, and tossed them onto my bed. Then, I began rummaging through my drawers for cute summer clothes to wear.

Taylor appeared in the doorway and laughed.

"Seriously? What are you gonna to do with that? It's an embarrassment," she said, then disappeared down the hallway.

She returned a short while later with a large, leather suitcase and laid it on my bed, pushing the gym bag onto the floor.

"Use this," she said. "What time are they getting here to pick you up?"

"About an hour or so," I replied, unzipping the suitcase. I would only be gone for a week, so I thought it was overkill. The gym bag would be big enough to fit a week's worth of clothes.

"Good. Do me a favor?"

"What?"

"Watch Ivy for me. I gotta go get something from somebody," she said.

"I'm not going to watch your kid while you go on a drug run," I snapped. I couldn't believe her.

"Yo, I'm selling my iPod to this dude I used to chill with in school," she said.

"*Right*," I replied in disbelief. "You sure it's not a quickie in the Taco Bell parking lot?"

"I need the money, Manda. I gotta pay for this thing at Ivy's pre-school and I don't have enough. I just started my new job. I won't get paid in time, and they need the money by next week, or she can't go."

I searched my sister's eyes for signs of a lie. Taylor seemed sincere. I cleared my throat.

"How much do you need?" I asked, my voice softer.

"Like a buck fifty," she said. "That covers her pre-k trip, plus gives me enough gas to last me till my first check, which is three weeks out."

"How much is the trip?"

"Seventy-five," Taylor replied. "It includes lunch."

"So you need seventy-five dollars in gas for three weeks? How far do you *work*?"

Taylor let out a long sigh.

"You're not driving yet. You have no idea how much gas costs each week. It's freakin' expensive. To be honest, that might not even be enough. If you ever get a car and a license, just wait till you get a job. You'll see what I'm talking about," Taylor said.

"Well, if Nana Jane has her way, I'll never drive," I replied, moving Taylor's suitcase out of the way and putting my gym bag back on the bed.

"You don't smell that? It's raunchy. Like Fritos and onion rings. Anyway, do what you want. I tried to help. And I can take you out driving for your license test."

"You've been saying that since I turned 15. I won't get my hopes up," I said.

"I will," she replied.

"When I'm collecting social security?"

"Take the suitcase, so you don't stink up your clean clothes. Seriously," Taylor said as she spun around to walk out of the room. "I'll be back before they get here. Ivy's in the backyard playing with her riding thingie."

"You left her out there by herself?"

Taylor glanced back at me, with one hand on the doorjamb.

"She's a big girl, Manda. She's not gonna break."

"She could leave the yard," I replied.

"Oh, no. Ivy knows better. I'd tear her little heinie to shreds," Taylor said sharply.

As she disappeared into the hallway, I followed behind her to head into the kitchen and out through the patio door to see if Ivy was okay.

She was sitting next to her riding toy in the shade on the concrete slab just in front of the door with her hair in pigtails tied with ribbons. Dressed in a yellow t-shirt and khaki shorts, she kicked her bare feet out in front of her.

She had been playing outside with no shoes on. Her little light-up Sketchers sat next to her with the laces untied, and her toenails were dirty.

I heard the front door open and close behind me as Taylor left. I pulled open the patio door.

"Hey, Ivy," I said. She turned around and looked at me with a smile.

"Hi, Auntie Manda," she said.

"You thirsty? It's kinda hot out here."

"Yeah," she said, standing to come inside. I let her in and closed the patio door behind her. Then, I pulled a plastic cup from the cabinet in the kitchen above the sink and poured her some sweet tea from the pitcher in the fridge.

She drank it down quickly, then headed back outside to the patio. I didn't relish leaving her out there by herself, so I sat down on the floor to keep an eye on her.

Becka showed up earlier than she said she would. When she rang the doorbell, I let her in. Momma didn't even budge, strung out on the sofa again.

"Hi, Ms. Rush," Becka said with a wave as she passed by Momma on the way to my room, knowing she wouldn't get a response.

"I haven't packed yet. I'm watching Ivy until my sister gets back," I said.

"That's cool," Becka said. "I can pack for you. Ain't like I don't know where everything is."

"You don't have to do that," I said as I headed back over to the patio door.

"Yo, *chica*, I got this," Becka replied, disappearing down the hallway toward my room.

Ivy yanked the patio door open and came back inside.

"You done? Hot out, huh?"

"Can I watch something on TV?" she asked.

"Yeah, I can put on the Disney channel. You hungry yet?" I asked.

"Yes," she replied. I motioned for her to sit at the table near the patio door and I rummaged through the cabinets for peanut butter. I took the loaf of bread from the bread box and reached into the fridge for a jar of jelly. Grabbing a butter knife from the drawer near the sink, I made her a sandwich and then cut the ends off.

I sliced up an apple on the cutting board and added them with a few Cheetos and the sandwich to a plate from the cabinet. Then, I set the plate down in front of Ivy, refilled her cup of sweet tea, and sat down with her while she ate silently, daintily playing with the Cheetos while she munched.

Becka reappeared into the living room with Taylor's suitcase and took it out to her car to put in the trunk. She returned with Taylor stepping into the house behind her.

"I found a stray out in the yard," Taylor said as she closed the front door behind her. Becka rolled her eyes and sat down in the chair beside me, waving at Ivy. Ivy smiled and waved back, then bit into an apple wedge.

"How was she?" Taylor asked.

"Fine," I said.

"I got two hundred fifty," Taylor said, triumphantly.

"How did you pull that off?"

"The guy thought I was selling it for three hundred and talked me down to two-fifty."

I looked at her strangely.

"Why didn't you just sell it to him for the three hundred?"

"Well, I didn't want to stiff him," she said.

I couldn't help but laugh. Becka grinned and shook her head.

"Well, now you can pay me for watching Ivy for an hour. Twenty bucks."

"You get paid with the experience of being able to enjoy time with your niece," Taylor said.

I laughed again.

"That's not how that works, but okay."

"You all packed up?" Taylor asked.

"Ready to go," I replied.

"Why you still here?"

I glared at Taylor, then stuck my tongue out at her. She returned the gesture, and I followed Becka out to her Camry.

Sliding into the passenger seat, I realized Becka's car smelled like Wayne.

"So, where's your boyfriend? What did you guys do? Make out before you came and got me?" I teased as I snapped the seatbelt buckle into place.

"You're a little detective," she said, starting the car. Becka put the car in reverse and backed out onto the street from the gravel drive. "He's back at my place, waiting for us with Pauline."

"Who's driving down?"

"Your boy's already headed down with his college peeps. We're going in two cars. You're riding down with Pauline. I'm taking Wayne with me in the hooptie."

"Why are we doing it that way?" I asked.

"Coolers, beach bags, beach chairs… all that's going in here with us, so the back seat and trunk'll be full. Pauline's car ain't gonna fit all that. So, you ride with her."

"Oh, okay," I said. "Makes sense."

"Sure does. Now I can fondle Wayne the whole way to Florida."

"You're gross. I don't need to hear all that," I said, crossing my arms across my chest.

"Sad that Maddie and Allie aren't going."

"Their family always goes to the Caribbean for Spring Break. Lucky. I've never been outside of Alabama and Florida," I said.

"*Yo!* We should go on a road trip. Just you and me," Becka exclaimed, sudden excitement in her voice.

"That would be nice. I'd like to go to California," I suggested.

"New York," she replied. "I have a whole lot of family up that way."

"You've told me about your cousins. A thousand times," I said.

"Yeah, a lot of my family came up from Puerto Rico and moved up there. I guess it was too *bama* for them here."

"Or too boring," I added.

"Yeah. That too," Becka said.

"I mean, compared to New York, I'm sure being down here is really lame," I replied. "Not as much to do, I'm sure."

"It does get a little played out, right?" Becka chuckled.

We pulled up along the curb behind Pauline's Mustang in front of Becka's house on Spanish Trail.

I got out, placed my suitcase on the ground next to the coupe and helped Wayne, Pauline and Becka load everything into the Camry.

Then, Pauline helped me stuff my suitcase in next to all of hers in the tight trunk and within a short while, we were on the road with Becka's car trailing behind.

As soon as we merged onto Interstate 10 from Interstate 65, Pauline rolled both windows down.

"Spring Breakers!" she screamed, sticking her head out of the window, honking the horn loudly. She threw up a peace sign and wagged her tongue, letting it hang out of her mouth. Cars nearby honked back noisily in protest.

I shook my head at her and laughed while she rolled the windows back up, switching the AC to a higher setting.

Pauline knew her way to Tampa and Clearwater, but she put in the address to the resort into the GPS navigation on her Blackberry Curve. She stuffed her phone into the holder that plugged into the cigarette lighter, right above the CD changer slot on the console.

According to the navigation, it would be nearly eight hours of sitting in Pauline's car getting throat massaged by the subwoofers, listening to her ring out the gears as she giggled like a little girl.

We wouldn't arrive at the resort until close to 10pm.

I settled back into the ribbed leather seat and smiled as Pauline switched to a 50 Cent song on her iPod, bobbed her head, dropped two gears and purposefully mashed the accelerator to tease Becka.

After three and a half hours of driving we made our first stop in Tallahassee at exit 199, the US 27 Monroe Street and State Capitol exit. Pauline and I followed Becka and Wayne into the Burger

King off of the exit to use the bathrooms and to grab a few Whopper meals.

The sun was creeping closer to the western horizon as we stopped to top off the tanks of both cars at the gas station on the other side of the overpass, amid a cluster of hotels.

When we merged back onto Interstate 10, Pauline turned the music down with her pinky finger as she clutched her burger.

"Hey. So, are you going to see your aunt while we're down there?"

I smiled and finished chewing a mouthful of ketchup-slathered onion rings before I spoke.

"I hope so. I miss her," I said. "This is the first time I've been down to Clearwater in a while."

"Do you get to see her a lot?" Pauline asked.

"Not as much as I'd like. We talk on the phone. She's always sending me nice stuff. And what she did for me, for Prom. I will never forget that."

"She's a better mom to you than your real mom, huh?"

I fell quiet for a while.

"I'm sorry. I shouldn't have said that," Pauline said, switching her Whopper to her left hand while holding the steering wheel.

"No," I put my hand on her arm as she downshifted to pass a line of semi-trucks trapped behind a diesel Ford pick-up pulling a huge boat. "No, it's okay. I mean, Auntie Beanie is *awesome*. She's more like me than anyone I know. And she understands me more than anyone I know."

"I'm glad you have her in your life. It's good to have people like that who have your back. I'm really close with my parents. But

I understand what you're going through. You told me before that your mom has had it rough since your dad bailed, right?"

"Yeah. I mean, it's been years. You have to get back up, you know?"

"Yeah, I get you," she breathed. "You excited to see Tee?"

"Terrell? Yeah. We didn't talk for a while after Prom. He thought I ditched him. Wouldn't take any of my calls. Becka had to drive out to his house and track him down."

"You don't think he's a little childish sometimes?" Pauline let off the accelerator after passing and moved back into the right lane.

"He just gets upset because it's harder to see each other now. It was hard already when I started basketball sophomore year. Then he started his internship last year. Plus, he has his job, and now he's getting ready to graduate in two months. This will seriously be maybe the second time I've seen him since Prom," I said with a long sigh. I watched as the pines seemed to stretch on forever, just a few feet from the freeway's shoulder.

"It's almost as bad as a long distance relationship," Pauline said. "I was with this guy a while ago who lived back in Cali, and six months in he was banging the flea market fixture in the condo across from him."

"How old was he?"

She smirked.

"Old enough. He was a freshman at Caltech. Or so he claimed."

"That sucks," I said with a chuckle. "I'm sorry for laughing. But Terrell's not a cheater. He's too busy for all that."

"I'm not trying to lecture you, but he looks like the typical frat slash momma's boy. Sometimes those dudes can be serious trouble. Trust me, I know. And he's graduating soon. That changes things. Just be careful," Pauline replied. She turned the music back up as we approached exit 225 for US 19, Florida-Georgia Parkway to Monticello and Perry.

US 19 would take us straight to Clearwater in about four more hours. I finished my Whopper and the last of the onion rings, then drank down my Coke while Pauline drove. When we finished our Burger King meals, I gathered all the wrappers and napkins and put them back in the bag. Pauline took the bag from me with a giggle and tossed it behind her seat. I shook my head at her with a smile, leaned my head back and closed my eyes to take a nap for the rest of the trip, with the bass from the car's Shaker system tickling the back of my neck.

I woke up to Pauline giving me a wet willy.

"What the hell, hooker?" I said, yanking my head away. I wiped at my left ear as Pauline snort-laughed. I glared at her, then sat up.

"Wake up, sleepyhead. We're here."

I adjusted myself in the leather seat and looked around. We were at the traffic light at the corner of North Fort Harrison and Cleveland. A five story brick building sat to the left on the other side of the intersection, across from a Starbucks.

I twisted in the seat to look behind us. The Camry was so close that the headlights were out of view. It looked as if it was touching the rear bumper of Pauline's car. Becka was laughing at something Wayne was saying, and their faces were a bright red, illuminated by the Mustang's brake lights.

I faced forward as we bolted through the light, sending Pauline a side-eyed look as she snapped the lever into second, then third gear, pressing us into the seats.

"Go ahead. Get a ticket, why don't 'ya," I muttered under my breath.

Pauline rolled her eyes and cackled as she slowed the car down to below jail term limits.

After a while, she made a right onto Court Street, and we continued on past the Pinellas County Courthouse and onto the Clearwater Memorial Causeway.

The night sky above us was a cloudless, clear black. Pauline hit the button to roll both windows down and I gazed out over the crystalline, sparkling water dotted with boats and yachts as we passed over the bridge.

After passing Island Estates, traffic slowed to a crawl, and I sat back in the seat, smiling as the Gulf breeze tickled my cheeks. Pauline had turned the music back up to drown out a motorcycle idling next to us.

Just then, her Blackberry rang. She turned the music back down, rolled the windows up, switched on the AC and put her phone on speaker.

"Yo, whassup, Spring Breakers!" Becka sang.

"Geez. I roll the windows down and it still smells like onion rings, mustard and armpits in here. And you guys are back there clowning," Pauline replied with a chuckle. "Do you *have* to tailgate me? You'll spazz when I brake check you. Better have some good insurance."

"You the one acting like you trying to reach escape velocity, *fool*. I'm just trying to keep up. *Anyhoo*, Terrell and them checked into a different resort. I copped the address," Becka said.

"Why'd they do that?" Pauline asked. "That was dumb."

"Something about roaches. Or naked old skeezers with saggy nipples. I dunno. But, now we gotta switch up our reservation."

"He could have told us that a while ago, instead of waiting last minute," Pauline sighed, annoyed. "Whatever. Let's pull over somewhere so I can take care of it."

"It's going to be hard to find something this late in the fourth quarter. Everything's probably booked," I said. "Is the resort we were staying at really that bad? Why don't we just keep the reservation we have and check it out ourselves?"

"I don't know. I'm pissed now," Pauline said. "I should have had my dad book us where he was originally planning to. We'd be pulling up to the Sandpearl valet right now."

We turned into a shopping plaza to the right and parked in front of a Wings beach store. Becka slid the Camry into the parking space next to us.

Pauline picked up her phone and pushed a few buttons, and her daddy answered after a few rings.

"Hello, Leenie," her daddy said.

"Hey, dad. I need a quick favor," Pauline replied.

"What's that? You okay down there? You're at the hotel now, right?"

"Well, that's the problem. I guess there's something wrong with the resort our friends booked," she said.

Her daddy exhaled slowly, then cleared his throat.

"I'll take care of it. Where are you now?"

"We just got off the Causeway. We're parked in front of the Wings in Clearwater Beach, when you first get off of the bridge."

"Okay. Stay put. I'll send you the reservation number to your email. Let me know when you get it," her daddy said.

"Hi, Mr. Davani," I said loudly.

"That must be Amanda. You doing alright down there?" he asked with a chuckle. "I'm sorry about the snafu with your hotel. But I think you'll like what I have in mind."

"Thank you," I replied.

"It's no problem. So this reservation is just for you three girls, right? I don't want to hear about any shenanigans. I'm not far from you, you know. Tampa's just a few minutes away. That's the only reason I agreed to let you change this little trip of yours. You originally said Pensacola."

"I know, dad. I told you, Pensacola's gotten too crazy. There was this big thing with the police this week. It's insane now. That's why we changed it to Clearwater. Plus, Amanda's aunt lives down here, too," Pauline said.

"Why didn't you just stay with her?"

"She doesn't have the space," Pauline lied. "Plus, she's super busy."

"I see. Well, sit tight. Call me back when you get the email," Mr. Davani said. "Love you, Leenie."

"Love you, dad," Pauline replied, and then she hung up.

"Awww, you guys are cute," I said, cooing.

Pauline smirked as she rolled her thumb to click open her Gmail. I sat back again and waited while she kept refreshing her email screen.

Suddenly, her Blackberry rang again. It was her daddy.

"Okay, Leenie. I've got two options for you. I called in a favor, and I can get you in at the Sandpearl, but they are renovating. They're also doing some work on Pier 60, so there will be some noise. But, the other option is, we have a house. It's on Eldorado.

Your mother doesn't know about it, so don't say anything. It's a surprise for later," Mr. Davina said.

"Oooh, Spooky. A mysterious house no one is supposed to know about. How creepy can you be, dad?" Pauline asked. Mr. Davina straight up ignored her comment.

"I can have someone bring over a key and meet you there. She's a contractor that's been doing some work on the house for me. She's also the real estate agent that handled the deal. Two birds in one stone. Anyway, you can stay there as long as you don't mess anything up. I've been making updates to it, so some of the work is still ongoing," Mr. Davina said.

"Um, we'll take the house for six hundred," Pauline said.

"That's what I figured. Saves money on a hotel stay. Just leave the house the same way you found it. Meaning, clean up after yourselves. No wild crazy parties. And don't break anything. I'm serious, Leenie."

"I hear you dad, I got it," Pauline said, letting out an exasperated sigh.

"Okay then. I'll text you the address. Call me when you have the key."

"Okay," Pauline replied, hanging up.

I chuckled.

"You know. If I didn't know any better, I'd say your daddy was over here in Tampa hooking up in the secret bachelor pad," I teased.

"Ha. Ha. Hilarious," Pauline said as she stared at the screen. The text came through with the address and she slowly backed out of the parking space. Heading back out onto Causeway Boulevard,

Becka followed close behind as Pauline creeped through traffic into the circle, and veered right onto Mandalay, next to Hooters.

We continued on for a while, past the Caretta and Belle Harbor resorts, past Mandalay Park on the left, to the next roundabout at Acacia into North Beach.

Circling around the roundabout, Pauline took the second Acacia exit heading west to where it became Eldorado.

A few blocks later, we pulled up onto the tiled front driveway and parking area of a stucco two story Mediterranean-style estate home with a two car attached garage, Spanish tile roof, balconies, and columns. Two tall palmettos towered over the house to the right.

Becka parked the Camry next to us and she and Wayne got out to look around, awestruck.

"This house is gorgeous," I said with a whistle. "How freakin' loaded *are* you?"

I decided that one day, when I was at the height of my career, I would get a house just like this on a beach somewhere in California. Maybe even Florida, so I can be close to my Auntie Beanie.

"I'm not loaded. My dad's family is," Pauline said.

"That means you're loaded too," I replied.

We waited for a while in silence, watching Becka and Wayne snuggle each other to death on the hood of the Camry.

My cellphone buzzed in my pocket, so I pulled it out and answered.

"Whassup, girl," Terrell breathed on the other end.

"Hey," I said.

"Where you at?"

I smiled.

"Pauline's dad hooked us up with a sweet beach house," I replied.

"When ya'll comin' through?" he asked.

I glanced over at Pauline.

"I don't think it will be tonight. We're all kind of tired."

"Becka's bringin' my bruh over here after ya'll get settled in. Why don't you ride with them? I can drop you back tomorrow after we chill," he said.

"You've got all your college friends over there with you, drinking and partying and all that. I don't really feel comfortable being around them all night like that," I replied.

"Girl, you're trippin.' Ain't nobody gonna mess with you. You're with me," he said with a chuckle.

"I get that, but I'm super tired tonight, Terrell," I breathed.

He was quiet for a moment. Then, he spoke.

"Aight, well. I'll let you go so you can get your rest. See you tomorrow at the pier?"

I nodded.

"Yeah. See you tomorrow," I said.

He hung up.

The inside of the car lit up as someone pulled up behind us. I turned around to look, and an Infiniti M45 sat along the curb, blocking us in.

A tall, deeply tanned older woman with feathered blonde hair to her shoulders climbed out of the car in a white designer outfit and matching white heels. She reached into her purse and pulled out a key.

Pauline stepped out to shake the woman's hand and take the key.

"You must be Pauline. I'm Dorothy Hayes. I work with your father," she said, handing the house keys to Pauline.

"It's nice to meet you," Pauline replied as she accepted the keys.

"You as well. So, about the house. There's plenty to love. Excellent community. The balcony in back is impeccable. The views are fantastic. Anyway, I'm talking like I'm selling it to you when your father has already bought it. Let me show you inside," Dorothy said with a laugh.

I got out to follow Pauline and Dorothy to the front door of the house as Becka and Wayne began unpacking the Camry.

We stopped in front of the white gate that protected the front patio, beneath a curved second level balcony. It was framed by two columns on either side and steel embellishments to match the front gate.

Dorothy pointed out which key was the one to unlock the gate, and Pauline inserted the key into the lock, then pushed it open to produce an ear-piercing screech coming from the hinges.

We stepped into the porch area beneath the balcony as Dorothy again pointed out which key opened the front door. Pauline unlocked the bolt, turned the latch and we stepped inside the cool front foyer. The house smelled like fresh paint.

Dorothy quickly disarmed the alarm and gave Pauline the security code written on a slip of paper.

While she showed her how to alarm and disarm the alarm, I helped Becka and Wayne bring in luggage and beach supplies inside as they brought them through the gate from the Camry.

After both cars were unloaded, we locked them and looked for Pauline and Dorothy, who we found standing out on the lanai beyond the first level summer kitchen, taking in the view of the Gulf of Mexico.

The grand balcony was above us, flanked on the north side by a spiraling staircase. The tiled patio on the first level expanded out with a step leading to a large outdoor entertaining space. Arranged next to each other, several beach chairs and chaise loungers sat overlooking the beach.

Palmettos flanked both sides of the back of the house, and the sand of the beach was just beyond the lanai.

"This house is ridiculous. How many bedrooms is it?" I asked.

Dorothy smiled.

"Technically four bedrooms. Three baths. Mr. Davani is using some of the additional space for six bedrooms total. Did you see the master suite?"

I shook my head.

"No, I didn't. Or, wait. Maybe I did. There was a whole upstairs area with columns," I said.

"Yes. The second level has a formal living room, dining room and the chef's kitchen. The master suite is on that level," Dorothy said.

"I call the master suite," I said. Pauline looked at me and laughed.

"Sorry. I love you, but… I'm not sharing," Pauline said.

"I don't want one of those first floor rooms. They look like kids' rooms," I said, simply.

"I'll take the first floor," Becka said. "That way I can get to that huge fridge, quick and easy. And sit out on the patio."

"There are three other bedrooms on the second level," Dorothy said. "I'm sure I can guess which one you'll pick. Well, if you need anything, my number is on that card I gave you."

"Thanks," Pauline said as she turned to walk Dorothy back out to the front through the house.

I stood out on the patio with Becka and Wayne, taking in the fresh gulf air, watching people of all sizes and shapes walk back and forth along the beach in the night. Many of them brandished glow in the dark neon bracelets and necklaces, or pulsing brightly colored flashlights.

Yawning, I turned to go inside. I located my sister's suitcase and dragged it up the stairs to the second level.

After a quick survey, I picked the largest room opposite the master suite, with its luxurious bathroom decked out in marble and a queen bed that seemed made for the stars.

Or so I imagined as I tossed the suitcase onto the floor next to the bed, climbed on top of the comforter without getting undressed, and curled up like a baby.

As soon as my head hit the pillow, I quickly drifted off to sleep, dreaming of Davina money.

twenty five
ONE WEEK WON'T HURT ♡

After Wayne and Becka creatively stuffed themselves behind
Pauline and I in the Mustang's backseat, I twisted around to look at
their situation and laughed hysterically. Wayne looked like he was
about to eat his kneecaps.

"You alright back there? You look a little smooshed," I said,
wiping at a tear in the corner of my eye. "Like an angry dwarf."

"You got jokes. I'm good," he said with a loud huff as he
crossed his arms. "I'll just sit back here and do nasty stuff to Becka."

"No, you won't. Touch me and you walk," Becka replied jokingly.

"I ain't walkin' nowhere. *Bruh*," he replied.

"I know you did *not* just call me *bruh*. Yeah, you about to walk
back to Bama," Becka said as she punched Wayne in the shoulder.

"Okay, *Lexi*," I chuckled as Becka shot a sneering glare in my
direction.

"Yo, wouldn't that be crazy if she showed up? He *did* say all
his peeps were here. That would include her, since she's his roadie
from the hood."

"If she's here, I swear I'll scream," I said. "That would be *beyond* messed up."

Pauline sniffed.

"Are you guys done? I'm about to drive now. I don't need anybody distracting me. I gotta dodge these crazy Florida drivers. Not trying to wreck," Pauline said, gripping both sides of the steering wheel tightly. The gear shifter sat perched in reverse gear.

"My bad. We good. Go 'head. Do your thing," Wayne replied, laughing.

Pauline lifted off the clutch with her left foot as she stepped into the accelerator, and smoothly backed the car out onto the street. Then, she grabbed the shifter with her right hand, nudged it down, over and up into first gear, and we bolted forward, lurching when she shifted into second and third.

"See. Now you actin' crazy. This ain't Midnight Club," Becka said with her eyebrows furled into a frown.

Pauline ignored her, banging the shifter back down to second gear when she approached the roundabout.

Wayne began making fake orgasm noises as he leaned over and nuzzled his head against Becka's neck.

"Boy! Stop!" Becka yelled, pushing him off of her. "I swear, you play too much. Ya'll gonna have to hurry up and get us out this car before I lose it."

"It's a short drive. You'll be alright. Wayne. *Behave,*" Pauline said.

"Ya'll need to chill. Ya'll can't *all* be raggin' it at the same time. For real though," Wayne said, then laughed loudly as we came to a stop behind a line of cars in the right lane, waiting for someone ahead to turn into the hotel parking lot near the corner of Rockaway Street.

Somehow, we ignored his obnoxiousness for the rest of the ride down Mandalay to the next roundabout where Pauline veered right onto Coronado.

Once we reached the public parking lot near the Visitor's Center, Pauline found a space next to the buildings along the main walkway of Pier 60.

After we climbed out of the car, we darted in between the Visitor Center buildings and emerged onto the main walkway near the bike racks, across from the sheltered children's play areas.

As we walked along the sidewalk next to the Visitor's Center, I saw Terrell standing with a group at the steps to the gift shop. Posted up right next to him, was Lexi.

I cut a searing glare at Becka and pursed my lips, smacking her on the arm.

"What the *hell*, Manda," she spat, but stopped walking abruptly when she saw the look on my face. I nodded toward the group, she followed my glare, and the light of understanding dawned on her face.

She cussed.

Pauline stopped walking ahead of us, realized we had halted and turned to see what was up. When she saw Lexi, she turned to look back toward me and immediately rushed over to my side.

My face was getting hotter by the second.

"I thought they were broke up," Pauline said, a confused look on her face.

"They were. They *are*," I said.

"So why is she here?" Pauline asked.

"They grew up together and are supposedly besties, even though they aren't together," Becka said.

"Yo, you mad, huh?" Wayne grinned. "Don't worry about her, yo. No need to get your panties in a bunch. She's old news. For real," he said.

I cut an equally dangerous sneer at him.

He put both his hands up in defense.

"For real. Yeah, they been roadies since diapers, dude, know'm sayin'? But they just chill. He got eyes for you, *ma.* On my *life*," Wayne said. "I know my bruh, and I'm tellin' you, he's all 'bout that *Manda*. He ain't even pressin' Lexi like that."

I shook my head.

"Why would he bring her knowing I'd be here? I don't care how long they've known each other. That's just *rude*," I said, suddenly marching ahead, my steps hard against the concrete. I heard Becka cuss again behind me as they followed.

Terrell, heavily immersed in conversation with the group posted up near the steps with him, looked over and saw me as I approached, and he grinned from ear to ear.

His smile faded quickly when he saw the look on my face. Then, he looked over at Lexi, then back at me, and his eyes went up toward the sky as he rubbed his forehead.

"What's up?" I said as I stood in front of him.

"Hey," he replied, his voice low.

"So. What's *up*?" I said again, with a tinge to my voice. He caught on and, looking around at the group, reached for my arm, nudging me to walk with him.

I followed him to an area along the walkway out of earshot of his friends.

"So what's going on?" I asked as he squinted at me under the blazing sun. He shielded his eyes with his right hand.

"Not much," he said.

"Why is she here?" I asked.

"Look, I didn't think it would be a problem if she came down with us. She's staying in her own room," Terrell said. "And we're just friends. You know that. I've known her my whole life, way longer than I've known you. She's like family to *my* family."

"Usually when two people break up, they don't take vacations together. Especially when one of them has moved on with someone else," I said. "Unless you're Bruce Willis and Demi Moore."

"This is Spring Break. We came down with a big group in three SUVs. In ours, I drove most of the way, she sat all the way in the back. It's not a big deal, and you're making it into something it's not. I'm not trying to hurt you," he replied. "Everyone is doing their own thing. Most of them still up in their rooms passed out."

"But you knew I'd be upset if I saw her here with you," I said. "I mean, you guys were together for a long time from what you've said to me before. So put yourself in my shoes. See it from *my* perspective."

He blew out a long breath, slowly, with his head hung low before looking back up at me.

"I'm sorry. I don't know what you want me to do. Send her back on a flight?"

I shook my head.

"No. Too late now, she's here. I'm not happy about it, but you know, you do you," I said, crossing my arms.

"Why you gotta be like that?" Terrell asked.

"I'm not being like *anything*," I replied sharply.

"Yes. You are. I'll just tell her to leave. Or you and me can go do whatever separate from everyone else. I can leave my rental here with them. You and me can head up the beach and chill. Get something to eat, whatever you want."

"And leave my friends? No. I'm not doing that," I said.

"So, then what do you want me to do?"

"Nothing."

Terrell raised his head toward the sky and closed his eyes, rubbing his temples with both hands, before turning to head back over to the group.

Pauline and Becka were watching me with concerned looks on their faces. Lexi was watching me as well, with a blank expression.

I shuffled back over to Pauline and Becka. Pauline put her hand on my arm. Becka stood close enough to me to touch her arm to my arm.

"You want to leave?" Pauline asked. "We can do that. I'm good with it. We can go Spring Break it in Naples. I know a place. I can get us there in two and a half."

"I'm good with it, too," Becka said.

"What about Wayne?" I asked, frowning at Becka. "I'm not going to do that to you. I want you to have fun."

"This can be a girls only Spring Break. I see Wayne all the time. One week won't hurt. And he gets on my last nerve, so I could use a break, anyway."

I stood there silently for a while, then turned to see Terrell watching me with a tortured expression on his face.

"I'm good. Really, ya'll," I said. My cheeks still felt like they were on fire, and I did everything I could not to stare Lexi down.

"Okay. But if you change your mind, or she does one thing out of character, it's gonna be *Flo-ride-or-die* down here," Becka said.

I looked at her strangely, then laughed so hard that it made me snort.

"Did you think that one up all by yourself? You've got smoke coming out of your ears from concentrating so hard," I said with a chuckle.

"Haha. *Hoe-larious*," Becka said with a sniff as we joined the group.

Terrell stepped toward me as Lexi looked away.

"We good?" he asked.

"I don't know," I said, as Pauline and Becka flanked me on either side. I turned and headed down the walkway toward the pier.

Terrell walked behind me in silence, followed by Lexi, Wayne and the rest of the group.

To the right, a man stood near the stone wall surrounding the play area, dressed in a Hawaiian print shirt, jeans, sunshades and a ball cap. He played and sang Marvin Gaye's "Mercy Mercy Me" on an acoustic guitar that looked similar to the one my daddy gave me.

His voice was brassy as he sang into a microphone, plugged into an amplifier perched on a stand nearby.

He was surrounded by a large crowd, and more people approached from the concrete sidewalk running along the beachfront.

I stopped to watch him and Pauline nudged me in the arm.

"He's not as good as you. You still play?" she asked. "I don't know 'cause we stopped going to Village, obviously."

"Don't ya'll go to that new church, near that huge house your family built out on 41? Up there with all those rich people?" I asked.

"Valley Hill? Yeah. It's right on the same road, just down a little. So, you still play on Sundays?"

I smiled.

"Youth Sundays, I lead worship. Regular Sundays, Pastor makes me do a solo and play during the songs," I said.

"So, you play guitar, cello, bass. What else?"

"Piano and drums. But only at church and just sometimes. When someone on the worship team is sick, I might cover for them and play their instrument," I replied.

"How the hell did you learn to play all those instruments like that?" Pauline asked. "I never asked you that. Always wanted to know."

"Daddy said I beat all the kitchen stuff when I was little. Pots. Pans. Bowls. Whatever," I said. "Then he bought me that little Casio keyboard. I played that and somehow just figured it out. It broke, though. Then he bought me the guitar. I started playing in church in third grade. As you know, did band in middle school and then high school."

"That's insane. You gonna be the next Taylor Swift?"

I chuckled.

"I don't know about all that," I replied, realizing the group and Terrell had walked down the pier and were clustered around one of the benches.

We headed over to join them, and I felt Lexi's eyes on me as we approached.

Sitting on the bench was a man frantically scratching away in a sketchbook with a graphite pencil. Terrell and Wayne were bent over watching him as his right hand moved swiftly across the paper. Lexi continued to watch me as I pushed past the others to stand next to Terrell so I could get a closer look.

The man was sketching a caricature of the two brothers, with their arms around each other's shoulders, throwing up what looked like gang signs. They were in bikinis and holding lifeguard floats, like a scene from a Baywatch rerun. He drew Wayne with dreads and huge pimples on his face, and Terrell with knobby knees and hairy legs.

I burst into laughter at the hilarious portrait.

"Yo, it's funny, but dude got skills. Look how fast he's doing that," Wayne said, reaching into his pocket to pull out his wallet. He produced a twenty-dollar bill and flicked it with his thumb.

When the man finished the sketch, he signed it and reached under the bench to pull out a black frame from a duffel bag hidden beneath. Unclipping the frame from the clear plastic face, he placed the sketch inside and neatly secured it.

Wayne handed him the twenty, and the man smiled, wrapped the framed sketch in tissue paper, and gave it to him.

Terrell laughed, passing an additional ten-dollar bill to the artist.

"We should hang this up on Mom's picture wall when we get back while she's sleep. See how long she takes to notice it," he said.

"Yo, she'll see it right away. You can't flip the sugar around in the cabinet without her bugging out about it," Wayne said.

"Your mom's OCD?" Pauline asked.

"She is *way* beyond that," Becka said. "My first time going over there, I saw every label facing forward. Toilet paper edges folded into a little triangle. And she throws out the toilet bowl brush each week and buys a new one. For each bathroom."

"How do you live with that?" Pauline said. "We don't even go *that* far, and my parents are ridiculously anal."

Terrell laughed.

"My mom had me pressing my own suits for church before I was even in school," he said. "She's strict. We got beat with extension cords growing up."

"That's straight up child abuse," Becka said.

"Yo. *He* got beat with extension cords. She was nicer to me," Wayne said. "I got the switch."

"That's 'cause I was always getting beat for the stupid stuff *you* did," Terrell said. "Covering for you."

"I didn't tell you to cover for me, bruh," Wayne replied.

"Don't get beat down out here in Clearwater, my dude," Terrell said. Lexi put her hand on his arm and smiled at him knowingly.

When I saw her movement, I sucked in a breath, and felt Becka's hand quickly grab my arm. I turned and let her and Pauline lead me away toward the Pier Bait Shop, where we paid the dollar admission.

After stepping outside back onto the pier, we pushed past two white-haired guys in shorts with mangled gray hair bursting through their button ups standing in the middle of the entrance.

They eyed us as we pressed through the turnstiles and continued across the pier's expansion nearly seven hundred feet out over the water.

Walking in silence, we meandered through the obstacle course of pedestrians on the pier, mom's pushing strollers, kids stuffing their faces with confections from the Visitor's Center, rowdy

Spring Breakers, dudes with their kids fishing over the railing and old people slowly shuffling along.

A nauseating mash up of cotton candy, fishy smelling tackle boxes, jumbo pickles, cheap cologne, even cheaper perfume and sweaty adolescents and children were a full on assault on my nostrils.

Eventually, we made it to the end of the crowded pier, surrounded by the Gulf of Mexico on all sides, not including the walkway. Seagulls were everywhere and people leaned over the railings to peer out over the calm gulf.

Above us, the bright sky was cloudless, open and vast. In the distance, a ship sat motionless against the horizon. We found a space between a couple taking pictures of seagulls arcing out over the shimmering waves and a group of kids dropping loogies from the railing.

We squeezed in closer to the couple and huddled up together to watch a group of pelicans following behind the seagulls, dipping low along the waves, heading up the beach.

"You okay?" Becka asked after a while.

"Yeah, I'm fine," I said.

"No, you're not," she countered. "I know you, Manda. You ain't *fine*."

"I told you. We can leave. Do our own thing," Pauline said.

"I'm good," I replied, shifting my weight onto my right leg as I squinted against the sparkling light of the sun reflecting from the waves.

Terrell tapped me on my shoulder. I didn't know he followed us out to the end of the pier.

I turned to look at him.

"Mind if I join you? Or are you still mad at me?" he said.

I nudged Pauline, and she slid over just enough to let him nuzzle up next to me.

He looked at me and leaned in.

"You look beautiful today," he said.

"Mmm hmmm," I replied. "Corny."

"For real. I wanted to see if you wanted to walk along the beach for a bit, then get lunch. There's a place called Crabby's heading toward where we're staying. We can walk there from here," he said.

"Just you and me, or with the entourage?" I asked.

"Well I mean, we'd *all* be going," he said. "Just the people I grew up with and your squad. Like I said, everyone else is passed out. They were all up late last night, gettin' hammered. So they won't be coming out of their caves anytime soon. Not till tonight, more than likely."

"Do I have to sit next to your ex?"

"No."

"Are *you* going to sit next to your ex?"

"No."

"She gonna be all touchy feely the rest of this week? If she is, I'm gonna seriously *freak*," I said.

"I already talked to her about that. She knows the deal, and said she's sorry to offend you," he replied.

"Okay, then. *Don't* piss me off," I said.

He leaned in and I let him kiss me. Then, he pulled away but stayed close enough for his breath to make my skin shiver.

"I won't," he said.

twenty six
CRUEL FOR THE SUMMER ♡

Keeping a straight face as we crossed under the US 90 overpass in Pauline's Mustang was an exercise in restraint. With the windows down, she dropped the clutch and shifted into the lowest gear the transmission could handle, then mashed down with her right foot. The unmistakable howl of the V8 reverberated off the concrete supports as she slapped through the gears.

I couldn't help but yelp with excitement as the torque pressed us into our seats, leaving Becka and Wayne far behind when she finally let off the gas and slowed back down to five over the speed limit.

By then, we were well on our way across the bridge over the delta where it emptied into Mobile Bay. To the left, flanking the north side of Bay John, was Meaher State Park, where in fourth grade we had taken a school trip to the Five Rivers Delta Center, and where Granddaddy liked to go fishing and camping to male-bond with the boys.

After crossing the Blakeley River, Apalachee River, and Chacaloochee Bay, we crossed over US 98. By then, Becka had caught up to us in the Camry and we were cruising at a more re-laxed pace.

As we passed over the bay at the mouths of the Tensaw River and Spanish River, the USS Alabama sat docked off to our left as the three prominent skyscrapers of Mobile gleamed in the evening sun.

The return trip home from Clearwater took just under eight hours with all the stops we made on the way back. We left after grabbing breakfast at eight. Pauline had successfully won the argument on which way to take, and we left Terrell's college caravan behind as we cut through Tampa to follow Interstate 75 through Ocala and Gainesville to link up with Interstate 10 in Lake City.

When we reached Tallahassee, Wayne checked in with Terrell and his squad to discover that they were approaching Perry, going back the same way we came.

As we neared Downtown, Wayne texted his brother again at the Government Street exit to discover that Terrell and the college entourage had just left Pensacola after stopping again for the last time.

The sun was making the last three and a half hours of its journey toward the horizon when we entered the claustrophobic George C. Wallace Tunnel.

I absolutely hated traveling through it and wished Pauline had taken Old Spanish Trail to pass through all the industrial terminals and cross the Cochrane Africatown Bridge over the Mobile River. From there it was a short drive to Interstate 165 at Bay Bridge Road in Prichard.

Pauline didn't roll the windows down and floor it through the tunnel as she usually would. I imagined it was because we were stuck behind a lifted diesel truck with a vinyl Dixie flag stretched across the rear glass. It roared while coal rolling us, spewing out black fumes behind it from the oversized exhaust poking out from under the truck bed.

Thankfully, they continued on Interstate 10 as we exited to circle around over the freeway to Water Street in Downtown. We passed the Renaissance Riverview Plaza Hotel on the left and the Mobile Convention Center, where memories of Prom were fresh on my mind, to the right. Beyond that, the Battlehouse towered above us on the left.

After a while, we crossed through the traffic lights at the intersection at Beauregard Street. The historic Gulf, Mobile and Ohio Passenger Terminal sat on the corner, recently renovated and restored after being nearly destroyed by flooding from Hurricane Katrina.

Water Street became Interstate 165, and just a short minute or two later, I glanced through the side view mirror and watched Becka take the exit for US 90 to drop Wayne off in Prichard.

Before long, we merged onto Interstate 65, and a few minutes later, Pauline pulled up in front of my house in Saraland.

She popped the trunk, slid out of her seat, and helped me grab the bags from Auntie Beanie's shopping spree at the International Plaza and Bay Street shopping center in Tampa.

I spent my last full day in Clearwater hanging out with Auntie Beanie in Ybor City, where we had an Argentinian lunch of Arroz Chaufa de Carne at El Puerto on East Fifth. From there, we went to the Florida Aquarium, as we did usually once a year when I would visit her during the summer.

After shopping at the mall by the airport, we stopped in Clearwater to grab Chinese takeout from Asian Pearl before heading to her two bedroom corner condo in the waterfront complex on Coe Road.

We ate dinner out on her tiled terrace and girl-talked about anything and everything as jazz music played from the stereo speakers inside. The panoramic views of Clearwater Harbor were pristine from both the terrace and the windows of her condo. The Belleair Country Club was visible from the guest room where I spent the night.

Auntie Beanie dropped me back off just in time for breakfast with my friends before making the trip back to Mobile.

Momma's Buick was parked in its usual spot, the hideous sofa on the porch was still an embarrassing eyesore, and I desperately wanted to go right back to Clearwater as I stood on the porch, hesitant to try the doorknob.

Becka has been in the house many times, although it was still embarrassing when she would stop by. She said she understood, but that didn't change the fact that the sight of my momma sprawled out on the sofa, with no bra on and her titties hanging out her pajamas, drooling and spazzed out on prescription meds was sickening.

The smell of her unwashed, unkept hair, the funk of not having showers for maybe weeks and wearing the same old ratty Christmas pajamas stayed in your nostrils.

I'd be out somewhere with friends or at school and I swear I could smell her as if she was right in front of me, and it was nauseating.

Becka was around when things first started getting ridiculous, and she's even seen Momma at her worst. But it was another thing altogether for Pauline or anyone else for that matter to see just how bad my momma had become.

I made it a point to avoid opening the door wide when I found it unlocked. My plan to keep Pauline from peeking inside back-fired as I squeezed into the house and Pauline followed, carrying the rest of the shopping bags. I hoped she would just leave them on the porch.

I was met with a piercing glare from my momma as she stood in the living room, her hair looking as crusty and ragged as ever. She looked like she had just crawled out from under the house and her musty smelling blanket sat in a heap on the floor between the television and coffee table.

I suddenly smelled the pungent odor of piss and turned around to catch Pauline grimace with a sour look on her face. I winced and grew even more disgusted.

"Did you have a nice trip?" Momma said, harshly.

I frowned at her.

"Yes, I did," I replied.

"You didn't have sense enough to ask me if you could go any-where?" she said with a sniff.

I looked at her oddly for a second before answering. She was awfully coherent all of a sudden, although her speech slurred and she struggled to stand up straight.

"Um, I *did* ask you. In fact, Taylor was standing right here when I did it. You said be careful."

"I didn't say you could go anywhere, little girl," Momma said, pointing at me. Her wrist bent at an odd angle, and she looked like she was about to fall over. She was clearly blitzed on whatever she had been taking.

"You think you're slick, sneaking out of here going God knows where for an entire week, and didn't bother calling nobody or answering your phone. Nana's been over here losing her britches worried sick over you, and your grandfather nearly had a stroke," she added.

"Now I know you're lying, 'cause nobody called my phone," I replied, sharply.

Pauline's eyes grew wide as she watched Momma's face turn four different shades of red. Her eyes were piercing as I watched her chest rise and fall with every breath she took.

"And on that note, I'm gonna go. Call me later, Manda," she said, setting the bags down on the floor before backing away and stepping outside. She closed the door quietly behind her.

Momma waited until she was gone before stepping toward me.

"Who the *hell* do you think you're talking to?" she snarled.

"What's your problem, Momma? I was with Auntie Beanie for Spring Break. It's no big deal," I said.

"That wasn't your aunt dropping you back off, now was it? You think I was born yesterday, *little girl?* You ain't too old to get your butt tore up. You're grounded for the rest of the school year, and the entire summer. Hell, till the reelection."

"*What?* You can't ground me for that. You told me I could go! Call Taylor. Seriously!" I dropped my bags and pulled out my cellphone.

I was surprised when she quickly snatched it out of my hand, considering how tanked she was.

"Who you think you're calling? Grounded means no phone. TV. Nothing," she said, slipping my phone into the pocket of her pajamas.

I inhaled slowly, boiling over with fury and rage.

"You told me I could go!" I said, loudly. "You can't take my phone away from me. You treat me like some animal, and I'm sick of it! Give me back my phone!"

I lunged for her pajamas pocket and she twisted away from me.

"You'd better calm yourself," she said.

I noticed two empty pill bottles on the table with the cap missing from one. I reached for them. The first bottle was Momma's prescription for Hydrocodone. The other bottle was Morphine Sulphate extended-release tablets. The name on the bottle wasn't hers.

"Who is Dana Stauffer?" I asked with a frown.

Momma grabbed the pill bottles from my hand.

"Keep your hands off things that don't belong to you," she said.

"You're just acting like a crazy woman, feenin' 'cause you ran out of pills to pop. What? Is your little drug dealer on vacay? You gotta take it out on me?" I snapped.

Momma reached her arm out and slapped me across my face.

Shocked by the sting, I balled my fist up and without thinking, snapped my right arm and cracked my momma square in the jaw. She buckled to the floor onto her knees, stunned for a moment, before reaching up to nurse her face.

Momma slowly looked up at me in horror, her eyes wide and welling up with tears.

"Get. The hell. Out!"

I took a step back, not believing that I just straight up cold-cocked my own momma like I was in a barroom brawl.

The look on her face was one I had never seen before, and she began to shake and tremble uncontrollably.

"I'm not kidding, little girl. *Get the hell out of my house!"* she screamed.

Just then, Nana Jane stepped inside the house from the backyard. She saw Momma kneeling on the floor with her hand covering her cheek, and her eyes immediately went to my balled fist. It felt good to frost Momma's flakes, and I was ready to light her up again if she so much as flinched.

When the dawn of understanding illuminated Nana's face, she shuffled over to us in her house shoes and grabbed my arm.

"What did you do, young lady?" she said, sharply.

"She just hauled off and hit me. I told her to get out," Momma said. My old hag of a grandmother looked at me with a cold stare. I tensed up in case I needed to mop her grill too.

"Nana, she said I could go with Auntie Beanie for Spring Break, so I went. Then I get back and she swears she didn't let me go, and Taylor was here when she said it."

"You can stop with the *lying*. She walked her narrow behind in this house with one of her friends. She wasn't with Sabrina Gayle," Momma said.

"None of that is relevant, right now. Did you strike your mother?" Nana Jane asked me.

"Yeah, 'cause she hit me first," I said. "Freaking child abuse."

"Looks like you deserved it. Lucky that's all she done," Nana Jane said. "You lucky she ain't tag your little legs with a switch."

"You're siding with her? After I just stood here and told you she said I could go?"

"You ain't got no business laying your hands on your mother, girl, nor sassing anybody. I don't care what she done said or did, you ain't nothin' but a child, and a child should stay in their place,"

Nana said. "Lord says 'Children, honor thy father and mother, that thy days be long upon the land which the Lord thy God giveth thee.' If you can't respect your mother under her roof and out from 'neath it, then you need to find somewhere else to be. You best do what she said, and go on."

"And where am I supposed to go?" I asked, frowning.

"You *grown*, girl. You gon' have to figure that out for yourself," she said. "But you ain't stayin' here. You big girl enough to raise your hands to your mother, well, you big girl enough to be on your own."

I stared at her before glaring at Momma, who finally stood up looking victimized.

"You know what? Taylor comes and goes however and whenever she feels like it. She got knocked up, and you practically threw her a party. You let the boys get away with murder. But you both ride me so hard I don't even have space to breathe. Why do you treat me differently than everybody else?"

Momma sighed.

"You ain't everybody else. You don't get it. I expect so much more out of you, Amanda," she hissed.

"How are you gonna expect more of me, when you can't even get your own crap together, Momma?" I retorted.

She sighed again.

"Nobody's perfect. I'm trying to work on myself. I know my problems. But you got way more going for you than I could ever dream of for myself," she said. "You just don't know."

"You contradict yourself," I said. "Well, I need my cellphone back, so I can call a ride."

"You don't pay for that phone, no way. Always taking things for granted. I said *go on*," Nana Jane said, shooing me to the door.

"Ya'll are something else. Talk about the pot calling the kettle black," I snapped as I grabbed my shopping bags and luggage, setting them outside on the porch. "Standing there quoting scriptures like you don't do nothing wrong."

Nana Jane followed behind me and held her hand out at the entryway.

"You know what? She got like this 'cause you let her. Like you really care. She's out there copping pills off the street and you're getting on me about something she *said* I could do," I gave her the key, and she closed the door in my face.

"The next step down the ladder is *heroin!*" I screamed as I pounded my fist on the door. I heard the lock tumblers falling into place, and I shook my head.

Standing on the porch, I fumed with my heart pounding so hard and fast that I thought I might be having a medical emergency.

It would be a long walk to Becka's, and she may not even be home. I had no way of calling Pauline. My only option was to go to Maddie and Allie's house, in hopes they would be home and let me use their phone.

I combined what I could and slung my shopping bags over my shoulder and dragged my luggage as I walked over to the twin's house.

When I knocked on the door, their daddy answered. The twins weren't home and their momma was out running errands, but he let me use their house phone. I called Auntie Beanie first. After a few rings, she answered.

"Hello?"

"Auntie Beanie?" I breathed.

"Hey, sweetie. What's the matter?" she asked with her intuition in overdrive.

Mr. Wentzler gave me privacy and stepped out of the kitchen.

"Can you come get me? So I can move in with you? Please?" I asked, breaking down into tears.

"Why, baby? What's wrong? What happened?"

"It's Momma and Nana Jane. We got in a freaking fight and now they're cruel for the summer. They kicked me out. I hate them now more than I ever did."

My eyes stung as I told her what transpired back at the house.

After I finished talking, she was silent for a little while, listening to my sniffles.

"Listen, baby. I'm so sorry. I wish there was something I could do. I mean, I could come get you for the summer, but that would be something I would have to talk to your mother about," she said.

"She's buggin' the freak out, Auntie Beanie! She's never gonna agree to that," I said.

"I'll talk to her," she sighed. "Just go back home and I'm gonna call her right now."

"Oh, no. I'm not going back there. Ever. Not after today. I'm sick of it," I said.

"I know sweetheart, but life doesn't work that way. I can't just come up and get you without her permission. I have to talk to her first," she said.

"You know what? Forget it. I'm sorry I called," I said.

I hung up before she could finish her next sentence and called Becka's cell.

She answered on the first ring.

"Who dis?" she said, giggling. I heard Wayne talking in the background.

"Hey," I said. "It's me."

"What up, girl. That's a weird number. Where you calling me from?" she asked, smacking her gum loudly.

"I'm at Maddie and Allie's," I said. "Using their house phone. Me and my momma had a fight, she hit me, I stole her back, and she kicked me out."

"Dang girl. You over there Supermanin' your mom dukes. That's insane. You okay?"

"Yeah. I'm okay. You think I could stay at your place for a while?"

"Girl, don't even trip. I got you. We over here getting pizza at Benzi's. Wayne decided he was gonna chill up here after we dropped off his bags at his crib, so we close to you. Gimme a few minutes for this order to be ready and we'll be there. You hungry? I got two cheeses and two pepperonis. And wings. Cousins are over so, you know how they be eating," she said with a snicker.

"I'm not really hungry right now," I said.

"Well, if you want something later, we can go back out and pick something up. Or I'm sure there are leftovers in the fridge," she said. "Let me go so I can get this and get there."

"Okay," I said. "Thank you."

"Girl, it's no problem," Becka replied, before hanging up.

I put the cordless phone back on the receiver and stepped out of the kitchen. Mr. Wentzler was polishing his shoes in the living room.

He looked up when he saw me.

"Did you work everything out?" he asked.

"Yeah, Becka's coming to get me," I said.

"Well. I don't know the specifics of what's going on, but sometimes family can be tough. It gets better, though. I promise," he said, smiling. "You can wait here as long as you need. The Missus will be back any moment with Maddie and Allie, so you won't have to be bored hanging out with this old man for too much longer."

"Thank you Mr. Wentzler," I said.

"Don't mention it. Hey, listen, I've got to finish up a few things for church tonight. You're welcome to take control of the remote here and watch whatever you want. I'll get out of your hair," he said, passing the remote control to their big screen TV to me. "You know how to work the satellite box? We changed providers so it's a new one, but it's pretty much the same set up."

"I'll figure it out, Mr. Wentzler. Thanks," I said.

He nodded as he shuffled down the hall and up the stairs with his freshly polished dress shoes in hand.

I slumped down into the leather sofa facing the screen. My face was expressionless as I watched the 76ers playing the Orlando Magic. Neither one of the teams were playing like they actually wanted to win the game. Similarly, I wondered why I even tried.

Senior Year

twenty seven

EIGHTEEN ♡

The boat rocked against the boat slip as I stepped aboard. Pauline reached out to grab my arm as I stumbled to gain my balance.

"You don't want to fall in there. I can't save you," she said, laughing.

"Why would you get on a boat if you can't swim?" I asked.

"First of all, that's insane, 'cause you know I can swim. Secondly, I didn't say I couldn't swim. I just can't save you. I just got my hair done," she said.

"Isn't a little too cold to be out on a boat? It's not summer anymore," I replied as I found a spot to sit on the loungers along the boat's starboard side.

Pauline's brother, Javion, sat at the wheel, his shorts tight against his muscular, hairy thighs. He smirked at me when he noticed that I was eyeballing his Corona flip flops. I was trying to figure out why his toes were so dirty.

"It's seventy degrees. Quit being a baby," Javion said, pulling his sunshades down over his forehead to rest them on the bridge of his nose.

"It's colder on the water," I replied simply.

Javion mocked me, imitating my voice with whiny accuracy.

"Speaking of babies, why didn't you invite your Bae?" Pauline asked, settling down next to me. Becka and Wayne sat across from us on the port side and snuggled up under a beautiful Navajo print blanket.

"Yo, my bro's in Cali for that internship," Wayne chimed in. "He over there livin' that West Coast vibe."

"You talk to him? When did he leave?" Pauline asked me.

"Yeah, I talked to him this morning. He was out there all summer. He came back here and then left again after the Vigor homecoming game," I said.

After attending Satsuma's Homecoming game with Becka, where we lost miserably to Daphne by nearly nine touchdowns, I went to the dance and was, to the shock of me and probably everyone else, crowned runner up Homecoming Queen to Britt Wolfe, head cheerleader.

Chase Gonzales, crowned Homecoming King, asked for a dance with me. He made it totally clear that he liked me all through middle and high school. I turned him down, not just because I was with Terrell, but because the thought of dancing with a dude wearing an oversized tiara in a red tuxedo just felt weird.

Becka tripped out on me about it, saying "Don't be that girl, Manda. It's *one* dance." She made me feel bad, so I ended up caving and dancing with him to a fast Rihanna song.

The following Friday, I went with Becka to Vigor's Homecoming game to see Wayne play against Citronelle High, where Vigor won by a conversion. Terrell met us there. Becka went to the dance later that night, and I went out to dinner with Terrell at a Mexican restaurant in Tillman's Corner before he caught his flight back to L.A. the next day.

He asked if I would ever go home and make amends with my momma. I told him she had a better chance of beating Barack Obama in the next election.

I hadn't talked to my momma or anyone else in my family all summer. Auntie Beanie reached out to Becka and Mrs. Canales, but I told them I didn't want to talk to her either, angry that she didn't come get me.

I found her birthday present to me, a new iPhone 3G already activated with a stupidly generous data plan, sitting on Becka's bed in its packaging next to the box it was shipped in, along with new clothes.

I took the phone out of its box to be nosy and kept it out. It was almost fully charged and already ringing when we left the house.

I watched as Javion got up to untether the boat from the dock. We teetered with his every movement, and the wake from another larger boat sloshed against the bow. Overhead, a pair of seagulls cried into the breeze, and a line of pelicans swooped along the waves just beyond the pier, heading toward the Gulf.

"So, is he staying in Cali now, or what?" Pauline asked.

I sent an annoyed glance toward Becka and Wayne, who were wrapped up in their own nuzzling.

"You wanna answer that, Wayne?" I said, finally.

"Answer what?" he said, pulling his lips away from Becka's neck, looking confused.

"Umm, is Tee staying in Cali, or is he coming back here after his internship? He won't give me a straight answer," I said.

"You know just about as much as I do. He ain't said nothin' to me neither, know'm sayin'?" Wayne said, licking his lips.

Pauline sniffed, loudly.

"Well, that sucks," she said.

"I'm not worried about it," I lied, as Javion returned to the captain's chair and started the boat. He turned on the music to a hip hop and rap music radio station and slowly pulled us away from the boat slip.

As soon as we were away from the pier, I immediately felt foolish for not bringing something heavier than a hoodie. The temperature on shore was deceiving. Out on the water, it was much colder than I thought it would be. I hugged myself and tucked my hands into my sleeves, wondering how Javion wasn't growing icicles on his leg hair follicles.

Just then, I felt a weight on my shoulders.

I looked up to see that Pauline had draped a large beach towel over my arms.

"You won't need that long. It'll warm up some more. It's still kind of early," she said.

I nodded as Javion pushed the lever to speed up. The bow rose and I grabbed the handrail and braced myself in the seat. My hair whipped behind my head and against my neck as I squinted against the wind.

Now that the boat was stable, I leaned my head back a little and closed my eyes to the sun, pulling the beach towel tighter around my shoulders. I felt Pauline move closer to me, wrapping her arm around me. I opened my eyes to glance at her and she squeezed tightly.

"Happy Birthday, Manda Pants!" she yelled. I smiled and hugged her back, as the boat continued down Mobile Bay, past the Naval Complex.

We weren't on the water for long. We stayed close to shore and passed under the Coastal Connection bridge for Route 193 to flank the northern edge of Dauphin Island, heading toward the Mississippi. Then, we turned around and headed back.

After docking, we disembarked and headed inside Pauline's place to warm up in the living room.

Pauline and Javion lingered in the kitchen making hot apple cider and spiked lattes. As I leaned back and sunk into the cushions, I could smell cookies being baked in the oven.

Wayne and Becka disappeared upstairs, and I shook my head as I watched them.

"Don't forget to strap up!" I yelled through my cupped hands. They giggled like two kids in a schoolyard and I laughed harder.

Becka trampled back downstairs a few moments later, brandishing her phone.

"Yo, your aunt keeps blowing up my phone. You must've left the cell she bought you at my house. You should just talk to her," she said, shuffling her sock-clad feet across the wood floor to stand in front of me. She shoved the phone in my face as it vibrated insistently.

"How many times has she called?" I asked.

"Enough to make me want to peel my skin off," Becka replied, clicking the home button to answer.

I reluctantly took the phone and whispered a greeting.

"Sugarbear?"

I breathed deeply.

"Hey," I answered.

"You've had me worried sick about you. Why haven't you called me? Did you get the package I sent?" Auntie Beanie asked.

"Yeah, I got it. Thanks," I replied. "I left the phone at Becka's by accident. We're at Pauline's now."

"Happy Birthday, sweetheart," she said. "Are you enjoying your day?"

"You could say that," I said.

She was quiet for a moment, and then she spoke again.

"That's good to hear. Are you going to go back home? They're worried sick about you over there, too," she said.

"They know exactly how to find me," I replied harshly. "They're not as worried as they claim to be."

Auntie Beanie sighed.

"I'm sorry I couldn't come get you. That whole thing is… complicated," she said.

"Everything about Momma and my family is complicated," I said with a sniff.

"You could have flown down here for the summer," she said. "Why don't you come down for Christmas and Thanksgiving? I can book your flight. It's late, and it might be slim pickings, but I'm sure I can find something available."

"I don't really wanna fly," I said. "I'm good here."

"You don't have to fly. I can come get you, if that's what you want."

"I'm good here," I repeated.

"Okay. Well, if you change your mind, you know where to reach me. And don't worry about your minutes on that phone I sent, it's an unlimited plan."

"Thanks," I said.

"You're welcome. Have you thought about college? Where you want to go? There's the University of South Florida and the University of Tampa right here. You could move here so you can go to school."

I was silent for a moment, listening to Auntie Beanie making crinkling noises as she rustled around with whatever she was doing. Pauline walked over from the kitchen and handed me a cinnamon smelling, amber colored, hot alcoholic drink of some sort. I sipped it, burning my upper lip. It tasted like butterscotch.

Auntie Beanie continued.

"You're eighteen now and considered a legal adult which means you can do whatever you want to do. I'm sure you want to finish your last six months of school there. But you can come here when you graduate, and no one can have a say in it," she said. "It's your choice."

"Doesn't Momma have to sign for me to go to college?" I asked.

"No, now that you're eighteen, you can sign for yourself. And since you've been working a job since the summer, and haven't lived at home most of the year, you can file your taxes and possibly be an independent student. So make sure you file your own taxes in January."

"I don't know anything about that," I said, risking another sip. I was careful to blow on it for a moment before drinking.

"I can help you with that, when the time comes. And if you're not an independent student, you can register under me for financial aid."

"I might not need that. I talked to a recruiter. Or somebody."

"Military?" she asked, sounding horrified.

"No. NYU," I said.

"For basketball? I thought you quit the team this year?" Auntie Beanie sounded relieved. "It's a shame, 'cause you're good."

"Yeah, I quit. Recruiters aren't coming to see sucky Satsuma's joke of a women's varsity basketball team. The women's volley-ball, softball and soccer teams get all the airplay," I said. "It was for music. They got my application and video audition."

"Ah, I see," she said, her voice suddenly changing. "What did they say?"

"NYU is giving me a full music scholarship. As long as I grad-uate with a 3.5 GPA," I said. "Right now I still have a 3.9, so I'm good."

I could hear Auntie Beanie squealing and clapping through the phone.

"That's *great*, Manda! I'm so proud of you. But why so far away? You could probably get the same offer at a school here, if not academic," she said.

I breathed out slowly.

"I need a change. I need to get as far away from here as possi-ble," I whispered. Pauline was laughing at something Javion said, and Becka and Wayne were upstairs knocking boots, obviously, so no one would hear me.

Auntie Beanie was quiet for a few moments. Then, I heard her clear her throat.

"You have to do what's best for you. It's your choice, now, and it's your life to live. You live it to the fullest. If it's your dream to go to New York, that's where you should go," she said.

I smiled.

"Maybe I'll come down for breaks between now and gradua-tion," I said.

"That would be nice. And you really need to call home, let them know you're safe," she said.

"I'm not doing that," I replied.

"Just think about it," she said.

I didn't answer her.

"Okay, well, I'll let you go. Please use that phone to keep me posted on how you're doing from now on," she said. "I love you, sweet girl."

"I will," I answered. "And I love you, too."

After hanging up, I realized Pauline had gone to answer a knock at the door.

Shuffling in through the door, dancing with balloons in hand, Kayli, followed by Maddie and Allie, Lucas, Keisha and the rest of the Lady Gators basketball team, Becka's older high school age cousins, and a few other kids from my classes that I hardly talked to walked in bearing gift bags.

Javion turned the music up, and someone turned the lights down and lit up a strobe light. Smoke curled along the floor and the house became a party in an instant.

I stood up as Becka and Wayne came back downstairs with big smiles on their faces.

I walked over to Becka and handed her phone back.

"You've got one more surprise, chica," she said with a cackle.

"What?" I asked.

A hand tapped me on my shoulder. I spun around to see Terrell standing there in a button-up shirt and jeans. He smiled and handed me a bouquet of lilies.

"I know you love these," he said with a grin.

"I thought you were in Cali on an internship," I said.

"Yeah. I was. Now I'm here. With you," he said.

"For how long?" I asked. He leaned forward and lowered his lips to mine, kissing me forcefully. I accepted his kiss, wrapping my arms around his neck.

"Happy Birthday," he said with a chuckle.

"Seriously. For how long?" I asked again.

"Why? You trying to get rid of me already?" he asked, snickering.

"You're not funny. Can't give me a straight answer. Just like when I keep asking you if you're staying in Cali after your internship is over."

"See, I was trying to surprise you, and you're trippin'," he replied, kissing my cheek and neck.

"Just answer my question and I won't get worked up," I said, with a pout.

"Okay. Okay. So my plan was to finish up this internship, then see what you were doing after graduation. Depending on what kind of offers I get that way, I wanted to see if you'd come out there with me. I mean, I don't know where you were planning to go, if you were planning to go anywhere, but there are plenty of colleges out that way," he said, placing his hands on my waist. He nudged me to sway with the music, dancing in place.

"You want me to move with you to L.A.?" I asked, a broad smile splitting my face in half.

"Yeah, if I can get a good offer on a job in my field," he said. "More opportunity in L.A. than here, for what I can do. I linked up with some connections that might pan out."

I smiled again.

"Maybe," I said.

"*Maybe?*" he chuckled again.

"Maybe. I'm still mad at you," I said. He kissed me again, softer.

"Why you mad at me? 'Cause I left you all summer?"

"That's exactly right," I replied.

"You know I didn't mean to. I had to take an internship as part of my graduation requirement, and it was either Cali or DC. I can't get my actual diploma in my hand until I complete it. So I picked the better weather."

I nodded.

"I mean, I get it. I wouldn't pick DC either," I said with a giggle.

"Anyway, I got you a present, but you can't have it 'till later tonight."

"Oh, yeah? And what's that?" I asked, cocking my head to the side. He grinned, pulling me closer to him. I nuzzled my nose against his neck and breathed him in. I loved the smell of his skin.

"It's a surprise," he said.

"You and your surprises," I replied as Pauline tapped me on the shoulder.

"Forgetting something? Letting it get cold, over here," she said as she handed me my butterscotch tasting drink. "I nuked it for you."

"Thanks," I said.

Pauline looked at Terrell.

"Want one?" she asked.

"What is it?" He looked at the small clear mug in my hand and frowned.

"A little something something," Pauline replied with a cackle.

"Naw, I'm good. I've got to drive tonight," he said. "And I don't really get down like that, but ya'll have fun."

"You're such a *punk*," Pauline said as she spun around and walked away.

Terrell chuckled again.

"Your friends are crazy," he said.

"Tell me about it," I replied, leaning my head back to close my eyes.

We danced again for a few moments as if no one else was there, before rejoining society and snacking on the cookies and goodies Pauline whipped up in the kitchen with her brother.

Having everyone there with me made my birthday incredible, and I quickly lost track of time amid all the laughing, joking, clowning around, and hot alcoholic drinks.

I was getting tipsy, and Terrell began to keep a careful eye on me with his over protective vigilance.

Hours past midnight, after most everyone had left, Becka and Wayne retreated to one of the guest rooms, making out before they even got to the door. Pauline disappeared into the master bedroom. Javion passed out downstairs on the loveseat with the Playstation on.

Kayli crashed upstairs in the other guest bedroom with me after my failed attempt to get Terrell to spend the night.

"I'll give you your birthday gift tomorrow, when you're not drizzed," he said.

Angrily, I flung myself down on top of the comforter, groaning as the dizziness made my head spin.

He left quietly after tucking me in beneath the covers, and I quickly got irritated that he was such a gentleman, unwilling to take advantage of me being inebriated.

I felt someone lift the comforter and crawl into bed beside me and realized I felt soft bare skin. Groaning that it was obviously not Terrell with a change of heart, I twisted to see that Kayli had stripped down to her bra and panties, and put her icy feet against my leg.

Yelping from the cold touch, I kicked at her and she flipped over with a moan and thrust her butt into my lower back.

I woke up the next morning sweating through my clothes. Kayli had left already, and I could smell Pauline making a late breakfast.

twenty eight

CHAMPIONSHIP GAME ♡

Vigor V. Russellville at Legion Field

December 2008

The thunderous pounding in the stands echoed across the stadium as the Vigor Wolves erupted from the tunnel and smashed through the banner.

Colored smoke bombs went off at the feet of the players, the atmosphere was intense, and I was caught up in the wave of excitement, clapping until my palms hurt, screaming until my throat burned and jumping up and down next to Terrell, Becka and Pauline.

"This is freaking *nuts*," Pauline yelled in my ear. "The whole stadium is packed. You'd think we were at a college game."

"I know. And it looks like a college stadium," I said, feeling the chill in the air as I pulled the hood of my burgundy Lady Gators hoodie over my head.

"It *is* a college stadium. This is where UA Birmingham and Auburn play. You think this is insane, wait till you see an actual college game," Becka said.

"Oh *snap*, Crimson Tide and *Tigers!*" Pauline said with her hands cupped around her mouth.

"What you know about that Alabama football?" Terrell asked with a smirk.

"More than you think," Pauline said with a cackle. "My dad and his bro squad are always in front of the big screen when a game is on. Game night at my house is freaking ridiculous."

"Yeah, it's like that when I go to Maddie and Allie's place. Their dad is a die hard Crimson Tide fan. Flags out in the front yard, those little mini-flags flapping from the windows of their Explorer. Shot glasses and beer koozies. Grown man jerseys. All that," I said.

Terrell nudged me with his arm and pointed. I followed the direction of his finger and saw his brother, Wayne, waving at us from the field.

"I told him we'd be sitting in Section 35," Terrell said.

"What would have happened if there was no place to sit over here? Did you have a back up plan, genius?" I teased.

"Well, it worked out. Didn't have to Brody anybody for their seats. So there," he said with a chuckle.

"Hey you guys," Pauline interrupted. "Snack now or snack later?"

"Girl, you always hungry. Skinny as a potato stick," Becka said with a snort.

"You've got nerve, *Becka Snacks*. Every time I see you, you're always eating something. As a matter of fact, forget the concession stand. Whatcha got in that beach tote you're carrying around?" I asked, reaching to grab the bag from its perch next to her.

"Look here. None of your business," she said, as she grabbed the bag before I could get to it and plopped it down on her opposite side. I shook my head at her.

"How did you get that bag in here, anyway? They got rules about clear bags and freezer bags and all that stupid stuff. Blame 9-11," Terrell asked.

"For me to know, and you never to find out," Becka teased, sticking out her tongue.

"Probably your overnight bag. Guess you and Wayne gonna celebrate after the game with a little bed spring action, huh? You better be careful. Mess around and get knocked up. Kiss that medical degree *goodbye,*" Pauline said, producing a bottle of Coke. She twisted the cap and took a long drag.

"I'm like, never getting pregnant. We strap it up. And, truthfully, that's none of your business, Leenie, so stay in ya lane," Becka said with a cackle.

"She's right, though. Ya'll running around like jack rabbits. You better be careful," I added.

Becka cut her eyes at me.

"I know you ain't got room to talk, with you and T-Bone over there getting it in," she said with a smirk.

"Actually, they haven't done anything. Yet," Pauline said. "My girl's a certified virgin."

I cut my eyes at her and frowned.

"What? It's true," she added.

I rolled my eyes at her and looked at Becka as she tossed her head back and laughed.

"Oh my god, girl, you're still a *virgin*? I thought ya'll hit it on your birthday?" Becka said in hushed tones, covering her mouth.

"No. We *didn't*. Can we not talk about this right now? I'm going to the concession stand. Anybody want anything?" I turned to work my way through the throng, with Pauline right behind me.

"You know where they are?" Terrell asked.

"Nope. But I'll figure it out," I said.

"There are six main ones. Some on the ground level. We're closer to the ones on the second level. You gotta go up more. And they've got food trucks out in the Village. Want me to show you?"

"I don't need an escort. I got this," I replied. He threw his hands up in surrender.

"Everything's questionable. Just don't eat the hotdogs. They suck," he said loudly. "I'd go to the food trucks if it were me. At least that's *probably* real food."

"Girl, I'm so sorry for putting you on blast!" Becka yelled after me.

I was about to flick my middle finger up at her, but I thought better of it and shooed her away with my right hand as I continued carefully stepping toward the aisle.

We nearly clambered up the rows until we reached the second level walkway, then headed over toward the nearest gaping hole in the bleachers. When we reached the seven row high entrance through the metal stands to the second level, Pauline tapped me on the shoulder.

I turned to look at her.

"So, when are you gonna tell him about New York?" she asked.

"I'll get around to it. Plenty of time. I haven't made up my mind yet on if I'm going or not," I replied.

"Um, yeah. And yet, that's the only school you applied to. Even though you have mad offers on the table."

I frowned.

"I've got time," I said.

"No, you don't. There are application deadlines, and they're coming up fast, right after winter break," she said.

I quickly glanced back up at the scoreboard to see that Vigor had just scored their second touchdown against Russellville and I wasn't even paying attention.

"I know," I replied. We walked through the crowd of people until we reached the line at concessions and stood in place to wait.

"You say that, but. Look, I'm just looking out for you," Pauline said. "I think you really want to go to New York, but you're afraid to tell him 'cause you think you're gonna lose him. You have to put your future first. I mean, you could get to college and mess around and meet other people. It's different after we graduate. Things change."

"And how do you know," I said, spinning around to face her with my arms crossed.

"I've got an older brother. Or did you forget?" She raised an eyebrow as she chuckled. "He was seeing this girl, Roxanne, all through junior high and high. They were inseparable. I honestly thought they were gonna get married, have kids. You know. The whole gamut."

She exhaled, pulled her cellphone out of her bra and checked it before tucking it back in between her breasts.

"Then they both go off to college. She goes to University of Tennessee, he heads off to Louisiana State. They swore to stay together the whole time, but, I mean they didn't even make it through first semester." Pauline sniffed, reaching up to pick something out of my hair. It was lint. She flicked it away and focused her eyes on me.

"That's not gonna happen to us," I said. "And I don't know why you keep pressing me about it. We talked about this on the way back from Spring Break."

"Manda. He's already like, older than you. He just graduated college. He's doing an internship on the other side of the country from where you'll be. You see how hard it is for you guys to see each other, now, and you're just over half a country a way. Just wait till you're in New York," she said.

"When he's done with his internship, maybe he can take a job where I'm at," I said.

"You need to be realistic," Pauline replied. "I mean, you two haven't even done it yet, and I know how guys are. They're some needy little things."

"I'm not liking you too much right now," I said, feeling my cheeks getting red. She was starting to stress me out.

"I'm just being real with you, Manda. That's all. Just think about it. I don't want you getting hurt," she said.

There was a thunderous roar across the stadium. I turned to get a peek at what was going on. Where we were standing, I couldn't see the scoreboard or the field.

Two dudes walked by with their hats facing backward in forest green Wolves sweatshirts.

"Hey, you know what happened?" I asked them.

One of them looked me up and down like I was a slab of bacon sizzling in a skillet. His gaze dropped to my legs and my boobs, and I rolled my eyes at him and focused on the more polite one.

"Yeah, they just got another interception. Wolves got the ball again, and they're at the twenty," he said.

"Holy cow, they're on fire tonight," Pauline replied in a sarcastic tone. I looked at her with an odd look on my face and the two dudes scurried off to wherever it was that they were going.

"What's your deal?" I asked her, thrown off by her expression.

"I'm good, Manda. You know what you want? We're almost up. Well, in the next century, maybe. The line seems like it keeps getting longer."

"I think people might be cutting in front of us," I said.

"No, I think this line is actually, literally growing more humans," Pauline replied. "Look. Near the front. I swear I see an embryo sitting on the concrete. Just chilling."

It took what seemed to be hours before we were close enough to be in view of the menu. Standing there with my arms folded across my chest, I scrunched up my lips as I perused the menu. I had to squint to see it clearly. There wasn't much to offer, aside from the usual peanuts, popcorn, nachos, barbecue *something* sandwiches, hot dogs and sausages.

"I'll probably just get a bag of popcorn and a Sprite. You know what? Why does it seem like everyone here is cheering for Vigor?" I asked.

"Beats me. Maybe they need a win," she replied.

I lowered my voice.

"For your information, not that it's any of your business, but we *did* do it," I whispered.

She looked at me and her eyebrows soared to her hairline.

"How? When?" she snapped loudly. I shushed her, looking around to make sure no one was in earshot.

"Remember Spring Break? Lexi the Ex showed up. That night at the resort him and his college freaks were staying at, after we went to the Pier?"

"Yeah. We were all there. Who can forget *that* drama?"

"Lexi was still all up on Tee, and I went to the bathroom," I said.

"Yeah, you were pissed," she said.

"He came in after me to check on me," I said.

"Uh huh," she replied, rolling her arms in a motion for me to get to the point.

"We did it in the bathroom," I said. "On the floor."

"Holy cow, you little *slut*. All this time, you had everybody fooled thinking you were a marshmallow, and come find out, you're a little hoe skeez," she said with a giggle. "So *that's* why there were no towels."

"I don't want anyone to know," I said. "So, please keep it to yourself."

"You didn't tell Becka?" she asked.

"No. It's bad enough that I'm telling *you,*" I said.

"Well, *that* doesn't offend me at all," Pauline said with a sniff.

"I wasn't trying to offend you. I just don't want anyone to know," I said.

"You have nothing to be ashamed of," she replied.

"He's older than me," I said quietly.

"*And?* This is Alabama. Totally legal if you consented. Just don't cross state lines with that. This isn't 'cause he's *black* right? I didn't think that mattered to you."

I cut my eyes at her sharply and frowned.

"*What?* No. I mean, I don't believe in race. It's a concocted social construct, so that has nothing to do with it."

"I see you. All socially *woke.* You go girl. But you admit, you prefer chocolate?"

"You're being obnoxious," I replied.

"You afraid your family might find out? You don't even live with those crazies anymore."

"No, but I wouldn't put it past them to do something drastic. Especially my Nana. She's so against all things black, it's ridiculous."

Pauline shook her head.

"Girl, I think you're overthinking things. And going just a *little* overboard." She wrinkled her nose at a short dude as he walked by with something snuggled in foil wrapper. "On second thought, those food trucks might be a better option. Whatever that guy ordered didn't look appealing. It looked like Yoda wrapped in a camping tarp."

"That would mean standing in a whole other line, possibly until we collect social security," I replied.

"I think I'd prefer that over having my stomach pumped in the ER for ingesting whatever marsupial *that* was," she said.

"Don't order the monkey meat," I said with a shrug as we stepped to the front of the line to place our orders.

Carrying everything back to where we were sitting and getting through the throng to our seats proved to be a nightmare because more people got up with the same idea we had, joining the seemingly endless line at concessions.

The score was now 23 to 7 with Vigor leading.

Pauline and I munched on stale tasting popcorn that we immediately abandoned when Becka opened her snack sack. Becka, of course, had a plethora of goodies in her beach bag after all, sharing barbecue smokies with Terrell who had been eerily silent throughout the game.

Pauline and I went for the pizza and beef empanadillas that Becka's momma made. She passed a bag of Doritos around and I greedily hoarded it once it was in my grasp.

It was actually starting to annoy me that Terrell wasn't being his usual self, making ridiculous comments and jokes that only he thought were actually funny.

Nudging him, I raised my eyebrows, and he looked at me and grinned.

"What's up with you?" I asked.

"Nothing. I'm good," he said.

"No, you're not. You're operating at one-fifth the stupid that you usually do. What's up?" I teased.

He shook his head.

And then I saw it.

He was holding his cellphone screen at an angle so I couldn't see it, but I saw it before he caught me looking at it.

"Lexi's blowing up your phone? What does *she* want?" I asked, wiping my fingers with a napkin after finishing the pizza slice.

"Yo, she's just going through some stuff, so it's nothing for you to get upset about," he said.

"Why would I be upset that your freaking ex is texting you? I mean, it's not the fifties," I said with sarcasm. "Going through some stuff like what?"

"You know. Her mother passed away not that long ago, so she's been struggling with that. The anniversary is tonight," he said.

"I'm sorry to hear that. I didn't know," I replied.

"Yeah," he added, wiping at his nose.

"So why hide the texts?" I asked.

"I wasn't hiding nothing," he replied.

"Okay, Terrell," I said.

"It ain't like that, for real," he said, grabbing my arm. I looked at his hand and then cut my eyes at him. He let go, holding his hands up in defense.

I turned to face the field to see Vigor had lost its fire. Russellville made a twenty yard pass, a touchdown and were well on their way to another one.

Terrell leaned forward and put his lips close to my ear.

"Look, since we're in Birmingham, I thought we could chill downtown tonight. Have dinner somewhere nice. I booked us a room, so we could make up for your birthday," he said in hushed tones.

"What about your girl, *Lexus?*" I asked, sarcastically.

"You need to quit with that. I told you, ain't nothing," he replied.

"I'll think about tonight," I said. "Not sure if I like you too much right now."

Terrell sucked his teeth as he settled back and sat down on the bleachers. I clapped as the stadium erupted in cheers and Becka looked at me oddly.

"Dude. You're rooting for the wrong team. Russellville just made a touchdown," she said.

I laughed at myself, realizing Lexi had distracted me. Russellville, in black, kicked off far down the field for Vigor, in white, to take possession.

By the time we reached halftime, Russellville had taken the lead.

During the third quarter, after their quarterback made a ten yard pass, Russellville had scored another touchdown, but then Vigor became invigorated, bolstered their defense, and took back the lead with five straight touchdowns to win the Championship game against the Tigers.

Wayne walked away with an MVP. They made an announcement over the loudspeakers at the end of the game with Wayne's stats and the game's highlights, then revealed that Wayne had accepted a football scholarship and officially signed to the University of Alabama in a send off for his final season with the Wolves.

As we walked through the crowd to meet up with Wayne, Becka slowed her pace to walk beside me.

"So, I have to tell you something," she said.

"Okay," I replied, feeling suddenly anxious.

"It's not bad. I'm gonna be going here. To UA Birmingham," she said. "I figured what better place to tell you than right here. *In Birmingham.*"

"What? That's awesome, Becka," I said, excitedly clapping my hands.

"Yeah, so I'll be close to Wayne since he'll be in Tuscaloosa. A quick drive."

"That's great news. Did you tell Wayne, yet?" I asked.

She nodded.

"Yeah, he knows. So, what about you and T-Bone?"

I shrugged.

"I don't know what he's doing. He asked me to move with him to Cali if he gets a job offer. But I really don't think he has it figured out," I replied.

"Cali? That's crazy. You *sure* about that? What about New York?"

"I don't know. I really need to figure out my life," I said.

"Why don't you get at him tonight. I know he's got plans for ya'll 'cause of what he asked me earlier."

"What did he ask you?" I rose my eyebrows.

"I can't tell you," she replied.

"*Butt licker!*" I howled as I smacked her arm, and she opened her mouth wide in a silent "ow" before rubbing the spot.

"You're so *abusive*," she said, faking like she was near tears down to the sniffling.

"Everybody and these secrets, tonight," I mumbled.

Terrell walked ahead of us to get the Benz and pull it around close enough to pick us up. We exited the stadium at Gate 12 and found him parked near the sidewalk leading to Blazer Village, the food trucks and tents.

Since Pauline and Becka parked farther away near the basketball courts, he drove them to their cars to drop them and Wayne off, brandishing his outlandishly huge trophy. Once they both pulled out of their parking spaces, he turned to me.

"I'm assuming that, since you're still in this car with me, you wanted to take me up on my offer."

"You sound like you're selling a Lincoln," I said with a smirk.

"Seriously, are we chilling tonight?" he asked.

I looked at him and smiled, shaking my head. He was like a little kid asking his momma for ice cream.

"Tonight's not a good night, Tee. Last thing I need is Becka's momma bugging out on me for staying out all night. She's been really nice to me, and I don't wanna blow it."

"Is this about Lexi?" he asked. "I told you, that ain't nothing."

"It's *never* anything," I mumbled as I peered out the passenger side window.

"What's that supposed to mean?" he asked. I didn't reply. Instead, I focused on the football field's surrounding grounds.

The crowded parking lot was a mess as people left the game. I glanced back at the stadium and saw the lettering at the top, honoring it as the site of the 1996 Olympic soccer games.

Terrell sighed in response to my silence as we turned left onto Graymont Avenue West from Parking Lot D and headed toward the skyscrapers of Downtown Birmingham. From what I could see, the neighborhood surrounding the stadium reminded me of the blighted area going toward the one basketball game we played at Vigor High, with its small, crumbling boarded up homes and sagging roofs in disrepair. Eerie, empty lots lay gaping and void in the darkness.

I had never been to Birmingham before, and although the skyscrapers of downtown glittered beautifully in the night sky, even the stadium we left behind desperately needed updating and renovation.

We continued beyond 9th Street, where Graymont Avenue became 5th Avenue North and changed into a one-way street with four lanes just before it crossed 10th Street.

Merging onto I-65 South from 10th Street, the AT&T City Center, Regions Center, Wachovia Tower and Harbert Plaza, four of the tallest skyscrapers in Birmingham, dominated the night skyline as Downtown loomed on the left.

I leaned back to close my eyes as the city flashed by, and Terrell continued the rest of the drive with the music playing low. I could barely hear the car itself, as the big Benz quietly slipped through the night.

Three and a half hours later he nudged me as we exited onto Celeste in Saraland.

"You want me to drop you off at Becka's right?" he asked in a sad voice.

"Yeah. Please," I said as he slowed to stop at the light, slapping on the turn signal.

Two police cruisers sat at the Shell station across the intersection, facing traffic.

"You might wanna go the speed limit. Looks like they're out tonight," I warned.

"Yeah, no doubt. I got this," he replied, as the light changed to green.

Terrell slowly turned right and cautiously continued down Celeste toward Spanish Trace. Just before Forest Avenue, the interior of the Benz exploded with blaring blue lights and blinding strobes.

Blowing out a breath, Terrell pulled the Benz over into the grass along the side of the roadway.

"I wasn't even speeding," he said, sucking his teeth. "Geez. Here we go."

"Maybe you have a taillight out," I said.

"I doubt it," Terrell mumbled as he rolled down the driver's side window. He twisted the key in the ignition to silence the engine, reached into his back pocket and pulled out his wallet, then plopped open the glove box and grabbed his insurance card and registration. He left the glove box open and placed his hands on the steering wheel.

Another police cruiser pulled up behind the black Dodge Charger parked right behind us, and the officer in the Charger got out and walked up to the driver's side window.

"License and registration, please. Is this your vehicle, sir?" the officer asked. He was tall, trim and fit, with biceps bulging as he took Terrell's documents.

"Well, technically, it's in my mom's name. But it's my car," Terrell said. "She gave it to me for college, and she bought something else."

"I'll be back in a moment," the officer said with a nod, reaching for a pen tucked away in his shirt pocket as he stepped away.

I turned to look behind us as another cruiser joined the two.

I was getting nervous.

"There's nothing in this car that I need to know about, right?" I asked with a frown.

Terrell looked at me incredulously, shook his head and smirked.

"What? Hell no, ain't nothing in here incriminating. You know I don't roll like that," he said.

"Just making sure," I replied, steadily watching the activity in the rearview mirror.

It seemed like forever passed before the officer returned. This time, he had his hand on his holster.

"I'm gonna need you to step out of the car please," he said, taking a step back. One of the other officers stood close by, with her hand also on her holster.

"Is there a warrant for my arrest? I haven't done anything," Terrell said.

"Sir, please step outside of the vehicle," the male officer said firmly.

Terrell reached for the door handle and slowly stepped out of the car. The officers stood back to give him room.

"Do you have any weapons of any kind on your person? Anything you want to tell us before we pat you down?" the male officer asked.

"No, I don't have anything on me," Terrell replied as the officer raised Terrell's arms to the sides and began to search him. Carefully reaching into his pockets, he pulled out Terrell's wallet. After feeling along his belt and waistline, he rummaged through his wallet. I watched for a moment, before the officer led Terrell away.

Terell's cellphone sat on the middle console. I was about to reach for it when the female officer came around to the passengers side and opened the door.

"Ma'am, I need you to come with me," she said calmly.

"Why? I didn't do anything," I said, my nerves on edge. I could feel my skin heating up, and I felt myself getting nauseous as my gut began to twist into knots.

The female officer, a thin, short dark-skinned woman with her hair braided neatly and twisted into a bun at the nape of her neck, calmly placed a hand on my arm. I stepped out of the car and she began to search me.

"It that your purse?" she asked when she was done, nodding at my Coach bag perched on the floorboard.

"Yes, that's mine," I said.

"Go ahead and grab it and hand it to me. Slowly," she said. "You don't have any weapons of any kind, or anything in there I should be worried about, do you?"

I shook my head at her before I reached into the Benz and picked up my bag, handing it to the officer as I looked around to see where Terrell was.

Two male officers were talking to him standing by one of the other cruisers.

The female officer looked through my bag and rifled through the contents, pulling out the matching clutch to find my picture ID and examined it. She glanced back up at me, then returned the ID to its place in the clutch. Then, she tucked it back into my purse and handed it to me.

"You're still a student at Satsuma High right? I saw your student ID. Do you have someone who can come pick you up?" she asked. "It has to be a legal guardian. Although you're eighteen and technically an adult, you're not an emancipated minor, and you're still a high school student. In the state of Alabama you are under the age of majority, which is nineteen."

I shook my head.

"What does that mean?" I asked.

"It means you need a parent or legal guardian to take you home."

"What's going on with Terrell?"

"Do you have someone you can call to come pick you up? Mother? Father?" she said, ignoring my question. "You can make things easy for me, or hard for me. Either way, one of your parents picks you up here, or you sit in the station waiting. Not a fun place this late at night, I can tell you that."

"I can call my momma, but I doubt she's gonna come get me," I muttered.

"You'd be surprised," she said, handing my cellphone to me.

I called my momma's number. It wasn't programmed as one of my contacts, but I knew it by heart. It hadn't changed for as long as I could remember.

She answered after two rings.

"Hello?" she breathed. I was genuinely shocked that she actually answered the phone. Then I suddenly became suspicious, because she *never* answers her phone.

"Momma?"

"Child, where are you?" she asked.

"I'm up the street. On Celeste. Near the gas station. Cops are here. Said you gotta come get me," I said.

"I'm on my way," she said. "Just sit tight."

It was a little unnerving that she sounded normal. Something was up.

"You okay to drive?" I asked.

"I ain't the one driving," she said before hanging up.

The officer nodded and led me over to her police cruiser, where she instructed me to sit down in the back seat.

I tried to guess what the officers were saying to Terrell. I wanted to go to him. He was standing there nodding, but I could plainly see the fear on his face.

Just a few moments later, the Buick pulled up and parked along the street on the opposite side with the hazard lights flashing. Other cars slowed down as they passed to be nosy.

It was too dark out, but I knew people in their houses were peeking out of their windows to see the spectacle of a line of police cruisers splashing bright blue light on everything in sight, parked along the street behind a shiny, black S Class Mercedes that could easily be a drug dealer's car.

The female officer came around to open the door to let me out, handing me my Coach bag. She placed a hand on my elbow and escorted me across the street to Momma and Nana Jane, who were now standing outside of the car with their arms crossed.

"Are you her mother, ma'am?" the female officer asked.

Momma raised her hand up and nodded, reaching into her purse to pull out her ID. She handed it to the officer who reviewed it, handed it back, and led me to the back seat of the Buick.

"Ya'll drive safe," she said as she turned to walk back across the street to where Terrell was talking to a few of the other officers. I watched as the rest of them finished searching the Mercedes.

I sat back in the seat as Nana Jane and Momma got back into the car, and Nana Jane turned the steering wheel tightly to the left to make a u-turn and head back toward Forest Avenue.

"Are the rest of your things at Becka's place?" Momma asked.

"Yep," I said with a sniff.

"We'll get them for you in the morning. You need to be with family. Not running the streets," Momma said.

"You wait how long? Six months to pull something like this? You knew where I was the entire time. Why are you doing this tonight?" I snapped.

Momma shook her head and didn't respond, feeding my anger.

"None of that matters now. You need to make better choices," she said.

"Look who's talking," I replied. "You two are the ones who kicked *me* out. You're both hypocrites."

"No. You chose to leave. People get angry all the time, and say things they don't mean," she said.

I shook my head as we pulled into the gravel in front of the garage at the house.

That's no excuse.

My thoughts and heart raced as I glared at the ugly red sofa, beat up rocking chair, and the rickety card table on the porch. I felt my stomach twisting in knots over the unknown. What were the police going to do to Terrell?

Stepping out of the car, I stomped into the house and straight to my room. It had been cleaned, but otherwise everything was as I had left it.

I pulled out my cellphone and stared at it, waiting for Terrell to call me and tell me everything was okay.

twenty nine
OUT WITH A BANG ♡
Graduation Day, May 2009

"I'm so done," I said as I settled back into the metal folding chair. The seat hurt my butt, and I squirmed as I tugged on the graduation gown, shifting the fabric so it wasn't so tight against my thighs.

"I know, right?" Becka said with a chuckle.

"That was the longest speech *ever.* Leave it to Stacy Freeman to act like she's leading a Republican primary."

I reached up to tuck a strand of hair back into place beneath my cap. Becka looked at me and grinned.

"It's all good, Manda. It'll be over with before you know it. And you're wearing your tassel wrong. Let me fix it," she said, reaching up to move it to the right side of the cap. She adjusted one of the bobby pins holding my cap firmly on my head while she was at it.

I let her style my hair instead of Pauline, and she managed to tame the crazy and put it up in a nice updo that had me looking like I was going to Prom all over again, complete with glitter on both my hair and face.

Watching as the third row down from us stood to line up for their walk across the stage to the podium to receive their diplomas, I turned to Becka.

"No one seems to notice that I'm totally not sitting in the right seat. I'm supposed to be way in the back," I said.

"Yo, girl. Keep cool and then, when this row is called, just squeeze back there in the back like 'oops, my mistake. My bad.' No big deal," she said with a giggle.

"I don't know, man. They might arrest me. You see all the cops posted up on the sidelines like this is a peaceful protest? I feel like we're in Selma."

"It's just 'cause of all the school shootings. Safety protocols or whatever," Becka said.

"I remember Virginia Tech during Sophomore year, and everyone knows about Columbine. That's it, right?"

"No, there's Red Lake when we were in 8th grade. There was a college or something in Illinois and one in Arizona I read about that happened last year. Chicago and Baltimore probably have school shootings daily. A lot of them don't make the national news," Becka said.

Just then there was a tap on my shoulder. I twisted in my chair to find a freckled kid grinning at me. He pointed down his row and I followed the direction of his finger to see Pauline waving a few feet away. I waved back, and she looked at me oddly and nodded toward the back rows.

I grinned at her and mouthed the words '*I know, I'm going back there in a bit.*' She laughed and shook her head at me as the second row down from us stood to join the procession.

When our row was called, I stood up and followed Becka to the outside aisle near the football field sideline, and spun around to shuffle toward the back rows. It was a struggle to maintain balance in my heels walking on the football field's turf. I should have worn flats like any of the other sane girls on the field.

One of the faculty members eyed me, shook her head, and watched me wearily as I carefully moved down to the correct row, sidestepped to the empty chair where I was supposed to be sitting and plopped down between two dudes who both snickered at me.

"They're gonna kick you out of here," one of them said. I recognized him from the men's varsity basketball team. It was Chad Mauldin. We were stuck together as partners once in a lab assignment during freshman year where we had to use graduated cylinders to demonstrate buoyancy, volume and density. He dropped both the cylinders and the beakers, and never heard the end of it.

"Might as well go out with a bang, right?" I replied.

"Mike drop," he chuckled.

I rose an eyebrow at him and wondered if he even understood what he just said. The basketball may have hit him one too many times in the paint.

The school administrator that was reading off the list of names called *Rebecca Denise Canales* and Becka stepped out from the line and onto the stage. Roaring applause, hooping, screaming and hollering exploded from the stands as she shook the principal's hand and accepted her diploma.

When I twisted around in my seat again, it wasn't hard to locate Becka's friends and family. They took up a whole section of the football field's bleachers.

The principal, Dr. Nordeman, interrupted the racket, seizing a microphone from somewhere nearby and speaking loudly into the microphone to address the field.

"May I have your attention? Please respect those families who are waiting for their graduating senior's name to be called by keeping the applause and excitement to respectable levels. Outbursts won't be tolerated, and you will be escorted off the football field, courtesy of the Satsuma Police Department. Thank you for your cooperation," she said, then gestured for the administrator to continue to call names.

The breeze picked up, sending seniors clamoring for their graduation caps and not long afterward, Pauline's name was called. Her family and friends disregarded the threat the principal made and proved to be louder than Becka's family as they stood and applauded, screaming and yelling. Pauline covered her mouth in embarrassment as she took her diploma, strolled the rest of the way across the stage in her expensive stilettos and down the steps on the other side.

I marveled at how well poised she was walking in the grass in three-inch heels, like the ceremony was a red carpet event.

Annoyed, several police officers looked over at Pauline's group in disapproval. I'm sure it was because of who they were that they didn't make good on the principal's threat.

Near where they were sitting in the stands, I found Momma, Granddaddy, Nana Jane, and my brothers sitting in old beat up lawn chairs in the grass next to the bleachers. I wouldn't dream of my daddy showing up and Taylor and Ivy were nowhere in sight.

Momma had long been back to her regular state, laid back on what were probably Ercs, Purple Drank and Biscuits in her raggedy pajamas, crusty dry skin and her busted looking house shoes. Her hair was a hot mess, all over the place and looking like it had never seen a comb or a brush in its entire lifespan.

I felt my cheeks burning with shame, and I watched a group of people pointing and laughing at my momma and them as they sat watching the stage.

It made me want to forfeit crossing to the podium to avoid them making a scene.

When the row I was sitting in joined the line at the edge of the stage, my stomach did somersaults and it took everything I had not to vomit in the grass. I focused on maintaining my balance in the soft turf.

I looked over at Becka, who nodded and sent me a thumbs up. My eyes went to Pauline, who put her fingers to the corners of her mouth and pushed up, reminding me to smile.

The smile I sent back was a weak one, and we edged closer to the stage quickly as the last of the seniors began accepting their diplomas.

The administrator finally called my name, and I adjusted my dress beneath my gown, walked up the steps and onto the stage, shook the administrator's hand and clacked across the platform in my heels toward the principal. She smiled at me broadly as she shook my hand and I accepted my diploma to loud, thunderously wild applause across the football field.

I turned to look and found everyone standing up, clapping their hands, drowning out and completely hiding my family from view.

Smiling, and silently thanking Heaven, I descended the stairs on the other side and carefully followed the others around to our row.

After the last name was called, and the last row returned to their seats, the senior graduating class stood and was met with loud screaming, yelling, and applause. Some of the other girls wiped tears from the corners of their eyes, as did I, knowing that this was the end for me, and by this time tomorrow, things in my life would be drastically different.

Dr. Nordeman announced the graduating class of 2009, and we collectively moved our tassels to the left before several seniors tossed their caps up into the air to the marching band playing an upbeat song.

The rows were dismissed one by one, and Becka joined me at the sideline. I slipped off my heels and kept glancing over to make sure my family didn't see me as I stayed hidden among a large group taking pictures.

"I got one thing to do and then we can bounce," she said. I nodded as I followed her around the bleachers in my bare feet, opposite where my family was waiting for me.

"You know they're expecting to get pictures with me," I said.

"I thought you didn't want them anywhere near you? Considering how crazy they looked over there, I don't blame you," she replied.

"It's crazy 'cause I might actually be kinda glad she never showed up to any of my stuff. My games, concerts, parent-teacher conferences. Most people don't even know they're my family, and I was born and raised here. I don't know if I should be relieved, or disappointed," I said. I hated that really, I felt like crying. My eyes started burning with the familiar sting.

Becka sensed it in my voice and turned to me, reaching her arms around me to hug me tightly.

"It's okay. In the end, they're the ones losing out," she said as she pulled away. "My mom's taking pictures of us with her new camera." Becka shielded her eyes from the sun and slapped her cap against her leg, looking for her group.

Once we found them, Becka ushered us all to a corner of the school away from the crowd and the football field, near the auditorium.

Against the brick, Becka took pictures with her family and friends, and urged me to get in most of them, then Mrs. Canales took some of just me.

"Where's Wayne?" I asked Becka as Mrs. Canales put her camera away in its bag. "I thought I saw him earlier."

"He was here, but he had to leave early to go to work. They're short staffed," she said. "I already said my goodbyes. Plus, we gotta get back to your house to get your bags before your peeps get home."

"That won't be for a while. I was smart and told them I was getting pictures with you first 'cause you had to leave right after. They're still over there waiting. They'll be waiting a long time," I said.

"That's so evil," Becka said with a giggle. "You're mean, Manda."

"They deserve it," I said. "After everything they've put me through, that's what they get."

"It's your choice. They can't stop you from leaving now. You graduated. I still think you should at least say goodbye. So does my mom. I mean, people will think you eloped."

"Eloped with who? You? That's funny." I replied. "No good-byes for suckers."

Becka shrugged as she led me away toward the parking lot and her Camry.

We made the quick drive to my momma's house, where the luggage I got from Auntie Beanie was packed and ready to go. I grabbed the bags and the guitar I got from my daddy, putting the guitar in the back seat and the bags in the trunk next to Becka's duffel and backpack.

We left from there and headed to Becka's, where we climbed out of our graduation gowns, changed out of our dresses and heels and put on something comfortable for the long drive ahead. I wore sweat shorts and a tee shirt while Becka wore yoga pants and a sleeveless top.

Not long afterward, we were on the road to make the eighteen hour drive to New York, and I was determined to never look back.

"Take therefore no thought for the morrow: for the morrow shall take thought for the things of itself. Sufficient unto the day is the evil thereof."

MATTHEW 6:34

thirty
DEFINITELY NOT A PELICAN ♡

He handed me the bouquet of lilies and I accepted them, then slapped him with them in the arm, destroying the flowers and sending the fragments all over the boat dock.

He put his arm up in defense, smiling as if it were funny.

I wasn't laughing.

Angie, alarmed, rushed to my side.

"AJ? Who's this?" she asked, looking like she was ready to throw down. "Do I need to call the cops?"

There was nothing left of the bouquet but the broken stems I was holding, so I stopped and breathed deeply.

"This is the butt licker I was telling you about," I said.

"Butt *what?* Who?" Angie asked, looking confused.

"Terrell. The one that's supposed to be dead or whatever," I said.

He chuckled, brushing the remaining bouquet fragments from his arm and chest.

"Well, I'm not *dead,*" he said. "I don't know who told you that."

"What are you doing here, Tee? I haven't seen or talked to you in like ten years," I said, crossing my arms.

He sighed.

"I've been in Cali. Where *you* been?" he replied sarcastically.

"I've been in New York," I replied.

"You were supposed to come with me to Cali," he said.

"I never said I would," I said sharply. "What happened that last night I saw you? The cops?"

"Yeah," Terrell said, looking away. "About that."

"About that," I smirked, shifting my weight onto my right foot as Angie defensively stepped closer.

"Remember Lexi?" he asked.

"Your trifling ex-girlfriend from college? Yeah."

He chuckled again.

"It was all a big misunderstanding. She wasn't thrilled about me telling her I wasn't taking her with me to Cali, and that I invited you to come with me. It was her dream to go to L.A., and she got salty over it. Did something stupid and out of character," he said, sitting down on the bench next to where I was standing. I turned to look down at him.

"Out of *character?*" I sniffed. "What do you mean by that?"

"She called the cops, told them I had a runaway minor with me in the car and gave them a description of the Benz. She didn't realize what she was doing could have gone really sideways for me. I don't know what she was thinking. Luckily, the cops that pulled us over in Saraland were decent," he said.

I felt my face getting hot. I had a five letter word that started with a B that was a perfect fit for what I thought about Lexi.

"So what did they do?" I asked.

He sighed again.

"They took me to the station, and once they cleared everything up, they let me go, but my mom got involved and didn't want me going back to Saraland. She told me that your grandmother and mother were threatening to press charges 'cause you weren't emancipated, still in high school, and were a runaway or something."

I raised my eyebrows in disbelief. I shouldn't be surprised, but I never would have guessed that they would go that far. Especially since I hadn't even been home for an entire summer and almost half the school year. I knew something wasn't right that night.

"I mean, I knew something was up. The police didn't arrest me, but it scared me anyway. You know I'm black dealing with white people. So, to squash the beef with your family, my mom made me stay in Cali," he said. "I guess she figured out of sight, out of mind."

I nodded, glancing at Angie for a moment before returning my gaze to Terrell.

"She didn't want me to end up like my pops. Apparently, he got caught up with the cops on some racial bias out in the county somewhere. He was with this white girl after he and my mom had been split up for awhile. It was in the news."

"That's some straight up garbage," I said.

"Tell me about it," he replied. "So I went back to Cali and then you were gone, I had no idea where you were, things went bad between my bro and Becka and she stopped talking to me too for a long while. She wouldn't tell me where you were or give me a number to try to call you after things cooled off," he said. "And to be honest, your family had me shook."

"My family sucks," I said.

"I wouldn't say that. They obviously care about you," he said. "No family is perfect. Mine sure ain't."

"You really don't know my family. How's Wayne?" I asked.

"He's good. On that NFL game out in Arizona. You know he play for the Cardinals," he said.

"Yeah, Becka told me. Which makes me mad that they knew you were back here and didn't tell me. Somebody's getting cut."

"Don't be mad at them. They were just trying to surprise you," he said. He leaned forward and reached his hand out to Angie. "I'm Terrell. My peeps call me Tee."

She accepted his hand and shook it.

"Angie. You're lucky 'cause I thought I was gonna have to toss you out there with the gators," she said.

"Naw, don't do that," he said with a laugh.

"She's one of my best friends from New York. I met her in college," I said.

Terrell nodded.

"So, how did you know I would be here, exactly?" I asked.

"Well, I was already in town visiting my mom. I was actually heading back to Cali on Monday night. Took a three day weekend. So, yesterday, I ran into Becka at this spot over on Wilson everyone's been raving about, Big White Wings. You been there?"

I shook my head.

"Yo, it's on point. The food is for real, and them stupid fries are on point. You gotta check that place out. Anyway, we linked up and she told me you were back and she got my number and hit me up today to let me know ya'll were headed over here. So I came through."

"I see," I said.

"You gonna sit down? You're making me nervous standing over me like that," he said as he laughed, rubbing at his beard.

"Good. You should be nervous. All this social media, you didn't think to look me up?"

"I'm like Jennifer Garner. I don't do social media," he said. "Nothing but negativity and drama. Ain't about that life."

"It isn't all bad," I replied.

"I beg to differ."

"I'm heading back to the house," I said, grabbing Angie's arm.

"Wow. It's like *that?*" Terrell asked, sucking his teeth.

"They already know you're here, right? You were already invited."

"Dang, girl, why you being so cold," he asked.

"I feel like there's something you aren't telling me, and I'm pretty sure I'm gonna hate you when I find out what it is," I said.

"Seems like you already hate me," he sniffed as he stood up and followed us down the pier toward the house.

Pauline grinned as we walked back onto the patio and I slumped back down into the chaise lounge I had been sitting on and reached for my mimosa to quickly finish it off.

"Well, that's definitely *not* a pelican," Becka said with a giggle.

"I hate you guys. All of you are total jerkettes," I said.

"Now, now, we will have *none* of that," Pauline said, refilling my glass. "You know, Tee, I have a front door. I would've heard the doorbell. No idea why you decided to be the Babadook and hide out on the dock trying to creep people out."

Angie held her glass out to be refilled. Terrell pulled a chair up near mine and sat down.

"How long were you sitting over there watching us, creeper? And where'd the flowers go?" Pauline asked, her face frowning.

"Awhile. And she destroyed them," Terrell said in a mock British accent. "In a fit of *rage*."

"Why'd you do that?" Pauline asked me.

I shrugged.

"So you guys knew he was back and thought you would *surprise* me, knowing I thought he was dead or something? You'd rather traumatize me?" I asked.

"Oh, don't be so dramatic, Manda," Pauline said. "You two were like peas in a pod back in the day."

"Not exactly," I said.

"What's that supposed to mean?" Terrell interjected, leaning forward in the chair.

I ignored him.

"So, what aren't you guys telling me?" I asked. "Like, there's a tension I can't put my finger on, and I feel like something's up."

Becka shrugged.

"I honestly don't know what you're talking about. I didn't peg you for a lightweight. The mimosas ain't even that strong for you to be trippin' like that," Becka said.

"No, seriously. There's something up. I can see it in Terrell's eyes."

"You're like *super* accusational. What's up with you, Manda?" Becka asked, her eyes going to Pauline.

Pauline looked down, and that's when I knew.

"Leenie, you said you went to University of California. In L.A.," I said.

"Irvine. Yep," she replied, bringing the glass of mimosa to her lips.

"And Terrell just said he was in L.A.," I said.

"Um hmm," Pauline replied.

"Terrell? You wanna go 'head and tell me how you *really* knew I was back?" I said.

He cleared his throat.

"I did run into Becka yesterday and we caught up. When she found out you were here, *she* called Leenie and then Leenie called me. She and I didn't know you were back until today."

"So you lied, basically," I said.

"When my mom sent me back to Cali for good, I was trying to get hired on through my internship. That didn't work out, so I decided to go for my master's degree at UC Irvine. It was the year after you guys graduated," he said.

I adjusted myself in the chair and sniffed. He continued.

"I saw Pauline on campus on my way to the library. I didn't know she was out there until then. We started hanging out, she hooked me up with a place closer to campus in a way safer neighborhood than where my family stayed at. Their house was in gang territory. She also had a connect for a much higher paying job and got me in. We started hanging out and got close after awhile."

"What do you mean by *close?*" I asked.

"We started chilling," he said.

I nodded, understanding exactly what he meant, and I glared at Pauline.

"We didn't know where you were, and never thought we would ever see you again, Manda. You were gone a long time," Pauline said.

"You *did* know where I was, Leenie. You liked and commented on my posts on IG."

"That was later, though," Pauline replied.

"You didn't think to tell me that?" Terrell asked her, after a brief silence.

Ignoring him, I sat quietly for a moment. Angie watched me with growing concern on her face. Becka's gaze went back and forth between me and Terrell and Pauline.

"So, it really wasn't that long," I said, finally.

"Come on, Manda," Pauline said. "That's not fair. I didn't move back to Cali until about a year after graduating. I didn't even know Terrell was in Cali, let alone attending the same school. And we didn't start talking until like, the following year. Like he said."

"Yeah, it isn't fair," I said, standing up. "You already knew I was going to New York, so when you ran into Tee in Cali, and later started following me on IG, you were *never* going to tell me you knew where he was. Now I'm starting to understand those cryptic convos we had in high school, about how you so disapproved of our relationship."

"It isn't even like that," Pauline replied.

"I mean, I came here to see *you,*" Terrell said, simply.

"How does that work? What, did you guys break up?" I asked.

They were both silent, looking at each other oddly.

"Okay, so Pauline, you're headed back to Cali for good, right? After you help your parents? And Tee, you're heading back on Monday, right? And I'm in New York. So, tell me. Really. How was that supposed to work?"

I turned to fully address Terrell.

"You guys haven't really broken up or whatever, officially, and you're handing me a bouquet of flowers like what? We're just gonna pick up where we left off? What'd you expect? A threesome?"

"It isn't like that, Manda. And we all got the flowers for you 'cause they're your favorites. As a welcome back gift."

"Uh huh," I replied, backing away as I clutched the glass of mimosa, then quickly downed it and set it down on the patio tiles.

I spun around to walk back into the house and up the stairs to the guest bedroom to retrieve my bag. Angie followed close behind me.

"Oh my god. *For real,* Amanda? Don't be like that. I ain't even a part of this drama. I didn't know anything about what they was doing in Cali," Becka said. I could hear Terrell's footsteps behind me and Angie.

When I stepped into the guest bedroom with Angie, Terrell grabbed my arm.

"Come on, Manda," he said as I glared at him. "This is BS. We should talk about it. Leenie didn't tell me she knew where *you* were and was in contact with you either, so that's not fair to me."

"What's there to talk about?" I said sharply as I grabbed my luggage.

"Look, I like Pauline. A lot. But I was in love with you, and that night happened and everything got jacked," he said.

"That was a long time ago, Tee. And now that I can put two and two together, she's really had a thing for you as long as I've known you," I replied, clutching my bag as I brushed past him.

Angie followed me out and down the stairs in silence, pulling out her phone to click on the Uber app.

"I don't know your mom's address," she said.

"You don't have to do that. I can give you a ride. There's really no need for you to leave. You haven't seen your squad in years. Why don't you stay, and if it's that much of a problem, *I'll* go," Terrell said, following us as we clamored down the stairs.

Becka and Pauline were in the living room, pacing back and forth. Pauline had her hand covering her mouth. She looked upset, and I could care less. When they saw me and Angie, followed by Terrell, Becka stepped in our path to stop us from making it to the front door.

"You're being ridiculous," she said.

"Move," I hissed with my lips pursed.

"I'll drive you back to your house," Becka said.

"I already offered," Terrell muttered behind me.

Becka held out her hand.

"Stop. Please. Just wait," she said. "We're bigger and better than this. You can look at Leenie's face and see that she's tore up. Obviously, she's really sorry."

I wasn't hearing any of it. I pushed past Becka and shuffled my way to the front door, unlocked it and flung it open, and marched out onto the gravel drive.

"The driver is two minutes out," Angie said from behind me.

I nodded as I led the way down to the end of the driveway.

A brand new looking, black Mercedes AMG S63 sat parked in the gravel sitting on large black rims and low profile tires behind Becka's Range Rover. There was no guesswork needed to know who it belonged to.

Terrell was still behind us, the rocks crunching beneath his feet.

"Amanda, stop," he said.

"So I see you've got your flashy baller car here. What did you do, drive all the way from L.A.?" I asked.

"Thirty hours," he replied.

"To stay for three days? Why didn't you just catch a flight?"

"I'm good. Rather drive. I like the scenery. You miss all that thirty thousand feet in the air."

I stopped walking and turned to face him.

"I had two really close, best friends all through high school. She was one of them, Terrell. You could have been more respectful of me and maybe dated someone that wasn't my best friend. No one half decent dates their girlfriend's best friend, especially after the way things went down between us," I said.

"It just happened. I never thought I would ever see you again. And I really wanted to," he said.

"She tried to warn me. And you should have tried way harder. I wasn't that hard to find. Becka knew exactly where I was this whole time. You could have reached out to her before her and Wayne were over. And, if that failed, there was one other way. Google me," I said as we reached the street.

Terrell stood silently watching me as Angie and I waited for the Uber driver to arrive.

When she pulled up, I walked around to the trunk and she got out to take our bags from us, placing them into the hatch of the Toyota Rav 4. I climbed in next to Angie in the back seat and Terrell stopped me from closing the door all the way.

"I thought you had moved on. If I had known, I would never have been with her. I would have moved to New York to be with you," he said.

"A little too late for that, don't you think?" I sniffed.

"It's never too late. At least take my number. So we don't lose touch again," he said.

I looked at him and shook my head, pulling the door closed as he stepped away.

Giving the driver the address to my momma's on Martha Al-leyn, I sat back in the seat and laid my head against the headrest.

Angie was silent for a few moments and then she twisted around in her seat.

"I wasn't going to say anything back there, but I think you maybe could have handled things a little differently," she said.

I cut my eyes at her.

"I'm on your side, no matter what. Just think about things. I think they're sincere and really feel crappy about it all. And it's the past. You moved on all these years in the city, doing your thing. Right? Over in the NYC being all Lipstick Jungle." Angie said, nudging me in the shoulder. "You were being an outright hoe, to be honest. And you could have googled him, too. Just saying."

She smiled at me, and I gave a faint smile in return. I know I was out in New York doing my thing, but after all these years, it still hurt. It took me a long time to get over him. Ten years later, I don't think I ever truly did.

I don't really know why I never tried searching for him online. Maybe it was because I was afraid of the unknown. That last night we were together, he had planned this incredible evening, and I shut him down over his ex-girlfriend texting him. After that, why would I have reason to think he'd ever want to see me or talk to me again?

Leaving all of Saraland behind was the easier way. Leaving my family, not reaching out to my friends, not coming back to visit. I began to wonder what my life in New York would have been like if I had kept in contact with Becka, Pauline, Kayli, the twins. Terrell.

What if Terrell had left Cali to be with me in New York? Where would my life be right now? It's been ten years. Would I be married by now with little kids running around a Brooklyn brownstone?

Angie interrupted my thoughts.

"How you feel, knowing he's alright? Think about how he feels, going all this time thinking he would never see you again, and eventually moving on, with someone familiar and close to you because of the connection your bestie had with you," she said.

I looked at her, and she grabbed my hands.

"Sometimes you have to see beneath the surface of what things look like. There's more to the story, and you should maybe take time to really listen to them. They both knew you. Maybe that's why they got close."

"That doesn't make me feel any better," I mumbled.

I settled back into my seat as Angie kept a hand on mine.

The rest of the drive to my momma's was filled with silence as I looked out at a city that had changed so much since I left. It seemed to be much bigger than I remembered, and I was seeing things I didn't see on the way to Pauline's riding in Becka's Range Rover.

There were so many new things that weren't there before, but beyond all the growth and renaissance, so many things hadn't changed at all.

Police officers stood in the middle of the street, directing a line of traffic into the church parking lot that began beyond the light at the freeway intersection. Momma planned to arrive early to find a good space, but it seemed as if everyone else had the same epiphany.

Lot attendants waved us over to a line of empty parking spaces near the tree line at the edge of the parking lot in the shade. Momma was ecstatic to park her Benz in a place sheltered from the sun's heat. I could tell from the beaming grin on her face.

"You got any gum?" Ivy asked as she put the Benz in park. Momma reached for her purse at Ivy's feet, plopped it down on the middle console, rifled in it for a package of 5 gum and handed Ivy a piece. Then, she twisted in the seat and passed the pack to Angie and I seated behind her in the second row.

Angie took two sticks and handed me one. I unwrapped it and popped it in my mouth as Momma handed me a beautifully embossed, brown leather-wrapped Bible.

"I couldn't find your old one, so I bought you this. It has study tools in it and a concordance in the back, like mine does," she said.

I unzipped it and found that she had written a dedication to me inside of it.

"Aww," Angie said with a smile.

Momma handed Angie a Bible that was also leather bound, but black.

"Got you one too," she said.

"I have one at home," Angie replied with a smile.

"Now you got two," Momma said, smacking her gum. She opened the door and climbed out. Ivy slid out of the passenger side.

I looked at Angie, who held the Bible out like it had bitten her.

"This ain't gonna be one of those culty things is it?" she asked.

I rolled my eyes at her.

"Stop being a ding dong and come on," I muttered, stepping out into the blazing sun. It was about to be the beginning of the fourth week of May, and when I checked the Accuweather app, it said it would be 84 degrees. It felt closer to 94.

I already felt sweat running down between my legs in my yellow sundress. Momma looked Southern chic in her large white hat, floral dress and wide white belt. Her hair cascaded around her shoulders beneath it.

Ivy's hair was styled the same way, but her dress was cream colored with contrasting dark blue heels. She wore a sapphire necklace and earrings that coordinated well with the shoes and her makeup. She was stunning, like her momma before things went south with Ivy's loser daddy.

Angie didn't do dresses. She wore jeans, red heels and a cute white lacy trimmed top. Her braids were twisted into an updo, and she could easily be mistaken for a Grammy winner.

When we reached the entrance, a pair of greeters held the door for us and we were graced with cool air as we stepped through the open glass doors of the church.

Inside, I breathed a sigh of relief as I looked around to see a mixed congregation. There were several interracial families with cute light-skinned kids that could pass for just about any ethnicity.

The smell of cinnamon buns and coffee had me turning my head to discover a cafe near a bookstore and gift shop at the front of the church near the entrance.

This was unlike any church I had ever been in. Resembling a large conference center and hotel, it was enormous.

I followed Momma and Ivy as they walked over to a set of open banquet hall doors. A woman stood at the entrance, handing out programs to those who stepped inside.

She beamed, handing a pamphlet to each one of us as we passed her, saying "Welcome and God bless you."

I smiled back at her and followed Momma and Ivy to a row of seats near the middle of the expansive auditorium that was the sanctuary.

A concert stage was at the front of the church, with large screens straddling each side and one IMAX sized screen in the middle hovering over the stage. Stage lighting pulsed and flickered from above it along the ceiling and off to the right corner, the musicians was making final adjustments.

Upbeat Christian music played from the massive speakers along the walls and perched up on towers on the stage.

I settled down into my seat and looked through the program as Angie looked around. Ivy and Momma were talking about something I wasn't really paying attention to. I looked up to see that the immense auditorium was quickly filling up to capacity.

Then, the lights went dark. An electric guitar began riffing. Lights dimmed over the stage and five silhouettes were slightly illuminated in reddish orange lights as smoke curled along the stage. I could make out three females and four dudes in the dim lighting. Two of the guys and one girl held guitars.

Above them and on either side of them, the screens came to life with imagery of sky and landscapes as more instruments joined the fray. The silhouettes nodded their heads up and down to the beat as the drums ignited, thundering across the sanctuary.

It was like a Santana concert.

Suddenly, the stage was bathed in light as the drummer hit the cymbals and the singers began singing an anthem to Christ, and everyone was on their feet, clapping and singing, shouting and praising.

Momma had her hands up and Ivy followed suit, her eyes closed and her head lifted toward some point beyond the ceiling.

The music, the sound, all of it penetrated my bones and my heart began to pound. It felt exhilarating.

Angie was already standing and mimicking what Momma and Ivy, and everyone else in the auditorium were doing. I was the only clown still sitting, so I got up and lifted my hands, waving them back and forth in the air.

The music was Billboard level. I wanted so badly to get up there with them and jam out on one of those sweet guitars they were blazing on. Or smash out on the drums.

If church was like this, I think I'd be there every Friday night. This was like a nightclub without anyone painting your top with their Cîroc. Or fighting in the alley.

Just a few minutes later, after a glorious Spotify worthy song, what looked like a cross between an athletic Sinbad and Chance the Rapper walked onto the stage with a mic and began to search the audience. He had swag, dressed in distressed jeans, Jordans, a slim fit button-up shirt, blondish-red tinted curly hair and light freckled skin.

His eyes landed on Momma, then me.

"Church, we have a very special guest tonight. I know from personal experience that this young lady can do amazing things with a number of musical instruments. I'd like to introduce you to Amanda Rush," he said, signaling for me to join him on the stage.

I looked at Momma.

"Did you put him up to this?" I hissed.

"I don't know what you're talking about," she said with a smile.

I shook my head and stood up, and boisterous applause erupted from every corner of the auditorium. All around me, people stood up and clapped, smiling at me as I shuffled down the row toward the aisle and approached the steps to the stage. I joined the pastor and he placed his arm around me.

"Many of you may know her from her time as the focal point of the Satsuma Sound. Or as the Power Forward that invigorated the Lady Gators some years back. I remember this little lady when I was a youth pastor for the Village. She was the youngest worship leader I've ever heard of, and man, when I say she could call down heaven with her gifts, I mean you could just see people pouring their hearts out to God when she was up on the pulpit. She has an anointing on her like you wouldn't believe, and I am praying that she would honor us by leading the rest of the Creekwood Worship experience."

He looked at me and smiled, holding his hand out to direct me toward the worship team.

A long haired brunette in a coordinating jean jacket, brown slacks and floral top walked up to me with a guitar and held it out while two other teenaged girls attached a mic to my top and sound equipment to my belt line.

"You're running the show now, so I'm gonna go back to my cave," the pastor joked as he stepped away.

My hands started to shake, I felt my body vibrating, and my stomach was flopping all over the place. It had been a long time.

I glanced down quickly and noticed the guitar was a Fender Auditorium series with a Getaria digital wireless system. Sweet.

"Hi, ya'll," I breathed into the air, the mic clipped to my top amplifying my voice across the sanctuary. I felt like I was in a freaking rock concert. "I'm not prepared for this, and I don't even know where to begin. Been a long time, so if I mess up, please don't throw tomatoes at me. This is my first time wearing this dress," I said. The auditorium burst into laughter and the drummer counted out.

The other guitars began to riff, giving me a baseline to work with. I hit a few chords and played with them by ear for awhile, just jamming to get my sea legs warm.

I thought about a song I remembered playing often at The Village Church, and the words came back to me. I strummed the guitar, hit a few chords and took a breath. The worship team knew exactly where I was going and followed on cue.

I belted out Third Day's "God of Wonders" as my throat began to feel scratchy. I pushed through and the female vocals near me joined in.

A warmth I hadn't felt in a long time seemed to burn in my chest, and I could feel the ripples and waves of energy raising the hair on my arm. The music was all around me, and through me, as I sang and played. I quickly found myself fighting back tears.

I led into a more recent song by Hillsong Worship, "From the Inside Out" as I quickened the tempo of the song to match the energy of the auditorium. It was one of the songs that Jackie and the women in her family sang while they blazed away cooking in the kitchen.

I didn't realize how much I missed being up on stage, and I was shocked at how well I sounded with the worship team, despite the mistakes I kept making. We did a portion of the song with the drummer all over the toms performing a solo to the vocals while we repeated the chorus a few times, then led back into the main part.

Four more songs later, the pastor came back onto the stage as the lights faded on me and the Creekwood worship team. The girl that gave me the guitar led me away to sit with them in the corner of the stage.

The pastor preached from the Bible about forgiveness, bringing up dramatic powerpoint on the screens to augment his teaching.

He brought up scriptures in Luke, chapter 17, moving on to second Corinthians, chapter 2, and started touching on how forgiving others was an act of love and kindness. He explained that in forgiving people, we were helping them and ourselves heal in the process.

The pastor told a story about how his daughters, Linna and Emmy, had done something that they were ashamed of, and were so torn up about it they punished themselves by not coming down for dinner one night. What they did had been so trivial in the pastor's eyes, but to them, it was like the ultimate mistake.

He said that we often beat ourselves up over our faults and failures, despite that we were already forgiven long ago at Calvary's cross.

I looked over at my momma and thought about the years she laid up on the couch, missing everything important happening in my life except things that annoyed me. Then I thought about how Daddy had left when he did, and how she struggled to get over it. She made a misstep at work that cost her the career she'd built, from not being able to focus on her work.

After that, she began going from job to job, and while hoping for Daddy to come back, she sunk deeper and deeper into depression.

Next thing I know, she is on all these meds barely functioning, and it all spiraled downhill fast from there.

I suddenly felt remorse. It was like a heaviness, and warm tears trickled down my face thinking about how mean and cruel I had been to my momma, adding to her pain. Knowing how I was to her, I thought about the way she was treating me now, as if I had never left and never did the things I did.

Maybe that was the freeing forgiveness that the pastor was talking about.

Just then, the pastor ended his forty five minutes of preaching and brought the band back onto the stage for another song as attendants began passing baskets through the aisles to take up offering and tithes. We performed Hillsong Worship's "Break Every Chain" as the pastor called for people to come to the altar for healing and prayer.

I glanced over in the middle of singing and playing the guitar and saw Ivy leading Momma onto the pulpit to join the pastor on the stage. He signaled for me and the worship team to play softer.

"There is a God of miracles," he began. "There is a God of miracles, church. He is a healing God, He is a deliverer, a conqueror. If you will just believe, He will provide healing for you today," he said forcefully. He took Momma's hand and signaled for one of the teenagers to give her a microphone.

"Tell the congregation what freedom sounds like," he said.

Momma had tears streaming down her face. She opened her mouth to speak but couldn't find the words from sobbing so hard.

"Well, since she's overwhelmed with joy and thanksgiving, I'll spill the beans. Not long ago, doctors found late stage cancer in Beth's ovaries. That's in addition to some heart problems she had been having. Church, there's nothing like trusting in an evil report.

"Numbers Chapter 13 tells us about how Moses sent a few good men into Canaan to spy out the land. We know that they came back from the land of giants gushing about all the fruit, milk and honey. But they also talked about the fierce, dangerous occupants of Canaan. Caleb was ready to take the land the LORD God had given them, but these other men had an evil report.

"Church, how many times has someone told us something negative in our lives? Filled us with doubt? How many times have we struggled to trust the LORD with all our hearts? Leaning to our own understanding?

"I'm here to tell you that GOD is a healer. Beth went to the doctor some days ago and they ran a whole bunch of tests. They couldn't find anything. They ran tests again. They couldn't find anything. They poked and the prodded, and still couldn't find anything, because GOD is Lord of all, including the doctors, and He has the final say. Come on, why don't y'all give GOD the glory," he said as he held Momma's hands up.

My eyes widened in shock and my heart pounded in my chest. I glanced over at Angie and found her wiping at her face. Tears had been streaming down her cheeks, and there was a woman sitting behind her who had placed a hand on her shoulder to comfort her after handing her a wad of tissues.

I felt warmth in my gut, as if I had just downed a shot of Wild Turkey and I looked at Momma, who was smiling at me. I couldn't take any more. I unstrapped the guitar and set it down, walked over to her and flung my arms around her, pressing hard against her as she sobbed against my face.

The pastor patted both of us on the shoulders as he stepped down from the stage and began praying for the people standing in line. I pulled away and looked Momma in the eyes as she brushed the tears from my face.

I felt like I was going to burst.

"Why didn't you tell me, Momma?" I asked, not realizing that someone had thoughtfully disconnected the mic.

"I didn't want to burden you with that," she said quietly.

"But you're my momma," I said. "You should have told me."

"I know. And I'm sorry. But I'm okay. Everything's gonna be alright. Go finish playing your beautiful music with the worship team. I'll see you in a bit."

I nodded and stepped back over to the guitar. One of the girls picked it up and helped me strap back in.

I decided to switch things up and led them into my acoustic, atmospheric version of "Say Yes" by Holly Starr. While we worked on Saturday mornings putting product into mason jars, Jackie put the song on repeat from her Spotify playlist. It quickly became one of my favorites, and playing it now brought tears to my eyes with everything that was going on.

I looked up for a moment as I breathed the words and saw my momma watching me with a deep look on her face I had never seen before.

We finished up the set with "Broken Vessels (Amazing Grace)" by Hillsong Worship.

When church service was over, the worship team gave formal introductions. I discovered that all of them graduated from Saraland or Satsuma a few years after I did, following the split from Mobile County Public Schools. All, except one. The girl that gave me the guitar, Geena, was actually my age and had moved here a few years ago from Selma. She looked like she was still in high school.

The pastor caught up with me outside just as I joined Momma, Angie and Ivy.

"Great job up there, young lady. You've still got it," he said, smiling broadly. "You remember me, don't you?"

"Yeah. You were the youth pastor when I went to Village. Pastor Eddie, right?"

"That's right. Good memory. My wife's around here some-where, but I'd like you to meet her and the girls. The one that set you up with the mic and all that, that was our youngest, Emmy," he said.

"Wow, I didn't know that," I said as Momma squeezed my arm.

"With that voice of yours. Didn't you go to NYU on a music scholarship? You doing anything with that degree?" he asked.

"I don't think anyone is doing anything with their degrees, re-ally," I said with a chuckle.

"Well, I have some people I know in Austin. I'd like to connect you with them. I record and livestream all of our worship experi-ences, and I was just told that they're blowing up my phone. I'm willing to bet it's about you."

"I don't know about all that," I said.

Pastor Eddie laughed.

"Well, you know, when you're called, it's up to you to listen to His voice. The door's open. Don't be shocked when they come knocking your mother's door down," he said.

"We'll see," I said with a smile.

"Alright, I'll hold you to that. You heading back to New York any time soon? If not, you should come back and visit us. Love to have you back up there with the team," he replied.

"I'd like that," I said.

He smiled and began greeting other people as they walked by and grinned at me, nodding.

"Girl, I knew you could play, but I didn't know you were Tay-lor Swift level," Angie said, slapping my arm.

"I wouldn't go that far," I replied.

"You're really good, Auntie Manda," Ivy said. "I loved watching you play in church when I was small."

"How do you remember that? You were only like what? Five?" I said with my eyebrows raised.

"I don't know. Just do," she said.

"So there's something you need to know," Momma said in a soft voice.

"What, Momma?" I asked.

"I'll tell you in the car," she said.

I shook my head. I hated suspense.

We greeted several more people before finally making it to the car.

As Ivy climbed into the passenger's seat, she beamed.

"So, we hit the mall for my shoes, then eat?"

"No, we're eating first, then the mall," Momma said.

"We won't have time," Ivy said.

"Sure we will," Momma replied.

I snapped the seatbelt in place, amazed at how hot the buckle was despite the Benz sitting in the shade.

"So, what's this mystery you want to tell me?" I asked. "No more health scares, please."

Momma adjusted the rearview mirror.

"Steven is not your father," she said.

"What do you mean?" I asked with a frown, glancing at Angie. She shrugged.

"My ex-husband, Steven. He's not your real father," she repeated. "And I'm not your real mother. I'm actually your aunt-in-law. And he's your uncle."

I looked at her, my eyes wide and my heart beating fast as I tried to get a grip on what she was saying, because it made no sense.

"I asked you to come here, and I wanted you to come to church today, 'cause there is something I've been struggling with telling you all these years, and it's been killing me. Literally," Momma continued. "Pastor Eddie? He's your biological father. Your uncle Steve's sister, Sabrina, or Beanie as you've called her since you were little, is your real mother."

I sat staring at the back of Momma's head for a while, not believing what I was hearing.

"Does he know I'm his daughter?" I asked, finally.

"Not yet. But if you want him to, and when you're ready, he will," she said.

"Why didn't Auntie Beanie- I mean, my momma, whatever, tell me that she was my real mother?" I asked.

Momma sighed.

"She was afraid. The circumstances were difficult for her," she said, lowering her voice.

"They had an affair when he was the youth pastor. She was a teenager, but he was older, and engaged. It's Alabama. Stuff like that happens here. Anyway, to protect your mother, Steven and I agreed to take you and raise you as our own. Your Nana thought it would be best considering the situation at the time. Things were different then, racially. There was still a big issue with acceptance, and with him being a minister, that just made things even more dangerous."

"So you did this because of racism?" I asked.

"Yes, that and your mother was young. We didn't want anything bad happening to her, or to you."

"What could have happened?"

Momma sighed as someone in a Dodge Challenger let her join the line in front of them. I looked at Angie, whose eyes were wide in shock as she grappled with the news I was getting.

In reality, I was even more shocked than she was, that I was handling things so well.

"I hate to even consider it. I've seen things. Your Nana has seen even worse. She grew up when things were segregated, so you can understand her fear."

"Is that why she had such a problem with me liking black shows and movies, and having crushes on black people?"

"Partly, yes. Mostly 'cause she was trying to protect you."

"By making me think I was white when I really wasn't?"

"Something like that."

"Well, that's lying."

"It is."

I sat there watching other cars make their way through the parking lot maze.

"So, that explains a lot. All this time I'm running around like a white girl, trying to figure out why my hair was nearly impossible to straighten. Otherwise it would be all over the place. But it's kind of dark blonde. I color it so it's lighter and for highlights, but black people don't have blonde hair," I said.

"That's not true. I've seen interracial kids with blonde hair. There's the light skinned kids on our street that have really curly blonde hair. Their father's white, mother is black."

"But, I'm *really* white looking. I even have freckles. I tan really well, but I'm not darker like other mixed people I knew or met. I'm like, so pale."

"Not everyone has the same skin, Sugarbear," Momma said. Angie nudged me.

"You know Halsey's black, right? I thought she was white for the longest before I read an article and saw pictures of her dad. She don't look black at all," Angie whispered.

"So what do I call you, then? Auntie Beth? 'Cause that just sounds so weird."

"Call me whatever you want to call me," she said.

"You won't mind if I call you a liar, then? Since I'm part of the family that lies. I mean, you've been lying to me my whole life," I said sharply. She closed her eyes tightly.

"We were trying to protect you," she said.

"No, I get it. It's like taking advantage of white privilege. I read a few articles about it. Racial passing. Except in my case, I was forced to pass for white when I just would have rather known what I really was, that's all," I said. "And I should have been free to explore and know my heritage."

"Shows and movies and hip hop music don't identify or define you," Aunt Beth said. "You identify and define who and what you are."

"I don't think I agree with that," I said. "So, why'd he leave?"

"Steven?"

"Yes."

"Your mother and father's relationship wasn't right in the eyes of the Bible and morality in general, and although your mother was the age of legal consent in Alabama, he was a person in authority over a minor being a youth pastor, so things for him would have been very bad if anyone had found out, or if we had pressed charges. Your uncle Steve wasn't thrilled about our decision, and wasn't as accepting as we believed he was. He couldn't handle it, knowing where you came from and ultimately it got the best of him."

I nodded as we inched our way toward the exit to the street.

"So, what happens if I don't want to tell him?" I asked.

"That's strictly up to you," Aunt Beth said.

"What about my real mom? Does she know you're telling me?"

"No, not yet," she said.

"Does she even want to be my momma?" I asked.

"Sugarbear, she's *been* being your momma all along, you just didn't see it. She's always taken care of you. When you needed things, she provided. When I was having a hard time with things, and was sick, she stepped up and was there for you."

"When I ran away, she said she couldn't come get me," I said.

"She was thinking about your needs first. She wanted you to finish up high school and graduate here. It made absolutely no sense to have you go all the way to Florida for your senior year when you worked so hard here. Transferring to another school in your senior year, in another state, that wouldn't have been a good idea," Aunt Beth said.

"So, what would happen if I called her right now and told her I knew she was my Momma?" I asked.

"I would imagine she would be on the first flight here to see you," Aunt Beth said. "In fact, I'm sure if you were to call her right now, you probably wouldn't reach her, because she's already on her way. When she found out you were here, she booked the next available flight. I'm sure she would've rather given you this news herself, but, well. It's done."

I sat back in the seat and looked out the window as we exited the parking lot.

Angie touched my hand.

"You still wanna leave Monday?" she asked, squeezing my hand.

I glanced back at her and saw the look on her face. She grinned broadly. Angie already knew the answer.

acknowledgements

First and foremost, above all else, I want to honor and thank Our Heavenly Father, the LORD God, for His Grace, His Mercy, His unfailing unconditional love, and for His steadfast hold on me. I am eternally grateful that no matter how much I lost, I always found myself gaining more in Him.

For my wife, I am grateful and appreciative of your love and support to encourage me to continue on this path that I have been given. When I wanted to quit, you kept me focused and on track. Through the pain, you made things better, and I will never forget how much you have blessed my life and been a light for my soul. So much of Saraland was influenced by your strength, womanhood, courage, and spirit. It is only fitting that it be dedicated to you.

To the pastors I have had along my journey, and to those pastors who have impacted me without knowing it, I am forever thankful that God has placed incredible leaders in this world.

To my family members and friends who have encouraged me and supported me throughout test and trial, I love you dearly and I am thankful to be blessed with such amazing people. An extra special thanks to my uncles Doug and Robin, my aunties Debra, Patricia and Mary, and my cousins Angel, Devon, Marc and Sherman.

To my mother, my father, my grandmothers Mary and Doris, and to my great grandmother Clara and my aunt Claudette, I will forever hold you all very near to my heart. You are tearfully missed. The books I write, and everything else that I accomplish in this life is with abounding love, in fond dedication and with deep gratitude to you.

To my ancestors who have sacrificed and endured so much to pave the way for me to enjoy the freedoms and liberties that I have today, I am eternally grateful, and I hope that my life's endeavors honors you all.

To my readers, fans and supporters, thank you so much for giving me a chance, believing in me, choosing to invest in me and for joining me on this journey as I follow dreams I have had since childhood. I am truly grateful and look forward to all that the future has in store, so that I can share it all with you.

To the brokenhearted, the hurting, those in pain, those who have suffered loss, those who don't know who they are or where they belong, those who feel like they have no place, those who feel lost- there's a Kind of Love. I pray that you discover how close that Kind of Love really is, as I have. It's been with you all this time. All you have to do is look up.

Writing this book was a unique challenge for me. I hope that I have honored the incredible gift that women are to this world by attempting to capture their essence and spirit, writing as a female narrator with respect, honor, adoration and love.

The I. Miller brand of shoes is an icon, made by I. Miller & Sons, a shoe manufacturing company valued at over 8 million dollars. Founded by Israel Miller, it now has sixteen retail shops in New York, 200 agencies throughout the United States, and two shoe factories.

Born the son of a shoemaker in East Prussia, near the border of Poland, Israel Miller arrived in New York in 1892 as in immigrant. He was in his early twenties at the time, and after working for four years as a cutter and designer in Paris, he became employed at a cobbler's bench in Union Square by John Azzimonti, a leading manufacturer of stage shoes.

Attributing his success to a lucky dollar he claimed to find in Union Square one morning in 1893, Israel Miller soon formed a partnership with an individual who had been acquiring orders for custom shoes.

Having received no orders, the dollar he found came just when he needed it most, and he fed his hungry wife and four children at home. After arriving back at the shop, orders began pouring in miraculously.

Israel Miller set up his own company, I. Miller & Sons, established in 1893, and within a short time, began providing custom shoes for the feet of Broadway dancers, performing artists, opera singers, silent film stars, glamorous socialites and the wealthy elite.

In 1911, he opened a small store in a brownstone at 1552 Broadway at 46th Street, which laid the foundation for the I. Miller & Sons brand.

During the first thirty years of the 1900s, I. Miller grew to nearly 230 stores across the United States, with the flagship boutique being the I. Miller building in New York, decorated with statues of four of Israel Miller's favorite high profile entertainment clients.

Alexander Sterling Calder, a Philadelphia sculptor, was commissioned to complete the statues, each to represent a branch in entertainment.

Marilyn Miller, depicted in her role as Sunny the circus queen in the Broadway musical, Sunny, was chosen to represent musical comedy. Mary Pickford, the producer and founder of United Artists, was chosen to represent motion picture film.

She was depicted in her role of Cedric in the film adaptation of Frances Hodgson Burnett's children's novel. Rosa Ponselle was chosen to represent opera and was depicted in her role as Leonora in the Verdi's opera La Forza Del Destino.

Ethel Barrymore, great aunt of the remarkably talented Drew Barrymore, was depicted in her role as Ophelia in Shakespeare's Hamlet to represent drama.

The I. Miller Shoes building still features the inscription, The Show Folks Shoeshop Dedicated To Beauty In Footwear, in honor of the incredible women in entertainment Israel provided shoes for.

Israel Miller's shoes were also carried in some of the most prominent shoe stores, stamped I. Miller & Sons on one insole, with the name of the shoe store and city location on the other.

Israel Miller died suddenly from a heart attack at the age of 63 in Paris on a Tuesday morning, August 15, 1929, just a few years after his famous flagship store in New York was opened.

The building was inaugurated on October 20, 1929. Following Israel's death, his son, George, took over the business, relaunching the brand with the help of designers that included Beth Levine and Andre Perugia.

I. Miller endures in American history as one of the most successful shoe manufacturers. During the 1950's, commercial illustrator and renowned artist Andy Warhol was instrumental in revitalizing the brand.

Throughout the years, a number of Israel Miller's shoes have been on display at the Metropolitan Museum of Art in Manhattan, and are currently cataloged.

In 1962, Genesco closed the New York factories of I. Miller following a strike by the United Shoe Workers of America. In 1973, Betty Davis, top recording artist, sang "Steppin' in Her I. Miller Shoes" on her self-titled debut single, but during the mid-1980s, the shoemaker closed its doors.

By 1964, shoes bearing the I. Miller brand were being manufactured by the Carlisle Shoe Company in Carlisle and Harrisburg, PA.

The I. Miller Building in New York, situated among the bustle of modern Times Square on the corner of Broadway and West 46th, was designated as a historical landmark in 1999.

The timeless facade of Israel Miller's flagship store still stands, looking much like it did a hundred years ago after an outside restoration and indoor remodeling effort in 2012 by fashion apparel company Express Inc. The I. Miller Building became Express' flagship store in June 2015.

The I. Miller brand of shoes endures in the modern era, available from JC Penney, beautifully adorning the feet of any woman or girl, for any occasion, who wants to look stunning and stylish enough to steal the show.

Mariposa

Veronica and Marisol Cartaya have never had it better, despite their country's fall into turmoil and violence. While starvation and chaos suffocate the rest of the nation, they enjoy the privilege and security of being a part of one of Venezuela's wealthy elite families.

The sisters have big plans. When summer is over, Marisol will leave her home behind and head for college in Barcelona, while Veronica finishes up her last year of high school. After she graduates, she will travel to Miami to attend the University of Florida to pursue her dream of becoming a lawyer.

But, no matter how protected they are behind their gated homes, secured schools and armored SUV's, when someone close to them betrays a potentially fatal secret, everything around them falls apart, fast.

Now, their mother is missing, their father has been murdered, and their home has been destroyed. With no one to turn to, no passports, and no documentation, their only hope is to escape the country at all costs.

While others have found status and refuge in Spain, Miami and the Caribbean, the only way out for Veronica and Marisol is with the assistance of cousins in far away Mexico.

Masquerading as migrants, the two set out on a treacherous journey in hopes of making it to the US Border, but danger and unbelievable evil await at every turn. They must survive a kind of hell far worse than the one they are running from, with perils they could never imagine.

MARIPOSA AVAILABLE SOON

Visit www.realglwilliams.com/mariposa for details.

Thank you for purchasing *Saraland*. I am truly grateful that out of all the books you could choose to read, you chose mine. I hope that it touched your heart and spirit and connected with your soul in ways only a dear friend can. If so, please share this book with your friends and family by posting about it on your favorite social media platforms. If you enjoyed this book, I would love to hear from you. Please take some time and post a review on Amazon and Goodreads. Your feedback and support will help me greatly improve my writing craft for future projects and make Saraland even better.

Click here to post a review of Saraland on Amazon
https://www.amazon.com/review/create-review/?
ie=UTF8&asin=057851513X&
and here for Goodreads
https://www.goodreads.com/book/show/49120904-saraland

I look forward to providing you with more compelling stories, introducing you to characters you can relate to and connect with, and taking you on journeys that reach deep into the farthest reaches of imagination.

Join me at *www.realglwilliams.com* where you can stay up to date and connected with me and other readers like you, gain exclusive access to featured author merchandise and swag, and be entered in random giveaways.

Follow, like and share on Facebook, Instagram, Pinterest, Snapchat & Tumblr *@realglwilliams*

With every purchase of my books or author merchandise, you are contributing to my efforts to support and advocate for urban and rural literacy, and to preserve the arts in public schools.

As founder of the GET LIT Initiative, I seek to encourage reading and help create greater access to high quality books and resources for the underserved. Please support your local or regional non-profit literacy organizations, libraries, local independent book stores and public school literacy programs, and give children in your community a chance at something greater.

With Warmest and Deepest Regards,
GL Williams

For more information on the Get Lit Initiative, visit
https://www.realglwilliams.com/literacy

www.ingramcontent.com/pod-product-compliance
Lightning Source LLC
Chambersburg PA
CBHW031630130726

47900CB00018B/74